# THE
# HEADMASTER'S
# LIST

## ALSO BY MELISSA DE LA CRUZ

*The Queen's Assassin*
*The Queen's Secret*
*Cinder & Glass*
*Jo & Laurie* (with Margaret Stohl)
*A Secret Princess* (with Margaret Stohl)

The Alex & Eliza Trilogy
*Alex & Eliza*
*Love & War*
*All for One*

*Because I Was a Girl: True Stories for Girls of All Ages*
(Edited by Melissa de la Cruz)

The Never After Chronicles
*The Thirteenth Fairy*
*The Stolen Slippers*
*The Broken Mirror*

Disney Descendants Series
*The Isle of the Lost*
*Return to the Isle of the Lost*
*Rise of the Isle of the Lost*
*Escape from the Isle of the Lost*

# THE HEADMASTER'S LIST

## MELISSA DE LA CRUZ

**ROARING BROOK PRESS**
New York

*For Mike and Mattie, always*

Published by Roaring Brook Press
Roaring Brook Press is a division of Holtzbrinck Publishing Holdings
Limited Partnership
120 Broadway, New York, NY 10271 • fiercereads.com

Our books may be purchased in bulk for promotional, educational, or business use. Please contact your local bookseller or the Macmillan Corporate and Premium Sales Department at (800) 221-7945 ext. 5442 or by email at MacmillanSpecialMarkets@macmillan.com.

Library of Congress Cataloging-in-Publication Data is available.

First edition, 2023
Book design by Aurora Parlagreco
Printed in the United States of America

ISBN 978-1-250-82738-8 (hardcover)
1   3   5   7   9   10   8   6   4   2

ISBN 978-1-250-89401-4 (international edition)
1   3   5   7   9   10   8   6   4   2

*In the end,*

*one of them was dead,*
*one was in jail*
*one was in rehab*
*and only one graduated.*


*Eighteen, headstrong and stubborn.*
*Seventeen, and headed to play soccer for Michigan.*
*Sixteen, and just got their driver's license.*
*Fifteen, and just along for the ride.*


*One of them was driving.*
*One of them was high.*
*One of them screamed.*
*One of them died.*

# ONE

SPENCER COULDN'T TAKE HER EYES away from the officer's pen as it hovered over his report, patiently waiting. The cap of the pen had been chewed like a dog toy. Her head throbbed, pain all over. She blinked, realizing he'd asked her a question.

"What?"

Spencer's mother squeezed her hand and said, "Can't we do this some other time?"

"I understand that, Dr. Sandoval. I truly do. However, a child died. We take these things very seriously."

Spencer's gaze landed on his badge. Officer Potentas, no, *Detective* Potentas. He'd introduced himself earlier. Her brain was hazy around the edges, like a cloud. How much time had passed? A second? An hour? The drip of the IV was cool in her arm. Spencer could sink right through the hospital bed and onto the floor.

"Okay, Spencer, let's try again. What happened last night? Can you walk me through it?"

*Scream. Float. Crash.* An eternity in the blink of an eye. Who screamed? Did she?

"There was an accident," she said, and swallowed, her throat dry. Her teeth felt too big for her mouth, or maybe it was the other way around. He wrote as she spoke. "We were at a party . . . Before school starts. End of summer. In the hills."

End of summer. End of *Spencer*. Her heart pounded. Why was it so hard to breathe? She didn't feel real. She wasn't sure she was talking; in fact, she wasn't sure she had a mouth and she folded her lips over her front teeth. Drip-drip went the IV, away-away went the pain. Cloud nine.

"Do you remember who was in the vehicle with you?"

"My boyfr—Ethan."

"The driver."

Spencer's breath hitched. *Scream. Float. Crash. Pain. Ethan.*

"Do you remember what happened next?"

When she screwed up her face, remembering, the skin on her cheeks pinched. Stitches from her cheekbone to her jaw. Sewed together like a doll. Chewed up like the detective's pen cap. "No. I can't . . . think."

"She's on sedatives, Detective," her mother said. Her brown hair was so shiny, like a penny. Spencer wanted to reach out to touch it, but her other hand was in a cast and too heavy.

"I know this is difficult. But everyone's story checks out. I'll be in touch."

One minute the detective was sitting at the foot of her hospital bed, and the next he'd teleported to the door where

Spencer's father stood, holding Spencer's sister's hand while talking to a doctor. The detective said something to him, and her sister Hope looked at her and something inside Spencer snapped.

She cried, blinked, reliving it all over again. *Scream. Float. Crash.* She had to go. Run for help. Her mother held her down and called out, and a nurse rushed in and pushed a button on the IV. More cold snaked up her arm. Sink into the bed. Let it swallow her up. Sleep came over her like a wave crashing on shore.

"Shoo . . . shoo . . ." Her tongue felt like a worm trying to crawl out of her mouth.

"He's going, sweetie. He's leaving," her mother said, squeezing her hand.

Her lids were almost closed, going bye-bye. *Scream. Float. Crash.*

Bliss took her away.

Los Angeles Police Department
Crash Report Form

## Crash Severity

Fatal / Injury / PDO

## Time & Location Information

Date of Crash: 03/SEP/2021

Time of Crash: 2:30 A.M.

Time Officer Arrived: 2:34 A.M.

Weather Conditions: Clear

Road Hazards: None

At Intersection: Sunset Blvd & Benedict Canyon Dr

Number of Motor Vehicles: 1

Number Injured: 3

Number Fatal: 1

## Section 1

Vehicle Year: 2019

Make: Porsche

Vehicle Type: Automobile

Use: Private Transportation

Airbag deployed: Yes

State: CA

Vehicle Identification Number: ███████

Vehicle Speed Est. 120 mph

Posted Speed: 45

**Section 2**

    Name of Driver: Ethan Amoroso

    Current Address: ▮▮▮▮▮▮▮

    Date of Birth: 12/NOV/2003

    Driver License Number: ▮▮▮▮▮▮

    Injury Status: Minor injuries, declined transport

    Drug & Alc. Test: Pending

**Section 3**

*Please Fill Out for All Other Occupants Involved*

    Spencer Sandoval—18—F—Injuries requiring hospital
        transport

    Tabby Hill—16—F—Minor injuries, declined transport

    Christopher Moore—15—M—Fatal

Officer's Notes: Vehicle 1 collision—damage extensive—no fire. No immediate danger to first responders. Impact with tree (standing). Light conditions dark-lighted. Weather clear. Driver sitting on pavement next to Passenger 2 prone, unconscious. Driver suffered injuries to head and shoulder. Passenger 2 had substantial injuries to arm and face. Passenger 3 emotionally distressed on curb, visible facial injuries. Passenger 4 remained in vehicle, fatal status. Resuscitation unnecessary. EMS arrived at 2:45 A.M. Driver and Passenger 3 declined transport. Driver claims they were coming home from a party in the hills. No tire marking to indicate brakes were applied. Driver tested for alcohol and drugs on-site. Pending results.

    Officer Diagram Attached

    Case Status: Open

**Get Salty: A True Crime Podcast with Peyton Salt**

*[Get Salty Intro Music]*

**Peyton Salt:**  Welcome and good listening, Salters. As always, I'm your host, Peyton Salt.

**Sasha Firth:**  And I'm your cohost, Sasha. You're listening to *Get Salty*, now the twenty-fourth most downloaded true crime podcast on Earworm, the world's most popular podcast hosting network!

**Peyton:**  Twenty-fourth! Incredible! Can you believe it? We love you all so much, Salters. Our fans are so supportive, and we look forward to getting some new merch available on our website as a special thank-you. Maybe some mugs or pins. We'll do a poll on our subreddit so people can decide! How does it feel, Sash?

**Sasha:**  Unreal. I get to share my love of true crime with all of you!

**Peyton:**  Oh, for sure! But this week, I've got a story for you, Sasha, that is as juicy—if not the juiciest yet, because this one is recent and hits close to home for me.

**Sasha:**  Oh yeah? Tell me more!

*[SFX: crickets, tires screeching, crash]*

**Peyton:**  In the early hours of September third, just a few days ago, a parent's worst nightmare—a phone call, informing them their child wouldn't be coming home. In a place like Los Angeles, the home of the rich and famous, one might be surprised to find themselves surrounded by death and tragedy. After a frantic nine-one-one call, EMTs arrived on the scene to find a black Porsche 911 Targa wrapped around a palm tree at the corner of Sunset Boulevard and Benedict Canyon, a scene of terrible carnage in the center of Beverly Hills's glitz and glamour. The driver and owner of the vehicle is Ethan Amoroso—

**Sasha:**    How do I know that name?

**Peyton:**    I'm so glad you asked! We covered a case a while back—

**Sasha:**    Oh! The house party!

**Peyton:**    Exactly. Episode one thirty-one, for anyone who wants to go back and listen. I know you Salters are already googling it furiously as I speak! [*laughs*] But for anyone who needs a refresher—the driver and owner of the vehicle is Ethan Amoroso, All-State athlete and millionaire's son and classmate of mine, the same Ethan Amoroso who two years ago was at the center of a huge scandal involving a serious accident at a party at his house in Brentwood, an incredibly affluent neighborhood in Los Angeles. Allegedly, the victim fell off a second-story balcony, suffering extensive injuries to the head, neck, and back, leaving the victim in a coma.

**Sasha:**    That's awful!

**Peyton:**    Usually we don't cover these kinds of cases, just because they're tragic if not common, but you can see why this one caught my interest. Star athlete, the Brentwood neighborhood, an obvious suspect.

**Sasha:** Now I know what you meant when you said this case was "juicy." Like OJ!

**Peyton:** [*laughs*] It's true, the murder of Nicole Brown Simpson did happen in Brentwood, but that's an entirely different case. We're not here to speculate, obviously, but you can see why I was so excited to share this! These kinds of things just don't happen in Brentwood. Ethan's involvement in one accident is a tragedy, but two accidents . . . let's say, my eyebrows are raised! Ethan hadn't been charged with anything before. Who knows what will happen now?

**Sasha:** What do you know so far?

**Peyton:** Ethan Amoroso and three others had been driving home from a party celebrating the end of summer, one last rager before school starts, in a residential development property called Highwood Estates in the hills when he crashed at high speed, shredding the car to ribbons. Only one person in the vehicle died. The victim, fifteen-year-old Chris Moore, was adored by just about everyone. He was about to start his sophomore year at a private school called Armstrong Prep.

**Sasha:** Ooh la la. Sounds fancy.

**Peyton:** [*laughs*] I know I risk doxing myself because I'm a junior at Armstrong, but I'd be doing a disservice to the community not talking about it. The tailored uniforms, the designer backpacks, daddy's money—definitely not my style, but it's the norm at Armstrong. Ranked top in the country in academics and athletics, Armstrong Prep is a private school for the rich and soon-to-be famous. Nestled among the meticulously green lawns of movie stars and tech moguls in the hills, it's the perfect spot for privilege to go unchecked, a sort of bubble from the real world. Ethan and all the others in the car are students there, one of them was even his girlfriend, I know them all personally and the incident has shaken me to my core. For sure, this is a tragic way to start the new school year.

**Sasha:** So the police don't think it was an accident?

**Peyton:** They want to charge Ethan for aggravated reckless driving and child endangerment, but they haven't arrested him yet. At the end of the day, I mean, it was an accident, but a senseless and selfish one.

**Sasha:** The cops sound real serious about this. Are they doing anything about it?

**Peyton:** Well yeah, an innocent kid died, Ethan put everyone in that car in danger. It could have been so much worse than it actually was. He could have hit another car even! Ethan had been going over one-hundred-and-twenty miles an hour before he crashed. I've got the police report right here.

**Sasha:** Drugs? Alcohol?

**Peyton:** It was a high school party in LA, of course there were drugs and alcohol. Duh. But the toxicology report on the driver hasn't come in yet. Since the case is so new, there's no other information to confirm, but it's safe to say that I won't be surprised if we find out he was drunk or high. He has a reputation after all.

**Sasha:** Horrible. What kind of person would do that?

**Peyton:** Someone who's not told *no* a whole lot. He actually just returned from a stint at a behavioral rehabilitation center—basically military school, but he came back to Armstrong Prep for his senior year. Could it be that he hasn't learned his lesson?

**Sasha:** Was Ethan the one hosting the party again? Like that accident before?

**Peyton:** No, for once. This party was thrown by the son of a multimillion-dollar housing developer, using the unfinished mansions like their own personal playground. Out in Mandeville Canyon, most of the houses are just skeletons of what their grandeur will soon be. Because they're empty and on winding streets up the mountain, with excellent views of the ocean by the way, it's the perfect location for a party to run wild. No neighbors to complain about the noise. No running water, no electricity, no rules. Rich kids just party different from the rest of us. Armstrong is like that.

**Sasha:** What makes the school so special?

**Peyton:** At Armstrong, there's this thing called the Headmaster's List. Only a few students are chosen every year, but everyone tries to make the cut since it's a surefire way to get into the best colleges. The Headmaster himself writes your recommendation. It's super competitive. Think of it as an honor roll but on steroids.

**Sasha:** Are you on it?

**Peyton:** No, sadly. I'd kill for a spot. But I'm too busy with this podcast anyway! Guess who is, though! None other than Ethan Amoroso. The crazy part is that everyone in that car was on the List too. The only one who wasn't was the victim, Chris Moore.

**Sasha:** That's crazy! I hope justice can be served, that Ethan will face the consequences of his actions.

**Peyton:** We'll see about that. His family is wealthy, like, absurdly wealthy. His parents are on what the school calls the "Headmaster's Circle," an exclusive club only for the richest donors to the school. It's easy for Armstrong to look the other way when you're in the Circle, especially when your family is helping to pay for a new stadium or the year's theater production. Is he on the Headmaster's List because of his daddy's money? Who knows. But I've been going to private school long enough to be cynical about these types of things. He's going to have a ton of resources on his side, but one can only hope that the case against him is strong. It's a shadowy reminder that privilege is a real problem. Being in Armstrong's good graces has shielded him from a lot of consequences. Affluenza is a disease! That's why I want to start a fundraiser for the victim's family, so I'll set up a link on our Instagram page where you can donate in their time of mourning. Maybe we'll add a pin or T-shirts, showing support and getting the word out about the case. Justice for Chris!

I plan to keep you and all our Salters up to date on this case as it inevitably proceeds. But first, a word from our sponsors . . .

*[End segment transcript]*

Update from the Uploader:

**BREAKING:** Ethan Amoroso has been charged with felony manslaughter! Stay tuned for more episodes!

# TWO

SPENCER WAS SECRETLY GRATEFUL THAT her parents had left her in peace for a couple minutes. If the doctors hadn't interfered, they would continue to fuss over her, constantly asking her every five minutes if she needed anything. Sleep. Lots of sleep. Maybe some more pain meds. A snack. And a book, something mindless. Her dad, chronically unable to sit still, went to the bookstore in the hospital lobby, no doubt picking up some reading material for them all, and her mom went to the cafeteria, hopefully grabbing Spencer as much cake and chocolate as her stomach could handle.

It was her younger sister Hope's first day of eighth grade at Santa Monica Middle School, so the lumpy chair she had draped herself in while flipping through channels on the television in the corner for the past week was empty. Things had been chaotic since the accident, but Spencer was starting to get into the rhythm of hospital life. Wake up, nurses make the rounds, a dietary aide asks her what she would like to eat for breakfast, eat breakfast that was unfortunately not sugary enough for her unquenchable sweet tooth, nap, check her pain levels, eat lunch, nap again, check her pain again, dinner, sleep, wake up with a nightmare, sleep, start over the next day.

Perhaps nightmare wasn't the right word. Night terror. Emphasis on the terror.

*Scream. Float. Crash.*

Memories of that night were still hazy, but the emotion was real. Her mind convinced her body that she was back in Ethan's Porsche, and she'd wake up in a cold sweat, screaming and crying, and the nurses would come running to make sure she wasn't being murdered. She couldn't help it. Flashbacks of the crash felt just the same as the real thing. Sometimes it would take a moment to realize where she was, but it would take hours for her heart to stop hammering in her chest and realize she wasn't actually dying.

It got bad enough that Spencer was afraid to close her eyes. She kept seeing the second before impact over and over again on a nonstop loop. They'd given her sleeping pills to help, but it could only do so much.

But being awake didn't solve her flashbacks, either. She couldn't stop it.

The doctors said she would need time.

While Spencer was alone for a glorious few minutes, she tried not to think about the crash and focused on counting the drop ceiling tiles. Two hundred six, if anyone asked. She was sick and tired of the daytime talk shows on every television channel in existence. Her phone had folded in half in the crash, completely destroyed, so she wasn't able to text anyone, hence her newfound interest in counting tiles.

Her phone had been such a fixture in her hand, sometimes she'd fumble around in the folds of the sheet trying to find it before she remembered that it was gone. She wanted to think about literally anything else other than the wreck that was her life.

Hospitals, in Spencer's opinion, were made for three things: sickness, death, and waiting, the last of which Spencer was extraordinarily familiar with. They'd kept her for a week for observation, and that meant Spencer didn't do much else but be confined to her hospital bed for the better part of a week, bored to tears. Already, the skin beneath the cast on her arm was starting to itch. The surgeon had done a good job, at least from what she could tell, putting the bones back into place inside her body where they belonged.

That meant Spencer would have to get used to this cast for the next four weeks at least, plus physical therapy to get back in shape enough for field hockey. She'd played field hockey year-round since she was fourteen, and she wasn't about to let a broken arm, wrist, and face stop her now. Even if she did have such a huge gash on her cheek it hurt to even smile.

Voices carried down the hall. They were muffled at first but got clearer as they grew closer.

"Oh, she's my sister, it's okay."

Before the baffled nurse could say anything more, Olivia's smile entered the room first, in her bubbly Olivia way, clutching a fistful of balloons in her hand. Olivia Santos definitely wasn't Spencer's sister, but they might as well have been. Ever since middle school, they had been next to each other on class attendance sheets, always had their lockers next to each other, and were practically joined at the hip. Muscles she didn't even know were tight loosened in Spencer's back when she saw her best friend in the whole world.

"Wow, you look terrible!" Olivia said with a grin, her cheerful face a welcome difference from the tired and professional expressions of the hospital staff.

"Hey, Liv."

Olivia snapped her gum between her teeth, dark eyebrows rising behind her round, gold-framed glasses. "Dang, you must be on some heavy-duty stuff. That's the best you can say to me?"

*Dang.* Olivia had the tongue of a sailor, more apt for a pirate with an eye patch and a peg leg. Even though she dressed like a woodland fairy when they weren't in their school uniforms and flitted into any room she entered because simply walking was too boring, she disarmed anyone who wasn't expecting it with her dirty mouth. She only censored herself when she was particularly upset, which was somehow more sobering than Spencer had anticipated.

Spencer hadn't looked at herself in the mirror since the crash, opting to avert her gaze whenever she hobbled to the en suite bathroom, like when she'd spook herself after playing a game of Bloody Mary at a sleepover and she was too afraid to look in the mirror and find out if the legend was true.

If it was as bad as it felt, Spencer didn't need to see.

Every time her fingers accidentally brushed over the stitches across her cheek to wipe away a stray hair, her thoughts immediately went to Frankenstein's monster. Children would see her in the street and scream and run for their lives. She couldn't blame them.

"It's not so bad . . . ," she said.

Spencer's eyes went to the IV bag, where more of the drugs were dripping through her veins. It was nice—the outside of her mind was soft and fuzzy, like the edges of a faded photograph.

"You look like you've lost about twenty IQ points. That stuff is making you dumber than you already are."

Their friendship was strong enough to consist of plenty insults-of-love, but Spencer didn't have the frame of mind to reply quickly. She felt like she would float away if not being held down by all these IV lines and weighted blankets.

"You better be bringing me coffee with that kind of roast," Spencer said, her lips lifting in a smile.

Olivia snorted and pulled out a Starbucks mocha-in-a-can from her purse, sweating with condensation and cool from the vending machine, and put it down with a flourish on Spencer's food tray, saying, "That better have not been a pun."

"I love you so much," Spencer said, cracking it open.

"Me, or the mocha?"

"It's not mutually exclusive." She always had a sweet tooth.

Olivia snorted and pulled up a chair to sit next to Spencer's bed. If Spencer hadn't gotten into the crash, she and

Olivia would be at the local café, Beans, right now—a ritual during their lunch break at school—and a privilege to go off campus grounds for the hour.

Olivia kicked her shoes off and rested her bare feet on Spencer's bed, as if she wasn't here because her friend had just suffered a traumatic car crash, but like she was lounging at the beach. Her blue toenail polish was chipped. Spencer wasn't sure why she focused on that detail—the painkillers made everything slow down, allowed her to hone her focus on the minor stuff, like seeing the detective's chewed pen cap that first night. She felt like her brain was processing information at half speed.

Spencer took a sip of her mocha and the sweetness of the chocolate instantly made her feel a thousand times better. She had been sick and tired of drinking apple juice out of the little plastic cups they gave her at mealtimes.

"For real, though," Olivia said, "how are you doing?"

"I'm okay. Surgery went well. No scissors left inside me, I'd call that a major win." She wiggled her fingers in her cast.

Olivia's eyes went to Spencer's cast. "I don't just mean your arm."

Spencer's lip twitched when she tried to smile. Blink. *Scream. Float. Crash.* The memory hit her just as quickly as the car hit the tree. She should never play poker; she wore her emotions on her face like a bright neon sign. "It's whatever."

That really was all she remembered of the crash.

Everything else was too out of her reach. Scrubbed clean. A blank slate.

Olivia's full lips were pressed into a thin line, but she didn't ask any more about it. From her purse, she pulled out a purple Sharpie. Olivia's bag was like Mary Poppins's, a nether realm of infinite space. Sometimes Spencer wondered what she *didn't* have in there—a severed and cursed human hand, a toboggan, the secrets of the universe? Olivia began absently drawing on Spencer's cast. She'd broken her left arm and shoulder in the crash, her dominant arm. Olivia decorating her cast would at least be an aesthetically pleasing temporary art piece in the meantime.

Olivia was a gifted artist, having won a series of art contests at Armstrong, her usual medium being charcoal, but her talent wasn't lost on the groove of Spencer's cast.

"Sorry I couldn't come see you earlier," Olivia said without looking up from her work. "They wouldn't let non-immediate family members in at first."

"I would have said you were my sister too, for the record."

"You better! We're practically twins."

"It's nice having you here. Things have been a little strict and all. Cops everywhere, trying to figure out what happened."

Olivia nodded soberly. "You really don't remember anything?"

"We talked to a neurologist, and a ton of doctors; they ran a bunch of tests. Apparently it's really common with head injuries after these kinds of accidents. I might get my memories back, I might not."

"Don't stress about it. Just don't hit your head anymore. You need all the brain cells you have left."

Spencer tugged on the end of Olivia's straight, platinum-dyed bob but let out a breathy laugh. Olivia swatted her hand away and stuck out her tongue.

"For real, though," she said, "do you remember that night?"

Spencer shook her head. "I remember the party. But, like, bits and pieces. I remember a fight with Ethan . . ." Olivia raised her eyebrows ever so slightly at that, but Spencer didn't point it out. Olivia always had opinions about Ethan, but she had kept them to herself, resigning herself to only the language of her eyebrows to indicate any sort of feeling.

Olivia hadn't been at the party. Though they were best friends, they didn't do absolutely everything together. Olivia's definition of fun ended promptly at teenage shenanigans and loud drunk people. Spencer simultaneously wished Olivia had been there, just so they could talk about it, but she also regretted that she hadn't decided to stay in with Olivia instead.

Spencer still couldn't wrap her head around the fact that Ethan had been charged for the crash. She'd heard police officers talking about it outside her hospital room a few days earlier. The tips of her ears burned at hearing his name. At one point not too long ago, her stomach swooshed with excitement hearing it. Now his name just left her feeling bitter.

"After that, I don't remember anything except, like, flashes. It's hard to explain. Like, I blink, and sometimes I remember it, the tree coming right at me. But the rest is just blank." *What with a literal gallon of painkillers coursing through my veins*, she thought.

"But you know about Chris, right?"

"Yeah. I know." The words felt like they took up a lot of space in her throat, and she had a hard time swallowing. She couldn't even take a sip of her mocha.

Chris Moore, everyone's little brother, had been pronounced dead at the scene. Killed instantly, was how everyone put it, taking away the implied edge of suffering. She didn't want to imagine the circumstances that would kill a person instantly, so she fought to keep that thought away.

It was hard for her to believe he was dead. Spencer could still see Chris's lopsided grin in her mind's eye. He was the son of one of her favorite teachers, Mr. Moore, and she'd seen the family resemblance from the start. Thinking he was dead now didn't feel right, like it was a fact she needed to disprove somehow because she'd just seen him the other day! He'd come to the Brain Freeze, the ice cream kiosk that she and Olivia worked at part time and on weekends, and he'd ordered a large chocolate-dipped cone, extra sprinkles.

He couldn't be gone, that just didn't happen to kids their age. And yet it was true; otherwise Ethan wouldn't be in so much trouble.

*Oh, Ethan . . .* Her stomach clenched wondering where he was now. It was a miracle he'd been able to walk away from the wreck with only a couple of scrapes, whiplash, and a broken nose. He was lucky. The bastard.

Spencer hadn't known Chris too well since he was younger than she was, but they mingled in the same circles, even though he was an AV kid glued to his computer.

"His funeral was today," Olivia said quietly, not looking up from her work on Spencer's cast.

There was nothing to say to that. Olivia cleared her throat and started coloring in the alien creature's face on Spencer's cast with crosshatch strokes.

No one expected Spencer to be at the funeral. She was still too injured to go anywhere except the five feet it took to get to the bathroom and back. The doctors were still concerned about her concussion and resulting memory loss. The last thing they wanted was for her to fall unconscious while in their care. The funeral was off-limits. She doubted Chris's parents would want to see her anyway. Seeing her might have been a bitter reminder of what their son wasn't—alive.

Olivia didn't mention Chris again the whole time she decorated Spencer's cast. Spencer had let a rerun episode of Steve Irwin's excitement over a venomous snake fill in the silence. In Olivia's own words, she didn't do well in the whole "expressing one's feelings" department; she'd rather put it on paper with charcoal. Spencer focused on her drink and finished it just as Olivia started sketching the outlines of a tentacled monster wrapping itself around Spencer's wrist.

In a mood to change the subject, Spencer asked, "How's the first week of school?"

Olivia rolled her eyes. "Typical. Spencer Sandoval gets into a freaking car crash and all she can think about is school and homework. Be normal, Miss Overachiever."

Spencer didn't deny it. Overachieving was in her DNA. "Please! It'll make me feel like everything's the way it used to be for a little bit." Spencer was one of the top students in her class, earning a coveted position on the Headmaster's List—the alumni of which went on to become Pulitzer Prize–winning journalists, esteemed artists, even US senators vying for the presidency. She'd worked hard for it.

Olivia didn't put up a fight. Who could argue with a bruised and bloodied girl in a cast? "Well, Becca Thompson got that nose job she was talking about. We've got a sub for history since Mr. Moore, you know, because . . . And the whole school is talking about the crash, like it's the next . . . Maybe we shouldn't talk about it." She went back to her drawing.

"What are they saying?" Spencer knew from her tone that it wasn't going to be good.

Olivia looked hesitant.

"Come on, I've got no connection to the outside world. I need to know."

Olivia took a long second, cringed, and said, "Let's just say people are . . . *happy* to see Ethan get arrested. Like, almost rabid with excitement. There was this viral video that went around online of the cops taking him out in handcuffs and people made memes and stuff. I just think it's so crass. I mean, a kid died, why do we treat this like some reality TV show? I know we live in LA, but come on."

Spencer's stomach dropped as Olivia spoke. A chill streaked down her back and she suppressed a shiver. *Scream. Float. Crash.* All other details hazy, but she could relive those few seconds over and over again without any control. Breaking up with Ethan that night was still as raw as the gash in her cheek. She remembered that much, but only bits and pieces of their fight before the crash. Breaking up with Ethan had hurt deeper than any physical pain she'd experienced.

When she wasn't remembering the crash, she was remembering the way Ethan had broken her heart.

"That junior, Peyton Salt?" Olivia said. "The one with the podcast. She's all over the story like it's her own ticket to fame. She's milking what happened for her own credibility. It's gross. She's making it seem like it's this story, and . . . well, it's working. Ethan is a bad guy everyone can hate."

It had been an accident. Why were people acting like Ethan had meant to hurt anyone? Sure, he drove a little too fast sometimes, and he got a few tickets now and again, but he wasn't a monster. Spencer and Ethan dated for two years, even when he was sent away to a behavioral rehabilitation camp. Two years of movie nights, and Valentine's Day presents, and texts goodnight. He had always been wild, full of life, and had a way of sending a thrill down her spine, but did people really hate him that much?

Olivia sighed. "Sorry, I didn't mean to unload all of that on you." As if sensing the shadow looming over Spencer's head, Olivia tried to lighten the mood. "You'd be happy to know that I've got a metric ton of homework for you in my bag, so you've got something to do, you crazy person."

Spencer smiled ever so slightly.

# THREE

SPENCER TURNED THE ORANGE PILL bottle over in her hands, worrying at the sticker label with her name on it with the edge of her nail. Vicodin was going to be her best friend for the next few months while she recovered. Earlier in the day, after passing all the discharge checks, she'd been cleared to go home and would start school tomorrow, Monday, a whole week late. Never did she think she'd be so eager to get back to normal.

"One or two tablets every four to six hours as needed," the doctor said while her mom packed Spencer's clothes and things away into a duffel bag she had brought along for the long stay. Spencer was finally going home, and she was more than ready to fall into her own bed and crawl under her own sheets. The doctor was sure to give her the rundown on what to do when not being looked after twenty-four seven. "Try not to take too much more than that if you can help it. Your clavicle will be sore for a long time since we can't splint it, so try not to move it too much."

"And that means no field hockey," her mom said.

The doctor nodded. "Especially no field hockey. Any sort of contact sport, really anything to do with your upper body, is off-limits. That means no carrying heavy things, like helping out with groceries, until we can make sure you're healing up right."

"What about school? I can barely hold a pen."

"I'll forward a note to your school. You'll probably have to have someone else take notes for you and carry your books until you're able to do it yourself. Spencer, need I remind you that you shattered several bones in your wrist? You need to take it easy and manage your pain until you can get back to your usual routine. You can't rush this."

Olivia had delivered Spencer's homework to her every day she couldn't attend, but her left arm was useless, and writing with her nondominant hand was harder than she'd thought. The idea that someone would need to take notes for her in class was more annoying than she wanted to admit. She had a very particular method of note-taking, and studying in general, that involved intense organization and color coordination. The person would need to be in all her classes, and be good at taking notes like she was, and be willing to tolerate her finely tuned strategies for maintaining her GPA. She couldn't afford to fall down on her grades, especially not now.

Her dream was to get into Caltech. She wanted to be an astrophysicist, even an astronaut if she could pass the tests, more than anything in the universe, and if she slipped up in even one subject, it could make or break her future. No one, nothing, especially not broken bones, was going to stand in her way.

"How long until I can play?" she asked. "Field hockey is

the only thing keeping me sane right now." Spencer didn't want to whine, but it hurt being told not to compete. She had been conditioning all summer long, running sprint drills in the park, footwork circuits with cones and jump ropes in her backyard, and going for hour-long runs before even the sun woke up. Being told to sit on the couch was about as easy as telling the sky not to be blue.

"Come back and see me in a couple of weeks when we get your cast off and then we can talk about physical therapy and getting you back onto the field. You want to have use of your hand again, don't you?"

"Yeah," Spencer said with a sigh. She knew field hockey wasn't everything, but a whole part of her life had been taken away in a single instant. Why couldn't she have broken the bones on the right side of her body? Even the surgeon had said he'd expected her right shoulder to have been broken instead, consistent with car crashes of this type, but of course she couldn't be that lucky. The important part was that she was expected to make a full recovery. That was what mattered.

The doctor went on, "I also want to help arrange a psychotherapist for your night terrors. PTSD isn't something that can heal as easily as broken bones, so you need a specialist who can help. Mrs. Sandoval—excuse me, Dr. Sandoval—I'll forward you a recommendation list so you can decide who is the best fit."

"Thank you." Mom and Dad were both veterinarians but still earned their titles as doctors. They were both from immigrant families, and Spencer and her sister were the first generation born in the States.

The doctor left, and her mom packed away the last of Spencer's things into her duffel bag before she held out a helping hand for her daughter to slide into a wheelchair, which Spencer thought was a bit overkill. Without delay, she wheeled Spencer out of the room, almost like she too was finally getting sick of the smell of antiseptic cleaner and soap.

The nurses bid her goodbye as they passed, which was definitely a nice touch on what Spencer could only summarize as being one of the most miserable times of her life, but she smiled and thanked them for their kindness.

In the elevator on the way down, Spencer twisted around to look at her mom. She wasn't wearing her usual green scrubs with a paw print embroidered on the breast. Sometimes it startled Spencer seeing both of her parents out of uniform, only because they were so often at the clinic. She didn't want to imagine how many hours they had to close its doors to take care of her.

Their vet clinic, a twenty-four seven emergency animal hospital called Paws Perfect in Culver City, was almost always busy. But Spencer had never seen dark circles as deep around her mom's eyes as they were now.

"I'm freaking out about school," Spencer said. "I can't miss any more days. The Caltech admissions office will probably look at my record and see a gap, and what if they don't care about what happened?"

Her mom only smiled in that tired but soft way that meant she understood it was Spencer's perfectionism getting the best of her. She squeezed Spencer's right shoulder assuredly.

"We'll figure everything out. Don't you worry. For now, there's someone special waiting for you at home."

The entire drive home, Spencer could barely open her eyes. She had them squeezed shut as she gripped the car door's armrest, willing herself not to panic. Every time her mom so much as tapped her foot on the gas, Spencer's stomach lurched like she was going to fall, and she gripped the armrest so hard, her fingers were numb and weak. Her hips were still bruised from where the seat belt in the Porsche had stopped her from flying through the windshield, and her sternum ached with the pressure the seat belt put on her chest now in her mom's Nissan Leaf.

"You okay, Spence?" her mom asked as they paused at a stoplight.

"Fine," she said through gritted teeth. "Just . . . go. Please?"

The light turned green, and Spencer braced herself. *Scream. Float. Crash.* Her throat was closing up and she tried not to go back to the crash, but it was easier said than done.

"We're almost home, sweetheart. Almost there." She eased the car forward once more.

Spencer was on the verge of tears but held her breath,

forcing herself not to cry. It burned in her chest. All she wanted was to fling the door open and throw herself out so she wouldn't have to endure it any longer.

She wondered if Tabby Hill, the other passenger who'd survived the crash, was feeling the same way about driving. Spencer knew Tabby, who was nonbinary, had just gotten their license. What if Tabby was too afraid to drive now? And Ethan . . . what was Ethan doing right now? Guilt was a monster roiling in her gut. If she'd been the one driving, what would have happened?

She wouldn't be deathly afraid of moving vehicles, that was for sure.

*SPENCER!* She heard Ethan's scream, echoing in her thoughts, a second before the crash. It was a new memory, one that punched her in the gut, and she remembered the terrified look in Ethan's eyes, the side of his face lit up as the headlights closed in on the tree before . . . His face was all wrong, all wrong, but she didn't know why.

Spencer covered her eyes with her hands and willed herself to breathe. She counted the seconds it took to inhale, and exhale, until her mom pulled them up to the driveway and turned the car off.

Their house, a cozy Craftsman-style two-story in West Los Angeles, was lit up in the bright blue afternoon sky. Spencer's car, a beat-up minivan (named "Gertie" because the van looked like a Gertie), which she'd bought off Craigslist when she got her license, would remain parked in the driveway for the foreseeable future. Hope and Dad were already home, waiting for them. She even spotted the flicker of the television through the living room window. Everything about the house seemed normal, and it occurred to Spencer that it was she herself who had changed.

Spencer tried to wiggle herself out of the passenger's seat, fumbling—thanks to her cast—with the lock on the seat belt. She couldn't get out of the car fast enough.

"Do you need any help, sweetheart?" Spencer's mother asked, a permanent furrow between her brows these days.

"I said I'm fine, Mom." Spencer unclipped her seat belt and opened the door. Her father had already opened the front door, waiting for them with a big grin.

Spencer's home was a much welcome change from the eggshell-colored walls of the hospital. The living room was the heart of the house, warm and vibrant with plush furniture and low-pile rugs that made one want to curl up with a book plucked from the wall of shelves. Her mom had put a mountain of candles inside the fireplace since they hardly used it. The couch in the living room looked like an awful good place to park herself after the arduous car ride.

Hope already had the right idea, sprawled on the couch with her phone playing a game. Usually she would be in the garage hammering away at her Rube Goldberg machine, but it seemed like she'd been called in to welcome Spencer home, though begrudgingly so. It was actually kind of a relief that twelve-year-old Hope hadn't changed a bit since Spencer's accident, being annoying as ever, because that meant some things could get back to normal. Her parents treated her like she was made of glass and might shatter at even the lightest touch.

"I already called dibs on naming her," Hope said, without looking up from the screen. Her phone dinged cheerily, as if mocking Spencer's confusion.

"Dibs? Naming her?" Spencer asked.

"Hopie . . . She already has one," Dad said. He kissed Mom on the cheek as she came into the house, carrying Spencer's things for her.

Mom threw Hope a withering look that didn't have any kind of heat behind it. To Spencer she said, "Your father and I—we talked with your doctors, and your father made some calls to get it fast-tracked. We had some old friends from school running a program out in Boulder."

"What are you talking about?"

"Why don't you go to your room and see for yourself?"

Spencer looked back and forth between her parents, whose faces were bright and excited, and she knew she wasn't going to get anything else out of them. Curiously, Spencer made her way upstairs, taking the steps carefully by holding on to the handrail for support, not intending to let her excitement put her back in the hospital, and headed toward her room at the end of the hall.

Her room, warm and inviting, the perfect place for her to throw herself down on the bed and stare up at the glow-in-the-dark stars above, glad that she didn't have drop ceiling tiles to count anymore. She had taken pride in decorating the room herself, in a soft robin's-egg blue peeking out behind all her band posters, and she'd even built her desk facing a large window of their quiet street, where she would gaze absently, ruminating over her essays or giving her eyes a break from staring at a screen for hours. She'd missed her room desperately and was glad to be back.

The newest and most unexpected addition to her room was waiting for her at the foot of her bed.

Small sounds of excited panting came from a large crate at the end of Spencer's four-poster bed and a copper-colored tail wagged through the metal bars. It was a fox-red Labrador, poking its snout through the slates of the crate, watching her with warm brown eyes.

"A dog?" Spencer asked, turning as she heard her dad come up behind her.

He leaned casually on the doorframe. "She's your service dog. She's going to be helping you through your recovery." He avoided saying the term "post-traumatic stress" like it was a curse word. Instead, her parents elected to use "recovery" and "struggles," as if it made what had happened to Spencer not as crippling as some might make it out to be. Her parents were trained medical professionals, but they were experts in the four-legged variety of medicine. They were trying to make Spencer feel better by lessening the impact of a word like "disorder."

"Are you sure?" Spencer asked. She'd never had a dog before. Even though they were vets, her parents were at the clinic most of the time, and with Spencer and Hope in school and doing almost every extracurricular offered, no one was home to take care of one. It was like the cobblers' kids having no shoes. No pets for vets.

Her dad moved toward the crate and put his palm flat against the bars, letting the dog lick his hand. "Of course we're sure! She's here to help. Our friend from school runs a charity in Colorado specifically training dogs to care for people with psychiatric needs. Like pressure therapy, disrupting emotional overload, reminding you to take your medicine, and even waking you up from nightmares, if you have them." He said *if*, but he really meant *when*. Spencer had already woken up every night from flashbacks so real, she'd start screaming in her bed loud enough that the nurses came running. Spencer could hardly contain the bubble of emotion swelling in her chest.

She wanted to feel grateful, but she couldn't help that instead she felt resentful, and she hated herself for it. It wasn't the dog's fault, or her parents', for that matter. But the dog was a reminder of what had happened. Not only would the evidence literally be on her face, but now she would have a dog at her side, broadcasting to the world that she was . . . broken. Everyone would treat her differently. Everyone would see just how badly her life had been ruined.

Dad unlatched the crate and the dog ambled out, heading straight for Spencer, tail wagging expectantly. The dog was already wearing a vest with patches sewn onto it specifically saying SERVICE DOG and DO NOT PET and I'M AT WORK. She licked Spencer's hand, then nudged it with her wet nose. Spencer wiped the drool on her jeans. Labs were always so slobbery; she'd seen her fair share at her parents' clinic, and the coldness of it jarred her.

Her mom appeared behind them, already having swapped out her contacts for her grandma glasses everyone so lovingly teased her about. "We still have to sort it out with the office at Armstrong, because you'll need to take her out at least once during the school day to do her business, but your doctors agreed, a service animal is a good idea."

"That's right, but remember, Spence," Dad added, "this isn't a pet. It's serious. She's a working dog, doing an important job. She's your friend, but she's also here to help you. She's to perform specific tasks and not play with your classmates. Understood?"

All manner of thoughts swirled in Spencer's head. She really wished that things could go back to normal, and a dog right now was feeling like a lot, on top of having to constantly be reminded about what Ethan had done every time she moved her shoulder wrong or caught her reflection in passing. Hesitantly, she asked, "Do I have to?"

"What's the matter?"

Spencer worried her lower lip with her teeth. "It's just another reason for people to stare."

Her parents glanced at each other before her mom said, "Sweetheart . . . It's for the best. Truly. Once you get used to it, you'll see."

"But what if I don't want to get used to it? What if I want things to be like they were? Normal?"

"This is normal. Lots of people have service dogs. There's

nothing to be ashamed of. This doesn't change who you are. You're still you, only now you're you with a little sidekick."

Dad said, "We'll feel better if you had some help when we're not around. You'll have more freedom too, especially at school."

Spencer dreaded the thought of school now. What would everyone at Armstrong think? *Poor little Spencer Sandoval needs special treatment, boo-hoo.* The dog looked up at her, eyes bright, tail wagging, waiting for a command. If things had been different, maybe Spencer would have been more excited about it, but pain in her shoulder was making her grumpy. It wasn't the dog's fault that she was in this mess. If this dog could help her focus on her schoolwork and get her back on track for Caltech, she guessed she could give it a shot.

Spencer took a deep breath and relented. "What's her name?"

"Ripley, like from *Alien*. Apparently, her handler was very into sci-fi movies. I think it suits her, though."

"Ripley, huh," Spencer said, testing it out. The dog's tongue snapped back into her mouth at the sound of her name, and Spencer smiled. It helped that Ripley was cute.

They would have a lot of work to do together.

# FOUR

**THAT NIGHT AT DINNER, RIPLEY** sat under Spencer's chair at the dining room table, exactly as she was trained to do, while they all ate together as a family, a Sunday evening ritual that seemed more important than ever according to Mom. She'd ordered takeout from their favorite Thai restaurant—a special treat after all the hospital food everyone had been eating for the past two weeks—sure to add some desperately desired spice to Spencer's craving for flavor. The egg rolls smelled divine, and she almost swallowed them whole without chewing first. Even with a week's worth of practice, it was still hard using her right hand to eat. Chopsticks were impossible to manage, so a fork had to do.

No one spoke for a while, as if no one was sure what to say anymore. What else was left besides the treacherous topic of Spencer's ex-boyfriend having accidentally killed a kid?

Spencer was thankful that no one said much while they ate. She wasn't in the mood to talk about it, she was so tired, and she absently rubbed her foot on Ripley's back, raking her toes lengthwise down her spine. Ripley's leg thudded excitedly on the floor as Spencer hit just the right spot.

"What's this around Ripley's neck? It doesn't look like a normal collar." Spencer referred to a black band with a plastic rectangle on it, sitting above Ripley's leather one with her ID tag on it.

"Oh, it's just a GPS thing, all service dogs have them." Her dad shrugged.

"So when will you be normal again?" Hope demanded. She was using her chopsticks like two spears, one in each hand.

"There's nothing wrong with her," Dad said matter-of-factly. "Besides, it's not what we say about these kinds of things. There's nothing wrong with Spencer."

Hope ran her tongue over her braces and added, "Well, my friends at school are talking."

"Is it talking or is it just rumors, Hopie?" Mom said.

"What's the difference?"

"Rumors mean it's not true."

"They say Ethan was drunk or high, which means he's definitely guilty."

"Can we talk about something else?" Spencer interrupted, trying to put on a smile but failing. She hated how her heartbeat accelerated at the simple mention of his name.

*Scream. SPENCER! Float. Crash. Pain.*

She blinked furiously, scrubbing Ethan's terrified face out of her mind's eye. If she'd been holding wooden chopsticks, she was sure she would have snapped them in half, her grip was that tight.

"Okay," Hope said, and shrugged, eyeing the last egg roll on the plate. Spencer didn't blame her; she was at least saying what was on her mind rather than hiding behind a false sense of normalcy. The pain radiating from Spencer's shoulder gave her something to focus on. She needed another dose of Vicodin. The one she'd taken at the hospital was starting to wear off.

"How are you feeling about going to school tomorrow?" her mom asked. "You can stay home another week if you'd like . . . Get back into the swing of things slowly."

"No, I want to go. I need to. I don't want to be stuck in bed anymore."

"I can drive you," her dad offered, but Spencer shook her head. Usually she took Gertie the Van because she had field hockey after school, but she didn't want to be in a car again.

"I'll ride my bike. It'll be a nice workout before class at least."

"With Ripley?"

"She can run alongside. It's not *that* far to school," she said. They lived below Pico, whereas most kids who went to Armstrong Prep lived right by school in the tony neighborhood where it was located. "Right? I can't . . . I don't want to get into a car again. At least, not for a while."

Her parents glanced at each other. Mom tipped her head and murmured, "Riding home was rough for her today."

Dad looked at Spencer in a way that made her heart break, so she stared at her plate. "Sure, kiddo," he said. "Anything you need. Ripley will be with you the whole time, but if you ever feel like you need to come home early or if you're not feeling well—"

"I'm not made of glass, I swear, I'll be fine."

Her parents exchanged looks, but they didn't fight her—there was no winning against Spencer's determination.

Dad said, "The doctors mentioned that it will take a little while for you to adjust to everything, and we don't want you to push yourself too hard."

That used to be Spencer's every day. She had always needed to give everything of herself and more at work, school, and at field hockey practice. She'd enrolled in almost every club possible: debate, yearbook, chess, pi club, somehow able to fit everything into the day and still have time to work and eat and sleep. For her, taking it easy was not, in fact, easy. Some people might call her stubborn and hardheaded, and she was not used to asking for help.

With her broken arm now, though, she didn't want that to slow her down, although inevitably it would. She needed to focus on getting her applications done for college and she couldn't miss the deadline. Caltech wasn't going to wait for her. They wouldn't care if she broke her arm and was late on submission. Besides, Spencer hated being late, more so when others were late. Nothing else put her in a bad mood more than someone showing up later than they said they would.

Injured or not, she was going to get everything in on time.

"Weren't you guys the ones who said I needed to get into the best school?"

"That was before . . . ," Spencer's mother said.

"Before what, a debilitating car crash that killed a kid and almost killed me?"

Shocked silence.

After a moment, Mom barely managed to say, "It was an accident, Spencer. You need to go easy on yourself. It wasn't anyone else's fault but Ethan's. He's made some mistakes and now he's suffering the consequences. It's not up to you to decide what happens to him next. You need to focus on yourself and your future."

The way she said it made it sound like Ethan's future was already decided for him. Again, she saw his face, lit up in her memory, the surprise, the panic . . . He'd looked at her, right before impact, like he'd wanted to see her right before it all went dark. And something about it didn't feel right. She didn't know what, but she kept seeing his face every time she closed her eyes, like he'd been the one who died, and not Chris. His beautiful face was haunting her.

"May I be excused?" Spencer asked. "I need to get my stuff ready for school tomorrow."

Her parents exchanged another round of looks. She expected that would be happening a lot in her presence. Her attitude could use a check, but she had pity points she was willing to cash in. No one argued with her when she pushed back from the dining room table and Ripley moved out from underneath, following her up the stairs, taking the steps with her at her side. Only two years old and already so well trained, it was like Ripley knew what Spencer needed at all times.

When they made it back to her room, Ripley took up

a spot at the foot of Spencer's bed and watched as Spencer moved around her room, gathering her notebooks and supplies for her late start at Armstrong. Her uniform hung on a hanger, pressed and ready in her closet.

It was a nighttime ritual she looked forward to. She always put her things in her bag the night before school, sorted her books by smallest to largest to fit in the largest pocket, stowed her pencil case on top, and double-checked that her headphones were wrapped neatly in their case. Organizing everything the night before meant that it was one less thing she had to worry about in the morning. Even being five minutes early for something was considered late according to Spencer—a fact that Olivia liked to heckle her about. Olivia had a casual relationship with schedules. But Spencer was adamant. Her future was on the line.

In fact, when she'd taken the SATs just last month, Spencer got pulled over for running a stoplight, which forced her to have less time before the test to study, giving her only forty minutes when she'd planned on having a full hour. She didn't want to admit that it threw her off her rhythm. It'd be all her fault if she lost five hundred points on the test because of it.

Spencer wiggled her fingers in her cast, analyzing just how she would be able to put on the long-sleeved white blouse over her cast and decided it would be a problem for tomorrow. She turned to Ripley lying patiently on her bed, her head lowered between her front paws but watching Spencer with eyebrows raised, ready to jump into action at the first sign.

"What am I forgetting?" Spencer asked, mostly to herself but directed at Ripley. It was an attempt to jog her memory.

She moved to her closet, making sure she had everything for her uniform, and instead she found one of Ethan's hoodies, hanging on a hanger. Her stomach dropped at the sight of it. Evidence of him kept popping up, she couldn't escape him. In one move, she pulled the hoodie from the hanger and looked at it. Green, his favorite color, with a white stripe down both sleeves. She'd loved wearing it, especially at night when she could curl up in bed, pretending he was next to her. It still smelled like him, and she frowned.

Her parents hadn't approved of Spencer's relationship with Ethan, but they never stopped her from dating him. She knew they thought he was spoiled and irresponsible even though they never said it out loud. They had rules about people being over when they weren't around, as well as a keep-her-bedroom-door-open policy too, in case anything got too wild. They might have hoped that she would outgrow him, see that they just weren't compatible. At the end of the day, Spencer supposed they were right, but she would never admit it to them.

With a noise of disgust, she crumpled up the hoodie, threw it into a corner of her closet where it landed in a heap on the floor, and yanked the closet door shut, sealing her feelings away.

"I can't stop thinking about him, Ripley," Spencer said, keeping her voice low in case Hope had her ear pressed up against the closed door, which was an all-too-common occurrence in the house.

Ripley just looked at her, eyebrows moving as if trying to analyze the look on Spencer's face, trying to figure out if she needed help. Spencer wasn't sure this was the kind of thing Ripley would be able to help with. Everyone had said that the crash was an accident, but Spencer had the strangest feeling that things didn't happen the way everyone said they did.

*Scream. SPENCER! Float. Tree. Ethan. Crash.*

It was so strange. She remembered seeing the palm tree, lit up, brighter and brighter, as the headlights went careening toward it. Ethan's face, his eyes. The roar of the engine. Like an old VCR she could pause and rewind the memory.

She wasn't able to place a concrete reason as to why, but it felt like a pinprick in the back of her mind that something was wrong.

She still had no memory of the crash, or some of the hours leading up to it. The last part of that night she specifically remembered was breaking up with Ethan, screaming at each other, her back to the party raging behind them, Ethan's face slathered in guilt. His hands, the bounce of his hair as he shook his head, the dot of light in his dark eyes as he pleaded with her to forgive him, the way his cologne washed over him. It was a memory so real, she could touch it. But she couldn't remember getting into the car with him. Why had she gotten in his car if they were fighting?

*Scream. Float. Crash.*

And then the next thing she remembered was being in the hospital. It was like her brain was a thousand-piece puzzle and she was missing five hundred pieces and the box with the picture on it had been thrown away. No guide. There were so many questions that she needed answers to, and none of it made any sense.

"I know I'm probably overthinking this," she said to Ripley, knowing full well it wasn't any use talking to a dog, but it made her feel better saying the words out loud. "I just can't help but think it isn't right. I can see Ethan in my mind, but something is wrong. Something . . ." In her memory, he'd been wearing that hoodie in the crash. How could it be possible, though? Unless memories were overlapping one another, of driving with him before . . . Something else about his face was wrong, but she didn't know what. She couldn't trust her own mind anymore.

*SPENCER! Crash.*

Ripley tilted her head at Spencer, the folds of her ears raised curiously. Of course, she didn't know what Spencer was saying, but it was funny to think she did.

"You believe me, right, Rip? You don't think I'm crazy?"

Ripley's tongue lolled cheerfully.

"It's okay if you do. I think I'm crazy."

Ripley yawned and put her head on her paws, blinking drowsily. It was getting late.

So Spencer went to bed with Ripley warming her feet, staring at the glowing stars on her ceiling, seeing the lines of the tree and hearing Ethan's voice, until she fell asleep.

# FIVE

**SPENCER PARKED HER BIKE AT** the rack in front of the east entrance at Armstrong Prep and caught her breath, wiping the sweat on her brow with the back of her wrist.

The school, a building in Romanesque Revival that exemplified the elite education that would be taking place inside its walls, sat on the edge of a hilltop surrounded by dense forest and gardens. It radiated excellence. Anyone who looked at it got a sense that this was an important place to be. To Spencer, it was just school.

Ripley waited patiently for Spencer to lock up her bike, panting after having jogged alongside Spencer the whole thirty-minute ride from her house to school.

She'd had to pedal fast to get there on time. Even though she had prepared for her return to Armstrong, she still scrambled to remember things before she could head out the door, like taking her medicine, and showering without getting her cast wet, and making time for her mom to help her with her braids because she couldn't do it with one hand. On top of that she couldn't find her favorite flats, the sparkly ones with bows, which Hope insisted she hadn't borrowed, which made Spencer have to settle for her old loafers. The medicine made everything soft, made her feel like she was losing track of everything.

She'd needed to figure out the safest route, avoiding the busiest streets and taking mostly neighborhood roads past the hedged estates and gated lawns, down the street where she worked at Brain Freeze, passing by St. Mary's with its marquee letter sign out front saying PRAY FOR JULIANNE, though groundskeepers were switching out the name with the beginnings of CHR, riding past the tents for homeless vets erected in the park, and taking a shortcut through the parking lot of the Brentwood Place Shopping Center. Admittedly, when she wasn't swerving out of the way of cars either oblivious to her presence or intentionally trying to get as close to her as possible to scare her, the ride itself was quite peaceful, what with the warm sea breeze slicing through the early morning sunlight that countered the dreamy haze of the morning's dose of painkillers. Spencer had quickly learned that the city was not designed for bikes. By the time she pulled up to school, she only had a couple minutes before the first bell.

Spencer cradled her cast to her chest as she fumbled with the bike lock's key in her right hand, trying to turn it but failing. This was one job Ripley couldn't do without opposable thumbs, but Spencer even had *those* and still struggled. She didn't want this one thing to fluster her, but she couldn't help the feeling of eyes watching her.

Before school, students often gathered on the front lawn,

sipping from their ventis and enjoying the last bits of the morning before the first bell ushered them into first period. Spencer was in the minority in riding her bike to school. It was more common to see BMWs and Teslas in the parking lot than her dad's old Schwinn on a bike rack, but that wasn't the reason people were staring at her now. She was capital *I* Involved in the crash that killed Chris Moore. Of course, she had prepared herself for this moment, ever since Olivia had said it was all the school talked about, but it didn't ease the tension that coiled in her gut when it was actually happening. Spencer tried to keep her head high, but no matter what, everyone knew. How was she supposed to get back to a normal life if she was forever labeled as That Girl from The Crash?

Even if they didn't know her name—which was wasn't likely since Armstrong's class sizes were small—they'd see it all over her face. The stitches in her cheek weren't going to be taken out for another week, but Spencer couldn't stand to miss out on any more school than she already had. It was her senior year, the most important to maintain her perfect GPA, and college application deadlines loomed. If she fell behind, even with her grade point average being one of the highest, she couldn't risk letting that be the deciding factor of her getting into Caltech or not.

She cursed under her breath when the key wouldn't twist in the lock. Would Caltech even want someone who failed at such a simple task as locking up a bike?

"Do you need some help?"

Without looking up, she said, "I got it." The key still wasn't turning. She wasn't going to be some damsel that needed Prince Charming to swoop in and save the day. Especially not Jackson Chen, Ethan's best friend.

"You sure?" Jackson's scuffed-up Vans appeared in her field of view as he stepped toward her. She lifted her eyes, squinting into the sunlight, landing on Jackson's gentle smile. Personality-wise, he was the polar opposite of Ethan. Whereas Ethan lived as if the runway was coming up short, Jackson's whole demeanor was more suited to the carefree surfer lifestyle. He had his skateboard tucked under his arm. Like Spencer, he'd opted to leave the car at home. He, however, lived closer to school than she did. He didn't look like he'd even broken a sweat.

"I'm fine." She wiggled the key, but it refused to budge. She thought about asking him how he was feeling, knowing his best friend wasn't coming to school, currently under house arrest, but she didn't quite know how to phrase it without sounding nosy. She settled on: "How are you?"

"Oh, you know. Here," he said with a shrug. Everyone knew that when a person said that, they were the opposite of *okay*. She knew that feeling all too well.

"Cute dog," he said about Ripley. Her tail slapped happily on the ground, as if she knew he was talking about her.

"Don't pet her. She's working." Spencer didn't mean to sound so clipped; her temper was shorter these days because everything wouldn't stop hurting.

"Of course. I can read, you know." He was referencing

the patches on Ripley's vest. "Doesn't change the fact that she's cute, but I'm not sure a service dog can turn a key. Are you sure you don't need a hand? Having two might work."

Spencer was about ready to kick her bike over in frustration before she took a deep breath. Riding her bike, especially so soon after the accident, may not have been such a great idea after all. Her legs already ached. But she'd never been in the habit of asking people for help. All her life, she'd been independent, getting a job scooping ice cream for some extra cash, picking up Hope after school in Gertie the Van, making dinner when their parents were working late. Asking for help was not in her user manual.

Before she could say anything else, Jackson kneeled down, setting his backpack and skateboard at his side, and pulled the chain tighter into the lock, allowing Spencer to twist the key.

"Thanks," Spencer said. She slipped it into the small pocket of her own backpack and picked up Ripley's leash.

"I get it. I broke my wrist skateboarding when I was ten. I don't think I have to tell you about the hassle of going to the bathroom . . ." The corner of his mouth quirked up, creating a little dimple in his tanned cheek. Unlike Ethan, he took a lot of the same AP courses that she did, but their schedules never lined up.

Spencer couldn't stop the smile that spread on her lips even though thinking about Ethan sent her stomach into knots. She'd known Jackson already for a few years, and seeing a friendly face eased her nerves.

Jackson was always the mild-mannered one whenever

Ethan would invite his friends over to swim in his pool, often the one to mellow out Ethan's high-octane energy with an easy laugh. He was on the soccer team with Ethan and was always over at his house. She had always thought he was cute, but seeing him now just reminded her of Ethan.

"Spencer!" Olivia's voice carried over the grounds. She was crossing the green lawn, waving her arm over her head.

Spencer thanked Jackson again before she and Ripley headed to the low wall where Olivia waited.

"And so she returns!" Olivia sang with a twinkle in her eye and together they headed into the building just as the first warning bell rang, giving them ten minutes to get to first period.

Coming back to Armstrong as a senior, Spencer expected much to stay the same. The long stretch of hallway branching off into classrooms lined with lockers painted burgundy to match school colors, the school crest in the tile underfoot, the posters broadcasting the upcoming homecoming dance and auditions for the school plays. School was back in session.

As Olivia guided her to where their new lockers would be for the year, Ripley made sure to keep the swell of students crowding through the halls at bay, a trained behavior that Spencer was more than a little thankful for. Obviously, people stared, both at Spencer and at the dog at her side. The crowd often parted like the Red Sea to get a better look. The flush on her cheeks stung. Her first day was already starting to be more overwhelming than she expected. The first thing she saw was a reminder of the crash.

A locker in the middle of the hall was covered in posters and flowers, messages left behind for Chris.

NEVER FORGOTTEN

MISS YOU FOREVER

LOVED YOUR SMILE

A group of sophomore girls stood in a circle close by, comforting another who was in tears, sobbing as mascara streaked down her cheeks. "I just m-miss him so m-much!" Her shoulders bounced with each hiccup.

Spencer kept her head low as she walked past. Chris's school photo was featured on a huge poster, smiling at her from the grave. He looked so young, especially for being only fifteen. It was a bitter reminder that he had just been a kid. Her stomach was threatening to rebel against her breakfast, but she kept walking. Everyone stared. She saw a couple of people wearing buttons with Chris's name on them. Voices carried, despite being hidden behind hands.

"—see her face?"

"Ethan's girlfriend—"

"Can't believe she's here . . ."

Spencer kept her focus firmly on the polished tile floors beneath her every footstep. Ripley bumped into her, encouraging her to keep going. Olivia eventually showed them to Spencer's new locker, conveniently right in front of the library entrance, and as expected, it was right next to Olivia's because of their last names. Spencer was grateful for the things that stayed the same today. No surprises.

Spencer gathered her things for homeroom. Per tradition,

Olivia and Spencer had synchronized their schedule, taking all the same classes, the only exception being homeroom— art for Olivia and study hour in the library for Spencer.

It took three tries doing her combination before Spencer got the locker open. She kept getting distracted by the unnerving feeling of stares on the back of her head.

"Just ignore them," Olivia murmured, gathering her acrylics from her decorated locker. This year's theme was apparently cottage core aesthetic, complete with a real daisy chain and pressed flowers on colorful construction paper collages taped to the back of the door. She always took the time to make her locker look pretty, saying it was a way to decompress in the middle of institutionalized academia designed to brainwash her into corporate life.

Spencer, however, liked the routine and schedule of school. Her binders were always color coordinated based on the subject, her notes meticulously organized and filed, and who didn't love a brand-new set of stationery at the beginning of the year? As words such as "anal-retentive" were thrown a lot whenever her name was brought up, Spencer preferred the term "chronically prepared."

Ripley pressed her body up against the back of Spencer's thighs, a gentle reminder that she was there, and Spencer nodded to Olivia, unable to find words that didn't make her feel like puking. She wanted to talk about the crash, about how it didn't feel right, but she didn't know where to begin. The bubble of anxiety in her chest was about to burst.

Before she could say anything, though, Olivia switched gears. "So, birthday."

Spencer was relieved for a subject change. She'd almost forgotten. "Right! Did you have anything in mind? How do you want to celebrate the big one-eight?" Olivia's birthday was at the end of October, but she liked planning for it ahead of time, for once taking a page out of Spencer's book.

"I'm thinking a huge party, maybe in Malibu? Vegan barbecue and a chocolate fountain, and a DJ. Maybe a bonfire? We can have them at Carillo Beach. I haven't decided yet."

Spencer let Olivia talk but tried not to show the twitch forming near her eye. The idea of a party right now, especially after what happened the night of the crash, set her teeth on edge. She couldn't tell Olivia no, though. Best friends don't *not* show up for a birthday party. It wasn't her party; she didn't get to decide what it would be. But she would be lying if she said she wasn't hoping to spend it as a night in with Olivia and a handful of friends ordering pizza and playing video games all night.

"Sounds great, Liv . . . ," Spencer said, hiding the edge in her voice as best she could. "I can't wait."

Olivia rolled her eyes, grinning. "I know, I should just lean into the whole Halloween thing and do costumes, but I want something new. Don't look at me like that. I know I'm being a cliché having my birthday on the beach. But I figure I only have so long to live out my dreams of kissing people by the ocean with a full moon high in the sky like in a high school rom-com!"

Just after the first bell, a voice came on over the sound system. "Good morning, Armstrong Eagles! Spencer Sandoval, please report to the headmaster's office. Spencer Sandoval."

"Uh-oh!" some guy called down the hall, jeering. "Someone's in *truh-bul*." A smattering of laughter followed.

Another voice called, "Your boyfriend better not've killed anyone else!"

Spencer went rigid, the muscles in her back seizing up. She closed her eyes and tried to quell the panic rising in her chest.

*Scream. Float. Crash.*

*SPENCER!*

Objectively she knew that wasn't why she had been called to see the headmaster. Her rational mind understood it was unlikely. But her body was trying to convince her that she was back in the car, going too fast, crashing. Sweat beaded on her forehead. Ripley tapped her cold nose on Spencer's palm, and it snapped her out of it long enough to remember to breathe.

"Shut up!" Olivia called at the heckler, which was only followed by more laughter. "Don't you have a bridge to live under, troll?"

"It's fine, Liv," Spencer said, slamming her locker shut. "I'll see you in physics."

# SIX

IT GOT EASIER AND EASIER to make her way to the administrative office as people hurried to homeroom, clearing the path for her all the way to the west wing of the building.

Before she could open the door it swung away from her, and she nearly crashed into someone coming out. She took a faltering step back and said, "Hi, Tabby."

Tabby's expression morphed from startled to shocked to disgust in the fraction of a second upon seeing Spencer.

"Oh, it's you."

That was not the kind of greeting Spencer expected. Tabby Hill's face was a sickly shade of yellow, an attempt to cover the obvious bruise that remained from the crash, the makeup only hiding so much. Like their namesake, Tabby glared at Spencer through a sharp wing of cat-eye eyeliner.

Tabby looked down at Ripley with a scowl, then looked at Spencer like she was something unpleasant that had crawled out of a swamp. "See you're taken care of, huh. Must be nice."

The new kid at Armstrong, having enrolled mid-spring last year, Tabby was also on the Headmaster's List, an accomplishment in such a short amount of time, probably thanks to her parents being one of the biggest donors in the Headmaster's Circle. Like that podcast noted, money made things happen at Armstrong.

Tabby was in a different social circle from Spencer, usually hanging out with the emo and theater kids behind school near the emergency exit to vape and watch YouTube videos between classes. To be honest, Spencer didn't consider Tabby a friend, but rather they were friend*ly* toward each other. At least that's what Spencer always thought. Now she wasn't so sure. Tabby's attitude was frigid at best.

The way Tabby looked at Ripley made Spencer prickle, like Ripley was annoying or being a nuisance even though she was just standing there.

Spencer didn't know how to react. Did Tabby have some problem with her service dog? Her grip tightened instinctively on the leash.

Tabby didn't say anything else, just waited, staring Spencer down with a twist of the lips and folding their arms across their chest. At first, Spencer's mind went blank, processing what to do, until she decided to step aside. Apparently, that was what they had wanted all along.

Tabby pushed past Spencer and marched out of the administrative office, long black hair swinging. Spencer stared at the back of their head, wondering just what the problem was, but headed into the office.

The admin assistant, Mrs. Ross—a little old lady with round, Coke bottle glasses, barely tall enough to see over the counter where she sat—told Spencer that Dr. Diamond, the headmaster, was expecting her and that she could just "head on back there, okay, sweetie?"

When she did just that, Dr. Diamond, headmaster at Armstrong Prep for the past ten years, looked up from behind his grand oak desk, framed beneath a whole wall of books and accolades and awards from his tenure teaching at Oxford before taking up the task of molding the minds of future leaders in sunny California. His accent still had a hint of London in it when he spoke. He reminded Spencer of a chipmunk wearing a tweed coat, like something out of a children's picture book. He smiled at her and beckoned her to sit in one of the upholstered chairs in front of his desk.

Among his books were framed pictures of all the students on the List. It was a way for him to show off his best students, an academic humble brag of sorts, like a parent proud of their children. Spencer spotted a photo of herself in action, taken from field hockey state champs last year, mid-throw. If she could say so herself, she thought it was quite a good shot. She looked strong. The newest addition to the collection was Tabby's, with their acting headshot, looking as glamorous as an old Hollywood starlet.

Next, there was Jackson's photo. He was goalkeeper for the varsity soccer team, his gaze focused on a penalty kick coming from just out of frame, his gloved hands raised as he readied to leap. The shelf where one would normally see Ethan's photo celebrating a goal he'd just scored, clipped from the front page of the *Daily News*, was vacant.

"Good to see you're back on your feet, Miss Sandoval," Dr. Diamond said. Then he held up a finger as he paused, reared back, and sneezed loudly into the crook of his arm. It was so loud, Spencer actually flinched. She couldn't help it—loud noises had that effect on her these days.

"Excuse me," he said, sniffling.

Spencer hated that even the silliest thing like a sneeze could get her heart racing. Ripley rested her chin on Spencer's knee, grounding her back to reality. She was safe, everything was fine. She hoped he didn't notice how panicked she felt.

"I apologize," he said. He blew his nose into a tissue taken from a box on his desk. "I am terribly allergic to dogs."

Horrified, Spencer immediately moved to get up. "Oh, I'm—"

Dr. Diamond held up his hand. "Please, Miss Sandoval. It's no trouble at all. No trouble whatsoever. I understand your circumstance and support it fully. Ripley—is it?—is more than welcome in this building if it means your mental health is cared for. I'm afraid my own shortcomings are no fault of yours." He smiled but he sounded muffled, as his nose clogged up and his eyes watered.

Spencer smiled appreciatively, but she knew it came off as looking pained. The last thing she wanted was for someone's throat to close up because of her.

"How are you feeling being back at school?" he asked, swiping the tissue back and forth across his nose before throwing it into the wastebasket.

Spencer wanted to be honest, that being back at Armstrong was emotional to say the least, but she didn't want to admit to feeling like she was weak, or that she was seeking attention, or that she needed pity. She put on her best smile and said, "It's fine." She didn't want to think about Chris's decorated locker, or the girls crying in the hallway, or the stares that followed her wherever she went.

"If there's anything else I can do to accommodate for your condition, I'll be sure all the faculty know. No one should bother you about Ripley, either. Your doctor explained everything to me about your condition. If you need to step out of class at any time, take a break, as it were, feel free. Just don't go off campus or interrupt any other classes. Knowing you all these years, though, I don't imagine I have to worry about that." He sniffled and scrubbed his nose with pinched fingers, and it made a noise like a suction cup. "We want to keep our top student safe."

Spencer's cheeks grew warm. It was nice being reminded that all her hard work paid off.

"It's a terrible tragedy what happened to young Chris. I didn't know him that well, but he was a good boy. I know his family, his father is a fine teacher. He was a promising student, although he wasn't List material. Chris will be missed. Did you know him? Was he your friend?"

Spencer shifted in her chair. "Um, no. Not really." Chris was a freshman, and while she saw him around, she wouldn't go as far as to say they were friends.

"Ah. Well! So it goes." He sneezed again.

"*Gesundheit,*" said Spencer.

When people found out that Chris was practically a stranger to her, it changed the narrative that many of them had formed about the crash in their heads. Questions swirled. Why was Chris in the car with Ethan anyway? Ethan was a popular senior; Chris wasn't at that level. It didn't make sense.

"Thank you." He blew his nose again but sounded too congested for anything to come out. "Even so, I'm not sure you've been made aware, but the school is hosting a small memorial service for Chris this Wednesday. A small garden has been built in his memory and we wanted you to say a few words at the candlelight vigil."

Spencer's stomach clenched. "I'm not sure I'm the best person to . . ." The thought of a hundred eyes on her, inevitably thinking the same things: that she had been in the car with Chris, that her boyfriend had gotten him killed, that she got to stand there now, alive, while Chris . . . It made her feel like crawling out of her skin.

Dr. Diamond continued, "Of course, we had discussed it, figuring since you were headed toward valedictorian status that you could take up the task. And we assumed since you were in the car with him that you were friends—"

"I'm sorry, Dr. Diamond. I don't know if I can handle doing something like that right now." Her voice wobbled like a plane in turbulence. She hadn't meant to cut him off so abruptly, but the walls were closing in on her.

She knew the school wanted to trot her out like they

always did. As one of the few brown kids at Armstrong, let alone a brown kid with one of the highest GPAs, Spencer was the face of their hastily put together DEIJ initiative. She never felt more like a scholarship student than when she saw her face plastered all over the banners that hung all over the school, or in every brochure. If you clicked on the school website, her picture was on the home page. Ethan used to joke she was Armstrong's only student.

Dr. Diamond watched her with sympathy, folding his lips together in resignation. "I see. That's disappointing. If you can't perform your duties as ambassador to student affairs, we can ask Hailey Reed instead. She's been eager to be more involved. It would only be natural for you to step down from the position. Though I don't imagine it would look too good on college applications if you did . . ."

Spencer clenched her jaw. Caltech would wonder why she couldn't handle basic extracurricular responsibilities. Holding that over her head felt like a low blow, especially after what happened, but she couldn't say anything. He knew he had her. Not only that, but for Hailey Reed to replace her in yet another realm of Spencer's life . . . She tried not to think about finding Hailey with Ethan that night of the crash, but a simmering heat had taken up a permanent place behind her sternum.

Dr. Diamond smiled and went on. "Either way, we would love for you to be in attendance. I'm sure his parents would appreciate it."

Spencer highly doubted that. If she was in their shoes,

she wasn't sure she'd ever want to get out of bed again. But she didn't say anything to contradict him. He was too busy honking into a handkerchief to notice the queasy look on her face.

He clicked his tongue behind his teeth. "It's been quite the start to our school year. One can only hope to move on for the better."

Spencer's gaze flicked up to the empty spot where Ethan's picture used to be. The headmaster too had written Ethan off. He was an embarrassment, a loser, no longer wanted. One mistake too many.

Dr. Diamond continued without noticing the sour look on her face. "I understand that you don't want to speak at the ceremony; however, we need some photographs of him for the stage. Our printing staff will need high-quality photos and his family has already approved the request. We just need someone to pick them up, and seeing as you live close by, I assumed it wouldn't be an issue for you to take up the task."

"You want me to go to his house?" Spencer asked.

"Yes, is that a problem?"

Spencer's whole life was defined by trying not to be a problem. She even felt bad that she had inconvenienced the nurses while she was in the hospital. But she also wasn't one to say no to figures of authority, especially to someone like Dr. Diamond. She'd already said no to public speaking, so she couldn't say no to going to the Moore house now. Why was she such a people pleaser?

If she continued to disappoint, her spot on the Headmaster's List could be in jeopardy, and with college acceptance on the line, she couldn't risk it, not when there were others like Hailey who were so eager to take her place.

But she had a history with the Moores. Not only was Mr. Moore her favorite teacher, but Chris's older brother Nick used to babysit her and Hope when they were little. She couldn't avoid them forever; she'd have to see them sometime. Better it be her than a complete stranger.

"Um, no, I mean, I can do it," she said. She hoped he could hear the discomfort in her tone, but he perked up and clapped his hands once.

"Excellent! You're one of the finest students at this school for a reason. Your strength and courage will be an inspiration to your classmates."

Spencer crinkled her nose. The last thing she wanted to be was an "inspiration." She wished he had chosen a different word.

"Is that all you wanted to talk about?" Spencer asked.

"No, actually, I wanted to let you know that as well as having Ripley at your side, I've also arranged for a student to chaperone you while you recover. Someone who can assist you with your studies until you're well enough to do so on your own. I had to make sure the right fit was in all the same classes that you were, make sure the schedules were lined up, so they had to be at the top of the List."

"Who?"

"Ah, Mister Chen, right on time."

Spencer twisted in her chair to see that Jackson had appeared in the doorway, his hand hovering on the doorframe, prepared to knock. He looked worried that he'd interrupted.

"Sorry," he said, "I was told to come in—"

"Yes, indeed. Not a problem! Miss Sandoval and I were just talking about you. She would likely appreciate your help getting to first period."

Jackson's cheeks pinked but he smiled at her.

Spencer thanked the headmaster for his time and stood up, leaving Dr. Diamond sneezing as she followed Jackson, who had offered to carry her backpack for her. They left the office and headed toward the library together.

"So!" Jackson said, bridging the gap of silence between them. Spencer was still chewing on her unsaid words to Dr. Diamond. "I guess we should get started then, right?"

She nodded, gnawing on her lip.

Jackson rubbed the back of his neck. "I know it's awkward. They asked me to and—"

"No, it's fine. Really. Thanks. I'm just getting used to a lot of things all at once."

Jackson let out a breath. "Yeah. I get it."

She knew he really did. "I have to grab something I forgot in my locker."

Jackson jutted his thumb over his shoulder, still carrying her bag. "Okay, I'll meet you in the library."

Spencer hurried to her locker, Ripley's nails clicking on the tile along her side, and threw the door open. She wasn't upset that she needed help from Jackson; in fact, she was grateful that he was paired with her, but she was upset that so much had changed in such a short amount of time. Her independence was slipping away from her bit by bit, like water from a leaky tap, and she just wanted things to go back to the way she had planned. She wasn't ready to let go of her old life just yet.

She uncapped the orange pill bottle and popped one of the painkillers in her mouth. Things were starting to hurt again.

# SEVEN

**SPENCER STRUGGLED ALL DAY, DESPITE** Jackson and Olivia's help and all her meds.

She spent the whole first period in the library with Jackson, sitting diagonally across from each other at a workstation underneath the glass ceiling, her favorite spot in first period. While she caught up on her required reading for English, a slog through *Crime and Punishment*, Jackson finished his essay for AP psychology on his laptop, his keystrokes a soothing rhythm in the quiet of the library. He'd agreed to share all his notes with her, sparing her the arduous task of deciphering his "terrible, godawful, embarrassing handwriting" (his own words), which lightened the mood. He'd be sitting with her in every class, ready to add any notes that she felt necessary. Because first period went so well, she expected the rest of the day would go by just the same, sailing through second period physics class, getting into the swing of things with Ripley nearby.

In third period, history class, Spencer met their new teacher, Mrs. McNamara. She'd be replacing Mr. Moore. He would not be returning to teach for the remainder of the year.

"It's nice to finally meet you, Spencer," she said, smiling when Spencer walked in the door. Mrs. McNamara was much younger than Mr. Moore, probably in her twenties, but already had ribbons of gray streaking through her dark hair, tied back with a pin. She was strikingly pretty, which Spencer noticed immediately. "We'll get you up to speed in no time."

Spencer usually sat in the front, but Mrs. McNamara asked that she sit in the back with Jackson, so that they could coordinate their note-taking without distracting the other students. A fair request, Spencer agreed. She situated Ripley on the floor next to her chair while Jackson and Olivia sat next to her.

Faces turned to stare at Spencer, taking in the stitches and the bruises and her cast, seeing the echoes of the crash written all over her body.

One of those faces belonged to Hailey Reed. When their eyes met, Hailey moved to look away, but she gave one last look before turning to face the front of the classroom, writing in her notebook furiously, as if to give herself anything to do not to look Spencer in the eye.

Hailey Reed was a perky blond volleyball star, the always optimistic go-getter, a walking stereotype, a prime candidate to join the Headmaster's List now that Ethan had fallen off. Spencer had had no problem with Hailey before the night of the crash. In fact, they might've been friends. She'd been over to Hailey's house several times for birthday pool parties over the years, but now Spencer didn't even want to share the same breathing space as her. She knew she was being harsh, but she allowed herself to wallow in her hatred for a while.

Seeing Hailey here in class, after what Spencer had gone through that night before the crash, made Spencer's heart tighten. Heat burned her cheeks and it took everything in her power not to throw the desk across the room. Hailey had known that Spencer and Ethan were dating, so it wasn't some innocent mistake. And Spencer wanted to hate her for kissing Ethan, but she hated Ethan for kissing her back.

"Are you feeling okay?" Olivia whispered, leaning in so only Spencer could hear.

"Yeah, why?" she lied.

"You look pissed."

"I'm okay. Really."

Just then, a classmate, Brody Dixon, slammed his huge textbook down on his desk, obliviously laughing with his friends about something or other, it didn't matter. Spencer nearly burst into tears, her whole body as tense as a rubber band ready to snap. Olivia must have seen the flash of panic that slashed across Spencer's face. She was positive she was having a heart attack. All she wanted to do was run out of the room, get somewhere, anywhere, that felt safe.

Being her best friend, Olivia didn't need to see the silver tears lining the edges of Spencer's eyes to figure it out. Olivia reached across the aisle and squeezed her hand. Ripley too felt the panic vibrating through Spencer's body and put her paw on Spencer's lap. It helped somewhat, but it wasn't a permanent fix.

The bell rang, ending the break, and Mrs. McNamara called across the room. "Okay, folks, settle down. Let's get started!"

It took Spencer almost the entire class hour to calm down, wobbling on the verge of hysterics, and when she finally did calm down, she felt like she was constantly waiting for the worst to happen all over again. Her mind went to dark places, expecting more and more outlandish scenarios to happen, like an earthquake that crumbled the school into dust around her or an asteroid blowing up the earth. The longer she sat with her thoughts, the worse it got. It was just a matter of time before her brain went into panic mode, forced to repeat the crash, and that felt almost as bad as it happening for real.

*Scream. Float. Crash.*

It was embarrassing, being on the edge of a breakdown all the time, especially when her whole life she'd been in control, confident, strong. Her life had been perfect. A handsome boyfriend. A perfect GPA. Gunning for valedictorian.

*Scream. SPENCER! Float. Tree. Ethan. Crash.*

She knew people thought she looked crazy, especially crying in front of her classmates, who were just looking for any excuse to stare.

*SPENCER! Crash.*

She almost didn't notice when the bell rang at the end

of class and everyone started filing out to the hallway for lunch.

"Spencer," Jackson said, his voice overtaking Ethan's in her memory. His voice was gentle, helpful. He smiled at her kindly. She got the impression that he'd been saying her name a few times before she heard him.

She couldn't help it. The doctors could only sew up her body, not her thoughts. She was fraying at the seams.

"Tabby's probably just jealous, that's all," Olivia said before taking a bite out of a giant pretzel she'd bought at the stand parked outside of school.

Olivia and Spencer had decided to take their lunch outside, letting Ripley go to the bathroom and then lie down in the grass, soaking up the sun before having to head back into class. Spencer sat on the low wall looking out over the grass and took a sip of her sweet iced tea. She was grateful for a break from four walls bearing down on her. Olivia had a college brochure open in her lap, flipping through a giant stack of schools to choose from. Unlike Spencer, she hadn't yet decided where she wanted to go. She'd been trying to narrow down her options, but it felt like a never-ending list of choices. In a way, Spencer was a little envious of Olivia, just because Spencer was positive Olivia would flourish wherever she went.

Spencer had told Olivia all about her run-in with Tabby at the admin office and how awkward it was. Olivia and Tabby were familiar with each other, what with Olivia working on set decorations for the school play—this year's big production being *Beauty and the Beast*—and painting the stage murals while Tabby rehearsed for their big number as Belle.

"No—*duh*, who wouldn't want to have a dog at school?" Olivia added, talking around her mouthful of pretzel. "Tabby is just . . . Tabby. I wouldn't think about it more than that, honestly."

Spencer, whose appetite had disappeared over the course of the morning, sipped on her sweet iced tea and watched Ripley as she circled the grass a few times before choosing the best spot to pee. She didn't want having Ripley to look like special treatment, like Tabby had said. Ripley was here because Spencer constantly felt like she was teetering on the edge of panic at the slightest thing. It wasn't fun, or funny, or anything to be jealous about.

Ripley came back to Spencer's side and sat down on her loafer, keeping watch of the other students milling about the campus grounds in small groups. She'd done a good job so far of keeping watch on Spencer's needs, almost like she was reading her mind.

Her shoulder was starting to hurt again.

"How are you feeling?" Olivia asked, sensing Spencer's discomfort.

Spencer pushed her shoulders back as best she could, shifting painfully. "Managing." All she could think about was getting back to her locker to take some more Vicodin.

"I know you won't listen to me, but I say you should call

it a day. Truancy is a harmless endeavor. Go home early. No one will blame you."

"I can't. Besides, I've got practice. And I'm supposed to head to the Moore house later to pick up photos for the memorial."

Olivia cringed. "Are you sure you want to do that?"

"I said I'd go, can't really back out now. Dr. Diamond kind of dangled college in my face over it. It's fine."

"If you say so . . ." Olivia's gaze stretched out across the lawn, watching a few junior boys play a quick game of Frisbee, their blazers in heaps on the ground. A group of sophomore girls walked past, carrying paper bags from the burger place down the hill, and Spencer caught sight of a flash of a bright blue pin on each one of their lapels.

*#justiceforchris*
*Stay Salty!*

She'd seen those buttons earlier in the day but didn't realize what they were until now. The sophomores gave her lingering stares as they walked past, and not just because Ripley had rolled over onto her back at Spencer's feet, paws dangling in the air, rubbing herself in the freshly cut grass clippings.

"Are those the pins from Peyton's podcast?" Spencer asked, once they were out of earshot. She'd never listened to her podcast before, thinking it sounded more like gossip than journalism.

"Yeah, some sort of fundraising thing. They sold pins to help raise money for Chris's family. I've been seeing people wearing them all over town." Olivia flipped through the college booklet in her lap. "This one says it's got the largest recreation center in the nation, plus private training sessions and three different kinds of swimming pools. Don't know why you need three different kinds. Water is water, right?"

Talking about college was an attempt at normalcy, and Spencer was grateful for the diversion. She let Olivia go on about schools, debating which one had the better campus life based on the stock photos the school had provided, while Spencer finished off her iced tea. Ripley needed to burn off some energy, so Spencer took out a fresh tennis ball from her backpack, purchased specifically for Ripley, and waved it for her. Ripley immediately leaped up and Spencer tossed it across the lawn, awkwardly of course since it was her nondominant hand.

Playing with Ripley helped ease the tension in her shoulders. Ripley's joy was contagious. They did this for a while, with Ripley fetching the ball and bringing it back to Spencer's outstretched hand. Spencer had to admit, it was pretty fun.

"Uh-oh," Olivia said, making Spencer turn around.

"What?"

"Don't look now, but Peyton Salt is watching you."

Spencer froze, watching Olivia's gaze go past her shoulder to where Peyton was standing. "What does she want?"

"An interview probably," Olivia said. She hopped down from the low wall and looped her arm around Spencer's waist. "Let's get out of here."

Spencer let Olivia lead the way. "Come on, Rip." Ripley bounced after them, obediently coming to Spencer's other side. She knew she was imagining it, but she felt eyes on the back of her head and when she turned to look, she saw Peyton Salt gawking at her across the lawn, her phone clutched in her hand. She was a mousy girl with wavy brown hair, but her eyes were sharp behind her thick-framed glasses.

Spencer let out a breath, trying to loosen the knot in her chest. Of course, Peyton would want to know what happened. Spencer would be the perfect source.

*Scream. Float. Crash.*

She just wanted to be left alone, even though she herself wanted to know why she felt like she was missing crucial information about that night.

While they walked together before the end of the lunch break, Spencer figured she might as well ask Olivia what she'd been meaning to all morning. "Do you ever think that . . . maybe the crash didn't happen the way everyone says it did?"

"Why do you say that?" asked Olivia.

"I don't know. Just a feeling, I guess."

"Ethan was driving. He was speeding and he lost control of the car," Olivia said sharply. "End of story. Don't stress about it. You need to take care of yourself."

"Yeah, you're probably right."

# EIGHT

**FIELD HOCKEY PRACTICE WAS ONE** of the few things Spencer looked forward to, especially with the mess that was her life trailing behind her. Nothing would make her happier than to get back out on the field, but because of Spencer's cast, she wasn't allowed to play.

"Sorry, Sandoval," Coach Fray said. "You know I can't let you."

"Can I at least stand with you? I don't want to miss anything."

Spencer'd gotten dressed in her usual practice gear, minus her shin guards and cleats, in a show of support. But Coach Fray's eyes went down to Ripley sitting obediently at Spencer's feet.

"Does the dog chase balls?" Field hockey balls were made of hard plastic, a perfect chew toy for any dog to nosh on, but Ripley wasn't just any dog.

"She won't," Spencer said. "She's well trained."

"Even so, I think it'd be better if you took a seat over on the bench. You'll be back on the field in no time, I promise."

Spencer glanced at her teammates, all of whom encouraged her to take it easy.

"It's okay, Captain!"

"Girl, we're good!"

"Feel better!"

Spencer tried to smile. Being forced to watch from the sidelines while everyone ran drills without her was a particular kind of torture, but she knew it was no use putting up a fight. Coach Fray, also her AP calculus teacher, said the team couldn't risk her breaking her wrist again; they needed her to fully recover to even hope to get back on the field. Spencer didn't want to feel jealous, but of course she couldn't help it.

While on the bench she fought the urge to open a book and study, so she perched her chin on her wrist and did her best to pay attention to the drills as Coach ran everyone through the gamut, barking about how the team hadn't been working out as they should have over the summer, and how state champs were going to be harder to go for if they didn't pick up the pace.

Because she had been absent the first week of school, she'd missed out on the news that the men's varsity soccer team and the women's field hockey team had to share the grass field. The soccer field's Astroturf needed repair after a pipe burst underground, turning the once perfect soccer field into a temporary swimming pool. Major renovations had to be done before the season started in full swing.

The men's soccer team was currently at the other end of the field doing passing drills, and Spencer tried to quash the boredom that was slowly seeping into her muscles. Everyone seemed to be doing something except for her.

Her painkillers mellowed her out, smoothing the edges of her mind. She'd taken more at the first sign of her shoulder and arm aching, and it made the world go all fuzzy in a way that comforted her. Among the haze, she could, at least for a moment, be at peace.

But she couldn't bear to watch practice from one spot, so she decided to take a small walk around the track circling the field with Ripley. Stretching her legs wasn't against the rules.

The soccer team had started running through corner kick set pieces. Spencer was only mildly aware of how the game was played, and not too familiar with the strategy despite dating the star striker. Watching Ethan from the stands was always fun. She'd gone to every one of his games.

The team, as always, looked strong and fast, moving for the ball and charging for the net as a unit while the coach yelled instructions. A rotation of goalies waiting for their turn had their hands looped through the net, yelling encouragement, and a player took a rocket of a shot at the goal that the keeper expertly punched clear over the net. The ball bounced all the way to Spencer at the track, and she stopped it with her foot.

Ripley's tail wagged as Jackson jogged over, his dark hair already plastered to his forehead with sweat. He'd been the one in goal; the way he'd moved sent chills down Spencer's spine. He threw himself from one end of the net to the other, like he was flying, the last line of defense. Like Ethan, he was good, as one should be on Armstrong's varsity team. Armstrong's program, both men's and women's, was legendary. Parents from all over the country enrolled their kids just so they could be on the team, hopefully getting looked at by college recruiters.

Ethan had already gotten offers from recruiters from the University of Michigan. Though, now with everything going on, Spencer wondered if that mattered anymore. A lump formed in her throat, but she swallowed it down.

Jackson beamed at Spencer when she kicked the ball toward him.

"Sorry to interrupt your walk," he said. "Thanks!" He flicked the ball up with his cleat and caught it, then lobbed it over his head back to his team. He didn't rejoin them right away, though; another goalie was already rotating it. Seeing him in his soccer outfit, a complete departure from his Armstrong uniform, was a welcome surprise. Heat rushed to her cheeks when she noticed how good his legs looked in shorts. Without his glasses too, he looked different, not better, but different, and it made Spencer feel dopey.

"Are you okay?" he asked. He let out a heavy breath, winded from the exercise.

"Define *okay*." She gestured vaguely to her team practicing without her, then to her face with a flourish.

"Stupid question, sorry."

Spencer tipped her head and the corner of her mouth lifted. "It's okay, I'm just being dramatic. Olivia rubs off on me in ways. Just trying to keep myself from going crazy."

Jackson relaxed too and returned the smile. Spencer's cheeks felt hot, as a knot loosened in her belly ever so slightly.

"I don't think you're crazy," he said.

"I don't know, sometimes I'll fool even myself."

"How come?"

Spencer wondered how much she should say. But Jackson had the kind of face that made her feel like she could tell him anything, open and honest and true. "I keep seeing flashbacks of the crash. Not just that, but things I remember don't really add up. Like, I keep seeing Ethan behind the wheel, specifically wearing his favorite green hoodie, but it's impossible because the hoodie was still in my closet from when I borrowed it from him. It's like my head is stuffed full of these images and it's all jumbled up, like memory puke."

He looked at her, his brow knit with concern, but he appeared to take her seriously. "That's awful. I'm sorry."

"Yeah, well . . ." She gestured casually. "I'm dealing with it. Thanks, by the way, for helping me today. You made it easier."

It was Jackson's turn to flush. He smiled and looked at his cleats. "No problem." When his eyes came up and met hers again, she realized she'd been staring and she cleared her throat, forcing herself to get it together. She blamed the painkillers for making her feel warm.

"I wish I could have done something," Jackson said. "I feel bad for not being there. Like, maybe I could have changed what happened."

"Right. I don't remember seeing you there. At the party."

Jackson nodded. "I was in Santa Barbara coaching

at a kids' overnight soccer camp when I heard the news. Drove all day to get back to be with Ethan, but . . . he won't see me."

That struck Spencer as odd. "Ethan won't talk to you?"

"No, I went to his house, and he turned me away at the door. He's not acting like himself. That's what's bothering me the most."

Spencer's heart broke for Ethan all over again. Sure, they broke up, but she couldn't help it. If he didn't even want to be with his best friend, he was hurting, and she felt bad for him. She wasn't some heartless witch.

Jackson continued. "He's got to be really torn up about Chris's death. He liked the kid, looked after him. Honestly, I think he's devastated. Like losing a little brother."

That was news to Spencer. "Really?" She hadn't put too much thought into why Chris had been in the car with them.

"Yeah," Jackson said. "Remember? Chris was his frosh buddy?"

"Oh, right." Last year, incoming freshmen were paired with upperclassmen, and Ethan had gone out of his way to make Chris feel welcome at Armstrong. Spencer felt a little guilty at that. She'd hardly paid any attention to her frosh buddy . . . Ella? Ellie? Spencer was too busy studying, she'd figured Ella or Ellie would figure out Armstrong soon enough.

"Anyway, Chris would come over and they'd work on Ethan's car together or just hang out, playing video games.

I think Ethan wanted to look out for him. So yeah . . . he's messed up. He won't talk to anyone; his parents say he just stays up in his room all day and night. I'm not even sure he's eating. You haven't talked to him yet, have you?"

"We broke up. I figured you'd have heard . . ."

Jackson's jaw dropped. "Oh. Sorry. No, I didn't."

"Well, glad to know some people know how to mind their own business, unlike everyone else in this town."

He flushed deeply.

"Sorry," she said. "I didn't mean for that to come off so harsh."

Jackson waved his hands. "No, not that. I just . . . I get it. I've been there."

How could she forget. His father. David Chen was a notorious fraudster, convicted a few years ago in New York City. Spencer didn't know the whole story, but it had been huge news. David Chen had been some kind of hedge fund manager. Spencer wasn't sure what that meant, but it sounded like he was making enough money. Apparently, it wasn't enough money, though, because he was caught siphoning funds from his clients into his personal bank account. As far as Spencer knew, he was still in prison. Jackson's mom, independently wealthy, moved across the country after that, and took advantage of her celebrity chef status to open a cookie café in downtown Los Angeles. But everyone knew about the Chens, even before they set foot in town. They were treated like outsiders from the start, every-one wondering just how much they knew or were complicit in the crime. People had opinions, and those opinions were hard to change. Spencer didn't think it was fair, though, to judge the family on what Jackson's father did, but the inner circle in Brentwood wasn't always as gracious.

She cringed. She hadn't meant to, but she'd picked at old scabs in Jackson's life. "Sorry," she said again. "I—Sorry." What else was there to say?

"It's fine, really." Jackson's eyes met hers and she didn't see any animosity there.

"I'm just not used to literally everyone knowing everything about me."

"Yeah," he said, managing a small smile. "I'm with you on that."

"Thanks. I just wish I had all the answers, you know? I hate not knowing what happened that night, even if it's nothing. I want the truth."

"What are you going to do?" he asked.

"What I do best—study. I want to document everything that happened that night, the crash, just so I can fill in the gaps in my memory and prove . . . Just so I know."

Jackson puffed out his cheeks as he let out a breath. "That sounds like a lot of work."

It would be. If she needed someone to help her with schoolwork, she'd need someone to help her with this. "Will you help me? Think of it like an extracurricular project," she said.

Amused, Jackson said, "Only you can sell it that well."

Spencer allowed herself to smile.

"But Ethan told the police what happened?" he asked.

"He was the one driving, and he was speeding. He ran the intersection. What more do you need to know?"

Spencer's gaze drifted across the field, as if a giant sign might have been erected in the past few minutes that would spell out the answers for her, but all she saw was everyone else getting on with their lives, playing sports, living, and Spencer felt like she was stuck in the past.

After a moment, Jackson asked, "Why do you think there's more to the story?"

Spencer twisted her lips, thinking. "I don't know, I just do . . ."

Why did she get in the car with him if they were fighting? They definitely broke up, she remembered that much. Why was Chris in the car with them? Or Tabby? She hardly knew either of those kids. It just didn't make sense.

"Tell me," he said. His voice was soft, and it gave her a little boost of bravery. If she could tell anyone, she could tell Jackson.

"I'm just not convinced Ethan's responsible for Chris's death."

Jackson's eyes widened, but he took it in stride. "Why, though? Do you think something happened that night that he's trying to hide?"

It sounded like there was a conspiracy to Spencer. She wasn't sure she liked the insinuation that something dark was hidden deep in the secrets of secluded parties in the multimillion-dollar housing developments, but if no one else was going to give her answers, she needed to go look for them herself.

"I know it's not a lot to go on, but that green hoodie . . . You just have to believe me that I feel like something is off. I want to know everything about the party."

A dimple appeared in Jackson's cheek as he thought about it. "If there's even a chance that we can prove he wasn't responsible, that he didn't cause it . . . That it really was just an accident . . ." He met her gaze solidly. "If we can clear his name, I'll help in any way I can."

Spencer smiled, relieved. "Thank you."

"For what?"

"For making me feel like I'm not crazy."

Jackson smiled, then said, "Ethan always talked about what a badass you are. Here it is in action."

Spencer had never been one to quit. Some people called it stubbornness, others called it hardheadedness. It was a benefit on and off the field, in her nature from the start. Once she set her mind to something, she never gave up. This was no exception.

"Some might say it's my best trait." She batted her eyelashes and smiled.

"I don't know about that," he said, rubbing the back of his neck.

She blushed too, realizing how flirtatious she was acting, and she bit her lip. Flirting with her ex's best friend felt like trespassing, even though she and Ethan were so over, but she hadn't meant to in the first place. She didn't want to get hurt again.

"Chen!" Jackson's coach hollered at him from the field,

hands on his hips. "Are you going to invite me to your little social gathering? Get back here!"

"I gotta go," Jackson said, walking backward. "But you should talk to Ethan. If he won't listen to me, maybe he'll listen to you. You might be able to shake some sense into him. I'll see you in the library tomorrow?"

"Yeah, tomorrow." It was one thing she could look forward to after what she still needed to do tonight at the Moore house.

"See ya later, Ripley!" Jackson said.

Ripley's tail wagged at Jackson's words as Spencer waved, watching him jog back to his practice. Still holding her hand aloft for a moment, she let what happened sink in. Someone believed her. She didn't feel so alone after all.

### *Get Salty*: A True Crime Podcast with Peyton Salt

*[Get Salty Intro Music]*

*[Transcription note: truncated for length]*

**Peyton Salt:** Before we get into today's main story, I wanted to update our listeners about the Ethan Amoroso case from last episode.

**Sasha Firth:** Oh! Spill! I have been obsessed with this case since you first brought it up. Everyone at my school has been talking about it, too. Has anything new happened since he's been charged?

**Peyton:** No, unfortunately Ethan has kept a low profile since he returned home under house arrest, waiting to go in front of a judge.

**Sasha:** Oh, the horror, house arrest in a giant mansion. Gag.

**Peyton:** I guess now is as good a time as any to reveal to our listeners that this is the start of a new series we're calling *Lifestyles of the Rich and Reckless*. We'll be releasing an episode every week to shine a spotlight upon the toxic glitz and glamour of the privileged class. We've had an incredible outpouring of support about Chris Moore's tragic death, and we've gotten thousands of emails from you asking for more details about the fallout. Some big things are coming as we start to plan our episodes as the case unfolds, so be sure to subscribe, stay tuned, and don't forget to hit up our merch store. We've already sold out of our limited-edition buttons for the Chris Moore Memorial Fund, but we still have some other Get Salty swag that you can buy so you can help support the show.

**Sasha:** Maybe we can get some *Lifestyles of the Rich and Reckless* stickers up for sale soon!

**Peyton:** Oh, Sasha! Great idea. Rich kids like Ethan get it way easier than most people in his situation. I don't feel sorry for him in the least, especially not after I saw Spencer Sandoval, one of the passengers in the car, her first day back at school since the accident. You can see how violent the crash was on her face. It's horrible to look at. Everyone at Armstrong was buzzing. You couldn't walk down the hall without hearing her name on everyone's lips.

Spencer Sandoval is sporty and cute, her signature look being long brown braids that make her look like she's ready to spring into action at any moment. Like many victims, the ghosts of the past haunt her. She carries the burdens of her ex-boyfriend's actions on her shoulders. But she has some very special help from an adorable service animal and a surprising sidekick, Ethan Amoroso's best friend.

Jackson Chen is a strong but soft boy-next-door type. He hovers around Spencer, as protective of her well-being as Spencer's service dog, Ripley. He doesn't look like the kind of person who would want to be friends with the bad-boy Ethan Amoroso. With a face as easy on the eyes as his, one can't help but be reminded of a medieval knight, dedicating his life to chivalry and honor. To think the likes of the two of them could be friends with Ethan Amoroso is beyond me, but with Jackson Chen's family's history, I can't help but wonder . . . But that's for another episode.

Spencer was dodging me all day, declining to be interviewed, so I decided to ask what some of her peers were thinking about the whole ordeal.

*[SFX: student chatter, slamming lockers, school bell ringing]*

**Luca Navarro (senior):**

I always liked Spencer. She's nice, smart. She helped me pass my chem tests last year. I hope she gets better soon. It's really sad what happened. She's got a dog with her, though, it's really cool.

**Grace Winkelman (sophomore):**

Spencer Sandoval walked right by Chris's locker, didn't even stop at it. I was crying my eyes out all day, looking at his picture, and she didn't even look once. I was going to go to homecoming with Chris and . . . and now? It's not fair!

**Valerie Lee (freshman):**

It's so scary looking at her face. You just can't stop staring. Ethan really [*BEEP*]ed her up.

**Tommy Fernandez (junior):**

That girl? Spencer? So annoying. She's always so competitive. She's gotta be the best at everything and it's so irritating. And she's got her dog at school, too? Special treatment. Why can't I bring my dog to school? Oh yeah, cuz I'm not on the Headmaster's List.

**Hailey Reed (senior):**

I don't really want to talk about it. Spencer and Ethan are like . . . I don't want to say. I feel so bad. Sorry. I just . . . It's really hard to talk about it right now.

*[SFX fade out]*

**Peyton:**

I'll be doing my best to try to get an interview with Spencer and Tabby, the other passenger in the car that fateful night. I think it's super important that we let victims tell their own story, and I won't give up on an interview. And now, for our main story . . .

*[End truncated transcript]*

# NINE

**SPENCER LINGERED ON THE SIDEWALK,** pacing back and forth, staring up at the Moore family's front door like she was staring down a minotaur. Damn her and her instinctual need to please figures of authority. Why couldn't she just tell Dr. Diamond she wasn't ready for this? He should have understood the mental torture she was going through. But it was too late now. They were relying on her to gather some photos for Chris's memorial. No one else would.

Ripley sat at her feet, watching her for a signal, her head tipped curiously to one side. At least Ripley didn't seem intimidated by this errand. Spencer took a breath and steeled herself, then made her way up the driveway, pushing her bike past a car covered in a tarp, and headed toward the bright red door, a week's worth of newspapers gathered on the welcome mat.

She'd never been to Mr. Moore's house before. He was her teacher, after all. She'd only seen him occasionally at the grocery store, where her parents used it as an opportunity to chat and have a small parent-teacher conference while Spencer tried not to be mortified talking to a teacher out in the wild. The Moores lived in a quieter part of Mid-City, off Santa Monica Boulevard. Their Spanish colonial house with its red roof and white walls stood out in the verdant brush that surrounded the property. It was a medium-sized house, definitely bigger than Spencer's, but it had a large yard, a novelty in the area, for sure.

She looked up at the dark windows on the second floor and wondered, morbidly, which one had been Chris's.

The porch light was on, and she could tell that someone was home, the telltale flicker of the television going on behind closed curtains. If she were a coward, she might have turned and headed home, pretending she had never come in the first place. But she was here now. No going back until she got what she came for.

Spencer tamped down the sudden urge to puke while she rested her bike on the lawn. It was now or never. She needed to do this.

She picked up a few newspapers on the grass that hadn't made it to the front porch and stacked the rest in her hand. When she rang the bell, her knees shook and she nearly forgot to breathe as the door opened. Instead of seeing either Mr. or Mrs. Moore on the other side, she was relieved to see Nick, Chris's older brother, home from college. He must be taking a break from UC Irvine.

He looked surprised when he saw her. "Spencer! What are you doing here?"

What *was* she doing here? This had been a bad idea, but she managed to say, "I've been assigned picture pickup."

"Right, the memorial." His eyes landed on the stack of newspapers in her hand, and she gave them over. "Thanks."

Nick's eyes were rimmed with red, clashing horribly with his auburn hair, but Spencer didn't want to stare. Both Moore boys had inherited their father's classic Irish coloring and freckles dotting their long noses. She used to have a crush on him, an innocent one-way affection, and her stomach twisted into knots seeing him this way.

"Come on in," he said, stepping back to let her into the darkened foyer.

"If it's a bad time I can . . ."

"Please. No trouble at all." He set the newspapers in a pile near the door.

He didn't question Ripley's presence and led the way toward the stairs. The Moore house smelled heavily like flowers, the source of which being almost an entire flower shop's worth of lilies erected in grand displays in the darkened dining room just to the left of the entry. The TV murmured quietly in the living room to Spencer's right, but there was no sign of Chris or Nick's parents anywhere. *Probably for the better*, she thought.

She didn't say a word as she followed Nick quietly up the carpeted steps. Usually she asked if she should take her shoes off when she entered someone's house, but in this case she wanted to be in and out as quickly as possible. The longer she stayed, the higher the chance that she would run into a grieving parent. And seeing his grieving brother was hard enough.

Up the stairs and down the hall, Nick led Spencer to

Chris's room. He flipped on the light and Spencer lingered outside the doorway, unsure if she should follow. The room felt off-limits. Nick meanwhile went right for Chris's desk, messy, untouched probably since the accident, and riffled through a shoebox full of photos.

Spencer couldn't help but look around at Chris's room, at the life he'd left behind. It was exactly how she expected a teenage boy's room to be, full of dreams and ambition, now marked by a gaping hole with his absence. His bed made and the sheets tucked in, never to be slept in again, his closet full of clothes he'd never wear, a memorial to his life on pause forever. He had obviously been into computers; the components of several were stacked in a corner of his room and an Xbox sat beneath a TV, a thin layer of dust gathering on top of it. He wouldn't ever again wake up and pull back the curtains at his window before he got ready for school, or tinker with his computer, or worry about what he was going to wear.

Spencer felt unmoored, like she was seeing the room through a television screen, rather than through her own eyes. This could easily have been her own bedroom, with her own parents grieving for her, with flowers from her own funeral sitting in the dark, leaving Hope to sort through photos for a school memorial. Ripley pressed her wet nose to the back of Spencer's hand, and it made Spencer jump, but she was grateful for the reminder to breathe.

"My mom used most of the good photos for the funeral, but these are a few more I thought would be nice. Some from his computer camp, this one of him with his friends . . . oh, here's one with me and Julie," he said sadly. Spencer vaguely remembered Nick was dating Julianne Greene, the girl who'd had that awful accident last year.

"How is she?" she asked.

Nick shrugged. "The same." She'd broken her back and fallen into a coma.

"I'm sorry," she told him. His girlfriend. Now his brother.

Nick didn't reply. Now he was holding out a small stack for her to take, and she did, with shaking fingers. The top photo was of Chris smiling wide at a tech convention, his vibrant red hair caught in the purple and red lights from a stage behind him.

Spencer's whole body felt cold. Guilt held her like a straitjacket. She knew she needed to say something, anything, but what could she possibly say that would make anything better?

"Nick, again, I'm so sorry . . ." She felt stupid for even trying.

He swallowed thickly and nodded. "Thanks, Spencer. If you need anything else . . ." An edge coated his voice, teetering on the breaking point.

That was her cue. "This is fine. I'll be going."

"Yeah."

Spencer turned to leave, and she distinctly heard Nick's muffled sobs coming from Chris's room. She pretended not to hear and left in a rush.

# SNAPS

**@tiny_neil:**

#justiceforchris Catch and burn the one that did this!

**@Resslersomemore:**

It's crazy. Miss you man. @chmoore #justiceforchris

**@norma.likes.drawing:**

We can't rest until we get #justiceforchris. Look at this vid I found of Ethan's old parties. The guy was a maniac. Absolute moron.

**@chockablock.marva:**

He intended to do this! He didn't even brake at the intersection! Why aren't the lawyers getting on this? He's a sociopath.

**@tiny_neil quote:**

@chockablock.marva I heard Ethan Amoroso was talking about doing something like this a week before. He planned this!!!

**@derikathedreamer002:**

I don't want to throw around tea, but when it comes to Ethan Amoroso I have no limit to how much I can pour.

# TEN

**HOPE THREW HERSELF ONTO THE** couch, which wouldn't have been a problem if Spencer hadn't already been stretched out, wearing her ice pack hat to quell the oncoming migraine that was threatening to ruin the rest of her night. Spencer yelled out as all of Hope's one hundred pounds fell on her legs, laughing all the while.

"Ouch! Hope!"

Spencer had been feeling too sick to even want to watch some of her favorite journaling and studying YouTube channels, an admittedly nerdy hobby of hers. Her eyeballs felt like they were going to explode out of her head, the migraine digging into her brain like an icepick.

"Move. You're in my spot," Hope said as she slapped her palms on Spencer's fuzzy socked feet, tapping out an annoying rhythm only baby sisters would know the beat to.

"No, I'm not. Your spot is on the lounger."

"Guess what, I want my spot to be here. I'm cold."

"Then go put on a hoodie."

"*You* go put on a hoodie."

"There's not enough room."

"I don't care."

It occurred to Spencer that this was a way for Hope to be closer to her. She couldn't imagine how scared Hope had been when she was in the hospital, so she didn't complain when Hope lifted Spencer's legs up and crawled underneath, draping them like a blanket.

Ripley had been dozing in her dog bed and opened one eye to see what the commotion was about, but she didn't move when the sisters settled down again. The TV droned on, and Spencer tried to ignore that Hope was fidgeting against her, tapping her foot to an unheard beat.

"Did you do your homework?" Spencer asked.

"Yeah, I did, *Mom*. Did you?"

"What I could." She had tried to read some of her assigned chapters in her AP English literature homework, but pain was starting to flare up again and she couldn't focus. Hence the ice pack hat. It was a bulky beanie, and Spencer thought she looked like Blossom, a character from a TV show her mom used to watch reruns of when she had a rare day off from taking care of sick animals. Both her parents were out of the house and weren't expected to be back until later. Pizza money had been left on the table by the door and the girls were, as usual, on their own for food.

Hope stole the remote from Spencer's grasp, which she didn't fight her for, and she flipped through channels, finally landing in the middle of a rerun of *Murder, She Wrote*, with Jessica Fletcher flirting with reformed jewel thief Dennis Stanton. Spencer closed her eyes and let their delightful banter lull her into a soft, cozy twilight doze. All she could do was wait for the Vicodin to make it all better.

"Why were you at that party?" Hope asked.

It was an unprompted question that seemingly came out of nowhere, but Spencer knew which party she was talking about. *That* party. Spencer squinted to look at her. Everything was too bright. "Because I thought it would be fun."

"You never want to have fun. You're too much of a dork."

Spencer didn't argue about that. "I went because I wanted to." And she knew Ethan would be there. She wished she hadn't. She wished she'd just gone home after work like she usually would have. Ethan making out with Hailey intruded on her thoughts and she huffed, "Why do you want to know?"

Hope shrugged a noncommittal shoulder. "Did you drink a lot?"

"I might have had one of those alcoholic seltzers, but . . ." She couldn't remember if she had more than that. She'd always favored the sweeter drinks. "I'm not sure."

Hope snapped, her voice rising an octave. "Yeah, well, that's really dumb of you! You shouldn't have done that! You shouldn't drink! You shouldn't have even been there."

Both of Spencer's eyes were open now. "Why are you so upset?"

Hope shrank into herself and folded her arms over her chest, pouting like she used to when she was five. It took her a moment to answer. "We had a drunk driving assembly at school today. They showed pictures and stuff, and it was really scary. I think they wanted to talk to us about . . . They had a mom talk to us about her daughter getting in an accident a couple years ago and dying and I ..."

Hope picked at her fingernails as she spoke, unable to finish the words, not because she didn't know what to say, maybe, but because she didn't want to.

"Hey, it's okay—I'm okay," Spencer murmured. "I'm right here."

"I know, but what if you weren't?"

Spencer's heart dropped. Hope settled down in the space between Spencer and the couch, and even though it was uncomfortable, and her body weight pressed the air out of Spencer's chest, Spencer let her lie there until she started dozing off.

While the TV droned on, Spencer tried to wade through the memories, though her headache was making it particularly difficult. Things came back to her in pieces.

Rows of cars parked in a dirt lot.

A yellow Solo cup. Metallic tasting.

Music. But muffled, like it was in another room. Hazy, dreamy.

Kids sitting around the firepit, smoking.

It was coming together.

She was sure of one thing. She'd only had one drink that night. Why was it so hard to remember that night? Was her memory loss really from hitting her head in the crash?

*"Please, wait. I can explain."*

*"What else is there to explain? You and Hailey deserve each other."*

*"Spencer!"*

*"Go to hell."*

*A hand on her wrist.*

*Then.*

*Engine roaring. Speed. Out of control.*

*Ethan in his green hoodie. No, wrong. Why?*

*Bright light. Eyes wide, terror.*

*The tree. The lines in the bark. Trapped in the headlights.*

*NO!*

*Pain. Darkness.*

*Cold hands on her face, wet, covered in blood. So much blood. She couldn't breathe. She was dead. Already dead. SPENCER! Crash. Float. Scream. Cold, wet hands cupping her face.*

Wet nose, not hands. A wet nose, tongue. Ripley.

Ripley was on top of her, licking her face, waking her up, her body pressed against Spencer's chest. Her breath was hot on Spencer's face.

Spencer cried, sobs racking her whole body, rolling out of her in waves, thrashing in her bed. It had been another night terror. She hated feeling this way. Ripley buried her nose under Spencer's side, not giving up on her. *Get up, wake up!* Her rough paws felt like sandpaper on Spencer's arms. She tried to push Ripley away, she didn't want to be touched, yet Ripley refused to go. But Spencer actually did want to be touched, and she wrapped her arms around Ripley's neck and sobbed into her fur.

Her parents rushed into her room and flicked on the light, telling Hope to go back to bed as she lingered outside.

Spencer still felt like she was trapped in that memory, even when her parents assured her she was safe.

*SPENCER! Tree. Scream. NO! Float. Crash. Darkness. Pain.*

She needed to remember everything, even if it made her feel like dying.

## WHAT I REMEMBER

*Highwood Estates
Cars parked
Unfinished mansions—scaffolding, dirt, no trees
Skateboards in an empty swimming pool
Yellow cup
Firepit
Music?—live or no??
Ethan—cheater
Hailey—backstabber
~~Green hoodie~~

## WHAT I DON'T REMEMBER

Tabby
Chris
Between breakup and crash—totally blank
Why did I get in the car?

# ELEVEN

SPENCER STARED AT WHAT SHE'D written in her journal, tapping her pen on the paper as she repeated the thought: *Why did I get in the car?*

*Why didn't Ethan stop at the light?*

*Why were Chris and Tabby riding with us?*

Her bullet journal was a complete mess. Using her right hand made her writing look like it was done by a second grader, and she could only write for so long before her hand cramped. But when she journaled, it helped calm the thoughts swirling in her head. Last night's night terror had shaken some things loose.

The moment she'd gotten to school, she went to the library and wrote down everything in an attempt to organize her brain while Ripley lay patiently under her chair. Even though she'd loaded up on painkillers, she was surprised by how much she did remember. She'd had to cross out green hoodie, because it wasn't possible that she remembered it, and her eyes skimmed over the other details. What else might she have misremembered? A part of her wished she could believe she didn't actually see Ethan and Hailey making out that night but . . . that was definitely real. So why did she get into the car with him?

She needed to talk to Ethan, but she didn't know how. It wasn't as simple as going to his house. Facing him again felt raw.

She'd already purged all their pictures together off her new phone, a gift from her parents. Each photo she deleted from the cloud felt like a paper cut, and after deleting the thousandth picture of them framed in a mirror, his arms wrapped around her shoulders, his chin resting on the top of her head with his devil-may-care smile as he grinned for the selfie, the emotional pain had started to rear its ugly head again. He'd hurt her too badly and too deeply for her to want to see him for a long time. There was baggage now, and she was tired of carrying it. She wanted to move on, hence the list. She needed to document everything, for her own sanity.

"Good morning," Jackson sang, appearing seemingly out of thin air. She almost jumped out of her skin. "Oh! Sorry. Didn't mean to scare you."

"It's okay." She forced her heart to settle back down. Ripley had perked up at Jackson's arrival, her tail thumping as he took a seat across from Spencer's side of the table. Spencer was glad to see a friendly face so early, too.

"Getting started on solving the mystery already?" he asked as he opened his backpack and brought out his laptop.

"Nothing major." Spencer shook out the cramp in her right hand. "I had a nightmare last night, needed to get some thoughts out."

"Are you okay?"

"I am now." Though the reality of her situation was becoming more concrete. A person didn't have a mental health service dog because they were going to get over their disability overnight. Ripley was in it for the long haul, and Spencer was coming to terms with the fact that she would be waking up with persistent nightmares and suffering from more panic attacks for the foreseeable future.

She had started picturing Ripley living with her in the dorm at Caltech, curled up at the foot of her bed to wake her up for early morning lab work. It didn't seem so scary now. More manageable. Even though it wasn't something she'd wish on anyone.

Jackson started to work on his laptop and pushed his glasses up his nose with his knuckle. She liked how good he looked in both his school and soccer uniforms. He kept his tie cinched neatly, compared to how Ethan always wore his loose, like he needed breathing room. With his glasses back on, Jackson reminded Spencer of Clark Kent and she caught herself staring.

Mercifully, Jackson didn't seem to notice and said, "So since I'm all caught up on my psych homework, I figured I'd get started on helping you remember that night. Maybe I'll start collecting some news articles for you and we can look them over together later."

"That sounds perfect, thanks." Spencer was grateful that he was taking her seriously. He didn't make her feel crazy. Doing this alone would have been impossible. "I've been meaning to ask, how do you play soccer without your glasses? Like, how do you see the ball?"

"Oh, I don't," he said dryly, still staring at his computer. "I fling myself in a random direction hoping to catch the ball. The secret is that I'm lucky." His gaze slid from his laptop and he cracked a grin. He was teasing her.

The laugh that came out of Spencer sounded like a bark, and she covered her mouth, remembering she was in the library and needed to be quiet. It felt nice to laugh like that again after so long. "That was pretty stupid of me, wasn't it?"

His dimple reappeared when he scrunched his nose, laughing. "Nah. To be fair, a field hockey ball is a lot smaller than a soccer ball when it's hurtling toward your face, a lot harder to see it coming. How you're not terrified of getting whacked in the face is beyond me."

"Occupational hazard. All my front teeth are fake," Spencer said, grinning. This time she was the one who was joking.

In the sunlight cast from the ceiling window, Jackson looked like he was glowing when he laughed, and Spencer made herself look away or else the flush on her face would be obvious. She looked down at her notes with the intent of focusing on something else, but she couldn't help smiling too, even though it tugged on the stitches in her cheek.

"Okay," she said, and chanced a glance his way to find him still smiling at her. "Shall we get started?"

At the memorial, Spencer and Olivia joined the throng of bodies in the courtyard as the sun was just starting to set.

Hardly anyone spoke, and if they did, it was kept to a hush. Even the bugs that usually came out at this time of night kept their buzzing to a low hum. She and Olivia, being part of the student union, had been recruited to help set up for the ceremony. With Spencer's injuries, she was delegated the task of handing out candles for the memorial.

When the box was empty, Spencer hovered in the back of the crowd, trying her best to blend in with the brickwork pattern of the rear wall of the building, waiting for the event to begin, holding on to Ripley's harness. The candle wax had already begun to drip onto the paper disk protecting her hand. The sea of heads in front of her were all turned to face the stage. Chris had been more popular than she thought. Tears glinted in the candlelight, and boxes of tissues were being passed around to people who needed them. A sound system and microphone had been set up on a small stage near the garden and they were playing a song by The Beatles, Chris's favorite.

The garden was small, big enough for only a single bench, but there was a small looping path so a person could disappear into the high foliage for a second. It looked nice, peaceful. Spencer wished it never had to be built in the first place.

The Moores had arrived only a few minutes earlier, shaking hands with some of the teachers. Mr. Moore looked grayer than she remembered as he firmly grasped Dr. Diamond's hand and they said some words to each other that were too quiet to hear.

Olivia emerged from the crowd and joined Spencer leaning against the wall. "Mrs. Moore looks as hot as ever. Why do all the heinously evil people always look like cliché stepmothers from a Disney movie?"

"Liv . . . we're at a memorial."

"I'm just stating a fact. Mrs. Moore tried to fine my parents because the grass in our front lawn was half an inch higher than the neighbor's just yesterday."

That definitely didn't sound like the actions of a grieving mother. But Catherine Moore was a classic Karen, determined to nose into everyone's business and generally difficult to be around. Mrs. Moore had famously—or rather infamously—as a city hall elected official, published an anti-homeless proposal regarding a gathering of tents outside the VA's office near the Brain Freeze, where Spencer's after-school job was. It was controversial to say the least. She'd also been one of the leaders of the silent blacklisting of the Chen family when they first moved here.

"Come on," Spencer said. "She just lost her son . . ."

Olivia sighed and folded her arms across her chest. She knew how to hold a grudge, but she didn't say anything else about it.

Mrs. Moore stepped up to the microphone. She was remarkably put together in Spencer's opinion, given the circumstances. Her honey-colored hair was pulled into a low bun at the base of her neck, not one sleek hair out of place. She looked down at her index card, tapping the edges into place with French-tipped manicured nails. The microphone

whined with feedback as she leaned in, so she backed off
and waited a moment before trying again.

"Thank you all for coming," she said. "My son Chris . . .
He would have loved to see all of you here today. Thank you
to Dr. Diamond and the Parents' Association for this lovely
memorial to my son's life. We also want to thank the student
union for putting together such a lovely ceremony. Jonathan
and I"—she glanced back at Mr. Moore, whose head was
bowed low, he didn't notice—"are truly grateful for all the
support the community has given us in . . . in this trying time."

Mrs. Moore's voice sounded robotic, rehearsed, like she
was a politician at a town hall meeting.

Spencer's heart felt like it was about ready to burst out
of her sternum, like an alien exploding from her chest. She
wanted to be anywhere but here, but if she left now, everyone would stare, and everyone would think she was being
inconsiderate, so Spencer kept her feet rooted to the ground
and rubbed Ripley's head rhythmically. All she could do
was close her eyes and breathe. But she couldn't help the
thoughts that swirled in her head like a tornado.

No matter how hard she tried to accept the official ver-
sion of the crash—that Ethan was speeding, that he didn't
brake, that he was most likely driving under the influence—
she wanted to believe it was all just an accident. She wanted
to believe that something like this couldn't be misunder-
stood, but the feeling that something was wrong wouldn't
go away. It nagged at her, tugging at her insides, telling her
that something wasn't right.

*Scream. Float. Crash.* Pain all the way down.

If she ever hoped to get any kind of peace about what happened, she needed to know all the details of that night. She needed to fill in the blank pieces in her mind; otherwise she would always wonder if she had done something differently, if she had said the right thing, maybe she could have changed how it had ended. She wouldn't be able to rest until she knew the truth, and journaling would only get her so far, as much as she hated to admit it.

It was Mr. Moore's turn to speak. He came up to the microphone, and he said, too far away from the mic so it sounded distant, a gentle thank-you, before turning and stepping down from the stage with his wife.

With a sinking feeling in her stomach, Spencer watched as Hailey Reed took the microphone next. She lowered the stand so it was level with her mouth. "We hereby dedicate this garden to Chris Moore, calling this area the Chris Moore Memorial Garden."

Spencer couldn't help the scowl that pulled on her lips. She couldn't even look at Hailey without wanting to scream.

The crowd clapped politely. Spencer joined in, half-heartedly, stopping just short of rolling her eyes. Her skin crawled and she had the sensation of someone watching her. Lo and behold, Tabby Hill was frowning at Spencer through the crowd. Spencer tore her eyes away, just as Hailey was replaced on stage by Harrison Ressler, with his long, dirty blond hair pulled back into a ponytail, holding his guitar.

When Spencer looked back at Tabby, Tabby was gone. Spencer got the distinct impression that Tabby had seen the scowl on her face and probably thought the worst of her. If Tabby didn't dislike Spencer before, they definitely did now.

Harrison had been the host of the party that night, but Spencer hadn't known before that he and Chris had been close. They must have known each other somehow, though, as Harrison's low, velvety voice carried over the crowd. "Thanks, Hailey. And thank you all for coming. I'm sure he would have been glad to see all your faces. I'm going to play a song to Chris's memory." He readied his hand on the neck of his guitar and turned his eyes to the sky. "You were taken from us too soon. This one's for you, man." As he began to play "Hey Jude," the crowd raised their candles high into the air, and Spencer took the chance to duck out.

It didn't feel right to sing along with everyone. Spencer quietly led Ripley down the sidewalk that wrapped around the school, pain rippling through her arm, determined to figure out everything that happened that night. She had too many questions that needed answering, but most of all, she had to prove to herself that she wasn't crazy.

It was time to see Ethan and find out what really happened that night.

# TWELVE

**THE CLARITY OF MIND SHE** had when riding her bike from Chris's memorial felt incredible. The breeze cooling her skin, the sound of Ripley's claws scratching on the pavement as she cantered beside her, the sky turning a deepening shade of purple—all of it made Spencer feel surer than ever that it was time to see Ethan. It was long overdue that she got some type of closure or answers about what happened that night. She couldn't keep not knowing.

She needed to see him, even if it would be for the last time, but at least then she'd be able to take the first steps toward recovery.

The ride to Ethan's was a ten-minute coast down quiet Brentwood streets, the echoes of Harrison's rendition of "Hey Jude" at the memorial still echoing in her head. She only saw one or two cars on her way, which would have been a relaxing bike ride if not for the feeling that she was about to do something foolish.

The Amoroso home looked like a brick of cement, rectangular, with hard lines jutting out above tree cover. Typical of Californian modern architecture, it reminded Spencer more of a modern art museum than a house. Its many glass windows afforded plenty of sunlight, and some were lit up this time of night, meaning that someone was likely home.

The house sat behind a gate and a row of hedges, perfect for privacy. Spencer, however, still knew the code and punched it in before opening the gate just wide enough for her to slip her bike and Ripley through and shutting it behind her. How many times before had she sneaked out of the house to see Ethan past curfew, doing exactly this? The memory sat bitterly in her stomach.

She walked her bike up the drive, set it down on the front porch steps, and rang the bell. The moment she did it, she thought maybe she was being inconsiderate. It was just after nine in the evening, and maybe everyone was already getting to bed, but the foyer light came on and a shadow moved in the doorway window. The door unlocked and Ethan's father appeared in front of her. He had a phone held to his ear, but he put it to his shoulder when greeting her.

"Spencer," he said, surprised. Mr. Amoroso was a candy company executive, and he always had bowls of sweets and chocolates around the house, something that Spencer took full advantage of whenever she was visiting. Mr. Amoroso was the breadwinner of the family, or rather, Ethan liked to joke, he was the candy winner. This was the first time seeing him after the accident, and he took in her face with a graying expression. He looked like he'd been getting ready for bed, wearing plaid pajama pants and a T-shirt. "I'm just on the phone with Ethan's lawyers. Can I help you?"

"Hi, Mr. Amoroso, is Ethan home?" Dumb question, of course he was home. He was still under pretrial home confinement—aka house arrest—until he was brought to the courthouse for the first day in court. But she didn't care that she sounded stupid for asking.

"He's in the back," he said, tipping his head toward the backyard and stepping aside for her to enter the house. Inside, the house was much like the exterior, wide open and well structured, all lines and boxes, with everything in its place and a place for everything.

Mr. Amoroso went back to his conversation with the lawyer, talking about potential plea deals, leaving Spencer and Ripley to make their own way through the house. Perhaps he knew what she'd come here to do. She opened the sliding door leading to the yard and closed it behind her.

Just as his dad said, Ethan was in the backyard, laid out on a lounger by the glowing infinity pool. A small waterfall was the only sound as Spencer stepped forward, Ripley obediently at her side. As she got closer, she knew Ethan heard her coming, but he didn't stir. A few bottles of beer were open and empty on the ground next to him. A blunt rested in an ashtray half burned, and at first she thought Ethan was asleep, but his eyes followed her as she circled around the edge of the pool toward him. His lids were heavy, and he watched her approach without saying a word. They'd spent many days and nights here, swimming and playing and partying. *Kissing.* With a sudden flush to her cheeks, Spencer remembered the quiet night when they'd first started dating, sharing a kiss in the shallow end of the pool that literally stole the breath from her lungs. And then everything was ruined by another kiss.

Ethan was the type of guy whose wild and carefree aura made her feel like she could do anything, be anyone. He was charming and witty and a little reckless, but she wanted to be a part of that life, too. The money didn't hurt, either. With Ethan, they went everywhere—VIP tours at Disneyland, exclusive nightclubs on the Sunset Strip, his parents' private clubs where she'd see Harry Styles one day and Taylor Swift the next, and he hardly ever even looked at a bill. She'd felt different when she was with him. She felt important, like she mattered. She wasn't just some brown scholarship kid, a charity case. With Ethan, she felt like a movie star.

Then—Ethan's fingers twined in Hailey's golden hair, their mouths open wide like they wanted to swallow the other whole, Hailey's hand down the front of Ethan's jeans, and Ethan's eyes snapping open, then seeing Spencer standing there, her whole body freezing cold and boiling hot at the same time. While Hailey didn't even move her hand, she just smirked at Spencer. And somehow, Spencer knew—this wasn't the first time Hailey had kissed her boyfriend. That this thing between them wasn't new. It was just new to Spencer.

She clenched her jaw. Seeing Ethan again, in person, made the moment come back to her. She remembered that at least.

Was Hailey sleeping with Ethan? Because Spencer wouldn't?

It didn't matter. She still wanted to know everything. Still wanted to know what she couldn't remember.

"Hey, Ethan," she said quietly. Her throat felt constricted, and she was impressed she could even manage to say that much.

"What are you doing here?" His voice was gravelly low. She knew he'd ask that question, and yet she still didn't have an answer.

Spencer chewed on her lips for a moment and then took a seat on the chair next to his. He didn't stop her, instead taking a sip from the beer in his hand. She could smell it on him, the stale cloud of cheap brews hovering over his head like a storm. He must have been drinking all day, not caring that his parents were home, but then he never cared before. His face was shadowed, glowing blue from below, the light catching the slant of his nose in a way that made him look bruised. He didn't look at her now that she was close. She wanted him to, and maybe a little part of her wanted him to look at her the way he used to. But she was kidding herself—that wasn't going to happen anymore.

"I needed to see you," she said. He still wouldn't look at her. "How are you?"

He shrugged and hissed. "Great! Best time of my life. Going to jail instead of college!"

"Don't say that," she said.

"Why not? It's true," he replied.

Ripley sat on Spencer's shoe. Not protectively, more like she too was tired of his attitude.

"I found your hoodie," Spencer said. "Your green one."

"Keep it."

"I'll give it back."

"I don't want it. I gave it to you."

"Well, I don't want it, either. You can give it to Hailey."

He screwed up his face, as if that was the last thing he wanted her to say, and took another sip of his beer. He drained it empty and set it down with the others. "Did my dad let you in? I told him I wanted to be alone."

"Don't blame him. I came here on my own. I want to talk about what happened that night at the party."

Ethan rolled his head, exaggerating exasperation. "Of course you do! You're not here to see if I'm okay, you just want to find out all the details. Why am I not surprised?"

She let his anger slide. He was too wasted to even try to argue with. His T-shirt was wrinkled, and he was wearing old soccer shorts with paint stains on them. His ankle monitor blinked. From his spot on the floor, Ripley stared up at Spencer as she shifted in her seat. "Does your dad know you're out here drinking?"

"He doesn't care. It's the least of his problems right now."

"How about I get you some water."

Ethan sighed loudly. "Let me guess, Jackson put you up to this."

"No. But he is worried about you."

Ethan's smile cracked as he opened yet another beer. His gaze went skyward as he took a swig. "Why should he care? I'm a piece of shit. He's better off forgetting about me, same as you. You two might be perfect for each other, after all."

His self-loathing was getting tiresome, and she wanted to smack the beer out of his hand. "If you keep up that attitude, you're going to lose your case."

"Oh, I know I'm going to prison. I'm already packed, got my chinos and my toothbrush all ready to go." His attempt at a joke fell flat.

"No, you're not, stop talking like that. It was an accident!"

Ethan almost laughed but it came out like a wheeze. He still wasn't looking at her. The cut of his profile was something out of the history books. He looked like a timeless beauty, sculpted from marble and pure imagination. The shape of his cheekbones, cut against the dark sky, could send shivers down anyone's spine. If he wasn't so beautiful, she might have thought he wasn't real. How someone with a face like his could hate himself that much was beyond her understanding.

"Ethan . . ." She said it like a warning. His name was basically a warning on its own: caution, turn back, category 5. "It was an accident, wasn't it?" she prodded. "Or were you drunk?"

He snorted.

"The thing is, I know you, you wouldn't drive if you were drunk or high. You *wouldn't*." She firmly believed that. Ethan was wild and rich but he wasn't spoiled that way. He wouldn't deliberately put people in danger. Not when they lived in Los Angeles, where kids like him and his friends have been Uber-ing around since sixth grade. What was the point of driving drunk when you had Mommy's Uber Black account? "Did you?"

He stared her right in the eyes. "I didn't."

"So what happened?"

"You really don't remember?" He sounded genuinely surprised.

"No. I had a concussion. And lots of broken bones to remind me about it. The doctors say I might not ever remember the crash, and that makes it all the more important that I ask you."

"I was driving, I ran the intersection. I tried to brake, or I think I did, but the car didn't stop. So we crashed, what more is there?" he said with a shrug.

"That's it? There has to be more."

"Does it matter if there is?"

"It does. Because I say so."

Ethan actually cracked a smile, and he thumped the back of his head on the headrest, grinning up at the sky, still unable to look at her. "Well, there isn't, that's the whole story."

Spencer huffed, then said, "I don't care that you were cheating on me, just tell me the truth."

"For once in your life, will you just stop trying to find the right answer to everything? This isn't some test you need to ace, some perfect score at the top of your paper."

"Don't start with me, Ethan. I'm not here to fight with you. Why was Chris even in the car with us?"

Ethan shrugged. "I offered him a ride. He was totally out of it, he needed to get home. Maybe it was better that he was out cold. Couldn't feel a damn thing." He took another swig.

"Why though? He didn't seem like the party animal type."

"I don't know. Why does anyone do anything?"

"Jackson said you guys were close. I forgot he was your frosh buddy last year."

Ethan shrugged again. "He's a good kid." He caught himself and swallowed. "*Was* a good kid. All I ever do is muck everything up." He wiped beer from his lips with the back of his hand, just like he did after kissing Hailey. Wiping away the evidence.

"How long were you together?" she asked, keeping her tone level and strong, for her sake. "You and Hailey, I mean?"

Ethan wouldn't look at her.

"I just need to know . . . I need to know if we . . . if we were real," she said.

"We were real," he whispered. "But I was never good enough for you. Admit it. Miss Perfect with Mr. Fuck Up."

She grimaced. "And you and Hailey?"

He sighed. "We were fooling around for a year."

A whole year. Half their relationship, he was with another girl. "Were you sleeping together?" she asked.

Another long sigh. Then: "Yeah."

The pain she felt in her heart was harsher than in her body. She wanted to ask more questions, but she realized she didn't want to know the answers to them.

But it was Ethan's turn to ask a question. "Did you love me?"

Spencer clamped her mouth shut and sat back, shocked. She wasn't expecting him to ask her that. They had never said those words to each other. Did she love him? Was that why it hurt that much? She wasn't sure she could answer him. She folded her arms across her chest and sat properly on the lounger, legs crossed, back pressed into the recline.

She had been infatuated with him at first; like a lot of girls at Armstrong, she'd had a huge crush on him. But it had been more than that. She liked the way he smelled, the way he'd made her laugh, the way he always took care of her. And if she didn't love him, what was she doing here?

"I don't know," she said finally, because she didn't. "I thought I did."

Finally, she got her wish and he looked at her and she almost regretted it. Pain stretched across his features, his expression so hopelessly open. He took in the injuries on her face and it stole his breath away.

Slowly, he reached out and touched her cheek, tracing his thumb gently below her stitches. He'd done it so many times, a touch so effortless and true before.

*Cold, wet hands cupping her face. So much blood. SPENCER!*
She flinched at the memory.

Ethan's hand jolted back. His lip trembled, though he tried to hide it, and he turned away. He couldn't look at what had happened to her, what'd he done. "God, your face." He let out a small sob but sucked in his breath and held it. He was about to cry.

Spencer turned her head away from him too, just so he wouldn't have to see, and planted her gaze firmly on the waterfall burbling in the silence spanning between them.

Eventually, he said, his voice thick, "I don't even know what you see in me. All I do is hurt you."

Spencer couldn't argue with that, and she couldn't argue with someone who had five beers' worth of self-hatred churning in his belly.

"I just want all of this to make sense."

He snapped. "But there's nothing else to it! I killed Chris! I did it! I was driving too fast, like I always do. It's all my fault! There! Happy?"

"Don't say that! You didn't mean to, right?"

"You sound like my lawyer. Just because I didn't mean it, doesn't mean it didn't happen."

His outburst shocked Spencer enough, she closed her mouth.

"I'm not a good person, Spencer. I'm not like you. You've got a future, you've got dreams, you're going to do things. It's better if you just let me go. I'm only holding you back. This is how it's supposed to happen." His eyes looked like glass beads, dully reflecting the glow of the pool, but he wasn't really looking at it. It was like he was staring a million miles away and seeing absolutely nothing. "Everyone else knows it, when will you?"

Spencer didn't know what to say about that. She could say he was wrong, but he'd confessed. Everyone else in this town had given up on him, and so, it seemed, had Ethan.

**_Get Salty_: A True Crime Podcast with Peyton Salt**

_Lifestyles of the Rich and Reckless_ Segment Transcription

*[Get Salty Intro Music]*

**Peyton Salt:**   Ethan Amoroso had everything going for him, and like they say, the mighty fall hard. It's a long way down to the bottom.

The son of a prominent executive at Cooper Incorporated, the multibillion-dollar candy company based here in Los Angeles, Ethan grew up with a silver spoon in his mouth, constantly feeding him the sweeter things in life. Like so many of his ilk, the privilege of being rich and handsome meant doors opened for him, people gave him anything he could ever want—opportunities the likes of which you or me cannot even fathom were on the table.

Star striker of the Armstrong soccer team, Ethan had already been noticed by several college teams, with a professional career on the horizon so long as he didn't suffer serious injury preventing him from making it to the big leagues. Though, if we're telling all, even if his knee gave out, he'd still be able to fall back on being the sole heir to his family's immense fortune. Not exactly a bad backup plan.

Ethan's father, William, has his own fair share of controversies. A few years ago, he'd been caught sexting a subordinate, all while married to Ethan's stepmother, but the scandal was later swept under the rug, an all-too-familiar occurrence. Rumor has it that Ethan was cheating on Spencer Sandoval and she caught him red-handed the night of the crash. Like father, like son!

Ethan's fast-paced, carefree lifestyle paved the way for a recipe for disaster. After the incident with Julianne Greene, who attended a house party at Ethan's mansion and was left permanently paralyzed and in a coma, Ethan turned to drugs and alcohol.

The only two options were to send him to military school or to a behavioral rehabilitation program, and the elder Amoroso chose the latter. Ethan seemed to be far beyond what his father thought he could handle. A police report was filed because someone had set the house on fire when he returned home. The name was redacted on the report, but could Ethan have been trying to get back at his father for sending him away? Did his father get his name redacted in order to protect him, fearing it would cause greater embarrassment for the family name? Who knows at this point? We can only speculate.

As for us Salters, we can only look at the destruction caused by Ethan Amoroso and the hundreds of others just like him who see the world for the taking and will do nothing short of having it all for themselves. It doesn't matter who gets in the way—people like Ethan Amoroso are nothing but trouble.

# THIRTEEN

**THE FOLLOWING SATURDAY AFTERNOON, SPENCER** expertly filled the ice cream cone, piling it with vanilla and chocolate swirl before dipping it into the melted chocolate and rolling it in sprinkles, then handed it to the man and his son waiting on the other side of the plexiglass barrier.

She'd worked at Brain Freeze since she was a freshman, and by now she was an ice cream aficionado.

The kiosk, built in the '50s, had been designed to look like a cup full of ice cream, the roof like a swirl on top, with large cartoon eyes. Last year, some vandals spray-painted the roof brown, making it look like a pile of poop. Since the kiosk was right on the edge of the Brentwood Sports Park, it was a popular place for a lot of kids her age to hang out, taking up some of the plastic seating and tables, shading themselves under the pinstripe umbrellas, and spending the rest of their day doing absolutely nothing.

Before, Ethan and his friends would come over while she was working, but at least Olivia still worked there with her. Spencer wiped the back of her hand on her forehead, brushing the stray hairs from her Dutch braids off her damp skin. Ripley couldn't physically fit inside the kiosk, it was that small, so she waited outside under the shade of a nearby tree where Spencer could keep an eye on her and refill a water bowl for her every thirty minutes.

"So when did you want to go dress shopping?" Olivia asked.

"Dress shop—" It took Spencer a moment to realize what she was talking about and then it clicked. "Oh! Homecoming. I totally forgot about it."

"Yeah! We're still going, right? I mean, since it's our last one and all, I figured we'd be stereotypical teenagers and do it this once to say we did it, and then maybe my parents will stop calling me antisocial, even though that's not what *antisocial* means . . . Soccer game got out," Olivia said, tipping her chin toward a minivan with a soccer bumper sticker on the back. A whole gaggle of kids poured out, their knees scraped up and dirty from the game. "Showtime." Olivia leaned on the counter, ready to take the orders and ring up the money.

Thinking about going to homecoming, especially without Ethan, felt like their breakup was real. He couldn't go, of course, even if he wanted to take Hailey. He was still under house arrest. But the thought of the two of them together still hurt. She wanted to move on from him, she knew she deserved that, but would she really be in the mood to dance the night away surrounded by everyone who'd been staring at her the past week since her return?

"I figured it'd be fun," Olivia said, punching in the orders of a scrambling mass of twelve-year-old soccer players resisting being wrangled by a mom who already looked like she was starting to regret mentioning coming here. "You know, get a dress, like a revenge dress like Princess Di, so when you post it online Ethan will see it and he'll feel like such a dumb-dumb for doing what he did, and then you and me, we can live it up and party like there's no tomorrow."

Spencer had to admit, that did sound fun. Like Princess Diana, she could make her first big appearance after the breakup looking like a million dollars. She thought about it, filling up a dozen ice cream cups with various toppings and mixing, moving quickly despite her sling so nothing melted too fast, and before long the throng of hungry kids were enjoying their well-earned desserts under the umbrellas.

"Can't we just stay in? Maybe take it easy?" Spencer asked. Simply thinking about loud noises and crowds was exhausting enough. And she wasn't sure she could stomach seeing happy couples dancing with each other. And it seemed wrong to go to a party when the Moores had just planned a funeral.

"You still have time. We can decide later."

Pain shot through Spencer's shoulder. It happened more frequently, especially if she was pushing herself too hard. She winced and said, "I might be over school dances."

Another customer stepped up to the kiosk and Olivia took their order. "Still," she said, turning back to Spencer as she made the strawberry cone. "It might help you get your mind off things. I want things to go back to the way they used to be . . ."

Spencer couldn't agree more. They worked the rest of their shift, hardly able to talk again with the rush of eager kids wanting a treat after their games. Before long, the garbage can was overflowing.

Spencer went out the back to take out the trash, heading through the parking lot, when she spotted two people standing near the dumpster by the community bathrooms. Tabby Hill and some person she didn't recognize were speaking about something that looked important, their heads leaning toward each other. The stranger looked shady, to say the least. He wore a hoodie, despite the heat, and his hair was a greasy, stringy flop that shadowed his eyes. He handed something to Tabby, who handed something back. Without another word, the stranger left, and Tabby put whatever it was in the front pocket of their jeans.

Spencer's and Tabby's eyes met for a fleeting moment, and Spencer pretended not to have been staring as she hauled the heavy garbage bag into the dumpster. Tabby hurried off, not giving Spencer another glance.

# FOURTEEN

SPENCER HAD NEVER BEEN TO a police station, ever in her life. She'd had the privilege of not having to set foot through its doors to see the brown tiles or sit in the plastic-form chairs in the waiting area or smell the burnt coffee in the pot. When she walked in, naturally the eyes of people waiting in the waiting area and the uniformed officer sitting behind the desk fell on Ripley at her side, but no one said anything about it when they saw her face and the bruises still splattering up her skin like an ink spill. Her back was sweaty from the ride over, and she knew her hair looked like a rightful mess thanks to her helmet, but she didn't care. She was beyond caring about anything at this point.

"I'm here to speak to someone about an accident I was involved in," Spencer said.

"Was this recent?" The receptionist's eyes landed on the stitches on her cheek.

"No, my name is Spencer Sandoval. I'm here about the Ethan Amoroso case."

At the sound of Ethan's name, the officer's eyebrows rose. No need to elaborate. "Ah. I see. Then you're going to want to talk to Detective Potentas."

Right. Potentas. That was the detective who had visited her in the hospital after the accident. Spencer's memories of that day were still so hazy, but the moment she heard the name, she remembered.

"Please, have a seat," the officer said. "He's out getting lunch, but he'll be back any moment."

Spencer didn't have to wait long enough for the skin below her shorts to stick to the uncomfortable plastic seating before a man in a white button-down shirt and tie loose around his neck entered. She stood up and rushed over before he even had time to look up from the phone in his hand, his other clutching a Styrofoam to-go box that smelled like something fried. He looked tired and weary, which was understandable given his line of work.

"Detective Potentas, hello." Spencer's formality always came out when she was up against authority figures, especially ones who wore a gun on their hip. "My name is—"

"Spencer Sandoval, of course, I remember," he finished for her. "How can I help you? Is everything okay?"

"Yes, I just wanted to discuss the case I was involved in."

He glanced at the officer sitting behind the desk, who shrugged. "Okay, sure, let's talk in my office."

His office was more of a desk in the back corner of the open floor plan. Ripley padded along at Spencer's side while they walked down the aisle, listening to the furious typing of other detectives writing up reports behind their computers, or chatting with coworkers, or waiting for jobs in a copier to finish processing. It reminded Spencer more of a boring office setting than a hard-boiled headquarters for jaded police that she'd seen so much on television.

Detective Potentas fell into his chair at his desk and clicked away at his computer, typing in his login information, while Spencer took a seat in the stained chair next to his desk, awkwardly positioned in the aisle. Eventually, he leaned back in his chair, and it squeaked underneath him as he rocked. "What can I do you for, Miss Sandoval?"

"I was just wondering if I could look at the police report of the accident."

"Now why would you want to do that?"

Spencer wrung her hands around Ripley's leash as she lied. "School project." It was the best she could come up with.

At least Detective Potentas looked amused. "A school project . . ."

Lying to the police was a thing Spencer never expected to do, but she didn't know how else to ask for it. She tried to smile, but she knew it looked strained.

The detective sighed loudly, his nostrils whistling. "I'm afraid that's impossible. I can't share police reports for an active case." He must have read the disappointment on her face because he leaned forward, resting his elbow on the desk casually. "What's this really about?"

Spencer wasn't sure what to tell him. Would he believe her that she was certain something was wrong about that night? "I still don't remember what happened that night, and I want to know."

"I might be able to make a call to pull some strings, but this would have to happen after Mr. Amoroso's case is processed by the court. And by then, I'm not sure what good it will do you. I can tell you're looking for answers, but sometimes these kinds of things don't have answers."

"I spoke with Ethan, and something just didn't seem right. I think something else happened that night, I just need to know what."

"Miss Sandoval. I know you've been through quite a traumatic event, but it's better if you let us take it from here."

"Maybe if I saw even just a picture of the scene, I could start to remember, knock a memory loose."

Detective Potentas looked at his hands and took another breath. "I'm going to make an assumption here. You're a good student, right?"

"Yeah."

"I can see it, it's in your eyes. You're smart, you're driven, that's all good. This is probably the first time anything like this has happened to you, and I pray it'll be the last."

Spencer sank into the chair, feeling small. She knew where this was going.

"I'm going to say, for your own sanity, it might be better if you don't try to remember that night."

"I'm not here to ogle some dead body, Detective. There's nothing else you can share with me? Not even the written report?"

The detective looked resigned, and Spencer could tell, legally, his hands were tied.

"Sorry, Miss Sandoval. It's just not in my power to hand something like that over to you. I've already got enough to deal with, especially from some podcast that's been spamming my number for days on end . . ."

Spencer tried not to let the sinking feeling of failure weigh her down, but her options were getting smaller and smaller.

"Tell you what," he said. "Come back to me again after all this is over, once you've got some distance between yourself and the accident."

Spencer frowned. Another roadblock.

Detective Potentas took out a piece of gum from his desk drawer and offered a stick to her, but she refused. A first for everything. "I can tell you're a good kid," he said, popping the gum into his mouth. "You're not looking to start any trouble, but it's in my professional opinion to tell you that it's not worth it, getting hung up on this kind of thing. Crashes happen all the time, especially if the driver is under the influence."

"But we don't know that for sure," she said. "Ethan would never . . . he would never get behind the wheel if he was high. Maybe if he were alone, but not if he had other people in the car with him!"

"People make mistakes all the time," the detective sighed. "And once the toxicology reports come back, it'll prove that."

She chewed her lip. "But why can't I remember anything?"

"With crashes like these, head injuries are common."

"Could there be another explanation to my memory loss, though?"

Detective Potentas stared at her, analyzing. "Illicit drugs, maybe."

A yellow Solo cup, then the night being hazy after that. Spencer shivered. "I didn't take anything . . . At least, I don't remember."

"What can I tell you? We're living in a time where kids are taking fentanyl-laced pills," he said grimly. "They're all over the city. Check to see if the hospital ran any lab tests on you when you were admitted."

Spencer shivered again.

"Take care of yourself, Miss Sandoval."

# FIFTEEN

**THE FOLLOWING DAY AT BRAIN** Freeze, Olivia was finishing up an order just as Spencer arrived for her shift. "Guess who was asking about you," Olivia said as Spencer walked in and Ripley flopped under a nearby tree, panting from the ride over.

"Who?"

"Peyton Salt."

Spencer frowned.

"She asked about an interview. I tried to run interference, but she's persistent. She gave me this card." Pinched between Olivia's index and middle fingers was a business card with the words GET SALTY on them.

Spencer sighed and snatched it from Olivia's fingers, crumpled it up, and then threw it in the trash under the counter.

"Figured as much," Olivia said. "Listen, I hate to do this to you, but I gotta split. Emergency on set. Someone decided to kick a hole in one of the castle walls during rehearsal last night, so I need to patch it before tomorrow. Think you can hold down the fort solo?"

Spencer gave Olivia a thumbs-up and she left, humming as she skipped to her car.

Unfortunately, soccer, baseball, and football games let out in overlapping intervals, which meant that the line at Brain Freeze was seemingly endless as Spencer worked hard to keep up with all the orders while also counting out correct change and making sure that everything was clean. Time flew in the blink of an eye. By the time the line had let up, Spencer rested her head on the cool countertop and took a breath. Her head wasn't hurting, but the rest of her was. What had Tabby been doing by the dumpster yesterday? What did the detective say? Illicit drugs were all over Los Angeles, and Spencer knew how easy it was to order them from the internet. Most kids she knew just DM'd a plug on Snapchat.

She heard someone step up to the kiosk and lifted her head to see a familiar face.

"Jackson, hi," Spencer said, finding herself smiling, not just because he wasn't Peyton.

"Tough day?"

"You have no idea."

"Oh, I can imagine." His cheeks and nose were pink from being in the sun, and he was wearing a warm-up jersey with COACH embroidered on his chest. "Coaching kids is like herding cats."

"What can I make for you?" Pain was already flaring up her back and down her arm, throbbing annoyingly, and Spencer had completely missed taking her usually scheduled painkiller break.

"Oh! Nothing. You looked like you need a morale boost. I just wanted to say hi. So, hi."

Spencer smiled. "Want to take a break with me?"

"Sure! I've got a second."

She planted a sign down on the counter that said STAY COOL! BE BACK SOON! "Give me five minutes and I'll meet you under the tree."

With two tall ice cream cups in hand, Spencer joined Jackson at the table under the pin-striped umbrella near the shady tree. Ripley's tail wagged wildly from her spot nearby. She clearly liked Jackson, but he was good about not petting her. Spencer took a seat across from him, sliding the ice cream over.

"Reese's, my favorite!" he said. "How did you know?"

"I remembered. That night at the fair a couple years back, you and Ethan had a pretend fight about what was better: peanut M&Ms or Reese's—"

"Right! The incident with the clown is the first thing that comes to my mind about that fair. Can't believe you remembered my evidence-based and accurate argument in favor of Reese's and that I won by a mile." Jackson's smile sloped upward and he dug the spoon in eagerly.

Spencer dug into her own ice cream, mixed with cookie dough.

"How do you like working at Brain Freeze?" he asked.

"It's not so bad. What about you, *Coach?*" She angled her gaze toward his jersey.

"It's fun. Kids that age cluster the ball like they're chasing a butterfly."

Spencer laughed, and Jackson's dimple reappeared when he smiled.

"How much do I owe you? For the ice cream?" he asked.

"On me."

"Really?"

"No problem. Don't mention it to my uncle, though, he owns the place. He'd kill me if he found out I was giving out ice cream. He may look like a surfer dude, but he's a real hard-ass."

"Secret is safe with me." He put his hand over his heart.

Now that she had some food in her belly, Spencer fished her painkillers out of her pocket and popped one. She washed it down with another spoonful of ice cream.

"How did it go at the police station?" Jackson asked, watching her.

"Not well, they think Ethan is definitely guilty."

"Did you talk to Ethan?"

"Yeah . . . he says he's guilty too, he doesn't even want to fight it. But I just . . . I just don't believe he'd deliberately do something like that, do you?"

Jackson shook his head. "No, of course not. If I did, I wouldn't be friends with him."

Spencer raised a scoopful of ice cream. *Cheers to that*, she thought.

He asked, "Have you been getting harassed by that podcaster following his case?"

"You mean Peyton Salt?" She thought about the crumpled-up card in the trash can.

"Yeah, her. She came to my house earlier and wouldn't leave. She kept throwing her phone in my face, saying she just wanted to ask some questions, how I felt about the charges against Ethan, but I didn't want to talk to her. I almost called the cops on her; she looked like she was going to camp out in the garden, but she left after a while."

"Yeah, she was just here. I've been dodging her, though. I don't think it's any of her business."

"Fair. Plus, once it's out there, it's hard to control what people think of the story. I'm worried I'd just make it worse, especially with his plea hearing coming up."

Spencer hummed in agreement. "I wonder how she's getting her sources. She seems like she's got a finger on the pulse, access to info we don't have."

"Like police reports?"

Spencer raised her eyebrows by way of an answer. "She might have a connection to the police somehow. In one of her earlier episodes, she said she had the police report in front of her."

"I didn't know you were a fan."

"I'm not," she said. "I was curious, read a few transcripts, and I don't recommend it."

"Believe me, I won't listen."

She regretted looking into Peyton's podcast in the first place. After reading a transcript about what other people had to say about her, she'd had to dose up on her painkillers as a migraine threatened to make her head explode.

She swirled the vanilla ice cream around her mouth for a while, savoring the cold, as her thoughts went back to Tabby. "Something else that the detective said, though, bothers me. I asked him about my memory loss and he said it could have been because of drugs. Like, serious drugs."

Jackson stared at her, wide eyed. "For real? You think you were dru—"

"It's not a fun thought, but . . . I remember only having one drink, and the rest of the night is a mess."

"That's fucked up."

"Yeah. It just got me thinking maybe Ethan was on something, too . . . but he didn't know it. I mean, he basically stopped partying since the accident at his house last year."

"Yeah, and he quit smoking pot since it would hurt his chances with Michigan."

Spencer nodded. She had been so proud of him when he went cold turkey.

"He used to get his weed from Brent Lang. Do you know if he was at the party?" Jackson asked.

"I think so. We should talk to him, for sure."

Brent was a self-proclaimed guru, touting the importance of meditation and healing through yoga and breath work. He had a group of devoted followers, mostly girls, who all embodied the New Age lifestyle, having started a yoga club during lunch period. In Spencer's opinion, he gave off "future cult leader" vibes. No matter the weather, he always wore a beanie, even at school where the dress code prohibited hats, and he wore crystals on leather ropes around his neck, claiming they cleared energy and opened his chakras. His mom was a pharmacist, but he'd constantly bash quote-unquote Big Pharma and how it was making people sick and that "natural remedies were the way, man." Would he really be capable of selling anything more hard-core?

Spencer and Jackson fell into a contemplative silence as they continued to eat their ice cream, though with less gusto now that the topic of Ethan possibly being high when he crashed loomed overhead like a storm cloud. Spencer could access her own medical records, so nothing was stopping her from finding out if she really did get her drink spiked. But somehow she didn't want to know; it was too terrifying to think someone would do that to her.

She asked, "Do you want to come over tomorrow? We can figure out our game plan then? Maybe sort through all the stuff we know?"

"Sure! I'd say 'sounds fun' but . . ."

Spencer allowed herself to smile. She appreciated his levity, even if it was short-lived. Having him around made her feel better.

But persistent questions hung heavy over her mind. Could she really have been drugged that night? She hadn't been paying attention to her drink, didn't even remember who handed her the cup in the first place.

# SIXTEEN

AFTER SCHOOL, JACKSON ARRIVED AT her house, right on time, at five in the afternoon, after his soccer practice let out. Unfortunately, it had been Hope who had gotten to the door first.

"Spencer! A boy is here for you!" she hollered, her voice seemingly echoing through the whole house. Annoyingly, she sang it, too.

Spencer managed to get there only seconds later, bumping Hope out of the way with her hip. ("Hey!" she cried.) She definitely didn't need Hope blabbing to her parents that she had a boy over, let alone Ethan Amoroso's best friend, a double whammy of trouble in the making. He hadn't even gone home to change, evident because, when he arrived at her front door with his gym bag thrown over his shoulder, his hair was pushed back away from his forehead with sweat, thanks to the heat of the day.

"Sorry about my sister," Spencer said, flushed.

Jackson looked like he was trying not to laugh; his face was all screwed up but his eyes were bright. "It's all right. Hey, I'm Jackson," he said to Hope, who was thoroughly pouting.

"Hey yourself." To Spencer, Hope said, "Mom and Dad are going to freak if they find out you had a boy over when they weren't here."

"It's not like that," Spencer said, hoping that the heat wasn't showing in her cheeks. "This is a . . ." What was this exactly? She couldn't go around saying they were investigating when the police wouldn't.

"It's a project for school," Jackson said quickly.

"Right! A school project. So you don't need to go tattling to Mom or Dad about it."

Hope folded her arms over her chest. "What do I get for not telling?"

She was intent on being a pain in the ass today, but before Spencer could tell her off for it, Jackson asked, "Do you like video games?"

Hope's sneer softened, and she looked Jackson up and down, as if she was surprised a jock who looked like him was interested in that kind of thing. "Yeah. Depends though. Why?"

From his gym bag, he pulled out a Nintendo Switch. "See, I've got the new Zelda game and . . . well, let's say you can play it as much as you want, so long as you don't get Spencer in trouble."

Hope looked at Spencer and rolled her eyes, as if weighing her options and deciding which would be more fun: playing a video game or seeing Spencer get grounded for a few weeks. "Deal. You keep bringing Zelda, I keep my lips sealed."

Jackson smiled, the warmth of it reaching up to his eyes, and Hope scurried away to claim her usual spot on the couch, already firing up the system.

Spencer stepped back and let Jackson fully walk into the house. "Sorry about her. She can be such a brat."

"It's fine, really. With three younger brothers, I know the drill."

Spencer led the way down the hall, toward her warmly lit bedroom. "You can put your bag there," she said and pointed to the spot on the floor in front of her dresser, while she pulled an extra chair she had stolen from the dining room up to her desk. Jackson dropped his bag and looked around her room. Ripley's tail wagged on the bed upon seeing him.

"You're tidy," he said. "Hope you didn't clean on my accord."

"I like organizing. It keeps my mind at ease. I like it when things are neat."

"Clearly," he said, spotting her binders and color-coordinated folders on the shelf above her desk. One of the folders had a custom label she had designed: INVESTIGATION. "You're like a professional."

Putting a label on it helped remove the personal connection and made it feel like an assignment.

They both took a seat at her desk—Jackson insisting he take the dining room chair and Spencer take her swivel desk chair—and Spencer showed him what she had compiled so far. "I've sorted what documents I could gather into these three sections: The Party, The Accident, and Legal

Stuff. And then I typed up what I could to get us started." She flipped through, showing newspaper clippings of the accident, and she even drew her own map of the party and a line drawn toward the intersection at Canyon Drive.

Jackson's eyes flitted over the pages as she flipped through quickly. He looked at her, his smile filled with amusement. "You are such an overachiever."

"I know. Is that a problem?"

"Not even. What do we want to do first?"

"I figured we could go through the socials of everyone who might have been at the party. There's no cell reception up in the hills, so most people uploaded videos of the party when they got home and posted it to Facebook and Instagram."

Her heart pounded painfully in her chest. She hadn't gathered the courage yet to check her medical records to see if they'd given her a drug test when she was in the hospital. Part of her wanted to know what happened that night, but another part of her was afraid of what she might find out.

Plus, she didn't want to watch Ethan making out with Hailey all over again, as miniature in the grand scheme of things as it was.

Jackson seemed to sense this hesitancy, and he said, "How about I look through the videos and you start making a timeline of the party. Then we can start a short list of people we'd want to interview in person, maybe anyone who can confirm what happened, like Brent Lang and Harrison, and Tabby, too."

Spencer was grateful for his thoughtfulness and took out one of her gel pens from the bunch she kept in a cup on her desk and got to writing. Meanwhile, Jackson opened his laptop.

"Have you started to remember anything else about the party?" he asked.

"Some. The beginning of the night, I arrived at the party around ten. I hadn't planned on going in the first place and told Ethan so. He'd wanted me to come, but I'd just gotten off a shift at Brain Freeze, and I was tired, but I changed my mind. He didn't think I'd be there. I took a Lyft to the front of the neighborhood and walked. By the time I got there, the party was going hard. The firepit was lit, and people were skateboarding in empty swimming pools."

"Good, I mean—not *good*-good. But it's a start."

Spencer flipped to a new page in her notebook and drew a rough line down the middle of the page and started jotting down all the memories she could in her notebook, giving ample space to fill in the gaps. Her notes consisted of the following in her right-handed scrawl:

9:30PM–Brain Freeze shift ends
10PM–arrive at Highwood Estates
10:30ish–I buy a Diet Coke from the bar
10:45ish–I find Ethan and Hailey together
TIME?–Ethan and I break up
TIME?–we leave the party (me, Ethan, Tabby,
    Chris) in Ethan's car
TIME?–crash

Her pen stayed pressed on the paper after she finished the *h*. To think, if Spencer had just stayed home like she had originally wanted to, maybe everything could have turned out differently.

"Have you ever blacked out before?" she asked. "Not been able to remember a whole night?"

Jackson shook his head. "I bet it's scary, though."

"It is."

Jackson watched her thoughtfully. "Are you okay?"

"Just seeing it all laid out like this, it's surreal."

Jackson worried at a hangnail on his thumb with his index finger. "Is there anything I can do for you?"

"You being here is doing a lot more than you think." She smiled at him, and he smiled back, color brightening his cheeks. Her stomach swooped delightfully but she felt guilty. She shouldn't flirt with him. He was Ethan's best friend. It still felt off-limits, like she was somehow just as bad as Ethan—a cheater. Besides, Jackson was nice to everyone. Did she really think there was anything else there? She refocused by pushing stray hairs from her braid off her forehead and looked down at the page. "This is helping, though. It's bringing some memories back. Like, when I got to the party, I got a drink. They had a station on a tree stump with cups and snacks and everything, and I paid five dollars to get a cup."

"Five dollars, wow. Harrison must have made a killing that night. Remember when he used to charge five dollars just to get in the door and drinks were free?"

"No, I didn't go to parties freshman year," she told him.

"Oh," said Jackson.

"Anyway, we'd have to ask him, but yeah, everyone was pretty drunk and it was relatively early in the night." She massaged her temples, trying to remember. "People were playing corn hole, and there was a game of beer pong in a half-finished garage, and a few people were vaping on the lawn. I remember smelling cotton candy, from all the vapor. The details start to get a little hazy here . . . But I think I heard music." She flipped back to her notebook page about what she remembered. She still didn't know if it was live or a playlist on speakers.

Jackson already had an answer for her. "The Misstakes. They're tagged in this one video here. See?" He pointed to a recording of the band in front of a dozen people jumping to the beat. But Spencer didn't see anyone she recognized, including herself, in the video.

He typed The Misstakes into Google and pulled up their website. All the members went to Armstrong, like everyone else at the party. They did a lot of pop-punk covers that were a hit at those kinds of parties. Unfortunately, their website didn't have any footage of that night so Jackson went to their personal Facebook pages to find anything that might help.

As expected, there wasn't much to go on. The band had probably been too busy performing to take photos or videos during the party. Jackson let out a sigh that ruffled the bangs on his forehead. There was a lot of work ahead.

Spencer had an idea. "Do you want a snack? How about some popcorn?"

"That's . . . yeah, if it's no trouble."

"No problem! Be right back." He looked like he could use some calories after his practice. So Spencer went to the kitchen to grab a bag of popcorn from the pantry. Hope was still planted on the couch playing Jackson's Switch.

"Is he your new boyfriend?" Hope teased, without looking up from the screen. No need to elaborate.

"No." Spencer started the popcorn in the microwave and leaned on the countertop. While she was there, she spotted a fruit bowl with some grapes and nectarines, which she washed and put on a plate. "He's a friend."

"Yuh-huh," Hope said sarcastically. "Tell yourself that."

"You're twelve. What do you even know?"

"More than you."

Spencer scoffed and threw a grape from the fruit bowl at her sister's head. It landed somewhere on the couch and Hope retrieved it.

"Thanks!" Hope said, popping the grape in her mouth.

Honestly, little sisters.

Spencer returned to her bedroom and handed Jackson the fruit and popcorn, which he took with a smile. They shared the snack, quietly working side by side, and Spencer was satisfied knowing that this was exactly what friends did. There was nothing bigger happening between the two of them, both content with the ease with which they worked together as partners. Nothing more, she told herself.

"Spencer . . ."

The edge in Jackson's voice made her look up from her laptop. She'd joined in his efforts to do some more research, recording anything that might look like people were acting more drunk than usual.

Jackson pointed at his own laptop's screen of a paused video from Facebook, uploaded by Nea Varkaus, a junior at Armstrong. Nea was on the debate team, so Spencer didn't really know her that well, but she was a regular at Brain Freeze, and apparently had enough social standing with the kids on the Headmaster's List to be at the party.

It was hard to totally make out in the dark, and they weren't the focus of the video—Nea had been recording herself and her friends doing some sort of rehearsed dance for TikTok with the firepit in the background—but Spencer recognized her old bright white T-shirt, tossed in the trash long since the crash, and the back of Ethan's head. They were paused, both of them with their hands in the air, gesticulating wildly. It was hard to make out the details of her expression, but she remembered this moment clearly.

"Is this when . . . ?" Jackson started.

"Yeah, this was us breaking up."

Jackson didn't say anything, just awkwardly pinched his lips together. He took a moment but said, trying to lighten the mood, "It's lucky that someone caught it on camera, though."

"What are the chances, right? It's at least something. What's the time stamp?"

"1:45 A.M."

Spencer jotted that down, adding the time on the timeline. There were still so many gaps. "Is there any way we can track where we went from there?"

Jackson played the video, but the phone was too far away to pick up any audio of what was being said. Past-Spencer and Past-Ethan moved out of frame, Spencer throwing her arms up and stomping off and Ethan chasing, but the camera didn't follow.

"Maybe there's another angle?" Jackson suggested.

"Maybe . . ." She stared at her notebook, miles away in thought.

Jackson must have sensed the edge in her voice because he said softly, "Listen, if it's too hard to revisit all this, we can stop. We've been at it a while."

"No . . ." Spencer hated the idea of asking people about one of the most humiliating experiences of her life, but it was outweighed by her need to know everything. At least Jackson didn't seem to judge her.

"For what it's worth," he said, "Ethan's an idiot. Pretty sure I can certifiably confirm that fact. He doesn't even think Reese's is the superior candy."

Spencer's lips spread into an appreciative smile, and she glanced at him. She hadn't realized how close they had been sitting to each other as the hour slipped by.

Their heads were tipped so close together, nearly touching, she noticed that his eyes were a beautiful dark brown, with golden flecks toward the middle. She'd never noticed before how pretty they were, behind his glasses.

She cleared her throat and ordered herself to get it together. "We've got a pretty good start so far. But I still need to check my hospital records. I'll know for sure then if there was something in my system that messed with my memory."

"Okay," Jackson said, nodding, though he looked worried for her sake. "I guess it'd be one less mystery."

*From: patientservices@mynsghospital.com*

*Subject: Patient Login Request*

*Thank you for using the Northshore General Hospital Patient Portal. Your login name or password has been successfully updated. Please click the link below to log in with your new credentials.*

*Patient Details*

*Patient Name: Spencer Sandoval*

*Date of Birth: 09/02/2003*

*Patient ID: SAN0982311-B*

*Status: Completed*

*Blood: B+*

*Most recent visit: 09/03/2021*

*Allergies: None*

*Quick-Click Documentation*

*Operative Report: SAN0982311-B-oprep.pdf*

*Drug/Alcohol Test Results: Pending*

*Upcoming Appointments*

*Cast removal—10/24—Send Email Reminder*

*Requesting prescription refill? Click here.*

# SEVENTEEN

**SINCE ACCESSING HER MEDICAL RECORDS,** Spencer had asked when any of her blood tests would come back, and the hospital explained it might take a few more days. She was still unnerved by the possibility that someone might have slipped something in her drink that caused her memory loss. The next day at school, Spencer and Jackson, with Ripley bounding along at her side, left the east wing of Armstrong when the lunch bell rang.

As expected, they found Brent Lang leading a yoga session near Chris's memorial garden. A couple of freshman girls moved through their poses on brightly colored vinyl mats. They were in the midst of doing an elaborate stretch that involved arms and legs wrapping around each other in a way that did not look entirely comfortable when Jackson and Spencer approached. Brent was wearing harem pants and his usual beanie, his legs wrapped around the back of his head like a human pretzel.

"Deep breaths, everyone," he said, with his eyes closed. "Release the worries of today. Exhale the bad, inhale the good."

He must have sensed the shadow passing across his face as Spencer stepped in front of the sun, looking down on him.

Brent opened one eye and looked at Spencer. "Can you not bring that dog over here? It's going to disrupt my aura's energy." Brent waved his hands through the air like he was scrubbing a window.

"Uh, sure," Spencer said, keeping Ripley at her side. "Listen, Brent? Do you have a second?"

"Can't you see I'm a little tied up at the moment?"

Jackson chuckled. "Good one."

Brent didn't look like he was trying to make a joke, though. Jackson's smile died quickly.

Spencer said, "We just wanted to ask you some questions about that night at the party."

Brent sighed when he realized that Spencer and Jackson were not going to go away anytime soon. He told his yoga students, "Move into Savasana and work on finding your breath. I'll be right back."

The students moved to lie on their backs, spread-eagle on the lawn, while Brent followed Spencer and Jackson so they could talk more in private. Brent always had a sleepy-eyed look, like he might curl up and take a nap under a desk at any moment at school. People at school were convinced he was on drugs, but Spencer had a sneaking suspicion that was just how he looked, perpetually calm and at ease with his place in the world.

Before Spencer or Jackson could say anything, Brent clapped his hands twice, closed his eyes, and breathed deeply. "I'm just clearing the air between us. Give me a moment."

Spencer and Jackson glanced at each other, and Jackson shrugged a shoulder. They waited until he was ready to speak.

"The spirits around you are very loud," he said. "It's distracting being around all that noise. Your aura is an oil spill, one big mess, and could really use a cleaning, you know."

Spencer wasn't sure what to say to that. "Uh, okay. Thanks?"

Jackson was trying not to laugh. Clearly, he didn't buy into the New Age lingo, either. The best course of attack, Spencer decided, was to just get straight into it. "We were wondering if we could ask you some questions about your, uh"—Spencer glanced at Jackson. "Side hustle. Selling some weed. The night of the end-of-summer party."

"God, it's crazy. Just remembering that night, what happened to Chris. Can't believe it."

"Do you remember much of the party? Anything unusual?"

Brent jutted out his lower lip. "Not really. Pretty run of the mill as far as Ressler's parties go. Ressler's definitely lost his touch, though; his parties used to be a lot more fun then. I think he's trying too hard. Charging too much."

"Do you remember seeing me at the party?" Spencer asked.

"Besides you freaking out on Ethan? Making a huge scene and all? Your aura was all spiky and red, such a buzz-kill. But not really. Why?"

Jackson jumped in. "What about anything else that might have been weird? Anyone who stood out to you? Something that didn't feel right?"

"Just the usual private school circuit. Kids from Armstrong, Westwood Prep, Oakhill. Can't say it was any different than you'd expect. It's just weird to think back on it now and realize it was Chris's last night . . . Hope he was happy." Brent's gaze drifted up as he thought about it. "Now that I mention it, I saw Chris over by the cars, actually."

That surprised Spencer. "You did? What was he doing?"

"I don't know. I didn't think anything of it until the crash. I think that was the last time I ever saw him alive . . . He looked like he was trying to find something. Like maybe he'd dropped something. He kept walking up and down where the cars were parked. I wasn't paying too much attention, though. Didn't seem like something to pay much attention to, you know? Why bother."

"Did anyone else see him at that time?"

"Yeah, my girlfriend Alison was there with me. She'll tell you the same thing. We were . . . ahem, *occupied* in the bushes."

"Right . . . ," Spencer said, catching the hint.

Jackson was furiously taking notes in his notebook. She saw him write down Alison's name. Spencer had the same thought about asking her about that night too, just to make sure it was accurate. But Brent seemed like he was sure he'd seen Chris before the accident.

"Do you know around what time specifically?" she asked.

Brent shrugged a shoulder and shook his head. "Nah,

I wasn't really keeping an eye on the clock, you see. It'd be kind of rude. Besides, time is a construct invented to further capitalist agenda."

"Listen, dude, did you hook up Ethan that night?" Jackson asked. "Edibles, pre-rolls?"

"Ethan?" Brent asked. "No, man, you know he's been sober for a year now. If he was high that night he didn't get it from me." Then his face shifted and a shadow passed over his eyes. "But people keep saying he was high the night he crashed. Is that true?"

"We don't know." Spencer faced Brent directly. "Were you selling other stuff at the party?"

"What are you looking for?" Brent asked, suddenly shifting into business mode. "I don't have any on me right now, but I can get it to you later. You want to get a body high or are you trying to get more in touch with your ancestors and see God?"

"No, this isn't for us, no," Spencer said hurriedly. "We wanted to figure out who was selling drugs at the party that might have made me forget stuff."

"*Marijuana* is not a *drug*, she's a plant of the earth. Nature is all around us. Making a plant illegal is just another extension of the Man. They just want to keep us oppressed. We're all slaves to the patriarchy."

Spencer stopped him before the inevitable rant she could sense coming. "I get that, but did you happen to know about any other drugs being passed around at the party that night? Anything a little more . . . mind altering?"

"I only sell weed and shrooms. I don't do the harder

stuff. Won't touch anything that's been in a lab. But yeah. There was probably some Molly being passed around."

"From who?"

"Junior. I think the name is Tabby Hill? Tammy maybe?"

Spencer looked at Jackson. "It's Tabby. You were right the first time."

Jackson's eyebrows were raised sky-high. "Tabby's a plug?"

Brent went on. "Yeah, man. Sells a lot of 'scrip. You should ask them. Say, what's with the pat down? You guys snitches? Working for the cops or something?" Brent asked, looking back and forth between the two of them.

"Brent, we've been in school together since sixth grade," Jackson said with a small smile.

"Oh right." He blinked lazily.

Jackson glanced at Spencer, as if to say, *Can you believe this guy?*

Spencer asked, "What does Tabby sell?"

Brent's smile slipped wider. "Ooh, does Little Miss Four-Point-Oh Spencer Sandoval use some performance-enhancing drugs to ace all her tests?"

Spencer's face felt hot. "No, of course not." *And by the way, I have a 4.9*, she wanted to add. Brent had probably never calculated a weighted GPA in his life.

Brent held up his hands, defensively. "Just saying! I wouldn't be the first to think it."

Spencer didn't want to argue with him; she didn't come

here for him to start anything. She just needed answers. "You said Tabby sells 'scrips."

"Adderall, Ritalin, Xanax, Percocet . . . Don't tell anyone I told you, because it skeeves me out, but I heard they'd gotten their hands on some dark shit. Like, stuff that could land a person in jail, no doubt. Plus, there's a lot of dummy Xannys and Addys laced with fentanyl on the market right now. It's Russian roulette out there. But lots of their clients are people who want to focus up during the day and then decompress at night. So yeah, there were probably pills floating around. I mean, it's LA, man."

"Right," Jackson said. Spencer was feeling simultaneously nauseous and exhilarated. If someone had slipped her something at the party, that would explain her memory loss. It was their first lead, and she could barely keep her breakfast down.

Brent looked over his shoulder and licked his lips. "Look, you didn't hear this from me, but I heard that Tabby got expelled from their last school for some crazy shit. Their family covered it all up, but things leak. Heard they were selling coke, heroin, meth even. Whatever it is, you should be careful. Tabby has all this bad energy. You never know with folks from Arizona."

"Noted," Jackson said flatly. It appeared that his opinion of Brent was waning alongside Spencer's. He didn't sound like he believed Brent in the slightest.

"Look, I really gotta go," Brent said. "My students will fall asleep if I'm not back. Do you need anything else?"

Spencer said they didn't, and Brent returned to his group of yoga acolytes.

"Heroin? Meth? You think Tabby was selling that stuff?" Jackson scoffed. "Maybe coke, but come on. It's all a bit extreme. What is this, a show on HBO?"

"We can't rule anything out," Spencer said. "The best we can do is talk to Tabby."

"If they'll even talk to us."

"We have to try."

"Tabby called in sick from school today. We'll have to wait until they're back to talk, then." Jackson clicked his pen thoughtfully a few times before putting it between the pages of his notebook. He had a habit of clicking his pen when he was particularly flustered.

Hearing that Tabby might have had a hand in Spencer's memory loss was frightening to say the least. If Brent's suspicions were right, Tabby wasn't someone to take lightly. But Spencer wasn't in the habit of listening to rumors.

Spencer bent down to scratch Ripley's back and Ripley looked up at her, mouth open in a wide smile. Spencer felt like even the dog understood that they were on to something. It was a step, even if it felt like a baby step, toward piecing together what happened that night.

# EIGHTEEN

OUTSIDE IN THE BACKYARD, SPENCER focused the telescope, then pulled back to look at the moon with her own eyes. Living in Los Angeles, Spencer hardly ever saw more than three stars, two if the moon was full. The light pollution and smog always made the sky hazy and impossible to see through. One of her dream trips would be a visit to the Cosmic Campground in New Mexico, located in the Gila National Forest. She could camp and watch the night sky, getting as many photos as she possibly could with the astrophotography camera she'd been saving up for all summer. Hike and cook on an open fire all day, and sleep under the stars at night.

But for now, she was stuck at home, until she was finally able to sit in a car again.

The moon was full and bright, a rarity in the city, and Spencer had set up her telescope on the deck, Ripley watching curiously from the grass. The crickets were out, the air was warm, and Spencer finally got to have some time to herself. She had lit some candles to see by and could blow them out when she needed to. For now, she had some time.

"Hey."

She turned to see Jackson, emerging from her living room, sliding the glass door behind him and smiling, as always.

"Hey!" she said cheerfully. "You made it."

She had invited Jackson over for a study session for their AP psych exam. Her parents were out at work, so it shouldn't be a problem. Besides, they were doing things for school. Why would she get in trouble for that? But she had something else in mind before they got to work.

"Hope let me in," he explained. "What are you doing?"

"Come see," she said, tipping her head to the telescope.

When he approached, she could smell him. Whatever he used when he showered, she liked it, a pleasant combination of cedar and rosemary. It reminded her of a forest trail on the northern coast. She was thankful for the dark, concealing the heat in her cheeks.

He leaned down and peered through the eyepiece. "Whoa," he said, completely—for lack of a better word—starstruck. "It's so clear."

"She's beautiful, right?"

"Totally." Jackson pulled back from the telescope and smiled at her; then he looked through the eyepiece again. "It's—wow, amazing! You can almost see the ranges in the mountains. Everything is . . . wow!" Spencer smiled. She too sounded lost for words the first time she saw the moon with a telescope. By making the moon so large, one can really feel so small. It had the opposite effect of being alone in an empty room. Instead, it made her feel closer to the cosmos. Like she could reach out and touch it. If she were at a dark sky park, she imagined the night sky full of stars could open up and swallow her whole. Someday she'd get there.

Jackson looked up at her. "Is this what you do most nights when you're not studying?"

Spencer smiled. "As if I couldn't be any more of a nerd."

"Not like that's a bad thing. I think sometimes we see the moon so much, sometimes we take it for granted."

He had a point. "I'm curious, though. What do you see in the moon?"

"What do you mean?"

"Like, when you look at the moon, what looks back?"

He looked through the eyepiece and said, "I think I see a man. The eyes, and the mouth, making it look like he's surprised." He tilted his head up again. "Is this some kind of Rorschach test? Did I pass?"

Spencer lowered her voice and stroked her face, as if she had a long beard. "Ah yes, you see a man in the moon, therefore you are at war with your conscious and unconscious mind." She laughed and dropped the act. "I'm joking. It's just fun to ask what people see. Everyone sees something different. It's called lunar pareidolia. What people see in the light or dark spots of the moon." The dark craters of the moon could form the impression of handprints, or the profile of a dog howling; some people saw the face of a man, others saw a woman with an updo. People could argue for decades about which was correct, but in the end, no one would be right. The only truth was that people saw patterns in random shapes as a result of asteroids hitting the surface with no atmosphere. And Spencer found comfort in the idea that there was an inherent need in people to see patterns and faces in randomness. Everyone was always looking for answers.

"Really?" he said. "I always thought it was pretty standard across the board."

She nodded. "You'd be surprised. Tons of people around the world see different things. I see a rabbit. The ears, the little tail."

Jackson looked back through the eyepiece and *ooh'd*. "Now I see it! But I can't see the man anymore. That's wild." He kept looking through the telescope, completely drawn in. Spencer stood by, holding herself and smiling as she looked at the sky, too. A plane flew overhead, its wingtip lights blinking.

Spencer glanced at the time on her phone. It was almost time.

"This is amazing. I've never seen the moon like this before . . . What are you doing?"

Spencer blew out the candles and counted down the seconds on her phone. "You don't think I wanted you here just to look at the moon, did you?" she asked with a grin. "Look again. Three, two, one . . ."

Jackson lowered his gaze to the telescope and after a second, he tensed up. "What is—it's moving! What is that? It's so fast!"

Spencer smiled wider. "Right on time. Perfectly predictable."

Jackson looked at her, his expression tight. "Aliens."

Spencer laughed. "I wish! No, that was the International Space Station. Pretty cool, right?"

"For real?" Jackson moved back to the telescope, but it would have been long gone by now.

"Four-point-seven-six miles per second. That's how fast it's falling. Can you imagine that? Weightlessness? Zero gravity?"

"No, I really can't. I've never even been on a roller coaster. Freaks me out too much. Heights? No thank you. That's way too intense for me. But still, this was so cool. Thanks for showing me."

"I'm glad you could see it! The conditions have to be perfect; fortunately we didn't have any cloud cover. Sometimes things just work out when you need them to."

Spencer half-heartedly kicked a rock down the sidewalk. It rolled down the pavement a few steps away, for Spencer to kick it again. They had taken a break from their AP psych notes to take Ripley for a walk. The conversation turned back toward Ethan and the case.

The first day of his trial was coming up next weekend. Inevitably, it stirred up excitement for people who were paying attention to the case.

"It's awful reading what people are saying about him online," Spencer said. The phone lit up her face in the dim light of the fading evening. "Reddit is the worst. And everyone's private stories on Snap."

"Yeah, it's brutal, they all say he's guilty."

"Spencer?" Jackson asked.

"Yeah?"

"What if he is?"

Spencer put her phone away. "He can't be. He wouldn't. Even Brent said Ethan was sober."

"But he doesn't know if he was sober *that night*. And you don't remember."

"I just—I just don't want to believe it's true."

Jackson put his hands in the pockets of his hoodie. "Yeah."

"The faster we figure all this out, maybe the faster we can prove people wrong," she said.

Jackson pushed his glasses up his nose and took a breath. "You really think when faced with the truth, people will change their minds?"

Spencer didn't want to think about the alternative, that even with all the facts, people have already found Ethan guilty and there was no going back. She didn't answer his question and turned Ripley down the corner, making sure she didn't stick her nose in the lawns with the warning signs about spraying pesticides in the grass. In a way, going online these days felt like she was sticking her own nose in poison.

It was surreal to think that everyone had an opinion about Ethan's case.

After the fifth celebrity tweeting about how they wanted #justiceforchris, Spencer couldn't take it anymore. Truth was discovered in split-second decisions, posted online for all to see, no going back.

"Any luck finding more videos from the party?" she asked.

"We've collected most of what I could track down. I think we've got a pretty good timeline of events."

The streetlights overhead crackled on, one by one down the street, lighting up the road in a pale orange hue, and Jackson's glasses caught the glint of a passing car, their high beams on bright. The flashback hit her head-on.

*Ethan's face. Lit up. Shadows cast across his cheeks. Crash.*

Spencer took a steadying breath and gripped Ripley's leash tighter.

"What do you know about Tabby Hill?" she asked.

Jackson bowed his elbows out, maintaining his hands in his pockets while shrugging his shoulders. "Nothing really. They seem aloof and we've never had a chance to talk. What Brent said about them makes me think that there's a lot we don't know. But how do we get them to talk to us?"

Spencer explained seeing Tabby while at work the other day, and how suspiciously they were acting when Spencer even tried to look in their direction.

"Weird," Jackson said. "But are we being just like these strangers on the internet, trying to accuse people of things before we even have all the facts?"

"We're not doing this for fun. This is real. Tabby should

be able to tell us more about that night. The only way to know is if we ask."

But that was easier said than done.

All week at school, Spencer continued organizing the events of that night. She pretended to be listening in class, even going so far as to use her large textbook to block Mrs. McNamara from seeing that she was really watching videos from that night and recording her thoughts in her notebook. She'd gotten in deep with the investigation, tracking down all the videos that she could, sometimes even cornering people in the hall to get them to give up any videos or photos of that night. She kept all of it in a small black notebook, which she could tuck easily into her bag and whip out at a moment's notice.

The whole time, Tabby almost made a point to avoid Spencer at all costs, ducking out of sight whenever Spencer and Jackson drew near. It was like trying to catch a cloud.

Once, by random encounter, Spencer managed to find Tabby in the bathroom right next to the cafeteria. When Spencer opened her mouth to speak, Tabby shot her the coldest look Spencer had ever seen. It actually stopped Spencer in her tracks.

"Tabby, I—"

"I'm keeping my mouth shut. Same as you."

Spencer didn't know what to say, let alone try to stop Tabby as they pushed past her to leave, looking over their shoulder only once, glowering at Spencer like she was the filth of the earth.

### *Get Salty*: A True Crime Podcast with Peyton Salt

*Lifestyles of the Rich and Reckless* Segment Transcription

*[Get Salty Intro Music]*

**Peyton Salt:** I wanted to get a bigger picture about Ethan after several of you have flooded our inbox about this story. (Don't forget to hit us up online, even just to say hi! We love hearing from our fans!)

Tabby Hill, the acclaimed child star you might recognize from those cookie commercials, continues to decline any chance at an interview. We've been trying our best to get their side of the story, but it would appear there's nothing else to say about the matter, otherwise they would want to talk to us, right, Sasha?

**Sasha Firth:** That's right. We want victims to have the chance to tell their story, but we also want to make sure we get the full picture about Ethan. I have to admit, like so many others, I'm obsessed. This case has taken over my brain.

**Peyton:** *[laughs]* I too can't give up. I need to know why Ethan did what he did. Since I have almost exclusive access, I interviewed several people about him from Armstrong and beyond, including those directly affected by his reckless behavior, to get behind the psychology of the rich and reckless.

*[SFX: school bell rings, voices in a crowd, lockers closing]*

**Harrison Ressler (senior):**

Ethan's a cool guy. He used to throw the biggest parties. I learned a lot from him, but he's a bit of a hothead. Makes him good at soccer, though. Bet he could have made the national team. His dad's got enough money to buy it for him if he doesn't anyway. [*laughs*]

**Tracey Pujolaso (junior):**

I nearly got run over by Ethan in the parking lot at school last year. He came peeling into an empty parking space, nearly killed me. Oh my gosh. Do you think maybe he tried to?

**Abigail Brak (sophomore):**

Everyone said he was the hottest guy in school. I still do. I mean, he's a piece of [*BEEP*] but it doesn't make him any less hot.

**Nick Moore (victim Chris Moore's older brother):**

Ethan needs to be locked up for a long time. He got my brother killed, my girlfriend's in a coma because of him . . . The world would be a better place if he wasn't in it.

**Patrick Hackett (senior):**

I heard he got shipped off to military school or whatever, total maniac. They do that to seriously messed-up people, right? I also heard his parents were sick of him, too. I'm not surprised he's going to jail.

**Alejandro Rojas (junior):**

Dude's loaded. He just didn't care he was driving fast. If he got a ticket, he could just pay it off or whatever. A two-hundred dollar ticket is chump change. With people like him, it's either get out of the way or get flattened, simple as that.

**Teresa Ferrera (senior):**
I heard a rumor he had a stalker, but isn't that what all scumbag guys say about girlfriends? "That chick was crazy." I don't buy it for one second.

**Daphne Deargacha (freshman):**
I don't really know him, but he's been all over the news. If everyone's saying all that stuff about him, it's true, right? Why else would people hate him?

# NINETEEN

**THE DAY OF ETHAN'S FIRST** appearance in court, Spencer went to the garage, following the sound of the metal hammering coming from inside.

While Spencer always thought she was smart and got good grades because she worked hard for it, Hope was a real genius. It never bothered Spencer that Hope was naturally talented at all things engineering and invention. Math and physics came to her as easily as breathing came to most people. When she was four, she built her first robot. At ten, she made a solar-powered automata out of pinewood.

Her current obsession was Rube Goldberg machines. She used various mechanics, like bowling balls as weights, pulleys, and springs. A few times the neighbors complained to the homeowners' association about a raccoon infestation, but it had just been Hope scrounging around in their garbage for anything she could use to make her machine bigger and better.

Her current project was huge, spanning the entirety of the garage, so much so that both family cars had to be parked in the driveway because there was no room to fit either one.

Hope had entered a contest for young engineers and needed to submit a video for the judges showing her work in progress. She was in the midst of recording a video, testing the machine. The grand prize was four thousand dollars and an article about the winner written in a magazine. Hope had been working on her project all summer, spending most of her days and some nights in the garage, finessing every detail and planning out each stage in a stack of notebooks. If there was any doubt they were related, Spencer and Hope's love for notebooks was a dead giveaway.

Spencer kept to the edge of the garage, staying out of frame of the camera as Hope's machine had run its course, the final domino falling over. Hope got started setting up for another run.

Spencer asked, "Did you steal my shoes?"

"Which shoes do you refer to, oh great and terrible queen?"

Annoyed, Spencer said, "My flats, the dark blue ones."

"Oh, those. No, why?"

"I can't find them. I haven't seen them for ages." The last time she'd worn them was . . . Spencer couldn't remember, but it bothered her. She liked knowing where all her things were and that things were in their rightful place.

Hope shook her head. "Why would I take them?"

"Because you've taken my stuff for your projects before." Spencer glanced at their mom's old bra being used in the machine as an elastic slingshot.

"I told you, I didn't take them. Maybe Olivia did," Hope said, focusing intently on balancing the dominoes.

Spencer sighed. Hope was many things: a genius, an annoying little sister, and a total nerd, but she wasn't a liar.

"Need help resetting it?" Spencer asked, about to reach for a bobbing bird garden decoration when Hope barked.

"Don't—touch that."

Spencer held up her hands innocently and backed up. "Did you get this from Mrs. Piripi's yard?"

"I didn't steal it. I'm simply . . . borrowing it."

"Hope."

"I left a note. I needed something to flip the coin." She referred to the tail of the bird that would flip a coin into a bowl of water. The whole setup was extraordinarily elaborate. Hope had said she wanted to build roller coasters when she grew up, and based on the expanse of the Rube Goldberg machine, Spencer didn't doubt it for a second.

"Where are you going anyway?" Hope asked.

"Ethan's court appearance."

"Oh. Do me a favor and grab those dominoes for me." Hope pointed to a bucket near Spencer's elbow, resting on top of an old carpenter's workstation. Spencer got the dominoes, and Hope took out some more blocks.

"How's it coming along?" Spencer asked.

"Fine," Hope said with a sigh. Spencer noticed how much older she looked these days. What happened to her baby sister? She was becoming a grown-up faster and faster. She sighed like their mom did. "I still have more work to do. But I feel like it's missing something. Some pizzaz." She waved her hands in the air, as best she could with one fist full of dominoes, doing jazz fingers.

"Maybe add some lights? LEDs or something that changes color?"

"Maybe . . ." Hope's gaze followed the track of the Rube Goldberg machine, watching it execute its function in her mind's eye. "It's not very good, is it?"

"What are you talking about? It looks great."

Hope shrugged a shoulder and twisted her lips, looking bashful. "Flip that switch over there. No, not—yeah, that one."

Spencer did as she was told and stood back with Hope as they admired her work. The machine started up beautifully. A series of ball bearings rolled down zigzag ramps, growing larger and larger in size, intending to get all the way to a bowling ball at the end, moved through a series of falls, rolling down tracks, spinning through tunnels, all the way to a wooden train set that flew off the tracks and fell to the floor with a plastic clatter.

"It's not finished . . . ," Hope said, almost like she was embarrassed. "I feel like something is missing. I can't get this one stage to transition into another. It's like . . ."

"A gap."

"Yeah," Hope said, folding her arms over her chest.

"Courtroom number two," said the security guard at the Santa Monica courthouse as Spencer walked through the metal detector. Then he noticed Ripley. "Is this a medical service animal?"

"Mental health," Spencer corrected. She picked up her backpack as it left the X-ray machine, thankful they didn't make a fuss about the painkillers inside.

"Fine. But be aware that Judge Patel might request that you take the dog out if it causes any distractions."

Spencer doubted that it would be a problem, but she understood why. If anyone was allergic to the dog, like Dr. Diamond at school, she didn't want to be the one standing between Ethan's fair trial and justice. How would she feel if she was the one who got Ethan in trouble because the judge might be in a bad mood?

As she approached the courtroom, she recognized some people waiting in the hall: The Moores were talking with the lawyer in red-soled Louboutins near the coffee machine; a couple of fellow students from Armstrong had come wearing #justiceforchris badges; even Detective Potentas was there, standing by the staircase and talking on his phone. Spencer had come to the trial without her parents. They didn't think it was a good idea, but she was determined to show her face at the trial. She wanted to be there, make sure that no one thought she was hiding. It was a terrible crash, but she needed to be there. She needed to see it through to the end.

But she couldn't help the nagging pull in her belly, telling her to go home. She was embarrassed, and anxious, and a little lonely. She'd tried to dress appropriately, but she couldn't help but feel like no matter what she wore, she would stand out in the courtroom.

That was when she spotted Jackson leaning against the wall near the water fountain, folding and refolding the end of his tie nervously, head lowered, lost in thought. His dark hair was slicked back from his forehead, and he wore a white long-sleeved shirt and slacks. If he didn't already look like Clark Kent, he did now. She could only imagine the worry he must be feeling for Ethan.

She sidled up next to him, standing at the wall too, watching the parade of people in suits filling the hall. She knew that he knew she was there, but they didn't say anything to each other for a moment, simply standing in silence and taking a breath before the inevitable chaos that would be the first day of Ethan's trial. She had no idea what to expect. She'd only seen trials on TV and she didn't think it could be like that, could it?

Jackson was one of the few people she wanted to be with at that moment, and it helped calm her nerves a little bit.

Spencer ran the tip of her thumbnail through the groove on Ripley's handhold on her vest. It helped ground her into the moment, feeling like she was real. She liked the way the cement wall cooled the sweat on the skin of her back, and she wiggled her toes in her shoes. She was alive, she was here, and she could get through this. But even then, it still didn't stop the flashback from happening in the span of time it took her to blink, and she let out a shudder of a breath.

*SPENCER! Cold, wet hands on her face. Engine roaring. Crash. Float.*

Images and sounds rushed through her head, out of order. She'd had to take a double dose of her pain pills today. It helped take the edge off.

"This sucks," Jackson said finally. He blew out a sigh that ruffled a stray curl on his forehead.

She glanced at him, noticing that he had turned his attention to the crowd of lawyers and stenographers and general employees of the courthouse as they went about their business, moving from one office to the next, just doing their day jobs and thinking about other things, and definitely not worrying about this one case because it was just another sheet in a pile on their desk, and they just wanted to get home to their families. Spencer had an instinct to tell him everything was going to be okay, but would she have believed herself if she was in his shoes?

"Yeah." That was all Spencer needed to say.

The courtroom doors opened, and the bailiff let everyone inside.

It was time.

She and Jackson found Ethan instantly—he was already sitting with his lawyer, Ray Cardona, at a table on the right side of the courtroom. Mr. Cardona looked a lot different than he did on the commercials running on TV; his teeth weren't as bright and his hair wasn't as shiny, but he wore a very expensive suit that fit him well, and his shiny gold watch caught the harsh lights from above. He and Ethan had their heads tipped toward each other, no doubt discussing some last-minute advice before the judge arrived. Ethan's jaw was clenched, but he nodded every so often. He was wearing a suit and tie too, his best foot forward.

Spencer and Jackson chose to sit in the back where she

and Ripley could cause the least disturbance. A few glances here and there, especially at Ripley, was the extent of what Spencer could handle while her stomach wanted to protest.

Ethan turned around in his chair, perhaps looking for a friendly face in the crowd to give him some courage. The bruising on his face had subsided significantly, now just a shadow of the accident remaining. Their gazes met and Spencer tried to give some sort of sign of support, the slightest smile, but he clamped his lips shut and turned away from her, facing the front of the courtroom once more.

Spencer couldn't help but think he looked guilty.

Why was she even here? She should hate Ethan's guts. No one would be angry with her for not showing up. He'd hurt her, in more ways than one that night, so what was she even doing sitting here on his side of the courtroom? Her gaze fell to Ripley at her feet, and she clenched her fist tightly.

The judge entered the courtroom from a side door, obviously the judge's chambers, and everyone stood up respectfully. Judge Patel was an older Indian woman with gray hair and gold-rimmed glasses. She looked serious, no nonsense. Spencer couldn't help thinking that didn't look good for Ethan. She didn't seem like the type to go easy on reckless teenagers who lived their lives thinking they were invincible.

When everyone took their seats again, Spencer was surprised that everything was a lot different from what she saw on TV. In courtroom shows, it was a lot more dramatic and tense, but the atmosphere in the courtroom was clinical, businesslike, and—frankly—boring. The lawyers listed off various technical terms noted by the judge and Spencer couldn't help but zone out. It wasn't just because the painkillers were taking effect, it was because trials were unexpectedly so mundane.

While the proceedings started, Spencer's attention landed on the Moores. They were seated together; Spencer was only able to see the backs of their heads. They were holding hands, but Spencer couldn't help but notice that Mrs. Moore's fingers were tapping impatiently on the table in front of them, her manicure making a noticeable rhythm on the wood. It was almost as if she was impatient, waiting to do something more important with her time. Spencer furrowed her brows and tried not to read into it, but it struck her as somewhat odd. They were suing the one responsible for their son's death. What could possibly be more important than that?

The judge looked up over the top of her glasses. Her voice was firm, like a strict schoolteacher's. "I'd like to remind everyone that no recording devices are allowed in my courtroom and that I expect everyone to behave accordingly, otherwise you may be removed at any time."

Spencer noticed she was speaking in the direction of a person sitting a few rows ahead of Spencer on the other side of the aisle. Peyton Salt. She lowered her phone when she noticed the judge was speaking about her. She blushed and pocketed her phone.

Spencer tasted something bitter in the back of her mouth as she glared at Peyton. All the terrible things she'd said about Ethan, about the crash . . . Spencer forced herself to look away, otherwise she was afraid she would scream. At what point did journalism turn into exploitation?

The Moores' lawyer went up first, the one with the red-soled Louboutins Spencer had noticed earlier. Spencer got the impression that she was good at her job and had the fancy heels to prove it. She introduced herself as Thora Barancewicz to the judge, submitting her case documents to the court and stating the charges pressed against Ethan. All the while, Spencer kept watching the back of Ethan's head. He sat motionless, watching the lawyer present her case, and barely flinched when the lawyer gestured in his direction. Jackson too watched quietly, powerless to do or say anything.

Ripley put her head in Spencer's lap, and Spencer realized that while the prosecution was describing the events of the crash, her breathing had become ragged and shallow. Ripley reminded her that she was okay, that she wasn't alone. Spencer realized just how important Ripley had become in her life. She might not have been able to sit there if it wasn't for her.

"The events of that night could have been prevented," the prosecution said. "Ethan Amoroso, known in the community for driving without care, for racing, for partying, for inconsideration for his neighbors and fellow students. His pattern of reckless behavior is an unfortunate result of carelessness, callousness, and a lack of empathy for others. Your Honor, this case is solid. When will the community finally be able to rest?"

Ethan didn't even move. Spencer couldn't take her eyes off him. To hear the lawyer say it so plainly, it put everything that had happened into a perspective that Spencer hadn't been prepared to deal with. Ethan was in deep trouble. He'd accidentally killed someone. It wasn't just a matter of blaming it all on a freak accident. He wouldn't be able to pick himself up and move on. This was big.

Jackson fidgeted beside her, picking at a hangnail on his thumb, worrying at the flap of it so much it had started to bleed, but he didn't notice. He must have been so scared for Ethan. She could see it in his eyes, and in his jaw, too. She was tempted to reach out and hold his hand to stop him from further hurting himself, but she didn't want to cross a line and ruin their friendship, so she clasped her own hands together instead.

"Mr. Ethan Amoroso," the judge said, pausing a moment for his lawyer to gesture for him to rise. "You have been charged with aggravated reckless driving, child endangerment, and felony manslaughter. How do you plead?"

But instead of answering, his lawyer stood up. "Your honor, I have in my hand Ethan Amoroso's toxicology report from the night in question."

There was a murmur from the crowd.

"May I approach the bench?"

The judge nodded.

Ethan's lawyer handed the report to the judge, who studied it, face impassive.

The lawyer turned to the courtroom. "As you can see, Your Honor, Ethan Amoroso was not driving under the influence. His blood alcohol limit was 0.06 percent. He was well within the legal boundaries of the State of California to get behind the wheel. The crash occurred at a blind intersection where there have been many complaints filed to the city to put in a traffic signal instead of a mere stop sign. What happened to Christopher Moore was tragic, but it was not done with a wanton disregard for human life. It was an accident. Ethan Amoroso is innocent. We would like to file for dismissal."

The courtroom exploded with whispers and shocked gasps. The Moores looked downright furious. Mr. Moore looked like he was about to stand up and throw something, while Mrs. Moore looked like she was plotting his demise.

Spencer couldn't breathe.

She was right!

Ethan wasn't high!

He was innocent!

The judge ordered a recess, and when everyone filed back in, the tension was palpable in the air. Would the case be dismissed? Would Ethan go free? It was too much for Spencer, whose head was throbbing. She fished around in her backpack for her orange pill bottle. Before opening the cap, she tried to remember how many she'd taken already that day.

She knew she took some with breakfast, and again between taking Ripley for a long walk and Olivia coming over to swap notes for a group project for AP Spanish. But she hurt, and decided to take another, just to get her pain under control.

She noticed Jackson beside, her, gripping the edges of his seat, his knuckles white.

The judge returned, and everyone rose.

After everyone was seated once more, the judge addressed the court. "I have studied the evidence and the new information, and consulted with lawyers for the prosecution and defense. Although it's been proven that Mr. Amoroso was not driving under the influence, the state's charges of aggravated reckless driving, child endangerment, and felony manslaughter still apply. Mr. Amoroso, you have been charged. How do you plead?"

Ethan stood up and faced the judge. "Not guilty."

After the opening statements, the trial was over for the day. Spencer tried to catch Ethan's eye before he left, but he wasn't looking her way.

"Fuck," Jackson whispered. "I thought it was over."

"Yeah, me too," said Spencer. It was too much to hope, but the prosecution made the argument that even if Ethan hadn't been drunk, the facts remained that he was speeding and hadn't stopped at the intersection and had caused the death of a human being.

A voice carried down the hall, over the din of people chatting. Curt and courteous. "Spencer."

"Detective Potentas!" Spencer put her pill bottle back in her backpack as he walked over, looking somewhat distracted, as if he was thinking about someplace else he wanted to be.

"I'm not surprised I keep seeing you around. Don't you have school? Extracurriculars?"

"Why shouldn't I be here? I was in the crash." Spencer wasn't sure why she felt so defensive, but she couldn't help it.

Detective Potentas put his hands in his pockets and looked around. "You're still trying to find information on your boyfriend's case?"

"Yeah," she said.

"You should leave the investigation to the police. You're only causing more trouble."

Surprised, Spencer raised her eyebrows. "Why? Has someone complained about me?" Her mind immediately began filing through all the names of the people she had interviewed.

Detective Potentas rubbed his chin and sighed. He looked beyond her, warring with himself over his words. That was when Spencer saw Mrs. Moore standing behind him, halfway down the hall, but she was glaring in Spencer's direction. Her dark red lipstick was nearly gone, she was pinching her lips together so tightly in disapproval. Nick, Chris's brother, was standing next to her, rubbing her shoulder in an attempt to calm her down.

"Your name has been brought up," Detective Potentas said finally. "You're not exactly being subtle about it."

"I'm not trying to do anything but fill the gaps in my memory, and until I find out what happened that night, I'm not quitting."

*Why was she with Ethan if she had broken up with him?*

*Why was she in the car?*

*Why was Tabby with them?*

*And Chris?*

It just didn't make sense.

"I knew you'd say that. It's not just that, though; you're causing more pain for yourself. Take my word for it: There's nothing to this case. I haven't seen an easier case closed in a long time. We have our guy. You heard the judge, even if he had nothing in his system, he was still speeding. Going 120 miles an hour in a residential zone. He lost control of the vehicle and killed that kid. You're not a detective. There's nothing to detect. Move on from all this, believe me. It's for the best."

"What if I say no?" There were two Spencers, one Before, and one After the crash. If the Before Spencer had heard the way she was talking to a cop, she would have been shocked. The Spencer who had come out of that crash had a sharper tongue, especially with the pain radiating through her body, reminding her of everything she'd lost. Girls with her skin color didn't have too many good experiences with police.

But Detective Potentas just sighed, like he was talking to a petulant child who refused to eat her greens. "Take care of yourself, Miss Sandoval. Don't go looking for relief at the bottom of a bottle, either."

When Detective Potentas walked away, Jackson returned. His cheeks were shiny, she suspected as a result of him splashing water on his face in the restroom, and he lent her the smallest smile, but his face fell when he spotted Peyton Salt lingering halfway down the hall.

Spencer frowned when she noticed her, too.

"Come on," she said. "Let's get some air." She wanted to get as far away from Peyton as she could. Jackson didn't argue. He carried her backpack for her as they left.

Spencer wasn't like Peyton. Peyton treated the crash like a story, but this was Spencer's life. Didn't she deserve to know what really happened that night? She'd been living with the direct consequences. Her life had been upended, not to the same degree as the Moore family, but she was nevertheless changed.

But where would investigation end and invasion of privacy begin? She wanted to believe that she and Peyton were different on all fronts, but would she be able to stop if she started hurting people in the process of discovering the truth? She felt sick just thinking about it.

Would she discover some secrets worth keeping hidden?

# TWENTY

**THE NEXT DAY, A SUNDAY,** Spencer got her cast off. It was a relief too, couldn't have come any sooner. She might have been able to be happy about it, though, had it not been for what Detective Potentas had said at the courthouse. A part of her knew that he was right, that she was just digging up dirt that muddied the water. Ethan's confession was crystal clear, solid. It was Ethan's car. Ethan was driving. Was she just making it more difficult for the other victims to move on? How would Tabby feel knowing that Spencer was refusing to let the case be closed once and for all?

Spencer tried going about her day, taking full advantage of the time Uncle Martin had given her off from Brain Freeze for her arm, and focusing her attention elsewhere, but her thoughts always circled back to the crash, like water going down a drain.

When night came, Spencer tried to enjoy sitting on the couch with Hope, but she wasn't even registering what they were watching, a *Murder, She Wrote* rerun she'd seen a dozen times. Hope wasn't even watching, either. She was on her phone playing a game.

Spencer's mood had turned inward and before she knew it, she was lost in thought, staring at the empty, used plates where peanut butter and jelly sandwiches had sat on the coffee table in front of them. Spencer hadn't had the energy to make anything fancier for dinner. Hope didn't seem to mind; it seemed like she could tell Spencer was having an off day.

It was in the police's best interest to close cases as quickly as possible. The quickest way was a confession, and with Ethan's case, it was open and shut. He had admitted to being behind the wheel that night. He was driving and it was his fault. What more could anyone ask for? Wasn't it the perfect case? The job had already been done for them. There was nothing more to see, nothing else to look for but secrets that would complicate the matter. Ethan's fate had been sealed the minute he confessed.

Ripley pawed at the door to ring a row of bells hanging from the doorknob to the backyard, as she was trained to do whenever she needed to go out.

It was unnecessary, but Hope kicked Spencer's leg, nudging her to get up. Spencer was already moving by the time she made contact and Spencer swiped at the air above Hope's foot, half-heartedly, and Hope settled back in for more gaming.

It had been dark for a few hours now, pitch black on the other side of the sliding glass door. Because of it, it looked like a mirror. Spencer looked like a ghost moving through the reflection as Ripley waited patiently for Spencer to arrive. She felt like a ghost, too.

"Okay, let's go potty," Spencer said as she opened the door. The motion-sensor light on the back porch turned on as Ripley cut down the deck and into the grass. Spencer followed, closing the door behind herself, and hugged her hoodie closer to her body as she watched Ripley—nose down, tail up—make the usual lap around the backyard before relieving herself.

The crickets were loud that night and Spencer tipped her head back, breathing in the crisp night air, catching remnant whiffs of a neighbor's barbecue somewhere close by, and waiting for Ripley to do her business. A dog barked somewhere in the distance, but Ripley paid no mind and trotted back up the stairs of the deck toward Spencer.

"Good girl," she said, but before Ripley came within arm's reach, she stopped and turned around, staring into the dark of the yard.

Spencer hadn't noticed it before, but there was a dark shape just out of the light from the porch, a shape that shouldn't belong there.

The little hairs on the back of Spencer's neck stood on end. The shadow was vaguely human shaped, but unmoving. Spencer froze, straining her eyes to make out any details, trying to see through the dark. Had Hope left something in the yard from her Rube Goldberg project? Was it some yard equipment her dad had been using earlier in the week? She would have thought nothing of it, chalked it up to just a trick of the eye, searching to make out random shapes like lunar pareidolia, but the hackles rose on Ripley's back and she let out a low growl. Whatever it was, Ripley saw it, too.

"Hello?" Spencer asked.

It was unmistakable. The figure moved.

Someone was in her yard.

Head, shoulders, distinctly there, but no way to make out any details.

Had they been looking in through their window? They hadn't drawn their curtains. Spencer and Hope had been sitting on the couch, in full view, illuminated on the inside, visible to anyone outside in the safety of darkness. Static rage snapped everything into focus.

Spencer took a step forward, heart hammering. Ripley backed up, though, shielding Spencer, but Spencer moved around her.

Spencer blinked, and in that fraction of a second the shadow took off into the deeper dark, and Spencer jumped down the steps, rounding the house, blood rushing in her ears and drowning out all sensibility to go back inside, Ripley hot on her heels.

Spencer sprinted over grass slick with water from the sprinkler. But by the time she rounded the corner, coming through the alley between her house and the neighbor's, the shadow was already around the corner. Spencer stopped in the front yard, panting, scanning the hedges and fences for any sign, but the street was darker. With the adrenaline hot in her head, she couldn't see or hear anything. Whoever it was, they were gone.

Ripley came up to Spencer's side and pressed her body against her legs, whining. Spencer took an extra second to see if she could spot the shadow, but it was no use. They had vanished.

Spencer looked over her shoulder as she brought Ripley back inside, but the street remained dark, and she tried to shake the feeling that she was still being watched as she locked the door behind her.

# TWENTY-ONE

**THE LIBRARY IN THE MORNINGS** at school was one of Spencer's favorite places to be. The skylights overhead filtered in the warm morning light, draping the desks in a comforting haze of dust floating in the air. The librarian, Mrs. Patton, with her beaded glasses chain, always greeted her while she was reshelving books, never bothering to check up on her frequently, knowing full well that Spencer was hard at work studying. She would usually sit alone during her free period, catching up on homework or rewriting her notes in neater script, using different colored pens to draw attention to important details, which was what she was currently doing with her right hand.

Even though she'd gotten the cast removed yesterday, her left wrist felt stiff, and she had to keep stopping to rest, opting to use her right hand so as not to break her flow of concentration.

She was shaking out her wrist and rereading her notes when Jackson took his usual seat across from her at the table.

"Hey!" she said, smiling. "Good morning."

"Morning! Your cast is off!" He put his backpack on the table and took out his textbooks and notebooks.

"Yeah, yesterday. It feels so weird. I'm getting used to having my hand back. When they took the cast off, my hand was all gray and wrinkly, like an old sock."

Jackson scrunched his nose and laughed, amused and disgusted at the same time. "Gross! I didn't want to picture that so early in the morning. Thanks." Seeing him was a breath of fresh air.

Spencer found herself smiling more easily, especially with Jackson around. She bit her lip, guilty of this newfound warmth in her belly, and lowered her gaze to her notebook. Ethan used to make her happy. Sometimes. His spirit infected Spencer's rigid habits, broke her down to bare desire. She'd wanted to date the hottest boy in school, and she did for a while. Did that make her truly happy, though? She wasn't sure.

Jackson busied himself with his laptop, tugging at his lower lip with his thumb and index finger, lost in thought, as his eyes flicked back and forth on his screen. She watched him for a quiet moment, admiring the lip-pulling habit of his. Was he even aware of it, or was it just as natural as breathing to him? He looked at her, and she lowered her gaze, feeling like a creep for staring so long. If he noticed, he didn't say anything.

"So, it took me forever, but I mapped out the entire night's events at the party. Almost down to the minute."

"Really? Great job!"

"Thanks! I mean, it's not really groundbreaking stuff.

Mostly drunk kids making out with one another and doing keg stands and stuff, but yeah. It's all done."

"What'd you find?"

"It occurred to me that maybe we've been focusing so much on recording your movement through the party, it'd be worth a shot looking for anyone else from the car. And . . . I found something that you might be interested in."

He spun the laptop around and Spencer saw a video pulled up.

"It took me a few viewings to catch it, but . . . here." He pressed the space bar and the video started. The video had been uploaded by Ed Hughes, a sophomore, featuring himself and his friends chugging cans of beer in record time in the unfinished kitchen of the housing development. The camera was shaking so hard that Spencer could barely make anything out except for the faraway looks of sophomore boys who were too drunk to realize they were basically walking blurs of bad decision-making. But Jackson pointed to a few frames when the camera swirled around to the crowd of people dancing in the yard. He pressed the space bar again and said, "Is that who I think it is?"

"Chris . . . ," Spencer said, eyes wide, jaw dropped. He was slumped on the ground, draped over a tree stump littered with what looked like red Solo cups, but the image was too blurry to make out for sure. There was no mistaking it, though, that was Chris. Spencer's stomach dropped, thinking that a couple hours after this footage was taken, he'd be dead.

"He looks wasted, right?" Jackson asked.

"Yeah, pretty par for the course at the party."

"Exactly. Which got me thinking. I went back through the night, working backward through all the videos in my timeline, to see if I could follow him, track his movements. I tried seeing how many beers he'd gone through, but . . ."

"Let me guess, only one."

Jackson nodded grimly.

"Harrison had it set up that you got different colored cups for what drinks you paid for, with little tally marks for how many you drank. Red was for beer. Every video I saw, Chris only had the one red cup with one red slash."

"So if he was drunk enough to be slumped over like that . . . you think he was drugged?"

"It's not out of the realm of possibility, is it?"

"But who would do something like that?"

"My thoughts exactly, until I found this video. It took me a while, but . . ." Jackson spun the laptop back to himself and used the track pad to pull up something else, before turning the screen back to Spencer. She couldn't help but lean in, like she would fall right through the screen and into the past.

It was a different video, uploaded by someone named Johnny Larchick, a name she didn't recognize. This time it was an Instagram video of a group of kids lip-syncing a song the band was playing behind them. They were acting like they were at a rock concert, and dressed for it too, singing along and throwing their hands over each other's shoulders, leaning against one another like they would topple over at any second, but Spencer could tell it was earlier in the night. People's hair and makeup were mostly intact, inevitably getting messier as the night wore on. Spencer unconsciously clenched and unclenched her left fist, stretching the sore muscles in her broken arm, as if she was ready to spring into action.

Jackson pressed pause again, and it was hard to see in the dark, but Chris's auburn hair was unmistakable, his white UC Irvine hoodie standing out from the crowd. His hand was outstretched, his face smiling, as a red Solo cup was being handed to him by none other than the new kid at school and Spencer's latest nemesis, Tabby Hill.

"No way."

"That's what I said."

Spencer couldn't believe it. "Why would Tabby want to drug Chris?"

"Guess we should ask Tabby."

Spencer twirled her pen expertly between her fingers, a trick that she did whenever she was trying to keep her thoughts from going a million miles per hour. "Could Tabby have been in my yard last night?"

Jackson paused, then did a double take, blinking hard, processing what she just said. "Wait, someone was in your yard?"

Spencer shifted in her chair, making the wooden legs creak beneath her. She was worried he'd react this way, but she couldn't keep it from him. "Yeah, but I chased them off."

"You chased—Spencer! Did you call the police?"

"It was no big deal. The person ran away. Not like the cops would do anything about it anyway." There had been a Peeping Tom in the neighborhood a few years back, several reports of people seeing a pale face looking in on them through a dark window, nightmare fuel. But the most the cops did at the time was tell people to close their curtains at night and not to change clothes near the window. Spencer never found out what happened to the Peeping Tom after that; for all she knew, he was still out there. What happened then didn't seem to match what happened last night. If it was Tabby, they must have been a track-and-field sprinter to get away that fast from Spencer.

"No big deal? Spencer, that's . . . really creepy." He shivered visibly. "Why would someone do that?"

"I don't know. But . . . something tells me it's not a random incident. I think it means that we're on to something with Ethan's case."

Jackson's brow twisted with worry. "You mean someone is trying to stop you from asking questions?"

"Let's talk to Tabby as soon as possible."

# TWENTY-TWO

"TABBY!" SPENCER BELLOWED ACROSS THE lawn, Jackson hustling right at her side.

Tabby whirled around, hair flipping expertly over their shoulder like a shampoo commercial. Their eyes narrowed after realizing who it was. Immediately, Tabby glowered at Ripley.

Spencer could hardly wait to talk to Tabby, but there wasn't a good opportunity during class sessions, or any time when Tabby didn't disappear like a ghost in the wind. Lunch was the only chance they had. Mostly everyone was out grabbing food, meaning students who had permission could leave campus to eat at any of the nearby restaurants or go home to have their private chefs whip up something before they had to be back in time for fourth period. It was unusual for a junior like Tabby to get permission to go off campus, but being on the Headmaster's List came with specific perks that other students in their class didn't get. They were headed to their car, a perky little VW bug, and Spencer and Jackson had only managed to catch up in the parking lot just in time.

"What do you want?" Tabby asked, barely repressing a

sneer. They glanced over Jackson, curiously, before settling a level gaze on Spencer. They folded their arms hastily across their body, or—Spencer thought—made an unconscious move to put up a barrier between them.

"We wanted to ask you some questions about the party the night of the crash," Spencer said.

"Not without backup, I see."

Obviously, they were talking about Jackson, who lowered his brows at the accusation that he was here because Spencer couldn't do it on her own.

"We just want some answers," Jackson said. "Saw something pretty interesting that we wanted to get your side of the story on."

Tabby's face went white, all the color draining away. They swallowed. "I don't know what we have to talk about."

Spencer watched Ripley at her feet. Ripley didn't react to Tabby at all, no sign of raised hackles or growls. In fact, Ripley seemed at ease. Maybe Tabby hadn't been the one standing outside her house watching from the shadows.

"We have video of you giving Chris a drink that night," Spencer said.

"So?"

"Pretty soon after that he started acting drunk, way more than he should be. We heard that you might know more about that."

"I don't know what you're—"

Jackson stepped forward. "Come on, Tabby. Enough lying. Did you put something in Chris's drink?"

Spencer glanced at the other students walking by. Some turned their heads toward them at the name Chris, but none stayed to eavesdrop any longer. A sheen of sweat had appeared on Tabby's forehead. Their eyes darted back and forth, cornered.

Spencer was about to worry that Jackson had come on a little strong and was about to try to convince Tabby everything was fine, but Jackson's tactic ended up working.

"Okay," Tabby said, sneering. "Not here, though. Let's go somewhere private."

"I didn't roofie Chris, if that's what you're thinking."

Tabby sat on the upper row of bleachers at the soccer field, Spencer and Jackson one row below. There was no one within earshot, save for the groundskeeper drawing new paint lines on the field with a spray can attached to a cart, but that was way too far for anyone to overhear.

"But I wanted to, I was planning to," they told them.

"You were going to roofie him?" Jackson asked. Spencer was grateful that he asked; she was too busy trying to figure everything out to be able to form words at the moment. She absently patted Ripley's side.

Tabby shrugged. "Yeah. He was blackmailing me."

Spencer's eyebrows shot up, same as Jackson's, and they both looked at each other before Spencer asked, "What are you talking about! Why would Chris Moore—one of the nicest guys at Armstrong—blackmail you?"

Tabby sighed, their shoulders slumping, and looked out

over the field, trying to find the words. "It's so dumb, I'm honestly so embarrassed about it. Don't know how he found out."

"It's okay, Tabby, you can tell us," Jackson said. His words were soothing, and the look on his face was encouraging but open. Even Spencer felt like she could tell him anything. He had that way with people.

Tabby worried their bottom lip, spinning the rings around their fingers. They looked like whatever they wanted to say, it was something worth keeping a secret for.

"We promise, we won't tell anyone. This doesn't have to leave here," Spencer said. Jackson gave an encouraging nod.

Tabby sighed. "Fine. I got expelled from my old school because I was caught selling Addy to some students."

"Adderall?"

Tabby nodded. "Back in Arizona, the school was kind of like Armstrong, and there was a lot of pressure for kids to get good grades, just like here. I have ADHD and figured I could make some extra cash on the side. The school found out and expelled me."

Spencer frowned. "Aren't you rich or something? Why do you need money?"

"My *parents* are rich. And strict. I barely have an allowance. But once I started selling extra pills from my prescription, I couldn't stop. It was . . . it was a high, making my own money. So I knew a plug who could get me some more, but not just that, he could also get other stuff, shrooms, Molly, coke, whatever. Then Harry—Harrison Ressler—asked me to make the party more fun; he knew I could get some of the good stuff."

"Coke? Molly?" Jackson asked.

Tabby nodded. "Don't look at me like that. Listen, I'm not a bad person. I mostly sold Addy, but if someone asked for some other stuff, I didn't care so long as I got paid. People can do whatever they want with it. I'm not going to ask questions."

Spencer didn't agree with that moral justification, but she didn't press it. She needed Tabby to keep talking.

"You sold roofies at the party?" Spencer asked.

"No, I only had one on me. I was planning on using it on Chris."

Spencer saw Jackson's reproachful look, but he didn't say anything about it, either. He looked just as judgmental as she felt.

"Why though?" he repeated.

"My parents donated an insane amount of money to Armstrong's sports program to get me in and keep my record sealed. And it was enough to get me on the Headmaster's List, too. Somehow Chris found out about it. I don't know how, but that doesn't matter anymore. He cornered me one day, said he'd use it against me, said that he would tell everyone at school that I was a drug addict if I didn't pay him money every month to keep his mouth shut."

Spencer's jaw dropped. Everyone's little brother really knew how to play.

Jackson asked, "How much money?"

"Two hundred dollars at first, but over the summer he came to me asking for more, three hundred now and he wanted it every two weeks. I was sick and tired of being yanked around, so I wanted to scare him. I wanted to show that I wasn't someone he could mess with. So at the party I thought I'd spike his drink."

Spencer and Jackson shared another look. "But you didn't?" Spencer asked.

"No, man, you know what was in that cup he was drinking? It wasn't beer. He was drinking straight vodka. Like almost an entire bottle of vodka in one of those cups. Sixteen ounces of vodka in, like, twenty minutes on an empty stomach. I was handing him a cup of water so he could sober up! He was drunk as fuck because he was drunk as fuck. A total mess. It was too pathetic so I figured I'd get my revenge another day. Then he was all over me, and I just wanted to get away from him. I saw you and Ethan heading home and asked Ethan for a ride, figured it was time for me to go home anyway. I was kind of high and out of it, too. We carried Chris to his car. Ethan was worried about him, asked him if he was okay. He cared about him . . . He was in the middle of the fight with you. Don't you remember any of this?"

"No," Spencer said, shifting uncomfortably. She felt disconnected from her past self; hearing about it from someone else made it seem like they were talking about someone else. "So if you didn't use the roofie on Chris, did you use it on me?"

Tabby looked appalled. "You! No! Of course not. Why would I do something like that?"

If they were lying, they were exceptionally good at it. Tabby looked more disgusted about the accusation than anything, which actually worked in their favor for Spencer to believe it.

"What happened next?"

"I got into the back seat with Chris—he was lying down on the seat—and I waited for you and Ethan to stop fighting. You two were really going at it. You've got some pipes, girl. I bet the whole Westside heard you yelling at him. Hailey Reed, huh."

Spencer couldn't help the flush in her cheeks.

"Around what time did Ethan get in the car?" Jackson asked.

"I don't know. I fell asleep waiting, you guys took so long. You were so dramatic. 'How could you do this to me?' 'You betrayed me!' 'I trusted you!' You know the drill. I'd pay an admission fee to watch if I wasn't so high myself. Next thing I knew, I smashed my face into the back of the passenger's seat when we crashed. And Chris . . . well . . ." Tabby gestured with their hand, leaving the rest unsaid.

Spencer sighed.

Tabby seemed disconnected from the accident, as if they had nothing to do with any of it. Sure, Tabby hadn't caused the accident, but did they have to be so blasé about it?

"I feel bad about what happened to Chris, I really do," Tabby said, "but to be honest, I'm kind of relieved, too. He wasn't the nice guy everyone thought he was. He was dirty. I feel like I can finally breathe again."

*But he was only fifteen, just a kid,* Spencer thought, remembering the hollow eyes of Chris's parents.

"You won't tell anyone about any of this, right?" asked Tabby. Their dark eyes flashed, a hint of a threat peeking its head out from the cat-eye eyeliner. "About me I mean."

"No, your secret is still safe." Spencer kept her voice flat, emphasizing her disapproval. It was tempting to call in an anonymous tip to the police about Tabby's illicit activities. What if someone else got hurt because of what they were dealing? But Spencer had a feeling that Tabby would get caught on their own one of these days. Besides, Tabby was planning to hurt Chris to protect themselves. Would Spencer want to risk Tabby's wrath by calling the cops? Even though Tabby was innocent with regard to the accident, did Spencer want to push Tabby's boundaries of what they were capable of in moments of desperation?

Ripley watched all of this, her head raised, as if she knew what everyone was talking about. She was one of the biggest clues about what happened last night with the stranger. She had acted instinctively to protect Spencer then, putting herself between her and potential danger. If Tabby was stalking her, threatening her, Spencer needed to know.

Spencer had one more question. "Where were you last night?"

Tabby answered easily. "Rehearsal for *Beauty and the*

*Beast.* I was in the auditorium until eleven or so. Why? Did you want to buy anything?"

Jackson scoffed in disbelief.

If they were at the play, starring as the lead in the musical, there were obviously witnesses who could account for her whereabouts, meaning Tabby was unlikely the person who had been standing outside Spencer's house. Spencer wasn't sure if that made her feel better or worse, knowing that Tabby wasn't some criminal mastermind. Even though it was a relief, whoever had been watching her from the shadows, trying to scare her, was still an unknown, and that made her skin crawl.

Spencer was getting tired of Tabby. They had clearly thought they weren't in the wrong and didn't contribute to Chris's death in any way. Of course, they'd been trying to do the right thing in getting him home safely, right? Tabby's hands were clean, relatively speaking. At least, they thought so.

If Chris hadn't wound up in that car, if he'd been buckled safely into his seat, maybe he would still be alive today.

"I can get you more Addy. Best price in town," Tabby said.

"No," Spencer said coolly. "I don't do drugs."

"You'd have me fooled. I see how many pills you've been popping," Tabby said, with a careful eyebrow raise. "Better keep your habit in check there, girl."

Spencer's face felt hot. "I'm not—"

But Tabby perked up and waved, signaling to a group

of friends who were calling toward them. The three of them had been talking for so long, they'd completely blown through the lunch period. "I gotta go," Tabby said, and without waiting for anything more to be said, left.

Jackson watched Tabby step down the bleachers and disappear with their friends, shaking his head. "I can't believe Chris would be capable of blackmailing Tabby . . . He struck me as the harmless type."

Jackson's thoughts had been in line with Spencer's. She was trying to put all the pieces together, staring distantly, putting the events of the night into context.

Was Chris really such an angel? Everyone seemed to think he was, but what else didn't people know about him? If he was capable of blackmailing Tabby, could he be capable of blackmailing more people? Maybe someone else who had a grudge? There was more to Chris than she thought.

"Is Tabby right, though?" Jackson asked. "About your medicine?"

"I don't have a problem. I'm not an addict." Spencer thought of people with addictions as having an uncontrollable urge to repeat destructive behaviors, couldn't help that they were doing it. Spencer could stop taking her pills any time she wanted to, couldn't she?

Jackson's face pulled tight with worry, but he didn't say anything. Polite as ever. "What do you want to do next?"

"I think we have a lot more work to do than I thought."

# TWENTY-THREE

**SPENCER SET HER PEN DOWN** on the page and massaged her eyes, which ached deeper than any late night cram session she'd done before. The lead with Tabby was a bust, but it opened a whole new can of worms about Chris. Why would everyone's little brother resort to blackmail?

Looking into Chris's past felt like she was digging up dirt from his grave, but she needed to know more. She learned that he'd been talented with computers, with dreams of starting his own software company when he was out of college, dreams that now would never be realized. With someone as good with computers as he had been, it made sense that he could find records about people's past.

Then she found it. It was nothing—a throwaway comment Ethan had made a while back—about how some kids he knew were getting into poker online. Spencer knew the site Ethan used and with a little help from Hope, she found the jackpot.

Chris was one of the top players on the site. He was a gambler. He was blackmailing Tabby to feed his addiction. Money made people do nasty things. She had no way of knowing if there was anyone else Chris had been black-mailing, but it raised some ugly questions about the crash. What if Tabby wasn't the only one who might have wanted to get back at Chris for something that he had done?

She took a chance and emailed Nick Moore, asking if he had any other information for her, maybe mysterious behavior or an influx of cash. He'd responded with no more information, just that Chris had been to a computer sum-mer camp that July, but he didn't know about any other side hustles he might have been working on.

*If you have any other questions, let me know*, Nick wrote in the email. *Don't hesitate to ask. I understand it's hard to move on, but I want to help.*

She appreciated the offer, but she was in too deep. The puzzle seemed to be getting more complicated the longer she looked into things. She was becoming an expert in every-thing about Ethan's case, inside and out, and she had hand-written nearly all her notes, compiling them into her binder. The binder was thick and heavy enough that she could slam it into the library's study table and probably break it in half.

She'd barely gotten more than two hours of sleep last night, despite Ripley's best efforts to calm her down, but admittedly the case was wearing on her. And every time she closed her eyes, she saw legal words floating behind her eyelids. If she didn't find answers soon, she wasn't sure how much longer her body could take it.

Jackson appeared from between the aisles of bookcases holding two to-go cups of coffee.

"Caffeine time," he said cheerily. Instead of wearing the Armstrong uniform, he was wearing his warm-up sweats for soccer, a burgundy getup that all the teams wore on game days. It made them stand out from the blazer uniforms but was still an acceptable outfit for the dress code. A small pang pinched behind her heart as she remembered she'd have to sit out her field hockey games this season.

Jackson handed her the coffee, and she took off the lid. The whipped cream had deflated a little on top of her latte, but she was grateful that he'd thought of her.

"I owe you one," she said, taking a sip. The whipped cream tickled her upper lip and she wiped it away with the back of her wrist. "Big-time."

Jackson took a seat across from her. "You deserve it. I'm the one that owes you. Look at all this! You are really thorough." He gestured to the binder, eyebrows raised, impressed.

"I had some free time."

"Some free time? I don't even want to know what you're capable of if you did this as a career. You're kind of scary. I mean, you found Chris's dirty secret in what, a day?" Jackson hadn't been surprised when she'd told him about the poker addiction. He said he was just surprised it wasn't bitcoin trading.

"Does that intimidate you?" Spencer asked, teasingly sticking her tongue out of the corner of her mouth.

"A little, yeah! In a good way, though."

Spencer laughed easily and was surprised by the warmth in her belly at his smile.

"So what did you find?" he asked.

Spencer took another sip of her coffee. "Let me show you!"

"You've got some, uh . . ."

He reached over, his finger crooked gently, moving toward her face.

Spencer's heart beat once, then twice, as Jackson too froze, arm outstretched, before realizing what he was doing.

"Um." Jackson pulled back and brushed his fingers on his own nose. "You've got a little whipped cream there."

Spencer scrubbed at the tip of her nose and wiped it clean. Jackson's light eyes caught a ray from the sunlight overhead and he bowed his head sheepishly, his ears flushing a soft pink.

What had just happened?

"Thanks," she mumbled.

Spencer tried not to let the heat fully consume her face as she returned to the screen in front of her. "So, anyway, I was looking into this camp that Ethan went to."

"Right. Camp." Jackson cleared his throat. Back to work.

"He attended one of their longer sessions offered, a two-month trip into the Chihuahuan Desert in New Mexico. I managed to do some digging and found a ton of stuff about the camp, some of it really shocking."

Jackson pinched his lips together with concern. "Like what?"

"So the reviews on the site itself say that it's all about promoting personal responsibility, character building, and reforming the lives of troubled youth, with hundreds of testimonies from graduates who went through the course. But there's a darker side. I found some reports of abuse, mental and emotional mostly, where some kids were punished, often going without food, if they weren't able to do certain survival techniques or didn't participate in 'camp' activities."

"Yikes."

"I cross-referenced a few names from Ethan's followers list with names from his camp, and figured out who his friends were. He follows them on Instagram."

"Ethan's never on Insta."

"Not anymore, but he used to be. His profile is still up." Spencer pulled up a page and spun the laptop around for Jackson to see. "This is what I found. Look at this picture and all the comments below it."

Ethan only put up one photo, but there were two dozen comments underneath it, most of them from the same person.

"'Dreamy Dayz'? Creative," Jackson said with a wince.

"The posts are dated after he got back from camp, which means they most likely met there. Look."

All the messages were from over the summer, mostly during August and at all hours of the day.

Jackson read the messages aloud. "'Can't stop thinking about you!' 'Call me when you get a chance.' 'Why are you ignoring me?' 'We need to talk.' Jeez. Whoever this person is, they sound obsessed."

"Keep going," Spencer said.

Jackson cleared his throat again. "'I'm warning you.' 'Don't make me do this.' 'You'll pay for this.'"

Jackson shifted uncomfortably in his chair. Spencer too felt queasy reading those messages. Whoever had sent them was definitely unhinged.

"So Ethan had a stalker," Jackson said.

"Yeah, check his tagged photos."

Jackson did as Spencer said and the muscles in his face tightened. "Oh."

The photo was graphic, to say the least. It was of Ethan's face, photoshopped onto a dead pig with his eyes scratched out with black *X*s. It had been uploaded by the Dreamy profile.

Jackson closed the laptop. He actually looked green, like he was ready to puke.

When Spencer had seen that photo too, she almost did. If she wasn't already a vegetarian, that photo definitely would make her want to be.

"That's just . . . sick," Jackson said.

"I'm sorry. I didn't want to keep this from you."

"No, it's fine. Really. I just wasn't expecting things to get that serious, you know? At first, I thought this was just an accident but . . . a lot of people didn't like Ethan, did they?"

"No. No, they didn't."

Neither of them spoke for a long moment. The library, quiet as always, felt particularly full with all the unsaid things that rushed through Spencer's head. What if someone had actually wanted to hurt Ethan? He kept saying he'd tried desperately to brake that night, but the car didn't stop—so what if—what if someone had messed with his car to make it look like an accident? The thought alone sounded like something out of a conspiracy movie adapted from a book she might read in the airport: fantastical. But could it really be out of the realm of possibility?

She'd heard of people, spurned by lovers, seeking revenge for less. Spencer liked to believe that people were generally good-natured at heart, but it would be foolish to deny that there weren't some real messed-up people walking the same earth she did.

Spencer remembered a specific case from the 1950s involving a housewife. Spencer didn't remember the name, but the woman had killed four of her husbands with rat poison and staged it to look like they were dying of a disease. They only caught her when the fifth husband went to the hospital on his own complaining about stomach cramps. She'd been using a fake name and identity for decades, avoiding suspicion before that. Who could ever suspect a poor, weak housewife of committing such heinous crimes?

"Do you think this person might have really wanted to hurt Ethan somehow?" Jackson asked.

"It's definitely worth looking into."

"That's crazy. Do you think he knows about this?"

"Like you said, he doesn't go on Insta anymore. Otherwise, he might have deleted these comments."

Jackson let out a low breath and leaned back in his

chair. He folded his arms across his chest and shook his head. "Should we tell him?"

Spencer chewed on the inside of her cheek. "You know him better than I do. How do you think he'd take it?"

"Not great! I mean, who would see something like this and laugh it off? I definitely wouldn't . . . But he deserves to know, right?"

"Yeah. I'd totally be locking my doors at night and constantly be looking over my shoulder."

"He might even be able to shine some light on it. Tell us who it could be. For all we know, it could be some practical joke."

"Not sure what kinds of friends would pull these kinds of pranks, though. Doesn't sound like anyone I would want to hang out with."

"Yeah, me neither . . . It doesn't feel right." Jackson's mouth dropped open. He looked like he'd seen a ghost, his skin went so pale. "Spencer, you don't think . . . Whoever wrote those comments knew that you two were dating?"

Spencer's stomach dropped. "Maybe. It's not like it was a secret. I'm not on Instagram either, and I don't think Ethan talked about our relationship online, but we were tagged in a few photos together. They might have been jealous."

"Do you think that they might have been the one at your house that night?"

A chill raked down Spencer's spine. She shivered violently and held her hands up in the air in forfeit. She needed a minute to process the idea that she might be in danger.

Was this person trying to intimidate her into giving up on Ethan so they could have a chance with him instead? Or give up on trying to look deeper into the crash so that Ethan was sent to jail? It was confusing. There were so many weak threads everywhere.

Was this even worth it?

As the detective had told her, even if Ethan wasn't under the influence, he was still driving recklessly. He was speeding way above the limit. The year before his party had gotten out of control, and a girl was in a coma. This time, he was reckless and someone died. Why did she keep thinking there was more to the story?

"I'm sorry," Jackson said, waving his hands apologetically. "This is just getting weirder by the day, and I want to make sure nothing happens to you. Maybe we should just drop it. He has a good lawyer, you know."

It was as if Jackson could read her mind. But she just didn't want to give up yet.

"Besides, my mom thinks it's crazy they're trying him as an adult. He's only seventeen. She thinks the case will be dismissed still."

"Wow, really?" Spencer asked.

"It happens. Anyway, you haven't seen them again since, right? The shadow person?"

"No, no sign. I wonder if me chasing them off might have scared them, too."

"Just don't do it again, okay? Next time, call the cops."

Heat spread on Spencer's cheeks again. She liked that

he cared so much. "Adrenaline is a hell of a drug. Besides, with you and Ripley at my side, I feel braver."

Jackson smiled sweetly at her. He looked down at Ripley and lifted his chin. "What do you think, Rip? You keeping her safe?"

Ripley's tail *thwapped* against the floor as she wagged it excitedly.

Jackson smiled, a big toothy grin, and looked at Spencer. When he smiled, truly smiled, his nose scrunched up and his eyes sparkled behind his glasses. Spencer diverted her gaze back to her computer. She felt rude for looking at him like that. He was Ethan's best friend. It felt as if she was toeing a line that instinct warned her not to cross, even though what she had with Ethan was long over. Besides, weren't there some sort of unspoken bro rules about this type of thing?

She also felt stupid for worrying about it. Ethan's whole future depended on her finding out the truth of that night. Complicated feelings couldn't get in the way.

Spencer pretended to focus on the screen, but she felt cross-eyed. "I'll have to do some more research, maybe find out who this is, or if they went to camp together and have a reason they'd want to hurt Ethan."

# TWENTY-FOUR

SPENCER CAME HOME THAT DAY to find a letter in the mail for her. It wasn't from Caltech, which immediately calmed her beating heart. It was from Ethan's lawyer, Ray Cardona, asking if she would be a character witness for Ethan's case.

They wanted people to take the stand to defend Ethan's character and potentially help with his defense that the crash was merely an accident. Spencer read through the letter a few times, thinking about it all night. She texted Jackson about it.

*Spencer: Did you get a letter too?*

*Jackson: Yeah. I found it taped to my door. At first I thought it was junk, from Peyton Salt again, but . . . I should do it right?*

Spencer nodded, reading his text, tucked in bed. She had her feet under the covers, and under Ripley, wiggling her toes as Ripley dozed peacefully. She couldn't help the queasiness churning in her stomach. As usual, the concept of public speaking made her want to crawl into a cave. And to speak about the crash, in front of a whole courtroom—it made her want to implode. She could already imagine the faces staring at her, judging her, even though she wasn't the one on trial.

*Jackson: You don't have to if you don't want to. I get it. He'd get it.*

"He," being Ethan.

Everything always circled back to Ethan. He was a black hole, whose gravity was so strong, nothing could escape his pull, not even light, not even someone as strong as Spencer. How she hated not being able to escape him. No one would blame her for wanting to hate him. She wanted to hate him. But she couldn't really ever hate anyone. Even him. Deep down, she knew she couldn't.

Spencer had every reason not to want to take the stand to defend Ethan's character. But she felt like it was the right thing to do. She needed to tell her story, tell her side of things, take back some control. Maybe then it would help her figure out a piece of the puzzle that would get her closer to closure.

*I'll do it too.* An idea struck her. She continued to type. *Maybe we can prep each other? We can ask each other some questions a lawyer might, just so we're ready.*

*Jackson: Sure! Just say the word, I'll be there.*

## Interview with Jackson Chen, Ethan's Best Friend—
## Recorded on Spencer's Laptop

*[muffled adjustment of microphone]*

**Spencer:**   Okay, you can talk normally.

**Jackson:**   Is this fine?

**Spencer:**   Yeah, perfect. Okay, you ready?

**Jackson:**   Where do you want me to start?

**Spencer:**   How do you know Ethan?

**Jackson:**   Well, we're best friends . . . Sorry, I can't help but feel like I sound stupid.

**Spencer:**   It helps if you don't look at the screen. Just look at me, talk to me like I'm a friend.

**Jackson:**   Aren't you?

**Spencer:**   What.

**Jackson:**   A friend?

**Spencer:**   Yeah. *[laughs]* Sorry.

**Jackson:**   It's just weird because, you already know all this, so I'm not sure what else there is to say.

**Spencer:**   Okay. Yeah, I know. I didn't want to make you write it all down for me. But I had to get a good biography of Ethan somehow for our notes. My notes on him feel incomplete. I know who Ethan is to me, but I want to know who Ethan is to you. Plus, sometimes just saying it out loud puts things into perspective. [*pause*] How about this, how did you two meet?

**Jackson:** Well, I met Ethan when we were in middle school, sixth grade. It's funny, I remember the exact date—February first.

**Spencer:** Why do you remember the date?

**Jackson:** It's my birthday. See, these other kids in our grade picked on me. I wasn't exactly the toughest kid on the playground, and I was a bit of a crybaby. Still am!

**Spencer:** No judgment! I love a good ugly cry now and then.

**Jackson:** [*laughs*] Anyway, my mom packed me this birthday lunch, with homemade cupcakes, and I was supposed to hand them out to my friends. They had sprinkles, and buttermilk frosting, my favorite. But before I could pass them out, one of the bullies—I won't dox him, it's not important—the bully saw this Tupperware container full of cupcakes and couldn't resist. He smacked the whole thing out of my hands. Right up into the air and onto the floor. *Blam.* Frosting everywhere, all over my shirt, in my hair, up my nose. Huge mess. I was embarrassed more than anything and didn't even know what to do. I stood there, covered in frosting, and before I knew it, Ethan comes flying out of nowhere and starts whaling on the guy.

**Spencer:** Oh wow.

**Jackson:** It wasn't really a fight. We were just kids. Ethan was way smaller than him anyway. We were in sixth grade, those kids were in eighth, and Ethan didn't stand a chance. Plus, you know the way kids fight, it was mostly just windmilling, no one actually got hurt. But it scared the bullies off. Then Ethan took the shirt off his back and gave it to me to wear.

**Spencer:** I didn't know that.

**Jackson:** Really? I mean, it's not like we talk about it every day, but it kind of cemented our friendship. But yeah . . . The rest of the day he wore his soccer uniform from his locker. We started playing on the same team the next season. Him being striker, me in the net. He actually got in trouble for fighting that day, but he never regretted it. Those bullies didn't bother me again and, me and Ethan, we've been friends ever since. He's always been there for me. If I could describe him in one word, though, it would be complicated. He rubbed a lot of people the wrong way.

**Spencer:** Do you think Ethan had a hard time making friends?

**Jackson:** Not really. He's the kind of guy that might throw you off, because you expect one thing from him, but then he comes out of left field, totally taking you by surprise. He got into trouble a lot at school, and at home. Maybe it was because his parents split up when he was younger? I'm not a psychologist, but that would mess anyone up. You remember, he got sent to that rehab camp.

**Spencer:** Right, the behavioral rehabilitation camp for minors.

**Jackson:** He hated that place. That summer before junior year was practically torture. He basically said so, but he wouldn't talk about what happened. Even when he was off this summer, he sent me letters.

**Spencer:** So you know about Ethan's camp experience? He barely talked about it with me.

**Jackson:** I wouldn't call it camp. It was more like juvie wearing summer-camp clothing.

**Spencer:** Right. They called it . . . what was the name?

**Jackson:** Camp Ervo. I think it's an acronym, but I don't know for what. It's where a lot of parents send kids when they get too much to handle. I don't know, I think it's just easier to send a kid away rather than deal with the fact that they might be going through some stuff.

**Spencer:** Going through some stuff, you mean . . . ?

**Jackson:** He never got over what happened at that party when Julianne fell. It wasn't his

fault that everyone was crowded out
on the roof. He wasn't even up there
when it happened. He was with me by the
pool when we heard the screaming. It
was horrible—when we found her there
in the grass, all splayed out. We all
thought she was dead. Ethan still beats
himself up about it, blames himself for
not keeping people from going up there.
Of course, no one pressed charges, it
was an accident. But he started smoking
weed to deal with his feelings about it,
drinking, too. His parents thought that
to toughen him up he needed to go away to
"camp" to learn his lesson. And when he
was back he was sober, straight-edge.

**Spencer:**   His parents, his dad and stepmom, were
they cool with what happened at the
camp? He lost a ton of weight; when he
came back he looked like a skeleton. He
sent me a few letters, too. He didn't
sound like he was having a fun time.

**Jackson:**   From what I could tell, they were
censoring his letters, too. Sometimes
I'd find a page missing, like a sentence
would cut off on one page and then it
would start up on another with a totally
different subject.

**Spencer:**   Right, I've got a few of them here.
They're in the drawer by your elbow. You
don't have to go searching for it, but
I remember reading those letters and
thinking he didn't sound like himself.
Like he was writing about things that he

knew he was allowed to say. Do you think he'd try to censor himself? In case he said something he didn't want to get out? Like a girlfriend? Would it really be so out of character for him to cheat on me with someone while he was at camp?

**Jackson:** I know Ethan. If he said nothing happened then, nothing happened. He wouldn't lie about it. Oh, wait. Did he lie about cheating that night on you?

**Spencer:** Well, I mean he couldn't lie, I caught him. But I guess he had been lying to me since it turned out he'd been seeing Hailey almost the entire time we were together.

**Jackson:** While I know Ethan's not a saint, it's not like he's some criminal mastermind, either.

**Spencer:** Do you think what happened to us that night was an accident?

**Jackson:** [*pause*] Look, I'm not saying I know all the facts. Ethan has a ton of speeding tickets on his license; honestly, I'm surprised it took this long for someone to get hurt in his car. I'm sorry, but that's the truth. He was driving, and someone died. Maybe we just have to accept that. We both love him, but we can't be blind to his faults.

**Spencer:** But come on, can you think of any reason why Ethan would be—Mom!

# TWENTY-FIVE

**SPENCER BOLTED TO HER FEET,** as if she'd been electrified. Standing in the doorway to Spencer's bedroom, still wearing her scrubs from work, was her mother. The expression on her face, stony and immovable, as she stared at Jackson was enough to send Spencer's heart hurtling into her stomach.

"Hi, Dr. Sandoval," Jackson said, already on his feet, too.

"Jackson." No smile, no lift of her voice, nothing.

Jackson was closing his laptop and moving for his bag. "I should get home," he said. Spencer could see the flush on the back of his neck, bright red.

"Yes, I think you should," was her mother's reply.

"We weren't doing anything," Spencer said.

"Of course not." Her mom was not in a good mood. The energy emanating off her body felt radioactive.

"Bye, Spencer. See you tomorrow. It was nice seeing you, Dr. Sandoval." Jackson disappeared down the hallway, showing himself the door. Her mom let him pass without moving a muscle. She simply looked at Spencer with a raised eyebrow.

If there was a good time to crawl under the bed, now would be it.

Dinner with the family was a tense affair after her mom had caught Jackson in her bedroom. Spencer sat at the table, fork hovering over her pasta, watching her parents silently pass dishes to each other, spooning piles of greens onto Hope's plate; her sister had already begun eating greedily. Spencer was waiting for someone to make the first move, say something so she wouldn't have to, but they were keeping quiet. Her dad impishly smiled at her mom, knowing that she was dragging out the torture of the silent treatment. What for? Spencer didn't have anything to be ashamed of.

"You're home early from work," Spencer said, trying to lighten the mood.

"We had a cancellation," her dad said. "What's this about a boy being over?"

Spencer shrugged. "No big deal. Can you pass the salt?"

Her attempt at deflecting was caught by her mom, who was an expert at detecting such tactics. "It wasn't 'no big deal.' I was just surprised seeing a new boy so soon."

"I promise, we weren't doing anything but working. It's not like that with him."

"Mom, they were totally making out. Eating each other's faces," Hope said, grinning.

"We were not! She's making that up! Don't listen to her!"

"Hopie, don't start trouble," her dad said with a look.

"He's helping me with school. He's nice, I promise."

"Then what were you doing?"

Spencer wasn't sure she wanted to tell them that she was turning into a private investigator, looking into Ethan's case. If they knew that she was obsessively compiling any information she could get her hands on about the case, she imagined they wouldn't react to it well, maybe even have her visit the doctor again. "Research for a project," she said. It was true at least.

"Yeah, anatomy," Hope said.

Spencer kicked her underneath the table. Hope let out a yelp.

"We weren't doing anything, I swear! The door was open the whole time. Mom, you saw."

Her mom just kept her mouth in a line, not saying anything. Even before the crash, her mom had been strict about a keep-the-door-open policy. If Ethan was over, there was to be no "canoodling" in her house. That was why it was more fun to go over to Ethan's anyway. His parents didn't seem to mind what he did with his girlfriends.

Spencer didn't mind the door-open policy. She respected it. The whole time they were dating, she hadn't gone all the way with Ethan. He definitely wanted to, but she kept wanting to wait. The timing never felt right. She felt the same bitterness about Hailey boiling up to the surface.

"Who is this Jackson boy anyway?" her dad asked with a curious lift of his eyebrow.

"He goes to Armstrong with me. He's on the soccer team."

Mom said, "You said his last name is Chen. Is he related to David Chen, that criminal?"

Spencer sank her shoulders. "Yeah, that's his dad."

Mom tipped her head back, looked down her nose, and made a noise halfway between a noncommittal grunt and a huff of interest. "I'd be interested to know what kind of person you become when your father is a criminal."

"Hey, now Gabby," her dad said. "Don't go making assumptions. Your father was a mailman. I don't see you handing out letters. Just because your parents do one thing doesn't mean you have to."

Mom threw up her hands. "I know, I know. Fair point. I'm just being protective of our daughter. You can see why I'm wary."

Spencer added, "He's not like his dad. He's sweet." She found herself thinking about his smile and the way he used his knuckles to push his glasses up his nose when they slipped down. Something must have crossed her face, because Hope noticed it.

"We should have him over for dinner," Hope said, eyebrows raised high, as if taunting Spencer with the prospect of introducing him to their parents.

"That sounds like a wonderful idea," her dad said, brightening.

Spencer glared at Hope, clenching her teeth, but she took a bite of her pasta to stop herself from saying anything. She didn't have to hide Jackson. She was being honest about there being nothing more to their relationship. He was just a friend. She agreed that she'd ask him if he was available sometime soon.

"How's school otherwise? Homework all done?"

"Mostly," Spencer said. "Just need to catch up on some reading."

"Good. Anything in the mail from universities?"

"Nothing yet."

"Well, that's the most important thing. Focus on school, then you can think about boys. You know what, I change my mind," Dad said with a teasing grin. "Nix that. No thinking about boys. Ever. In fact, no thinking about girls, either. No dating until you're married."

That got her mom to smile, too. "Ah yes, because that worked out so well for us."

"It did!" Her dad cheerily took a bite of his pasta.

Hope crinkled her nose as their parents nuzzled noses. "Ew. I'm going to the garage." And she hurried out of the dining room.

"Jackson and I are going to be character witnesses for Ethan's trial," Spencer said matter-of-factly. "We're helping each other get ready for it."

Her mom and dad gave each other looks, this time with less unspoken volume behind the eyes, and then Mom said, "Just remember to keep the door open."

Jackson had a second chance at redemption with her parents and that was more than Ethan ever got.

# TWENTY-SIX

**THE MOMENT SPENCER STEPPED UP** to the stand as a character witness, she felt like her knees were going to give out. Just like Jackson, who sat at the back of the courtroom, she'd taken a half day off from school. Now, sitting in front of the courtroom with Ripley at her feet, she twisted the hem of her skirt between her fingers as the lawyers went through all the usual legal proceedings, which mostly went over her head. The noise became a dull drone as anxiety took hold. She focused on the hairs on Ripley's back, attempting to count them to try to calm down, when Thora Barancewicz stood up and approached the bench.

"Spencer Sandoval, Ethan's ex-girlfriend, and victim," the prosecutor said in an accusatory tone.

Spencer's eye twitched at the word *victim*.

"Thank you so much for taking the time to tell your story. I can imagine how difficult it must be, sitting here, facing the one who did this to you."

Spencer absentmindedly traced the scar on her face. The doctors said it would heal, and in time, a good plastic surgeon could render it invisible.

Ethan was at his table, staring at the wooden surface, unable to look at her. Spencer blinked a few times. "Yeah."

"Can you tell us a little bit about your relationship with Ethan? How would you define it?"

Spencer thought about it a moment, careful with her words. The Vicodin was making things feel slow again. She'd had to take some to feel better. Even though her cast was off, everything still hurt. "Fun."

"Fun!" Ms. Barancewicz repeated, smiling. "I definitely know that feeling! Young love, first love?"

Spencer found herself nodding.

"And what about your relationship at the end? What made it all come crashing down?"

Spencer took a steadying breath and kept petting Ripley. "He cheated on me."

Ms. Barancewicz rolled her eyes. "Boys, am I right?" She was playing the "best friends type," trying to make Spencer feel like they weren't in the middle of a courtroom right now. Ms. Barancewicz continued. "What kind of person would cheat on a catch like you? You're attractive, you're smart, you've got a personality. You're the total package, wouldn't you agree? Straight-A student, Headmaster's List, Field Hockey Captain."

Spencer wanted to disagree, but the painkillers were making it difficult. "It's not my fault he cheated."

"No, it's not! And it's not your fault you got in that car with him that night. So why did you?"

"I still don't remember."

Ms. Barancewicz said, "Let me remind the court that Miss Sandoval suffered a major traumatic brain injury as a result of Ethan Amoroso's actions."

His lawyer protested the accusation and there was a bit of an argument between the lawyers and the judge, but Spencer wasn't paying attention. She was holding on to Ripley, afraid she was going to topple over the bench. Ripley was doing a great job putting pressure on her legs.

Ms. Barancewicz was able to continue. "Only someone whose moral character is a bit on the wonky side would cheat on you, right?"

Spencer shook her head. "Maybe."

"I don't know, Miss Sandoval. If I found my boyfriend cheating on me, I'm pretty sure I'd be furious."

"I was angry. No doubt. But him cheating on me has nothing to do with what happened."

Ms. Barancewicz sighed. "Maybe Ethan was ashamed about what he'd done to you. Maybe he wanted to apologize. Maybe he was distracted, emotional. We have some eyewitness reports from the party that you two were having a major argument right before, isn't that right?"

"I don't know! I don't remember!" Spencer yelled.

If only she could. If only she could piece together what happened, maybe they wouldn't be sitting in this courtroom right now.

"Regardless, he drove the car into that tree. His actions had consequences. A family was broken apart because of him. He could have broken yours too, if he hadn't already broken your heart."

Spencer's gaze landed on Ethan. He stared firmly at the table in front of him, refusing to look at her still. Then, as if drawn by a string, she found Jackson's eyes. He gave her the slightest nod of encouragement, and for a split second, she wondered what could have been, if she had been dating Jackson instead, and guilt spiked in her chest.

Ms. Barancewicz was done. She turned and took her seat with the Moores.

Ethan's lawyer, Ray Cardona, stepped forward. Spencer second-guessed everything she had said. Had she answered everything the way she wanted to? Could anything be misconstrued? Did she just screw up Ethan's case?

Ethan's lawyer only had one question for her, and he asked it, giving her a steady look. He got straight to the point. "Has Mr. Amoroso ever before shown reckless behavior or self-destructive tendencies that might have worried you?"

Spencer couldn't help the memory that rushed into her head.

"Careful, Ethan!" Spencer said, despite laughing.

Ethan surprised her with a drive to the mountains, making her squeal with delight as he took turns so fast they sent her stomach every which way. He blasted his music with the windows rolled down, and Spencer coasted her hand through the air, melting on good vibes and the beach air, singing along badly without a care. The bass thumped the whole car. She liked the Targa, how the leather seat seemed to hug her body, the purr of the engine vibrating beneath her sneakers, the hot metal smell of the car baking in the sun.

He took her down to the coast, weaving through traffic, the other cars turning into blurs as Ethan never let up on the gas. Spencer didn't care that her hair was coming out of her braids. The wind whipping through the car and the music blaring from the speakers made her ears hurt too, but she was young. And alive. With Ethan.

He took her to the mountains where they got out and walked on the dirt path, winding like a snake above Malibu.

Ethan jumped down from the rock ledge and scooped Spencer up in a kiss, pulling her hips toward his. Her smile pressed into his lips and she pushed him away playfully.

"Ew. You're all sweaty and gross," she said and stuck out her tongue.

"I thought you liked it when I was sweaty and gross." He raised a suggestive eyebrow and she punched him in the arm. His smile reminded her of her first taste of champagne: sweet and bubbly. She wanted more of it.

She kissed him again, for real, and he sighed into her lips.

When he took her hand, he leaned in and said, "Come on. We're almost there."

Together they jogged up the crest of the hill, coming upon a flat spot where a small bench sat beneath a tilting oak tree teetering over the edge of the cliff overlooking one of the best views of the city Spencer had ever seen.

For once the smog that usually hung over the landscape had been swept away in the wind, leaving the sky blue and unblemished without a cloud to ruin it. The ocean, a strip of blue in the distance, nestled up against the rest of the city. Ethan scuffed his sneakers in the dirt. There wasn't much to say except to enjoy the feeling of being very small in that moment.

Ethan balanced on the rock face, his arms outstretched for balance, as he showed off his athleticism. He always did that, showing off, climbing walls or dangling from trees, putting his muscles to good use, performing for the world at all times. He was so carefree and wild, down to the waves in his hair, which was still in the awkward growing-out phase after his head had been shaved for camp. Ethan walked right up to the edge of the rocky cliff and looked down. Spencer didn't have to know it was a straight drop down, not to mention, far. If he slipped, he could get seriously hurt. Or worse. But Ethan always had to look down. Spencer's nerves twisted in her belly. She sensed something that she couldn't quite put her finger on. He was always toeing the line. Ethan, never the coward, always had to look down and see for himself.

But Spencer didn't say anything. She held her elbows tightly, squinting in the sunlight. The sun burned on the top of her brown hair, and she had wished she hadn't left her baseball cap in the car.

"It's so weird, isn't it?"

She almost didn't hear him. He was talking away from her, his voice carried by the wind.

"What?"

"All this. Life. Living one minute, and the next . . . it's gone."

She didn't know what he was talking about, at least not at the time. Looking back at this memory, she knew he was hurting a lot. He never showed it, never talked about it, at least not with her. All she could do was stare at the back of his head, at the hair growing in slowly, returning to how it used to be but never quite the same. The shape of his cheek-bones set against the bright blue sky, turned away, still.

His voice was clear now. "One step. That's all it would take. One." Ethan stared at his shoes. The wind kicked up, the gust buffeting Spencer's hair from her braids. The Santa Ana winds were strong.

Maybe she did know, somewhere deep down, that he was in pain, and Spencer instinctively reached out and grabbed the back of Ethan's shirt as Ethan spread his arms wide. But he didn't jump. He just breathed deeply and tipped his head back, as if embracing the sky.

The wind cut all around them, spraying dust and dirt into Spencer's eyes. She turned away, but Ethan didn't. He was flying.

The courtroom waited, all eyes trained on Spencer.

"Miss Sandoval?" Ray Cardona had been waiting patiently. "Please answer the question."

"I'm sorry, could you repeat it?" Spencer's mouth had gone awfully dry and she swallowed.

"Has Mr. Amoroso ever displayed self-destructive behavior or any other pattern of thinking that might signal intent to harm himself or anyone else?"

Spencer squeezed Ripley's harness handle for support.

"No," she lied. "Never."

Ethan, finally, looked up and stared at her. She didn't look away, determinedly setting her jaw.

"Thank you, Miss Sandoval," Mr. Cardona said. "That's all for now."

Only after she left the courtroom did Spencer feel like she could breathe again. The judge had called for a lunch recess, and everyone exited the courtroom.

The floor beneath Spencer's feet felt uneven and she needed to take a seat on a bench in the hallway. She felt unmoored, untethered, and the Vicodin was a riptide pulling her into the deep, dark ocean, where it was peaceful and quiet.

Ripley placed herself on Spencer's lap, the whole half of her body weighing down on her, and Spencer almost didn't notice the shadow that had stepped in front of her. She looked up to see it was Ethan.

"Why did you lie?" Ethan asked, keeping his voice low.

"I didn't."

"Spencer . . ." He licked his lips and shifted his weight to his other foot. His gaze landed somewhere above her head. He knew she was lying, even now, but he didn't want to broadcast it in front of everyone. He glanced behind himself, at his father, stepmother, and lawyer talking to one another. "Don't make this worse."

Spencer's brain was taking a second too long to rev up. She couldn't find the words.

"Where's Jackson?" Ethan asked.

He didn't have to look any further. Jackson had appeared around the corner holding two paper cups of water. He saw Ethan and stopped. They stared at each other for a moment, then Jackson nodded.

Ethan bowed his head. He finally looked at Spencer with a deep understanding, one that Spencer wasn't even able to admit to herself. "It's better this way. I promise."

He looked at her with a sadness that twisted her insides, then left without letting her say another word.

# TWENTY-SEVEN

**THE REST OF THE DAY** went by in a haze, and then—just like that—it was over. Spencer barely registered that Jackson had answered the lawyers' questions. The painkillers had wrapped her in a safe cocoon and she spent most of the time watching Jackson, admiring his poise, distantly drifting off into a pain-free daze. The Vicodin started to wear off by the time the judge dismissed the court for the day.

She met Jackson outside where he was shrugging off his Armstrong jacket and undoing his tie. His white undershirt made him practically glow in the sun. He saw her coming and his jaw relaxed, as if the mere sight of her made him feel more at ease.

"How are you feeling?" she asked.

"Okay. How about you?"

"Better now." She still felt loose, but it was better than the throbbing pain in her shoulder.

Jackson managed a small smile. "Do you want a ride back to school?"

"No, thanks. I rode my bike. Maybe I should start a petition to the city to get bike lanes. I feel like that frog in that one video game."

"Frogger. A classic. You're heading home?"

"I guess. I don't really want to, though."

"You're sure you don't want a ride? It might be safer, especially with it getting dark soon and all."

Spencer waved her hand. "I've had enough of cars for one lifetime, I think."

Jackson nodded and mussed up his long bangs. He looked more like himself again. "Fair. It was worth asking. I don't really want to go home, either. I was just going to sit in an In-N-Out and stare at the wall. Today has been a lot . . ."

"How about we go for a walk? Ripley needs to stretch her legs."

Jackson smiled. "Anything for Ripley."

Together, they headed toward the pier, not intending to go anywhere in particular, just *away*. Jackson walked alongside Spencer, Ripley between them, as the sun started to sink in the sky. Someone gave Ripley a milk bone. Ripley had done a good job today, keeping Spencer calm during the proceedings. She deserved all the milk bones in the world.

"I felt bad, talking about the times I've been in the car when Ethan was driving. But I couldn't lie." Jackson crumpled up his napkin and threw it in the trash can.

Spencer shuddered. She had. She had lied. Jackson was a better person than she was.

They walked along the boardwalk, their footsteps thumping hollowly on the wooden boards beneath them, and Spencer watched the white crests of the sea where some surfers were catching a few waves. "He's off the List, you know," Jackson said with a sigh.

"Yeah." It was expected. Couldn't have a murderer on the Headmaster's List, could you? "Maybe Ethan is guilty. I don't know. It's kind of beside the point for me right now. I just want to know the truth."

"Maybe we'll never know," said Jackson.

"If we can at least prove with physical evidence that it wasn't his fault, it should help his case . . ." She was starting to have the shape of an idea.

They hadn't had a chance to go to Highwood Estates yet. With everything going on, getting ready for today, they hadn't had a chance to spend the day searching for clues like the Scooby Gang. They already had a dog; they just needed a VW bus to make the trip complete.

Jackson leaned on the metal railing, his face turned toward the sunset.

"I think a person can be good and still do bad things," Jackson said. He looked out over the ocean without really seeing it. His thoughts were elsewhere. She couldn't help but get the impression that he wasn't just talking about Ethan.

"Your dad?" she asked.

Jackson nodded.

"You don't have to talk about it if you don't want to."

"I guess I thought I was done with courtrooms. But that smell . . ."

Spencer knew that smell was the closest sense tied to memory. Any time she smelled exhaust, when the air was still, she was back in Ethan's car again, dying. It stood to reason that being in court would stir up a lot of emotions that Jackson had been trying to juggle all at once. Just like her, he was going through it and trying to pretend like everything was fine.

"He's a criminal but he's still my dad," Jackson said. "Sometimes the people closest to us can disappoint us the most."

Out of the corner of her eye, Spencer caught a flash of light, a reflection, and she looked over to see Peyton Salt lowering her phone, obviously having just taken a picture. A picture of her and Jackson standing together.

"Not now," Jackson said with a groan.

"Do you mind?" Spencer called, throwing her arms wide.

Peyton took that as an opportunity to walk over. Her #justiceforchris pin proudly glinted on the lapel of her Armstrong blazer, sparkling almost as much as her teeth. "You two make quite the pair. What are your thoughts on Ethan Amoroso?"

"Did you follow us?" Spencer asked. They had easily walked a mile after leaving the courthouse. Spencer tried not to think about how creepy that was. "I would really appreciate it if you didn't take photos without our permission for your show."

"Please delete whatever pictures you took," Jackson said. "It's not cool."

"What's the matter? It would look great on our website.

Especially if there was an exclusive interview to go along with it . . ." Her voice lifted to go along with her smile.

Spencer just scowled.

"I've been trying to reach you for a while now. I spotted you at the courthouse; you're a hard face to miss in the crowd, Spencer! In case you haven't been getting my messages, here's my card." She flipped it to Spencer, who robotically took it, operating on autopilot. "I think you'll find there's some mutual benefit to us connecting. Lots to talk about, lots to discuss. My live tweets about the case are already going viral. This is going to be huge."

Spencer's lunch was threatening to make a reappearance. Jackson huffed and turned his back on Peyton.

"Now's really not the time," Jackson said. He was trying to be polite, but Spencer could see his hands were shaking.

"Oh, for sure. I know it's been a troubling time, to say the least. But it'll be over soon!"

"Why do you want to talk to us anyway?" Spencer asked.

"Everyone wants to know everything about you, even what you had for breakfast. Trust me. You're a big deal. DM me whenever you're ready! I've got friends in a lot of high places around here. Just say the word, and I can get you anything you want, but you need to play ball with me, too. Don't be shy. I'm here to help."

With that, Peyton Salt turned and walked away. Spencer watched her go, dumbfounded. That was not at all how she expected the conversation to go.

She spun around to face the ocean with Jackson, turning

the card over and over in her fingers. They didn't speak again for a long while. Spencer wasn't even sure why she was still holding the card. She didn't plan on calling Peyton Salt anytime soon, but something she said made her continue flipping the card end over end through her fingers. *I can get you anything you want.*

"Do you think she could get us the police photos from the scene?" Spencer asked.

Jackson looked at her, surprised. "You really want to do that?"

"I asked Detective Potentas and he said no. But maybe someone with her influence can do what we can't."

Jackson tipped his head. "I guess, sure, but . . . it feels like asking a favor of the devil. Who knows what it'll cost in the end?"

"Yeah, maybe you're right . . ." She folded up the card and threw it into the cigarette bin nearby. Both of them were quiet for a moment again, listening to the waves hitting the legs of the pier underfoot, the caw of seagulls flying overhead looking for an easy snack, the cry of children wanting some cotton candy. If things were different, she might have been able to convince herself she was having a nice night. The breeze was warm, the surf was clear—it could have been a perfect day.

She thought about the disturbing photo that someone from Ethan's behavior camp had sent him. The one with the dead pig with his face on it. Before they had started dating, Ethan had been a player—someone who broke hearts wantonly, recklessly. He broke hearts like he was accused of driving—recklessly.

Which made her think of someone else. Someone else's heart he must have broken, was breaking. Hailey Reed.

She and Ethan had been secretly hooking up for a year, Ethan had admitted. What did that do to a girl? And what if . . .

What if Hailey had snapped, seeing Ethan leave with Spencer that night? Even after Spencer had caught him cheating?

What if . . . ?

"What do we do now?" Jackson asked.

Spencer dug her thumbnail into the groove of Ripley's leash, and Ripley looked up at her as if asking that exact same question. She felt like she was being pulled in several directions at once, but Ripley and Jackson were pointing her toward the right one. There was something they needed to do. She would look into Ethan's stalker later, and talk to Hailey even later than that. For now . . .

"It's time we go to Highwood Estates."

# TWENTY-EIGHT

**SPENCER STILL HAD TO PICK** up the things she had dropped off at school before going to the courthouse. She had a lot of things on her mind, including working on her college applications. She and Jackson had parted ways at the courthouse parking lot, and she rode all the way back to school, arriving just as the streetlights were coming on.

No matter how many times she stayed late at school, doing homework in the library, or dropping off something in her locker after practice, or roaming the halls during a school dance to get some air, she thought school after dark was creepy.

The absence of people crushing into the hallway, their voices carrying, the sound of lockers closing, the smell of deodorant—it made the school feel like it was missing a vital organ.

She moved around as courteously as she could, to avoid the freshly mopped spot the custodian Mr. Burnham was washing in the hallway. He waved at her with a smile while his headphones blared jazz loudly as he worked. They were both common figures to be seen after hours, and Spencer always said hello to him whenever she could. He looked busy, though, so she didn't bother him.

At her locker, she let Ripley sit so she could gather her things, and she was so busy thinking about what she wanted to eat for dinner that night, she almost didn't notice a piece of paper fall to her feet. She stooped down and picked it up, almost not opening it until she saw handwriting in red letters that definitely wasn't hers. In big, blocky script, it said something that made Spencer's heart pound.

*Stop looking into the crash*

*Or else*

She looked up and down the empty hallway, but the only person she could see was Mr. Burnham swaying his hips to the music while he worked, oblivious to the panic quickly consuming her.

The note obviously wasn't signed—who would sign a threatening letter?—and she didn't recognize the handwriting. Tamping down the bile determined to lurch out of her throat, Spencer scrunched up the paper and shoved it into the pocket of her backpack. All thoughts of her college applications vanished.

Ripley's eyes, amber and pensive, watched her expectantly, aware that something was wrong but unable to react to it. This was not in her training regimen.

Spencer slammed her locker shut and hurried out of the building as quickly as possible, continuously looking over her shoulder, wondering who might be watching her leave.

Wondering if the person who'd sent the note was watching her right now.

Jackson's brow was furrowed as he read the threatening letter.

Spencer had rushed over to his house, riding as quickly as she could, him being the first person she wanted to talk to about it.

When he opened the door, he looked as if he'd just gotten out of the shower. He was already in his pajamas, a plain white T-shirt and sweats, but his hair was damp and sticking to his forehead. He had been slipping his glasses on when he opened the door. The first thing out of his mouth was to ask her if she was all right, immediately seeing the excitement in her eyes. He let her in the house without hesitation.

His house was near the coast, up a winding hill with sweeping views of the Santa Monica coastline. His neighbors included several Hollywood stars, famous musicians, and models, looking for their own slice of heaven in the hills.

His mom, a celebrity chef, was filming a competitive cooking show downtown, so the house was mostly empty, save for one of Jackson's younger brothers in his room playing video games with some friends.

Jackson brought Spencer to his bedroom where they could talk in private.

She might have been embarrassed that they were in his

bedroom, but she was too amped up to dwell on it. She paced in his room, Ripley sitting obediently at Jackson's feet while he read the note.

Spencer kept looking out the window, stepping away and then returning, pushing back the curtains, wondering if there was someone watching from the shadows like before.

"I hate this so much," he said finally. He tossed the paper onto his desk and leaned back in his chair, massaging his temples. "Maybe you should tell someone about this, someone who can help."

"Don't you see? This is a good thing."

Jackson looked at her like she was speaking Klingon. "Excuse me?"

"That letter is proof that we're on to something."

"Spencer. You're amazing and everything, but I fail to see how that makes sense. This is scary. If I got a letter like this, I'm pretty sure I'd shit myself."

"Don't get me wrong, I'm so freaked out. But this is just the tip of the iceberg. Why would someone go through the effort of warning me to stay away if Ethan wasn't really at fault? What if it wasn't an accident?"

Jackson paused, staring at her, and blinked. "What are you saying? You think someone *made* Ethan crash?"

Spencer nodded. "Why else write that note? Not only that, but I think whoever wrote it is getting desperate. They just showed their hand."

"How?"

"How did they know that my locker is *my* locker? That I'm looking into Ethan's case?"

Jackson pursed his lips. If she wasn't so amped up, she might have noted how cute he looked. But her heart was racing, her adrenaline pumping so fast, that she didn't have time.

"You think it's a student," Jackson said, vocalizing her thoughts for her.

"Maybe a classmate. Maybe someone—"

"Who was at the party that night," Jackson finished for her. Their thoughts were in sync. Jackson was standing now, his eyes bright with newfound energy.

Someone at the end-of-summer party up in the hills, someone who wanted Spencer to keep quiet, someone who might very well be in one of the videos they'd been combing through for the past few weeks, someone who could have inadvertently opened up a new part of this case that Spencer hadn't considered.

One thing was clear. Spencer's memory was the key. And someone didn't want it opened.

# TWENTY-NINE

**THE TRIP TO HIGHWOOD ESTATES** had been long overdue. The threatening note was proof of that.

That Saturday, Spencer rode her bike all the way from her house to the new development, Ripley—as ever—jogging at her side, keeping pace with Spencer's pedal strokes. She and Jackson had decided they would go to the scene of the party early that morning.

Spencer had gotten used to riding around town, even though she felt guilty leaving Gertie the Van gathering dust in the driveway. She wasn't sure when she would willingly get into a car again, maybe not ever.

A fine sheen of sweat had already pooled at the small of her back, pressed up against her backpack, by the time they reached the start of the Mandeville Canyon trail.

Ripley led the way down the dirt path. Spencer, despite conditioning all summer for the field hockey season, huffed and puffed, appreciating all the downhill slopes as she scaled the dirt trail heading toward the location of the party. Dried shrubs and gnarly-looking bushes threatened to scratch Spencer's ankles and jam into the spokes of her wheels, but it was a relatively pleasant ride through the hiking trails and toward the neighborhood that would soon be called Highwood Estates. Harrison's dad, a huge developer of the area, was in charge of overseeing twenty houses on two-acre plots of hillside. The construction crews in charge of building the houses hadn't started their day yet, so hardly anyone was around, even as the sun started to lighten the sky from gray to a pale hazy pink.

She had arrived before Jackson and took a water break with Ripley (who happily lapped at a foldable bowl Spencer had brought along) under the shade of a tree by a clean-smelling port-o-potty. A couple of minutes later Jackson pulled up in his black Tesla.

He waved at her through the windshield before he parked and got out of the car with two to-go cups of coffee.

Spencer's smile went wide.

"Mochas, I got you some extra whipped cream, too. Hope that's okay," he said, handing her the cup.

"That's perfect, thanks!"

She appreciated the forethought of having some caffeine in them for the start of their investigation. Together, with Ripley leading the way, tail held high, they started to search for any clues about the party. Even though dawn was approaching, it was still too dark to find anything that might be too small or hidden in the shrubs, so Jackson used a flashlight to scan the area.

Remnants of the party had mostly vanished, either blown by the wind or scavenged by animals. What little evidence there was left of a party ever having been there was a large firepit, with some ashy, chopped logs and a single Solo cup still wedged underneath the teepee formation, and trash underneath some nearby brush. From atop the mountain, there was an incredible view of the entire city. If it wasn't so hazy with smog, Spencer guessed she might have been able to see all the way to the beach from here, reminding her of the date with Ethan atop the mountain.

"Looks like the party was a real rager . . ." Jackson said, using his foot to flip over a flat piece of rock, spooking a lizard from its nap and sending it scurrying into the dirt.

A twig snapped, making Spencer whip around. The sound had come from behind a small hill, out of sight.

Was it the shadow person who had been in her yard?

Jackson held out his arm in front of Spencer, instinctually, and stepped forward. Ripley's tail was up, alert, but when Jackson pushed back the brush, he saw who it was.

"Brent Lang?"

It was indeed the "future cult leader" Spencer had interviewed a while back. He wasn't alone. There were about two dozen other people, scattered about the terrain, using sticks with pokes on the end, picking up trash and putting it into bins attached like backpacks over their shoulders.

"What's going on here?" Spencer asked, though she could guess for herself.

"Collective action. After no one came out to clean the place after the party, we decided to do it ourselves. We're the Green Initiative." Everyone was wearing green shirts with SAVE THE PLANET on them or HUG A TREE on bandannas wrapped around their heads. It definitely looked like a uniform. "I sent out the word online to help clean this place up after the mess. You wouldn't believe the number of pounds of trash we've collected."

Spencer quickly got over her shock about seeing him here at this hour and asked, "Did you find anything that might have been out of place for the party? Anything at all?"

Brent looked confused at first, and asked, "Out of place?"

Jackson jumped in. "I know, it's a weird question to ask, but if you've found anything you might have noticed that wouldn't look like usual party trash."

"Me personally, no. But you're welcome to look through our bags if you want." He gestured to the backpacks filled with trash that the team had already collected.

Spencer huffed. Digging through the trash was not exactly on the top of the list of things she wanted to do this morning, but if they really had picked up all the trash from the party, what other choice did they have? She glanced at Jackson, who shrugged, seemingly on board.

"Okay. Do you have any spare gloves?"

"Incoming."

Spencer stood up and stepped back as Jackson dumped another bag of trash into the already heaping pile. She had to turn her head away, sparing herself an eyeful of dust. The stench alone was something Spencer was all too familiar with when taking out the garbage at Brain Freeze, a combination of sickly-sweet decomposing food waste in dozens of pizza boxes with discarded leftovers and the acrid stench of stale beer. Empty Juul cartridges, dozens of empty liquor bottles, broken beer bottles, smashed beer cans, open condom wrappers . . . *Yuck.* Spencer had been using a trash picker to move things around, having thought of bringing along seemingly everything in her backpack except for a pair of gloves. Brent and his team didn't have any extras. Jackson, a little more courageous than she, had picked up some of the cleaner looking bits with his bare hands.

"Is that the last of it?" Spencer asked, referring to the now empty bag in Jackson's hands.

"Yeah. Find anything?"

"No. Not unless you think someone leaving their retainer wrapped in a napkin is interesting."

Jackson scrunched his nose. "Not particularly."

Brent watched them with a bemused expression from afar. "You guys are going to pick all that up again, right?" he asked, calling from atop a nearby hillside. He and his group had moved on down the hill.

Jackson assured him they would, while Spencer stared at the mess they had made. The sun was almost entirely overhead now, close to noon, and all Spencer had to show for her efforts was an aching back, and she was stinking like garbage.

She wasn't sure what she expected to find here, and she felt a little foolish thinking she could find a clue like they do on television. Did she really think she was Sherlock

Holmes, analyzing footprints with a magnifying glass and smoking a pipe? She took a seat on the ground, arms resting on her knees, and Jackson plopped down next to her. Ripley, being the only wise one of the group, had sought the shade of a nearby tree, waiting for them to realize that they'd wasted the whole morning for nothing.

If she looked anything like Jackson, Spencer looked tired and sweaty and ready to call it a day.

She offered Jackson a granola bar and he waved her off. "I've got garbage stinking up my nose. I doubt I'll be able to eat for a week."

She couldn't blame him, but she was too tired to care as she ate her granola bar and sulked. With this much garbage littering the landscape, she was starting to lose faith in humanity.

"Well," she said, grunting. "Guess that was all for nothing."

As if taunting her, the wind kicked up and garbage rolled away in the breeze.

Jackson and Spencer both swore and gave chase, catching what they could, stomping on flyaway cups and fluttering napkins. But it felt like with every piece of garbage they caught, two more would go flying past.

"Go that way!" Spencer called to Jackson, pointing to trash that spread out down the hill. Meanwhile, she went for the garbage that had scattered across every flat space nearby. Shrubs snagged the lighter pieces and, thankfully, the wind died down enough for Spencer to put everything safely away into a large garbage bag.

She sighed at the task ahead of her, but she spared no time in collecting what she could. It was only after she picked up a napkin from the snares of a bush that she realized this place had been used as the parking lot during the party. Seeing it in daylight, and not through grainy, underexposed footage from phones, was different, but she was certain this had been where Ethan and everyone else parked their cars that night. She spotted the telltale tire treads of dozens of vehicles having sat in the soft dirt. Dozens of shoe prints showed just how many people had come through the area. No wonder there was so much trash left behind.

So much, in fact, that the volunteers had missed some hidden beneath some of the underbrush. Spencer got on all fours and found some glass bottles and even a sneaker. *Who just loses a sneaker and doesn't go looking for it?* The sight of the lone sneaker shook her memory—it reminded her of something, but she couldn't remember what exactly. She shook her head. She was just about to return to Jackson when something peculiar stood out to her.

At first, she thought it was just a broken branch; no wonder people missed it. But on second glance, it was too straight to be anything found in nature. She had to stretch far beneath the shrub to get it, but when she did, she realized what it was.

"Jackson!" she called.

He must have heard the excitement in her voice, because a few seconds later he came running over.

"What's wrong?" he asked.

"I think I found something."

She handed it to him: It was a pair of wire cutters, the handles dirty from being in the sand for a few days. But otherwise they looked like they'd just been left there.

"Where did you find them?" he asked, looking them over curiously. When she pointed to the bushes, he said, "Weird. How do you know they're not just junk?"

"There's no rust on the metal. They haven't been out here long enough."

"Unless they were left over by the construction workers, but . . ." His eyes widened when he realized she was right. "Oh my God, do you think . . ." Suddenly, as if he'd been shocked, he pinched the handle with just his index finger and thumb, holding it out like it might bite him. "What if it has fingerprints on it?"

"Only one way to find out."

# THIRTY

**DETECTIVE POTENTAS'S EYEBROW REMAINED RAISED** as he stared at the hastily wrapped pair of wire cutters, the only clean place to put them being in an unused dog poop bag, courtesy of Ripley. .

Jackson and Spencer had rushed over from the mountains to the police station as quickly as they could. She knew she smelled like a locker room, but she didn't care. She hadn't spent the day looking through garbage to stop now.

"What am I supposed to be looking at?" Potentas asked.

"Isn't it suspicious?" Spencer sounded breathless, even to herself. It was tempting to get into Jackson's car to get to the station faster, but she still opted to ride her bike. She probably looked like a mad woman storming into the precinct, helmet hair definitely not the most fashion-forward style.

"Walk me through your theory." He looked tired. Dark circles bruised around his eyes, and the wrinkles around his mouth looked deeper. He took a long, deep swig from a hand-painted coffee mug, glancing at the door. He appeared as if he wanted to be anywhere but talking to a couple of teenagers who had just been shoving trash under his nose first thing on his shift, but he indulged his curiosity.

"Someone *wanted* Ethan to crash, someone tried to kill him," Spencer said. "Did you check the car? See if anything was wrong with it?"

Detective Potentas pulled his lips tight, having taken another sip of coffee. "The car was a hunk of twisted metal, kid. There was nothing left *to* check. Besides, Ethan Amoroso confessed at the scene that he was driving. Nothing else to it. Otherwise, we'd be wasting manpower when we had everything we already needed right in front of us."

Spencer's mouth could barely keep up with her brain. "But it can't be a coincidence, not after I got this threatening letter about me looking into this case . . ."

"You got a what?"

Spencer flapped her hand. "Let me finish, hold on. But it got me thinking: How would the person know I was looking into it, let alone which locker was mine? They all look identical, unless the person knows it's mine because they go to school with us." She gestured to Jackson, and Detective Potentas's attention flicked toward Jackson and then back to her. He still looked confused.

Jackson continued for her. "So we figured, maybe the person who wrote the letter was at the party. Almost everyone was there that night."

"Ethan said that he tried to stop but that the brakes weren't working. Because the brakes were cut. With these." Spencer held up the tool.

"You really think someone sabotaged Ethan's car?" Potentas screwed up his face in a way that made him look like he was trying not to laugh.

"Don't you think Spencer getting a threatening letter is reason to think something weird is going on?" Jackson asked. Spencer was thankful he was at her side.

"Not really. Do you have the letter as proof?"

"No, it's at home."

"Right. So it could be nothing."

"Or you're wrong and it's everything!" Jackson said, his voice rising.

A few officers nearby looked up from their lunches, and Potentas waved them off. "Who are you again?" he asked.

Jackson settled his gaze. "Jackson Chen."

"Chen. As in Ethan's best friend? As in David Chen? That New York banker?"

Jackson's ears flushed red. "Yeah . . ."

Potentas seemed like he had all the ammunition he needed though, and he set his mouth in a thin smile. "You two really think you have uncovered some sort of conspiracy, haven't you?"

"Isn't it kind of weird that we found wire cutters at the scene of a huge party?"

"That is a huge stretch, Miss Sandoval. What you've found is essentially garbage."

"Can't you just run the prints? There might be something on there that's suspicious."

"Look, kid." Spencer bristled at being called *kid*, but she didn't have a chance to say anything as he went on. "It's not like what you see on TV. I can't just 'run prints' whenever. There are always prints that need to be run. There's a huge backlog in cases, and it could take weeks to even get it to the lab, if anything is worth salvaging. I would need to file a literal metric ton of paperwork, because the case has already gone to trial. But that's beside the facts. This. Isn't. A. Conspiracy."

He emphasized each word to make a point, and Spencer pinched her lips tightly together to stop herself from saying anything she might later regret.

"Your boyfriend was driving like a fool."

"Ex-boyfriend," she corrected automatically.

"Right. Ex. Which means it's probably in your best interest to remember why that is. Why are you so determined to keep doing this?"

Spencer didn't have a good answer. But she knew she wasn't going to get anywhere with Detective Potentas anymore. He was never on her side, never had been. She was always going to be a victim in his eyes, always looking for answers to a tragedy she had been helpless to stop.

But she had to know.

Ethan had been sober for a year. He wasn't drunk and he wasn't high. The toxicology report confirmed that. He wouldn't deliberately put people in danger. Maybe himself—he hated himself that much, but other people? After how badly he felt about what happened to Julianne? She just couldn't believe it. He had been her boyfriend for two years. Sure, he was cheating on her. He wasn't perfect. But he wasn't . . . he wasn't . . . he couldn't . . .

There was something wrong here. She just had to remember!

"So you're not going to help me?" Spencer asked. She hated that her voice cracked. Heat bloomed behind her eyes, a mixture of frustration and anger threatening to bring on the tears, but she refused to show it.

"No," Detective Potentas said. "I'm sorry. I'm not. Be my guest to look at the car in the impound lot, but take some advice. Leave it alone."

She shoved the wire cutters into her pocket, spun on her heels, and marched out of the precinct, Jackson hurrying after her.

Spencer still refused to cry, even when she got to the parking lot. Ripley looked up at her, her eyes soft, as if to say she was sorry too, and Spencer put her hand on top of her dog's head appreciatively. Jackson slid up next to her, standing just far enough that it wasn't uncomfortable but close enough that she felt reassured he was there.

She sighed loudly, wiping furiously at her eyes. She didn't want him to see. If he noticed, he didn't say anything. They stood together, watching the rows of police cars in the parking lot, not saying anything for a long while before Jackson broke the silence.

"I know why you're so determined to help Ethan," Jackson said, as if answering Detective Potentas's question.

Spencer smiled sardonically. "You do?"

"Yeah. You care, even when it's easier not to. You want justice in the world. You want to see the best in people. It's what I always liked about you."

Spencer let his words hang in the air a moment. *Liked me?* She figured it was just a slip-up, but Jackson's ears were still red. She chose not to bring attention to it even though her stomach was doing cartwheels.

"I don't care what Potentas says. I think we're on to something," she said. "Ethan loved that car. He would get it fixed if he knew the brakes were busted—it just doesn't make sense."

Jackson was silent.

Spencer's stomach went icy cold as another idea came to her. "I don't want to sound like a conspiracy theorist or anything but . . . everyone at the party was either on the Headmaster's List or vying for a top spot, right?"

"Yeah."

"What if . . ." Spencer swallowed. She knew what it would sound like and still she said it anyway. "I've been thinking of Ethan's stalker, and maybe even Hailey."

"Hailey? What's Hailey got to do with it?"

"Maybe she wanted revenge on him for being with me. I don't know. But now I'm wondering . . . what if someone was trying to clear the board? What if someone cut the brakes so a spot at the top would open up?"

She felt queasy saying it and Jackson looked like he was going to throw up, too. He let out a shaky breath. "That's . . .

super messed up. I mean, come on, the Headmaster's List isn't that big a deal, is it?"

"Isn't it? Everyone at Armstrong is obsessed with getting on it."

"Yeah, but come on . . ." He shrugged. "Half the kids at Armstrong don't need to go to college, they're all trust fund kids, they don't need to work a day in their lives."

"That's not the point—remember the Varsity Blues case? All those kids came from rich families, from families that didn't need their kids to go to Yale or Stanford or USC. One of those kids was already making a million a year as an influencer. She didn't need to go to USC! But all those parents still cheated. Still wanted the prestige of an elite school. And that's all people care about here. Prestige. Status. They'll cheat to get it. You know that."

Jackson looked stung.

She flushed.

He sighed. "You're right. People are crazy about stuff like that."

"I don't want to jump to conclusions, but we need to keep digging, right?"

"Yeah, but now I'm starting to get a little freaked out."

"That makes two of us." She took a deep, steadying breath and clenched her fist around the plastic bag holding the wire cutters. Scared or not, she wasn't going to give up.

# ETHAN AMOROSO CASE FILES
## Updated by Detective Potentas

Our records indicate the Amoroso family filed a restraining order against a young woman named Jessica Summers. She'd made several threats against Ethan's life, both online and in person, suffering delusions and episodes of psychosis involving a believed relationship with Ethan after they both attended Camp Ervo, a behavioral rehabilitation program for troubled youths. After Camp Ervo, she repeatedly made attempts to get Ethan Amoroso's attention, escalating to a point when she went to Ethan's house, climbed the property fence, and set a garbage can on fire that was next to the house. It didn't leave any permanent damage, but it was enough for us to step in. She was later arrested, but the family didn't press charges, insisting she receive medical assistance instead.

For the past two months, she has been receiving mental health treatment at a facility in Henderson, Nevada, called Calm Springs Ranch. Round-the-clock supervision there means all patients are kept under close watch to ensure they do not hurt themselves while receiving care, and Jessica Summers has not left the campus since she was admitted.

It is complete conjecture that she had something to do with the crash. There is no evidence to indicate she was anywhere near the area on the night in question.

# THIRTY-ONE

**"THAT'S THE CAR?" JACKSON ASKED**, nonplussed.

Spencer could hardly believe that a sports car could be so small when it was compacted into a cube.

The foreman at the impound lot just shrugged his shoulder. "Not sure what else to tell ya. That's the Targa. Shame. Real nice car, too."

Spencer's whole world felt like it had narrowed down to a pinpoint. Their one piece of physical evidence had been turned into a two-foot-by-two-foot cube of twisted metal and plastic. She could just barely make out the shattered glass of one of the side mirrors. Ripley sniffed at the cube curiously and sat in the dirt, as if confirming Spencer's worst fears. This was a dead end.

The foreman flipped through some papers on a clipboard and said, "We only got confirmation to strip it and then compact it a few days ago. The cops had already done everything they needed with it and, well, there you have it. Was there something important in there?"

There would be no way to tell if the brakes had been cut on the car. Not unless she had a time machine.

"Not anymore," Spencer said. She turned and headed down the aisle walled on either side by stacked, wrecked cars ready to be compacted next.

Jackson thanked the foreman and hustled after her, jogging to her side. Spencer's pace was breakneck. She needed to think of another plan, and quick. She was running out of time to prove Ethan wasn't at fault.

"Potentas knew the car was going to be destroyed. He could have told us. I'm so stupid."

"Don't be so hard on yourself."

"Just let me be hard on myself for a second. It makes me feel better," Spencer said. She didn't mean to snap, but she was getting frustrated. "I guess I have no choice, I'm going on that podcast."

"Come on, are you serious? She's a nut. We're not talking to Peyton Salt."

"I know, I know it sucks. But what if she has something that will help?" From what she had gleaned from overhearing conversations in the hallway, Peyton had the scoop on things that only Ethan's lawyers should have access to. Jackson had to admit, even though Peyton Salt was annoying, she had information they needed.

"Fine." He finally agreed. "But don't be surprised if I end up punching her."

Peyton Salt's smug smile instantly made Spencer question whether or not this was a good idea, but it was too late to turn back now.

They'd used Spencer's account and contacted her through the DMs of her podcast's official Instagram page (with an astounding 1.4 million followers), and Peyton replied so quickly Spencer almost thought she was waiting for them to reach out. They set up a time to meet later in the week at Beans at noon during their lunch break off campus.

Peyton Salt arrived late, only by five minutes, but it was already enough to put Spencer in a sour mood. She waved at them cheerily before she ordered the biggest cappuccino on the menu, which made her even later, then sat down across from them at a small table toward the restrooms. By the time she'd unpacked her things, Spencer had already finished her mocha and even the sugariness of the whipped cream wasn't enough to sweeten her mood. Peyton's #justiceforchris pin on her Armstrong jacket caught Spencer's eye.

"My fans will go absolutely rabid the minute they get your side of the story," Peyton said breathily. Ripley regarded her with an air of reproach that Spencer might have found funny if Spencer wasn't feeling so low as to reach out to someone like Peyton Salt for help.

"I was wondering when you'd reach out," she said, tapping her fingers pensively on the laptop sitting on the coffee table separating them. "You two make quite the dynamic duo, so cute in your matching uniforms." Peyton pointed her fingers at them. "The victim, the best friend, tragic connection, working together to solve a mystery. It's all very dramatic and I'm living for it."

Peyton liked to hear herself talk, so it would seem. She

barely paused long enough for either Spencer or Jackson to get a word in edgewise.

Jackson sat beside Spencer, his back rigid and his coffee untouched, but he didn't respond. Spencer knew this was only going to get worse from here on out. Peyton Salt—the podcaster, wannabe Pulitzer Prize winner—had the pictures from the scene of the crime. How else was she able to describe them so clearly on her podcast?

"You're finally ready for an interview?" Peyton asked, but Spencer shook her head no.

"Not just yet. We were hoping you could help us first."

Peyton Salt's eyebrow arched up. Curiosity lifted the corner of her mouth. "Oh? And what might that be?"

"How are you getting all the details for Ethan's case?" Jackson asked.

Peyton bobbed her shoulders playfully. "I have my sources. But a good journalist never reveals them."

"Come on, Peyton," Spencer said. "We know you've got an in with the case somehow. You have information and we need it, too."

"Like what?"

"Police report, crime scene photos . . . whatever you're using for your podcast," said Jackson.

"Morbid curiosity?"

Spencer tapped her finger on the table. "You could say that."

Peyton shivered with the excitement of it all. "I might be able to find a way to get you what you want, but I have something I want, too. I can't just give these kinds of things away for free."

"What do you want?" Spencer asked, although she already knew.

"An exclusive interview. Nothing more."

Spencer glanced at Jackson, asking for silent approval. He bobbed his head once.

"Fine," she said. "If we agree to that much, will you be able to get it to us quickly?"

"Depends. Why do you want to know about it so much anyway? It's nothing everyone doesn't already know."

"I need to see it for myself. I ... I need proof." Spencer wasn't sure how much she should reveal, so she skirted saying it outright. "We just want to make sure everything is normal."

Peyton took a sip of her cappuccino and smirked. "I'm not sure what else you're looking for. You of all people should know it's a pretty open-and-shut case. He was speeding, lost control, and crashed the car."

"We're not asking for much, just information that the police aren't willing to hand over so easily."

"Not asking for much? Girl, don't you see? This is asking for everything. It'll take me a few days to compile it for you, and even then, I'm not sure why you want to see that kind of thing in the first place."

Jackson spoke up. "We don't care how long it takes, right?" He added the last part, looking at Spencer, who nodded.

"Don't be surprised if by the time I get it to you, Ethan's already convicted." She shrugged, saying it as if it was a casual conversation about the weather.

Spencer furrowed her brow. "Aren't you always saying you're a journalist? Shouldn't you be impartial? Don't you want to know if there's more to it than that?"

"Listen, hun." Peyton leaned on the coffee table, resting her elbows on the top and linking her fingers together under her chin. "My listeners want to feel things. Everyone does. The root of my show is based entirely around emotion. A villain, a victim; a hero, a loser. It gets the heart pumping, gets the mind racing, gets people talking. The more people care, the more people engage. Everything doesn't have to fit into its own neat little box to be a good story. Once you tap into the heart of a story, you tap into the hearts of millions. Studios have already reached out to me, and it's going to be big. Like Netflix docuseries big. People want this."

"So you admit to sensationalizing Ethan's story," Jackson said, failing to hide his disgust. Spencer, too, seethed. Peyton was making money in the wake of her tragedy. No one asked her if she ever wanted to be a part of this.

"If people don't want to listen to me, they can just shut me off. Simple as that. But they don't. They love being mad, they love to hate, and—sorry, not sorry—but they love to hate Ethan. I just give them what they want."

Jackson let out a snort of a laugh and looked away, staring out the window. It was the best he could do to keep from storming out of the place, Spencer was sure of that.

She could barely control her own voice when she spoke next.

"So you want to use us, too."

"Use you? I see it as mutual promotion. You're the perfect victim, a tragic figure in this whole mess. Deceived by an unscrupulous, conniving prince, a woefully doe-eyed angel who has been caught up in Hurricane Ethan."

Spencer cringed. She didn't think she was perfect, far from it, and to hear that other people might think otherwise set her teeth on edge. Peyton seemed to sense that, leaned in, and touched Spencer's hand. Her fingers were cold.

"People are rooting for you, Spencer. They want you to win."

Spencer doubted there was any winning in this scenario, but it would be pointless arguing about that. Spencer plastered on her best smile and said, "I want to win, too."

At least it was partially true. Winning meant proving her sanity. Winning meant showing everyone she wasn't going to ignore her gut. Winning meant she had to play ball.

"Go ahead. Ask away."

**_Get Salty_: A True Crime Podcast with Peyton Salt**

_Get Salty_ Exclusive Interview Episode Transcript

_[Intro Music]_

**Peyton Salt [_voice-over_]:**

Wow. Wow-wow-wow. Y'all. Do I have a treat for all you lucky listeners. It must be fate because, lo and behold, I was fortunate enough to be contacted by two people directly affected by Ethan Amoroso's case—our newest deep dive into the scandals of rich and privileged Los Angeles life. Be sure to catch up on all our episodes. I met with Spencer Sandoval, Ethan's ex-girlfriend and passenger injured in the crash, along with Jackson Chen, Ethan's best friend, for an exclusive interview about how Ethan's case has affected their lives and rocked a small community to its core.

When yours truly arrived at the coffee shop, I had no idea what to expect from the interview, and definitely didn't expect to uncover a lot more than what I intended.

A little background—Spencer and Jackson have been investigating Ethan's case independently, determined to find truths where there appear to be none, caught up in the concept of innocent until proven guilty, despite Ethan's case being closed any day now with the judge expected to make her decision once proceedings are over. It's pretty clear what happened: He was speeding, he didn't brake, he killed Chris Moore. He's a reckless, arrogant brat. End of story. But maybe there's more to it than that, since two of those nearest and dearest to him are trying desperately to search for answers among the rubble.

Pictures from the interview will be made available on our Instagram page, including a transcript of the interview within the next few days.

What could these two possibly be doing to heal from this case? What kind of relationship do they have? A couple, thrown together by tragedy such as theirs, is bound to be looking for comfort. I myself have seen them spending a lot of time together around school, united in a shared cause, which has everyone talking. They agreed to sit down with me to have a one-on-one chat.

*[SFX: chairs scraping on pavement and the hum of cars passing down the street, a bell chimes as a door opens and closes]*

**Peyton [*voice-over continues*]:**
We sat outside a local coffee shop to hear their side of the story.

**Peyton:** Thank you both for being here. Spencer, can you tell me a little bit more about yourself?

**Spencer Sandoval:**
I'm Spencer, I'm a senior at Armstrong Prep, I play field hockey, and I plan to go to Caltech next year.

**Peyton:** And you, Jackson?

**Jackson Chen:**
Yeah, uh, I'm Jackson, Ethan's best friend. I also play soccer with him on the school team at Armstrong.

**Peyton:** So let's jump right into it. How does it feel to be at ground zero of America's latest true crime sensation?

**Spencer:** It's . . . It's a lot.

**Peyton:** Let's talk more about the incident. What was it like, the moments leading up to the crash?

**Spencer:** Ethan and I broke up that night. I was furious at him, but I don't remember most of the night. I have memory loss. This far out, I'm not sure I'll ever remember. I have no idea what happened in the car. I woke up in the hospital.

**Peyton:** Horrible! And your face, scarred . . . Do you regret getting in the car?

**Spencer:** Of course I do. But I can't change that. I wish no one had gotten in that car in the first place.

**Peyton:** And Jackson, do you regret not being there for your friend? You were at some overnight soccer camp?

**Jackson:** Yeah, I wish I was there, maybe I would have stopped him from driving. I still have nightmares about it, that maybe if I was there it wouldn't have happened.

**Spencer:** You never told me about that.

**Jackson:** Well . . . when compared to you, it feels minuscule. Like, why should I have nightmares? I wasn't even there. How can I have nightmares about something that happened to someone else?

**Spencer:** You should have said something . . .

**Jackson:** I didn't want to bother you. You're going through it as it is.

**Peyton [*voice-over*]:**
Spencer and Jackson can hardly take their eyes off each other. They find solace in each other's eyes. It's almost like I'm not even there.

**Peyton:** Have you two gotten close since the accident?

**Jackson:** Close? I mean, we were already friends before.

**Spencer:** Yeah, it's true, we do hang out more. Looking into Ethan's case and everything. But no, it's not a big deal.

**Peyton:** Does Ethan know?

**Spencer:** Know what?

**Peyton:** About you two? I imagine his ex-girlfriend and best friend getting together would be a source of some emotion. Has your friendship with Ethan changed over the course of your investigation?

**Jackson:** No. He says it was an accident, and we believe him.

**Peyton:** And nothing more has become of it?

**Spencer:** It's not like that. We're friends. We're not together.

**Jackson:** Why do you think we're together?

**Peyton:** Just a little hunch. Call it intuition.

**Spencer:** We have nothing to hide. But Jackson and I are doing this because we care about Ethan's case. We want to make sure everything sees the light of truth in the end.

**Peyton:** Of course you do! There's that Armstrong Preparatory School spirit. Which reminds me— you both attend Armstrong. Spencer, you've been on the Headmaster's List for a while now, and Jackson, you just got on, didn't you?

**Spencer:** Oh! You did? Congrats, Jackson, that's great.

**Jackson:** Thanks. It's a hard thing to celebrate, honestly.

**Peyton:** Everyone wants to be on the List, don't they?

**Jackson:** I wouldn't go that far again. Some people make it out to be a big deal, but it's really not like that.

**Peyton:** I find that hard to believe. Armstrong is pretty cutthroat. The Headmaster's List is a shortcut to the Ivies and Stanford. It's a pretty big deal.

**Peyton:** Do you think Ethan deserved to be on the List? Isn't it meant for future leaders of America, after all?

**Jackson:** That's not for me to judge.

**Peyton:** Spencer? What about you? Do you think

|           | Ethan deserved to be on the List? His grades weren't near what yours are, or Jackson's. |
|-----------|------------------------------------------------------------------------------------------|
| **Spencer:** | Of course he deserved it. |
| **Peyton:** | Did he? But it's common knowledge that if your parents write a big enough check, you can buy your way onto the List. Doesn't that make you mad, Spencer? That other people might be using other means to get what you've worked so hard for? |
| **Spencer:** | It would make me mad if they cheated, but— |
| **Peyton:** | Ethan is a cheater. Perhaps in more aspects of life than one! Shouldn't he be punished? |
| **Spencer:** | Are we done here? |

# SNAPS

**@chockablock.marva:**
Jackson is so quiet and awkward. Is he hiding something? Getting weird vibes from him. Red flags everywhere. Anyone find more info on him? #SaltyInterview

**@Turkiwi:**
Jackson seems so fake, it's not even funny. Why wasn't Ethan's so-called best friend at the party with him? He might just be looking for attention. I bet they hardly know each other IRL. #cloutchaser

**@OctoPuddle09:**
#SaltyInterview They are dating. Obviously.

**@Awolfe04:**
No mention of Chris? They don't even care about the real victim. Sketchy as hell. #justiceforchris #SaltyInterview

**@norma.likes.drawing:**
Jackson Chen is just like his dad, except instead of stealing cash he's stealing Ethan's girl! lolololololol

**@itslilylom:**
Who names their kid Spencer? I thought it was the dude at first!

**@Nidusrez2000:**
They're totally hooking up. #goodforher #SaltyInterview

**@Muhd_adLinsey:**
LOL why is this chick even bothering? Waste of time. THE DUDE WAS DRIVING. Guilty as sin.

**@laterhaterz:**
Team Spencer! Ethan is scum. #SaltyInterview
#menaretrash

**@anniehallcrocodile:**
Jackson Chen is so cute, I want to scream. Why
can't I get a hot guy to help me solve a mystery?
#foreversingle #SaltyInterview

**@petrichordreams:**
More of these interviews please! @GetSaltyPod You did
such a good job! Congrats on the Netflix deal!

**@AskAWalrus:**
It's finally time trash like Ethan pay for what he's done.
#justiceforchris #burninhell

**@leprecorn:**
Hot take—maybe we should all cool it? Doesn't anyone
else think it's weird that we're creeping on the lives of
private people? Those paparazzi style pics of Spencer
and Jackson? Kind of weird. We all want #justiceforchris
but this feels like harassment.

**@MorgenOgirl:**
Does this mean Ethan is still single? Asking for a friend.
#SaltyInterview

# THIRTY-TWO

**ANOTHER DAY OF THE TRIAL,** and Spencer took her usual seat in the rear of the courtroom. Ripley obediently lay at her feet, her warm fur brushing up ever so slightly against her bare calves. Jackson was next to her, his hands clenched between his knees, stopping himself from picking his nails until they bled. He had an unconscious habit of picking at his nails when he was worried. Spencer was worried, too. Ethan was taking the stand today.

Spencer had an instinct to reach out and hold Jackson's hand so he wouldn't hurt himself, but she stopped herself. It wouldn't be appropriate. Especially now that Ethan had been called up, and already sworn on the Bible, waiting for the lawyers to finish preparing for questions.

"Mister Amoroso," Thora Barancewicz, the Moores' lawyer, said, pausing for dramatic effect. Spencer took a short, shuddering breath.

Ethan looked paler than usual, sickly even. House arrest had not been kind to him. It wasn't just lying around the house and doing nothing, it was lying around in the house and worrying. The usual cut of his cheekbones had a sharpness that veered into gauntness, and his eyes had a hollow look to them that wasn't just the remnants of bruising from the accident. She could tell he was self-soothing, rubbing his hands together under the stand, and he stopped himself after realizing it was making him look guilty.

"Please state your name for the record," Ms. Barancewicz said.

"Ethan Alexander Amoroso."

"Thank you, Mister Amoroso. You're a longtime resident of the area, right?"

"Yes, my family moved here from London when I was two. I've lived here practically my whole life."

"And your parents, who are they?"

"My father works as an executive and my stepmother is in marketing."

"What of your birth mother?"

"She's still in London. I don't see her a lot."

Ms. Barancewicz rested her elbow casually on the witness stand, as if she was chatting with someone while out on the town. "Would you say you had a happy childhood?"

Ethan shrugged a shoulder but agreed.

"A privileged childhood, to be sure." Ethan nodded. Ms. Barancewicz walked back to her table and flipped open a folder, but she spoke too quickly to have read anything. She already knew the fact that she was pretending to look for. "It says your family is worth an estimated one hundred million dollars. That's definitely a lot more money than most people in this courtroom can even dream about."

Spencer had always known that Ethan's family was rich, it wasn't a secret. Sometimes it bothered her, simply because she felt intimidated inviting him over to her house. Her whole house could fit into his backyard. A lot of people cared about the money the Amorosos made; rumors that they'd made it illicitly were not uncommon when it was a slow news week.

"Having that kind of money, you probably weren't in want of too many things. Perhaps the word 'no' wasn't in the vocabulary."

"I'm not sure what—"

Ms. Barancewicz didn't let him finish. "It's no secret then that your family sometimes had trouble disciplining you. Records show you attended a behavioral rehabilitation camp, Camp Ervo, just this past summer, before the accident. A camp intended to reform troubled youth. Can you tell us more about that?"

The skin on Ethan's face got tight. "There's not much to say. We camped in the desert for two months. It . . . wasn't fun."

"Why not? A privileged kid like you, not used to living it up in the wild?"

Spencer could see Ethan's whole body seize up. He'd probably been dreading this topic. From what she and Jackson knew, the camp had a firm hand when it came to reform, sometimes letting the kids go hungry if they weren't able to build the fires correctly or sleep in the cold when the inevitable desert night came around. It was supposed to build character, but Spencer considered it more like pun-ishment.

"It's not my definition of a vacation," Ethan said. Spen-cer could hear the edge in his voice.

But what else was Ethan supposed to say? Lie? Tell everyone it was the best thing ever? How would he defend himself in this situation?

"What is your definition of a vacation? A getaway to the Alps? Jet setting in the tropics?"

"I hated it," Ethan said. "Two guys showed up at my house in the middle of the night, put me in the back of a van, and drove me to the desert until morning. They didn't tell me where we were going. I thought I was being kidnapped."

"If your parents resorted to sending you to a camp, it's a pretty good indicator that even they didn't know what to do with you." She said it with an unintended wink, like she was making a point that nailed his coffin closed.

Ethan's eyes went to his parents sitting on his side of the room. From Spencer's vantage point, she saw Mrs. Amoro-so's shoulders bouncing up and down, silently sobbing. Did she feel guilty for sending Ethan to that camp? Mr. Amo-roso sat rigidly still, as if his spine had been glued straight.

Spencer never had seen any evidence that his parents physically abused Ethan, but what kind of parents would send their kid away to a camp like that? Parents who might have thought they were doing the right thing . . . but Spencer didn't imagine she could ever send any future children she had away like that.

Ms. Barancewicz went on. "I understand that you're no stranger to this kind of environment, is that correct?"

"Y-Yes." He licked his lips. Spencer could see how dry his lips were from her seat all the way in the back.

"You've had your fair share of run-ins with the law. Tell us more about that."

"I . . . I drive too fast sometimes. I guess it's a bad habit."

"A habit, Mister Amoroso, is biting your nails, or grinding your teeth, or fidgeting. I wouldn't call driving recklessly, speeding into the triple digits, participating in drag races and such, as being a habit but rather active choices, choices that you are able to control."

Ethan had nothing to say to that.

"This is not an interrogation, Mister Amoroso," the lawyer went on.

*Really looks like it, though*, Spencer thought.

"This is an analysis of your character, and your previous history with accidents happening a lot around you."

"If this is about what happened to Julie—"

"Does that not reflect your moral character? A selfishness and lack of empathy for those around you?"

"Objection, Your Honor." Ethan's lawyer stood in a half crouch. "My client is not on trial for a case that has already been resolved as an accidental fall. How is this relevant to the case at hand?"

Judge Patel made a note with a flourish of her pen and said, "Overruled. This better be going somewhere, Ms. Barancewicz."

"It is, Your Honor. Two years ago, Ethan Amoroso threw a house party big enough that it made the headlines, is that correct?"

Ethan looked at his lawyer, his lips pressed in a thin line. The lawyer bobbed his head and Ethan took a breath. "Yes."

"Tell us more about that. What happened at your party?"

"There were about a hundred of us, mostly kids from my school—"

"Armstrong Preparatory School. One of the most exclusive private schools in Los Angeles, if not the best."

"Right. Yeah. A few friends came over for some fun, and I admit, it got a little out of hand."

"Out of hand? There are several police reports from your neighbors about noise complaints, underage drinking and smoking marijuana, and drag racing in a residential zone."

Ethan's cheeks pinked and he leaned forward into the microphone. "Haven't you ever thrown a party when you were a kid my age?" Spencer wanted to tell him to calm down; she could see the frustration bubbling up his throat. He couldn't snap, or look angry—the jury wouldn't like that at all. But all Spencer could do was sigh and hold Ripley's leash in her lap.

"I'm not the one on trial here, Mr. Amoroso," Ms. Barancewicz said. She spun around and walked back to the prosecution table, absently pushing papers on the desk. It drew everyone's eyes naturally to the Moores, sitting there, glaring at Ethan.

"When Julianne Greene fell off the roof, where were you?"

"In the pool house. With some friends. We were ... playing beer pong."

"Playing beer pong while an innocent teenager fell from your roof, breaking her back on the lawn. Let the record show that Mr. Amoroso nodded his head. Next time it'd be helpful if you verbalized your answers."

Ethan looked like if he opened his mouth he would puke.

Ms. Barancewicz didn't seem to care. "What did you do when you found out?"

"Called for an ambulance."

"After five minutes."

"We panicked. We all thought she was dead."

"But she wasn't dead. And if you had acted sooner, maybe she could have regained consciousness."

Ethan's chest heaved. He was getting more flustered by the minute.

"Your Honor," Ethan's lawyer said as he stood up again, half raised from his chair. "What does this have to do with this current case?"

"I'm getting there, Your Honor. I promise."

The judge looked unamused but gestured for Ms. Barancewicz to continue.

"Whose car was it when you crashed that night?"

"The Targa is mine."

"That your father paid for."

"Yes, but he didn't drive it."

"Certainly. He gifted it to you, is that correct?"

"For my sixteenth birthday."

"Interesting. Every boy's dream! And you imply that you have a complicated relationship with your parents. What kind of parents would send you away to a behavioral rehabilitation center, when only the year before, they gifted you an expensive sports car? Do you feel like the car was used as a tool to try to control you?"

Ethan stammered. "What? No!"

"Do you act out to get attention from them?"

"No!"

"Were you planning to wreck the vehicle to get back at your father?"

"No! I wasn't—" Ethan stopped himself short and clamped his mouth shut. For a millisecond, his eyes turned to the people in the courtroom, locking gazes with Spencer. Her heart seized up and she forgot to breathe. Ethan looked back at the lawyer, his calm demeanor returned. "No. It was an accident."

Ms. Barancewicz seemed content with what she had gotten out of him. She turned back to the court and said, "One accident is just that, an accident. Two accidents, though . . . This pattern of reckless behavior, of his admitted habit of speeding, instigated by a privileged youth who has evaded justice from the law time and again, emphasizes the lack of moral character we are all witness to here today. Ethan says he panicked when they found Julianne Greene fighting for her life on his lawn. Strange how he can only think quickly when he's behind the wheel of a fast-moving vehicle. It was only inevitable that it come to this. That is all, Your Honor."

# THIRTY-THREE

**SPENCER HATED TO ADMIT IT,** but she desperately needed a break.

She'd been working basically two jobs, one at Brain Freeze and one surrounding Ethan's case, plus school and field hockey practice (granted, she was still on the bench) and physical therapy, all while trying to keep on top of her pain, visit with her PTSD specialist, Dr. Alex, as usual, and still have time to sleep at the end of the day. It was starting to weigh on her.

She massaged her eyes after pausing a YouTube video she'd been watching about bullet journal spreads on her phone. Seeing how other people organized their thoughts and put them on the page eased her worries. She also got some ideas about how she wanted to organize her planner, now that she had her hand back, even though it was still sore and continued to cramp when she tried to hold a pen. She wondered if that would ever go away.

She and Jackson had been working on Ethan's case for the better part of a month. Time had flown by so quickly, she barely had time to register that Halloween decorations had already been put up—artificial cobwebs and plastic pumpkins galore. The school library had turned into a haunted mansion.

"How's it going?" Jackson asked, looking up from his own work.

"I'm okay. Thanks."

Jackson went back to his worksheet, filling out the questions in his usual scrawl.

He'd been working hard, too. Having to take notes for her, on top of all his other responsibilities was a lot. She had to repay him somehow.

"Hey, um . . . ," she started to say, and Jackson looked at her. "How would you like to go see a movie with me? I think the newest Marvel movie is out. My treat, for all your help with school and everything."

Jackson's cheeks flushed bright red. "You really don't have to do that. It's no trouble, really."

"Please, it's the least I can do for you, especially since you won't let me pay you any other way. Without you, I would have been so screwed this year."

Jackson smiled and dipped his head as he rubbed the back of his neck. "That sounds great."

"How's seven o'clock? Tonight?"

"I'll be there, for sure." His smile was so warm, and when he looked at her with those brown eyes, Spencer's stomach did a happy little flip.

With Ripley at her side, Spencer rode her bike to the movie theater, a restored classic building called The Pix, and locked it up near the 7-Eleven parking lot across the street. She was pleased to find Jackson already there, waiting for her under the brightly lit marquee. He was standing with his hands in the pockets of his jeans, his shoulders scrunched up toward his ears in the chill of the night despite his zip-up hoodie, but he relaxed and smiled when he saw her. Spencer had planned it out so they had plenty of time to get their tickets, get some snacks, and find their seats.

The Pix was her favorite movie theater to go to, ever since she was little, and she went almost every weekend with Olivia last year. She liked the old-Hollywood look of the theater, reminding her of a time long since gone. Her favorite piece of decor was the replica Hollywood sign being eaten by the *T. rex* from *Jurassic Park* in the ticket lobby. The theater often showed a lot of classic movies, but it also had some new ones, and Spencer wasn't too picky on what she wanted to see, so long as it would be at The Pix.

But when she went to buy their tickets, her heart dropped into her stomach. Just as another couple moved out of the ticket line and into the theater, Spencer saw, behind the counter, none other than Hailey Reed. Like every other employee at the theater, she wore a bellhop uniform complete with a hat on top of her head. If Spencer had to wear an outfit like that, she would have felt ridiculous; Hailey, though, made it look like the latest front-page fashion. Spencer had completely forgotten that Hailey worked at The Pix, and she wanted to turn and run before Hailey noticed her, but it was too late. Hailey's eyes widened ever so slightly when she spotted Spencer.

Jackson stepped up to Hailey's counter and Spencer forced herself to do the same. She automatically asked for two tickets, and Hailey looked at Spencer, then at Jackson, doing some mental calculations and assumptions in her head, but Spencer was trying to keep the wasps swarming in her throat from coming out and stinging everyone with all the words she wanted to say.

She clamped her mouth shut, trying not to remember the way Hailey's tongue slipped in and out of Ethan's mouth, and her lips went numb because she pinched them between her teeth so hard. Hailey didn't look at Spencer, which made Spencer feel a little better. *Good, let her feel ashamed*, Spencer thought.

Though she almost wanted Hailey to look at her, make her see the rage burning in Spencer's eyes. A punctuation mark on the events of that night.

But she didn't want to fight over a boy. She wasn't that type of girl, even though a petty part of herself wanted to be. She could imagine herself getting a good punch to Hailey's perfect nose, but Spencer knew it wasn't worth it in the end. She would just feel worse.

Hailey was about to ring them up when she gave a weary look at Ripley.

"You can't have pets in the theater," she said, her voice tinny through the speaker system through the plexiglass barrier.

Spencer had anticipated this kind of reaction. "She's not a pet. She's a service dog."

"I don't think my manager will let you, though."

"Come on, Hailey," Jackson said. "She won't make any noise. We promise. We'll leave if it becomes a problem."

"No," Hailey said. "It's against the rules."

"Are you serious?" Spencer demanded.

"I don't make the rules." Hailey turned away.

Spencer banged on the glass.

"What?"

"Are we going to talk about it?" Spencer demanded.

"Talk about what?"

"The fact that you were sleeping with my boyfriend for a year?"

Hailey came out of the booth, her cheeks red and her arms crossed. She looked at Spencer with utter disgust. "What's there to talk about?"

"I thought we were friends."

Hailey barked a laugh. "Friends?"

"Weren't we?"

"No."

"But I thought . . ."

"You thought just because we're in the same AP classes and all that crap that we're friends. You might even think we're alike. But no, Spencer, I'm not like you. Unlike you, I'm not deserving of certain privileges, even though we have the same GPA and I have even more extracurriculars than you do. No, I'm just another white girl in LA. But you— you're *special*." Hailey's eyes flashed with so much resentment, Spencer had to take a step back.

"My sister put herself through State, but her

roommates—both of them were minorities, so they didn't have to. My sister worked three jobs because our step-father wouldn't pay for college. She couldn't get financial aid, she had no help from anyone."

Spencer shook her head. "That's not my fault . . ."

"Yeah, but I didn't make the Headmaster's List and you did, and we all know why," Hailey bit.

Spencer did know. She was the happy brown successful face of Armstrong, and to be honest, she was happy enough to play that part when it suited her. But then again, there were a ton of kids on the Headmaster's List who got on because their parents were big donors or had some kind of connection to the school. She fit a certain bucket, but then, so did the other kids. But it was always easier to blame the brown kid for taking a spot, wasn't it?

"You know why Ethan didn't break up with you? Why he was with me but never made it public?"

Hailey didn't wait for Spencer to answer.

"It wasn't because he felt sorry for you. It was because he was *scared*. He thought people would think less of him for dumping sweet perfect Spencer Sandoval. That people might think he was racist for breaking up with you and dat-ing me. Even though I was better for him in every way. I loved him. You didn't even know him. He was with me for a year and you hardly even cared that he wasn't around. You didn't even notice."

Hailey sneered, then looked down at Ripley. "Fine, whatever, take your stupid dog inside."

With that, Hailey went back into the ticket booth.

Jackson jogged over with Cokes and popcorn.

Spencer had tears in her eyes.

"Hey, are you okay?" he asked. He looked at Hailey in the ticket booth. "Did she say something to you?"

"I'm fine, it's nothing," she sniffed. "Come on, movie's going to start."

With Ripley safely beneath Spencer's legs and Jackson sitting warmly at her side, their elbows almost touching, Spencer finally allowed herself to breathe.

She didn't notice Jackson watching her carefully, but she did notice Ripley shifting under her legs, the warm fur of her back brushing against the back of Spencer's calves. She tried to focus on that, but everything felt so loud, even the rush of blood in her ears as panic held her captive. She felt glued to her seat, unable to move, unable to think or focus on anything else except what was happening. Her memories of the past crashed into the present. The walls were closing in. All the air was sucked out of the theater.

She closed her eyes before she could see it happen on screen. All she heard was the scrape and crunch of metal, the oddly quiet moment when the car was in the air, spinning, the thump of the body thrashing around in the cabin, the shattering glass.

*Scream. Float. Crash. Pain.*

A whimper escaped her lips, and she squeezed her eyes tight.

*Engine roaring. Cold, wet hands on her face. SPENCER!*

*Twisting metal. Float. SPENCER! Tree bark. Ethan's face. Ethan! I CAN'T—! Cold. SPENCER!*

Pain. Nothing else.

*Don't, please don't, not here,* she told herself, in an attempt to stop her memories from flooding her brain like a failing dam. She didn't want to make a scene, she didn't want to draw attention to herself. But she wanted to run. She felt like she was dying.

"Spencer." Jackson's hand was warm on top of her own. Shocked, she opened her eyes, saw his own in the flickering lights of the screen, and knew what he meant. She rose to her feet.

He didn't question it. He held her hand as she stood, Ripley at her side, and they all quietly exited the theater.

"I didn't know there'd be a car crash in the movie," she said. "This was all my fault. I should have known going in, should have seen reviews or something. This is so embarrassing, I'm so sorry. I ruined everything."

Jackson waved his hand. "You didn't ruin anything. It's not your fault you got triggered. I'm not disappointed, I promise. Don't worry."

Spencer couldn't help but worry. That was all she did these days. She blew into the tissues and rubbed the top of Ripley's head. She sat on the curb, and the dog rested her chin on Spencer's lap and looked at her with those golden amber eyes, as if telling her it was all going to be okay.

Spencer took a breath and all she could do was wait for the panic to subside. The muscles in her back ached from crying so hard. She drew in a deep breath, forcing air into her lungs, and she realized that Jackson's hoodie was draped over her shoulders. He was sitting next to her in just his T-shirt. When he'd done that for her, she didn't know.

"Are you sure you—" She tugged at the sleeve, moving to take it off.

"No, it's fine. You take it. You need it more than I do."

"Thanks," she said, blushing.

Her gaze snagged on Jackson's mouth, at the gentle curve of his lips as he smiled. They looked soft, and she wondered, for a brief moment, what it would feel like to kiss him. The remnants of her panic flitted on the outskirts of her mind, still threatening to rage like a storm once more, but having him next to her made it feel less like she was drowning.

Jackson noticed where her eyes had landed and a flush went up his cheeks. He went very still as he watched her, shoulders tense like he was holding his breath, and she wondered if he wanted to kiss her back. His eyes were round and full in the marquee lights from the theater, and her stomach did a delightful cartwheel, but something held her back.

What would she be risking if she went for it? They were friends, but what if he just wanted to be friends? What if she was reading into everything? But her eyes landed on his lips again and a bubble expanded in her chest.

Ripley broke the moment by shoving her snout into Spencer's face, digging her cold, wet nose into Spencer's cheek, eager for attention, making both of them laugh.

*Jealous, much?* Spencer thought, amused.

If Jackson was disappointed, he didn't show it. He cleared his throat and rubbed his lips together, as if applying ChapStick. She wondered if maybe she had been wrong after all and let the moment pass. It felt safer this way.

"Anyway," Spencer said. "I should really be going."

"Tonight was fun, all things considered."

"All things considered," she repeated.

His eyes were still bright in the lights from the theater, and he smiled as he pulled his gaze away.

She couldn't help but smile, too. With him, it felt good.

By the time she got home, she realized she was still wearing Jackson's hoodie. It smelled like him, cedar and rosemary.

But she couldn't forget Hailey's icy gaze.

*You didn't even know him,* Hailey had told her. *I loved him. You hardly cared that he wasn't around. You didn't even notice.*

At least one mystery was solved.

Hailey cared about Ethan. She wasn't the one who caused him to crash.

# THIRTY-FOUR

**SPENCER USED TO BE A** morning person, but ever since the crash, it got harder and harder to wake up. She used to be able to jump out of bed, get dressed in her running gear, queue up her running playlist, and go for a half hour–long jog through the neighborhood, taking a break halfway through to do some more stretches and calisthenics in the park before heading home, about three miles total on an average day. For school, she'd been chipper and refreshed, ready to take on the day. She liked the routine of it, the predictability in a schedule, and it was a comfort especially when midterms and finals made a valiant effort to hack away at her spirit.

Ripley had been trained to jump onto her bed and lick her, nudging her face with her wet nose, once Spencer's alarm went ignored. Spencer could not ignore an enthusiastic dog weaponizing her cold nose before the sun was up.

"I'm up, I'm up," Spencer said, gently pushing Ripley's head away. Her hot, stinky dog breath could wake the dead. But Spencer was still so tired. She'd woken up in the night, as usual, but she felt like she hadn't slept at all.

She tipped a few of her pain pills into her palm so they would be working by the time she made it to school. However, there wouldn't be any school today. It was a scheduled in-service day for faculty, so students had the day off. Normally, Spencer would use it as an opportunity to catch up on homework (although it was likely she was all caught up) or use it as an opportunity to jumpstart on any essays or projects she knew were coming up, thanks to her bullet journal. But that wasn't going to be happening.

The temptation to take her medicine and go back to bed was powerful. It seemed to call to her, luring her back under the sheets, like a siren at sea. *You don't want to move. Stay here. It's safe. You don't want to do anything.*

If it wasn't for Ripley, she might have done just that, pulled the blanket up to her chin and gone back to bed. But Ripley was very good at her job.

Bed-headed and bleary, Spencer got up, threw on her bathrobe and slippers, and shuffled to the kitchen where she could let Ripley out into the back.

Her parents were, unsurprisingly, gone already. They'd left the kitchen with some cereal set out and ready for Spencer to have a bowl. Hope was already enjoying hers on the couch watching cartoons. Unlike Spencer, she had school today, but Spencer didn't have the energy to tell her to stop watching cartoons and get ready.

Spencer hugged her robe around herself as she let Ripley make a few laps around the yard, nose pressed down toward the grass, on the trail of whatever animal had made a journey through it in the night, while Spencer tried to wake up. A combination of sleep deprivation, obsession over Ethan's case, and the side effects of her medication was making everything feel like it was moving through molasses.

"Your phone has been going nuts all night," Hope said matter-of-factly.

Spencer had left it on the kitchen table when she got home after leaving the movie with Jackson, to prevent herself from getting distracted from her work reading over Ethan's case transcripts. It was dull work, but she couldn't let the phone tempt her from it.

She was curious, though, as to why her phone would be "going nuts" and Spencer picked it up off the table. Three missed calls, eleven unanswered texts. All from Olivia. With a sinking feeling, Spencer read through each one.

6:30pm–Hey! Don't forget to bring your sunblock. We are NOT having another Aloe Vera Incident.

6:54pm–Where you at?

Missed call from Olivia Santos at 7:01

7:02pm–Are you coming? People are here.

7:04pm–Cake is here! Strawberry and chocolate for miles!

Missed call from Olivia Santos at 7:22

7:49pm–Is everything okay?

8:04pm–Spencerrrrrrrr

8:10pm–I'm eating this whole cake without you!

8:59pm–You could have at least said you weren't coming.

9:12pm-People are asking about you.

10:07pm-Are you mad at me or something?

Missed call from Olivia Santos at 11:27

11:28pm-Don't bother coming.

Spencer had completely forgotten about Olivia's birthday party.

She immediately tried to call Olivia, but it rang once and then went straight to voicemail. Olivia wasn't just mad, no—she was hell-fire furious.

Spencer swore several times and tried again. It went straight to voicemail again. "Hi!" Olivia's cutesy voice said. "If you're not in immediate mortal danger, you know it's better to text me. If you're a spam caller, I look forward to blocking you!" *Beep.*

"Olivia!" said Spencer. "I'm so, so sorry. I can't believe I missed your party. I'm so . . . Please call me back."

She hung up and Hope was staring at her. While she had been going to a movie with Jackson, she had completely forgotten about her best friend.

"Am I a bad person?" Spencer asked.

Hope pouted her lips thoughtfully. "I'd say you're probably not great."

Spencer let out a groan and called Ripley inside.

"I feel so bad," Spencer said, leaning on the counter of Paws Perfect. She often visited her parents at their work, but usually they were too busy for it to be anything but a quick hello and dropping off a couple scones from the bakery next door.

"Don't be so hard on yourself," Dad said, typing away at the computer at the front desk. "These things happen. I'm sure Olivia will forgive you."

It was Halloween. As per tradition, kids in the neighborhood would visit various shops and businesses on the street for trick-or-treating, so he was dressed up and ready with a bowl of candy, which Spencer had already helped herself to. Even chocolate couldn't make her feel better.

He was busy working the front desk, scheduling and managing appointments, while Mom was in the back giving a terrier puppy his shots while dressed like a ketchup bottle. Dad didn't seem as bothered by what happened as Spencer was.

"You two have been friends for forever. It's not like one little thing can get in the way of that."

"Yeah, but she's so mad. She won't answer the phone or respond to my texts."

"Give her time. She'll come around," he said.

"I can't take you seriously with that outfit on."

"What? The mustard? You don't *relish* my costume?"

"Funny."

The next school day, Olivia hardly paid any attention to Spencer, even when they sat next to each other in history class. While Mrs. McNamara was busy teaching a lesson about fur-collar crime after the Hundred Years' War, Spencer slid a note over to Olivia. Olivia pretended not to notice, continuing to take notes, and Spencer nudged it closer to her. Olivia sighed dramatically and took the note.

Spencer had written: *I'm sorry. Please talk to me.*

After Olivia read it over, she didn't even look at Spencer. She crumpled the note up and stuffed it under her notebook. She put her hand up to her eye, blocking Spencer from view, as she kept writing. Spencer's chest tightened. She knew she had messed up, but Olivia was a grade A grudge holder, and the fact that she wasn't even letting Spencer explain herself had Spencer's insides churning up like they were in a blender.

Spencer, too, tried to focus on class, but Mrs. Mc-Namara's voice faded into the background as Spencer's blood rushed through her ears.

After class let out, Olivia tried to rush out, but Spencer caught up to her and pulled her to the side, out of the way of their classmates heading toward next period.

"Liv, please. I'm sorry," Spencer said. "I'll make it up to you."

She narrowed her eyes. "I think it's too late for that."

"When will you talk to me?"

"I don't know, Spencer. When were you going to tell me that instead of coming to my birthday, you were on a date with Jackson Chen?"

"How did you know that?"

"*Everyone* knows that. Snap Map? Duh! You forgot to ghost your avatar. Anyway, it's all anyone's been talking about. Maybe if you got your head out of your ass, you'd be able to hear them."

Spencer's eyes stung. She didn't want to get angry, but she could feel pain creeping up her throat. She tried to swallow it down and said, "I lost track of the days. I didn't mean—"

"No, I get it. Ever since the crash, you've changed. You're not yourself."

"Obviously, Olivia!" Her voice had risen loud enough that people started to stare. "Can you blame me?"

"You barely acknowledge my existence! All you do is hang out with Jackson and talk about Ethan, how he didn't do it, when it's obvious to everyone but you that he did! I know Chris died, but you didn't!" Her eyes were glassy and her voice wobbled. She was barely keeping it together, too.

Spencer got the feeling that this was bigger than missing a birthday party, but the rational side of her brain had been overtaken by wildfire. The pain in her shoulder flared. "I'm trying to help Ethan!"

"Are you really? Or are you just using it as an excuse?"

"An excuse for what?"

Ripley leaned into Spencer's legs and Olivia scoffed. People were full-on staring at them now.

"You coming to my birthday meant a lot to me, and I know it's just a stupid party, but you're my best friend! I wanted you there!"

"How many times do I have to say I'm sorry?"

"You don't get it," Olivia said, snarling. "You're obsessed and it feels like you don't even know it."

"Not everything is about you!" Spencer roared. She regretted saying it the moment it came out, but her anger burned hot on her cheeks. In that moment, she knew she had royally screwed up, and what was worse was that Olivia didn't say anything back that had nearly as much heat.

Hurt, Olivia took a step back. She flashed a pained smile. "Right, of course it's not. Because everything is about *you*. How silly of me to want a little attention from my best friend on my birthday," she said softly. "Bye, Spencer." And with that, she walked away.

When Spencer arrived home one day, mid-November, she found an unmarked manila envelope sitting on top of the pile of the rest of the uncollected mail. Spencer dumped the junk mail and catalogs onto the kitchen counter and tore open the envelope. She didn't need to know who it was from.

Peyton Salt had come through. Her and Jackson's interview had paid off. Inside was a stack of large photographs of the crash, a sticky note attached to the front photo.

*Thank me later!*

*Love–P.S.*

Spencer shut herself away in her room so no one could see what she was doing and try to stop her.

Looking at the photos, she expected that it would unlock some part of her memory, immediately put her back to the event and everything would click into place. She desperately, now more than anything, wanted things to get back to normal. She wanted to be a better friend to Olivia, a better sister to Hope, a better . . . *whatever* with Jackson. But looking at the photos now, it felt like she was looking at something in a textbook. The warped metal and plastic, broken glass, unrecognizable pieces of lives shattered in an instant. But it felt as if it had happened to some other person, a distant tragedy that hadn't affected Spencer as deeply as she knew it had.

She didn't remember any of this, how the car had wrapped itself sideways around the palm tree. Ethan had tried to turn the car, avoiding the inevitable, but the car folded in half like a cheap piece of paper. The photos, of course, were taken at night, the flash of the camera illuminating the polished black hood of the car, making everything else in the frame expand with a long shadow stretching over the street. No one else was in the frame. The photographer had moved around the car, taking in the scene as completely as possible before moving on to the details of the car, the driver's seat, too destroyed to . . .

Bile churned uncomfortably in her gut, and Spencer already tasted the bitterness in the back of her throat.

Her heart thudded painfully in her chest as she flipped through the photos, waiting for the inevitability that was sure to come. Brace for impact.

The next photo was of the driver's side, of the mangled steering wheel, chaos of the footwell now more bent metal than anything recognizable, broken glass everywhere, the seat almost flush with the steering wheel, the airbag deflated like a limp ghost. She remembered learning to drive manual transmission in that car.

The memory came back to her so suddenly, it almost

took her breath away for a different reason: a flash of the sun on her face, the smell of pavement baking in the heat, Ethan's laugh as she stalled the car once again. It had been in the school parking lot on a weekend in spring. The garden in front of the school had just been planted. She could still smell the flowers. Flowers, like a funeral. Chris's funeral. And just as quickly as it came, the memory left and she felt so hollow. She thought it had been a happy memory. She'd been with Ethan, she'd learned how to drive stick, they'd been so wild and free. All that, for this. Clinical, unemotional police photos of the result of a wreck. Shambles.

Spencer knew it was coming, she could feel it. Each photo moved her closer and closer to evidence of Chris's mortality, captured on flimsy photo paper. Her whole body went cold when she saw the distinct tuft of auburn hair. That was all she needed to see.

*Oh God.*

Ripley, sensing her mood, planted her body against Spencer's legs.

Spencer's vision darkened on the edges, and she reeled. The world was tipping underneath her. She tried to remember how to breathe, but she choked. She willed herself to move on to the next photo, and a limp and bloody hand greeted her. It was too much.

Spencer dropped the photos and dashed to the bathroom. She barely lifted the toilet lid in time before she puked deep into the bowl, her whole body purging what she'd just seen the only way it knew how. Her eyes watered as she gagged, her stomach twisting with each heave.

Ripley barked outside the door.

She regretted seeing the photos, but she knew she had to. It was the only way she could remember. And now it felt like it had been a fool's errand. It didn't unlock some deep memory or give her the final clue she'd been missing. Instead, she saw something she couldn't unsee. For what? What did she hope to prove?

She clenched the cool porcelain edges of the toilet bowl and heaved, but nothing else came up. All she was able to do was kneel down, wipe her mouth, and rest her forehead against her arm.

If she had any hope of facing what happened that night, she needed to be able to see those photos like a detective would. She needed to see the scene for what it was, rather than how it felt, removing the emotion from the situation. It was easier said than done, to divide a part of herself from that night, but she had to try. For herself. For Ethan. For Chris. Didn't they deserve closure, too?

She needed to prove she wasn't crazy, that she wasn't looking at the evidence and stirring the pot for nothing. If she didn't believe in herself, no one would.

She pulled herself up to her feet, rinsed out her mouth, and spit the acrid remnants of her lunch down the drain. The girl that stared back at her in the mirror was almost a stranger. The scar on her face was still healing, still pink, though the stitches had been removed long ago. Her skin looked dull, her hair flat, her eyes sunken. She splashed water on her face, the coolness shocking some nerve into her spirit, and took another breath.

What had happened, happened. Chris was dead. Looking into the case wouldn't change that. The photos didn't change that. That thought didn't make it feel any more real, but it did invite a new feeling of determination that swelled in her chest. Olivia could stay mad at her for it, for all she cared.

But she had to know what she couldn't remember. She couldn't let it go. She was going to do this. She needed to do this.

# THIRTY-FIVE

**SATURDAY NIGHT, SPENCER AND OLIVIA** closed up the kiosk. The air between them was as cold as the ice cream they served.

Spencer wiped down the plexiglass divider as Olivia picked the music to zone out by. It was a soft, bedroom pop playlist that she'd been obsessed with lately, making it easier to get into a cleaning rhythm. They had just had a huge rush of customers after a nearby baseball game had started at the sports complex, the whole time spending it without speaking to each other unless they needed to.

Every inch of Spencer was sticky. Her fingers were like glue, a result from seemingly the millionth chocolate shell cone she'd served up, having to fight the urge to lick her fingers clean. It was hard work, but it helped her focus on something that wasn't her crumbling life.

She was sad about the fight with Olivia, and not only that, but everything that had been happening lately bore down on top of her, like a mountain of weights pressing on her chest, squeezing the air from her lungs with each breath she tried to take. The podcast, the shadow person in her yard, the unending mountain of homework that awaited her at the end of every day. And she wasn't able to talk to anyone about it since it felt like it was all her own doing.

Her pain was particularly bad, too. Even though the cuts on her face had all healed, the reminder of the stitches in her cheek formed a faded stripe of darkening skin that she was sure would never go away, and the pain in the rest of her body never seemed to fade. She'd wake up in the night, feeling like she'd been trampled by a stampede and need to take another dose of Vicodin just to be able to fall back asleep, which would be lucky for her if she wasn't stuck staring up at the glowing stars on her ceiling, thinking about everything that was happening with Ethan and Jackson, and feeling like she was going to puke. Then she'd have to properly get out of bed and get ready for school to start the day all over again.

She knew she looked miserable; she hardly recognized the face she saw in the mirror every morning. These days in particular, she almost jumped out of her skin when she caught her reflection.

Olivia and Spencer finished up the closing down routine and locked the kiosk on the way out.

Spencer kept her bike locked up at the bike racks, as usual, by the baseball diamond. Olivia's voice made her turn around.

"You sure you don't want a ride?" she asked softly. It was the most she'd said to Spencer all day.

Even though they were fighting, it was sweet that she

still offered, but Spencer shook her head. "Thanks, but . . ." She couldn't finish the thought.

Olivia bobbed her head but said nothing else. Spencer ached for things to be better between them, and it was all Spencer's fault.

They parted ways, and Spencer and Ripley walked along the sidewalk looping around the parking lot. Spencer wished she could get Olivia to understand. It was harder and harder to remember things lately. No matter what she wrote in her bullet journal, some things slipped through the cracks. But it was still her fault. What kind of friend was she?

The bike rack, situated underneath the streetlamp, was in clear view of the street. Being a girl, naturally Spencer kept her wits about her when walking anywhere alone at night, especially near a parking lot. Now with the thoughts of some creepy Peeping Tom watching her from the shadows of her own backyard, she was extra aware of her surroundings. But Ripley didn't seem to be perturbed, and no one was lurking in the parking lot as far as she could tell. A baseball game was going on nearby, which also put Spencer at ease a little bit, listening to the crack of the bat and the cheer of the crowd in the stands.

She got her bike lock key from her backpack and put her helmet on and got to work unlocking her bike from the rack. Behind her, a car pulled up to the curb, its headlights blinding her a little bit, and she turned her back to it to see her bike lock better. Black dots from the light lingered in her vision for a second, but she got her bike unlocked and readied herself to go. She didn't think anything of the car whose headlights were blaring behind her, throwing her shadow in a long stripe across the pavement. When she turned to look at it, wondering if it was Olivia making sure she was okay, she couldn't get a good look at the car at all. It could have been black or red, it was hard to tell in the dark. The engine idled, its purr a low rumble. A lone person sat in the driver's side, indistinguishable in the dark. Maybe they were waiting for someone at the baseball game, ready to pick them up, so Spencer didn't worry too much.

Calculating, but still ever cautious, Spencer wheeled her bike off the sidewalk, Ripley taking a moment to scratch herself before trotting to Spencer's side.

*Always be aware of what's around you,* her mother would often warn. *You never want to be unprepared. Make a scene if you have to, apologize later.*

She couldn't explain how she knew it, she just felt it, an intuition that was as mysterious as it was real, a warning prickling on the back of her neck to tell her that someone was watching her. She wanted to think that she was just being paranoid, already jumpy and looking for killers wherever she went, but she couldn't shake the twist in her gut telling her that something was off.

She glanced at the baseball field, flooded in bright lights, and wondered if she should go there, where there could be more witnesses, or even help if she needed it. But would she be overreacting?

The logical, rational side of her brain told her that she was being silly, start riding, and she would see soon enough that she was just being paranoid. So she did just that. She took a breath and left the parking lot, Ripley jogging happily nearby. But the car followed.

The headlights washed over her as it turned, inching behind her down the street, getting closer.

She tried to tamp down the panic that was bubbling up in her throat. If this was Olivia, playing some sick joke on her, or to get back at her for missing her birthday, Spencer was going to lose it.

The car engine revved behind her. Cold fear gripped her.

*Please go around. Please go around,* she thought.

The car felt like it was right on her back wheel. The engine was so close, and she could almost feel the heat radiating off it.

Instincts that she had been so determined to ignore were practically screaming at her. Her whole body was tight. She tightened her grip on the handlebars.

Then she took off.

The car wheels screeched after her, accelerating.

She stood up on her bike, pedaling as hard as she could as she took a turn down the street. Ripley kept up, galloping in stride, and still the car was right on her.

She didn't have time to think about how she should have stayed at the field, maybe waited for her mom or taken that ride with Olivia. She just had to get out of there fast. Her heart pounded, her breathing hard. She pushed herself fast, but the car, of course, was faster.

It was so close, the headlights were so bright, but she kept going. She couldn't stop. If she did, she'd meet the hood of the car in an instant. The engine was screaming at her, drowning out all other noise. Her legs burned with the effort, but fear had taken over.

*Help, please help me! Anyone!*

Something told her to jump, and she did. The instant she flung herself off her bike and into the bushes, the car clipped her bike with a horrible crunch, and took off down the street, its red taillights disappearing as it sped away.

For a moment, all Spencer could hear was the hollow pulse of her heartbeat raging in her ears and the dull echo of Ripley's barks as she lay in the bushes, the branches painfully stabbing her in every part of her body. But she was safe.

The pain was immediate and constant, but Spencer pulled herself out of the bushes. Ripley was barking furiously at the car, unhurt but frightened, and then she immediately went to Spencer's side. It took a moment for reality to set in.

Spencer had almost been run over, narrowly avoiding a direct hit.

Someone was trying to kill her.

# THIRTY-SIX

**SPENCER CAME HOME TO FIND** Mom and Hope on the couch, curled up watching an old rerun of *Murder, She Wrote*, a fitting and somewhat ironic thing, given Spencer's current circumstance. Spencer could hear Dad in the shower. She was still dazed, not quite sure what had just happened.

Mom leapt to her feet when she laid eyes on Spencer. "What happened to you?"

Spencer inspected herself. The scrapes and bruises on her knees and elbows were clear in the light of the house now, and her mom rushed to her, fussing.

She pulled a leaf from Spencer's hair. "What is this? Are you hurt?"

"I'm fine, Mom. Really." The bike, not so much. To avoid any more cars, Spencer had cut through a few alleys (in hindsight, not the wisest decision, either) and climbed over a few neighbors' fences so as to stay out of sight of whoever had tried to run her down.

But she told her mom everything, and without hesitation, her mother immediately rushed to the couch and grabbed her phone. Hope sat by, looking at Spencer with shock.

"What are you doing?" Spencer asked.

"Calling the police."

Spencer groaned. "Mom, don't."

"Why not? Someone needs to look into this." She held up the phone to her ear. Spencer could hear the line ringing on the other end. It was already so late, she didn't expect that too many officers would be available to take a call to the non-emergency line.

"Seriously, it was probably just a drunk driver." Spencer doubted her own words, but her mom didn't need to know. It felt like an attack.

"That's worse, Spencer. They could hurt someone else. This town has enough drunk drivers as it is . . ." She probably hadn't meant to say it, but her eyes widened when she realized that Spencer was putting two and two together. Ethan. Of course, Ethan. "I didn't mean . . ." But it was too late.

"It's not worth it," Spencer said. "I'm fine. Ripley's fine. I just want to go to bed."

"Are you hurt? Do you need to go to the hospital?"

The last place Spencer wanted to be was inside another car, and she shook her head.

Mom wasn't through with the interrogation. "Well, did you see who did it? The car?"

"I didn't get a good enough look, just the taillights as it sped off. It'd be impossible to find them."

The lines around her mom's mouth deepened as she frowned. She wrapped Spencer in a tight hug, which made

Spencer wince in pain, but she didn't pull away. Finally, someone on the other end of the phone picked up.

Mom stepped away. "Yes, hi, hello," she said. "I'd like to speak to a Detective Potentas—Yes, I understand he'd be at home, can you leave him a message? It's about my daughter, Spencer Sandoval."

Spencer didn't hear the rest. She went to her room and called the person she wanted to see most right now.

"Wait, wait, back up. You almost got run over? Are you okay?" Jackson's voice was nearly drowned out by the sound of one of his younger brothers playing some kind of shooting video game and yelling taunts at the other team. Jackson moved away from the ruckus and closed a door, probably to his room. It was quieter now, and she heard the squeak of a mattress as he sat down.

"I'm fine," she said, nodding, assuring herself. "Can I send you a picture?"

"Is it a photo of the driver?"

"No." Spencer flipped open to a blank page of her bullet journal and started sketching. "I didn't get a good look at the car, or who was driving, but I did get a look at the taillights. Do you recognize this shape?" She took a photo with her phone and sent it, waiting a moment for Jackson to see it.

She wasn't an artist, but she was able to sketch the general outline of the long, rectangular-shaped taillight, broken up by what looked like a series of lines like a cage.

But Jackson sighed. "Sorry, I don't. I'm not really a car guy. But I know someone who is."

Ethan did not look happy to see them. "What are you two doing here? It's almost midnight." He glanced at his watch.

"We just had to ask you a question, it'll be really quick, I promise," Spencer said. She'd slipped out of the house, forgoing her bike until she could get it fixed, and ran to meet Jackson in front of Ethan's house right then.

"If this is about . . . God, Spence, please, just go home. You too, Jax. You shouldn't be here." He moved to close the door, but Spencer kicked out her foot and it jammed on her sneaker. Ethan looked shocked, but he didn't try to push her away.

"I just need your expertise, please. It's one question."

Ethan sighed, his lips pressed together. Then he glanced at Jackson.

"Please, man," Jackson said. Whether he meant to or not, Jackson flashed the best puppy-dog eyes in the world, and Ethan's shoulders dropped, relenting.

"Fine, what."

Spencer handed him the paper with her drawing on it. "Do you know what kind of car would have this taillight?"

Ethan scrubbed his chin thoughtfully, then said, "That's an old-school Dodge Charger. Probably R/T 440. I'm guessing from 1968 or so. That kind of car is super hard to find, you've got to restore it. I don't know anyone who has one. What's all this about?"

Spencer's heart pounded. "You're sure? You're positive that this is a Charger?"

"Well yeah, they have a really distinctive rear light."

"They couldn't be confused with any other type?" Jackson asked.

"No, like I said, they're pretty unique. Why are you asking me this?"

Spencer looked at Jackson, her eyes bright, his too. It was their first real break.

But Jackson's phone rang in his pocket, and he answered it, stepping away. "Hey, Mikey. What's up?" Spencer could hear one of his younger brothers' voices on the other end. "Yeah," Jackson said. "I'll be back in a few minutes." He hung up and looked at both Ethan and Spencer. "I left my brothers at home, and I shouldn't leave them alone too much longer or they'll set up a booby trap for the Wet Bandits. I need to go."

"I'll explain everything," Spencer said.

Jackson tapped his phone in his palm. He clearly looked like he wanted to stay, but other responsibilities were pulling him back. "You'll tell me if you figure anything else out?"

"Absolutely."

"What is going on?" Ethan asked as Jackson waved and crossed the lawn to his car parked in the driveway.

Spencer let Ripley walk first into Ethan's house and she followed after. He didn't argue. There was no sign of his dad or his stepmom, but Spencer didn't care if anyone overheard. She wasn't planning on staying long anyway. She took a seat on the couch in the living room, overcome with exhaustion. "Someone tried to run me off the road. I didn't see the car except the taillights."

Ethan looked horrified. "What? Oh my God, are you okay?"

"I wouldn't be here right now if I wasn't. Do you know anyone who drives that car?"

Ethan put his hand on the top of his head, in shock. "No. Why would someone do that?"

"I think whoever it is, is trying to scare me."

"Why?"

"Because I'm looking into what happened, finding the truth, about the crash."

Ethan groaned and threw his head back. "Why am I not surprised."

"I need to know, Ethan!"

"I told you what happened!"

"But . . ."

"And now you're almost run over by some lunatic. What if they don't miss next time?"

Spencer clamped her mouth shut and glared at him. Being angry with him was easy, but she had more pressing things to worry about. "I found wire cutters at the party. I think the brakes on the Targa were cut."

Ethan actually laughed. "That would explain a lot."

"Do you know of anyone who might want to do that? Maybe your stalker?"

"She's not involved in this."

"How do you know?"

"I just know, okay? She's getting help. She wouldn't do that."

Based on the firmness in his voice, she knew he was telling the truth. She didn't have the full picture, but Ethan did, and he seemed convinced enough. She took a breath. "Fine. I just can't help feeling like I'm so close to figuring it all out. I got a threatening letter in my locker, and someone's been lurking outside my house—"

"Fuck, Spencer!"

"You can see why I'm a little freaked out! The police don't believe me, so Jackson's been helping me figure out what made you crash. I think whoever is behind this is afraid of the truth coming out."

Ethan sighed and took a seat on the floor across from her, his elbows on his knees. He looked wary, not from lack of sleep, but a deeper kind of tired that made him look older somehow. "Do you believe me?" she asked softly.

"I *believe* you and Jackson make a good pair. You two seem to be getting cozy with each other," Ethan said, smirking.

Spencer huffed. "You've been listening to too much of the *Get Salty* podcast."

Ethan put his hand to his chest mockingly. "You wound me." But then he smiled, and her heart fluttered with excitement. She hated how his smile still had that effect on her.

Ethan's smile fell and he looked at her, concern furrowing his brow. "Come on, Spence. None of this is worth it. Leave it alone."

"You know I can't."

"I'm begging you," Ethan said, eyes shining. "Please. If not for me, then for Jackson."

"Why?"

Ethan paused before answering. "What if that nut job tries to go after him next?"

Spencer's stomach dropped. She hadn't thought about that. The whole time, she'd been so selfish, caught up in her own world.

Ethan continued. "Come on, if someone is trying to hurt you because of me, wouldn't they go after him, too? And if they succeed . . . I won't be able to live with myself."

A chill raked down her spine. *If they succeed . . .* She shook her head. "I've come too far to give up now."

Ethan pressed his lips together and sighed. "I knew you'd say that. I figured I might as well try."

Guilt wrapped a cold hand around her stomach. If Ethan was right and whoever was trying to intimidate her tried to hurt Jackson, she'd feel responsible. Her crusade for truth could get other people hurt and it'd be all her fault. She looked at Ripley, who looked back at her, eyebrows raised expectantly. After a beat, she took a steadying breath and looked at Ethan. She couldn't let whoever was behind this win.

"What does your lawyer say? About the verdict? What are your chances?"

"Because I wasn't driving under the influence, it's harder to prove 'wanton disregard for life,' especially in a blind intersection like that. Even if I was speeding, there's still a chance it wasn't my fault. So the onus is on the prosecution to prove my character. That I'm the type of guy who would do this, who would willingly speed without thinking about the consequences."

Spencer nodded. "And . . . ?"

"He thinks my chances are fifty-fifty."

"I'm sorry, Ethan."

"Yeah," he said, resigned. "I'm sorry, too."

# THIRTY-SEVEN

**"I KNOW WHAT I SIGNED** up for," Jackson said the next morning. Spencer had told him everything that she talked about with Ethan as they walked together toward the police station, Ripley panting happily at her side. "I can't give up on him. Or you."

"You're not afraid?"

"Oh, I'm terrified. But it's too important to me now to see this through."

She was glad he was as stubborn as she was, but a prickling sensation of worry creeped along the back of her neck. She hoped she wasn't dragging him into a mess that was quickly growing out of control. Having him with her as they walked inside the station was like a lifeline at sea, and she was grateful he had been with her throughout everything so far. She didn't want to lose him, too.

Detective Potentas didn't try to hide the groan that came out of his mouth when he saw them come in.

There wasn't any time to call him out for it. She needed to speak, or else she felt like she was going to explode. She could barely sleep the night before and couldn't wait to show him what she'd found. "Detective, I have something you might want to look at—"

"Not another piece of garbage . . ." He tried to move around them, carrying his mug of coffee for a refill, but Spencer and Jackson followed. It looked like he'd been there all night, or he'd never gone home.

"It's not! I almost got hit by a car last night—"

"Yes, I got your mother's message."

"Then you know I've been targeted by some maniac on the road. The car they're driving is a Dodge Charger from 1968. We need to be on the lookout for anyone who has one, who might know Ethan and would have a reason to want to hurt him."

Potentas rolled his eyes. "This is a separate, unrelated incident. Please file your report to the receptionist and we'll get right on it."

"Yeah, right," Jackson said, rolling his eyes.

Potentas shot him a look, then to her he said, "Miss Sandoval, I have tried being polite, tried being open-minded, but I'm at my wit's end. I can't help you anymore. I just can't. I have more cases that I need to worry about, and this isn't something I can help you with."

"She's being threatened, Detective," Jackson said.

"By whom? Exactly? A mysterious stalker? I've been in my line of work for fifteen years, and I've never had one single case with circumstances as outlandish as yours. For all I know, you could have written this so-called letter yourself, seeking some sort of attention."

"You don't believe her?" Jackson asked. Anger coated his voice.

"Frankly, Mr. Chen, I've got too much of a caseload. I'm not in the business of humoring a couple of teenagers looking to play Scooby Doo."

Spencer was desperate. "Someone tried to run me over, Detective! Don't you care if they're actually successful next time?"

Potentas sighed. "I wish I could tell you what you want to hear. But I'm sorry. Don't come back here."

Jackson and Spencer sat on the steps of school, the first bell having long since rung. The lawn was empty, everyone already having gone to class. After the police station, neither Jackson nor Spencer felt like sitting in the library for an hour. Ripley dozed on the grass, her ears twitching now and again, as if she was lost in some dream.

Spencer hugged her knees to her chest, feeling the need to hold herself for fear that she might crumble to pieces otherwise. It was over. Detective Potentas was not going to do anything.

"Why won't they listen?" Spencer asked. "I did everything. I gave them more evidence, more things to consider, and they look at me like I'm wasting my breath."

Jackson let out a small laugh.

"What's so funny?"

"Nothing you said, it's just . . . I used to want to be a police officer when I was little. I used to believe that the world could be just, that the good guys would always catch the bad guys. Like in the movies. But after everything with my dad, with Ethan, now you go to them asking for help and . . . Is this what growing up feels like?"

Spencer rested her cheek on her arm, watching him as he spoke. He was looking toward the horizon, the morning softening his face with warm colors despite the sadness in his eyes.

Spencer hesitated, but thought it was only polite to reciprocate. He had offered a shoulder for her to lean on; the least she could do was offer the same. "Do you want to talk about it?"

Jackson shrugged, but he didn't get angry at her or defensive when she asked. "What else is there to say? With my dad, I . . . I looked up to him for my whole life, and then like that, it was gone. Like it was nothing. Something like that changes you, especially when you're a kid. There was me before, and then there's me after. And no matter how much the world changes around me, I don't want it to change me where it counts."

She'd felt the exact same way about the accident. They didn't talk again for a long beat. Spencer wished she had taken the time to get to know Jackson earlier. She couldn't do anything like this with Ethan, something as boring as sitting on the steps at school and talking. There always had to be movement, action with Ethan, never a moment to breathe. But with Jackson, time slowed to a comfortable pace, a pace that Spencer could feel the edges of and hold on to.

Jackson snapped her out of her thought spiral when he asked, "What about you? What did you want to be when you grew up?"

"An astronaut," she said. "Always have. I want to be the first person to land on Mars."

"And come back to Earth after that, I hope!" Jackson said with a laugh.

"How else would I get all that fame and fortune I so desperately desire?" Spencer said dryly with a wave of her hand, which made Jackson laugh harder. She smiled too, basking in her ability to cheer Jackson up even just a little. "Don't tell anybody, but I actually wanted to be an astronaut *princess* when I was little. What will NASA think?" Jackson snorted and nudged her with his elbow. Spencer let the good air hang for a moment before continuing. "All my life I've been working toward my dreams; then this one thing happened and it put everything into perspective. I don't want anything else to get in my way."

"You'll make it."

Jackson was looking at her now, with a level gaze and a proud smile. He said it so assuredly, it almost took her aback.

"That's one thing I'm sure of in this world now," he said. "Once you've set your mind on something, God help us, Spencer—you're unstoppable."

Spencer smiled and her cheeks felt hot. They'd been doing that an awful lot lately whenever Jackson was around.

He rubbed his thighs nervously, smoothing out invisible

lines in his slacks, and cleared his throat. "Sorry, I'm just grateful for everything you've done so far. Without you, I might never have done nearly as much to help Ethan. I don't think I've ever properly thanked you for it, either. So thank you."

"So much good it's done for him now, though."

"Maybe there's something we missed. We can keep trying."

Spencer wanted to believe him, and the way he was looking at her made it easier. "I wish we'd gotten to know each other at school before this whole thing."

Jackson's voice was soft. "Yeah, same. But to be honest, I've always liked you, Spencer. I've had a crush on you forever."

Spencer blinked, surprised. "Really?"

Jackson nodded. "Ethan beat me to it. He's always faster than me. Faster to act, faster to do things that might scare me, faster to go for what he wants. I always felt guilty, though, for liking you. It felt wrong after he asked you out. But I couldn't help it."

"Jackson, I . . ." The words felt full in her mouth.

The blush was bright on his cheeks. "You don't have to say anything. I've been waiting to tell you for a long time, so . . . now you know."

"Yeah, the thing is, I . . . I feel the same way."

Jackson's eyes were round behind his glasses, his lips slightly parted in shock.

She liked Jackson. She couldn't deny it now. She really *liked* him. She liked the way he worried his fingers over his lower lip when he was deep in study, she liked the way his nose crinkled when he laughed, she liked that he cared about her and propped her up, helping her take one step forward, together. She had thought she had her whole life mapped out, and still it found ways of surprising her. Jackson was helping her in so many different ways.

Her heart galloped wildly in her chest as she leaned toward him, and he leaned toward her. She felt like she could fly. They were close enough now that Spencer noticed a small scar below his right eyebrow, more pronounced now that his eyes were closed.

All she had to do was close the gap; their lips were already a hair's breadth away. She could feel his breath on her skin, tickling the small hairs on her cheeks. His lips looked so soft. All she yearned for was to close her eyes and lose herself in his touch. She'd never felt like this about anyone before, including Ethan. She wanted to kiss him more than anything.

But something held her back. It tugged at the back of her thoughts, and she pushed against it, but deep down, she understood. She couldn't do this yet.

"Jackson . . . ," she whispered. It was like a magic spell had been lifted.

Jackson pulled back and smiled softly. He knew it wasn't right, too.

Spencer touched her fingers to her lips and took a breath. Her heart felt so heavy. She was holding herself back because of Ethan, again.

Jackson ran his hands through his hair bashfully. "I'm so sorry. I—"

They talked over each other. "I wish we could but . . ."

"I'm Ethan's best friend. I can't do this to him. What am I doing?"

"It's not that. Ethan and I are so over, but I need more time. I want to kiss you. I don't think you know how much I do."

"Really?"

"Yeah," she said, smiling. "Really. I need some time to . . . heal? It sounds dumb but—"

"No, I totally get it. No pressure."

Jackson's expression softened. When he looked at her, she felt real. His smile melted her heart, but she could feel the distance spanning between them growing further. She wanted to move on from Ethan, but everywhere she looked, all she could think about was him. In a way, she hated Ethan for that. She couldn't move on because of what he'd done. It had affected all three of them so deeply; Spencer needed even more time to shake off the debris so she wouldn't get hurt again.

Jackson looked over his shoulder to the empty hallway. "We should get going. Second period will start soon."

# THIRTY-EIGHT

**THE DAYS PASSED, AND THEIR** investigation into the crash had come to a screeching halt. They had nothing else to work with, now that the police had shut the door on both of them. Ethan's case was drawing to an inevitable end, and it was only a matter of time before his fate was sealed. They were running out of options, but there was no place left to turn to. They had run out of leads.

That morning, Spencer was at her locker, gathering her books while Ripley sat at attention behind her, and she thought about everything that had happened. Olivia still wasn't speaking to Spencer. She avoided her at every turn, never being at her locker when Spencer was there, and it made most mornings lonely. Her absence was an ever-present ache.

Everyone else at Armstrong went about their morning, laughing and chatting, like it was any other day, but Spencer felt like she had blinders on, only able to focus on the task in front of her. Her world had narrowed to a singular point, and guilt pressed at her from all sides. She wished she had all the answers, that she could fix everything, but she couldn't, and it felt awful.

With a sigh, she closed her locker and moved toward the library to meet Jackson as usual, but instead, she saw Jackson coming toward her, looking like he'd swallowed something nasty, his skin waxy and pale. He gave her one look, and she knew. Something was wrong.

"Are you okay?" she asked.

He nodded stiffly. It was obvious he was lying.

"Jackson."

Whatever it was, he didn't want to say it aloud. He reached into his pocket and pulled out a folded piece of paper and handed it to her. It was in the same handwriting as the note that had been shoved into her locker.

*Stop playing Watson*

*Or Spencer Sandoval will pay*

"It was on my porch this morning," he said, his voice thick.

Spencer felt like she'd been punched in the head; her ears were ringing. Ripley pressed herself up against Spencer's thigh, worried she might fall over. Ethan had been right.

Spencer grabbed Jackson by the hand and walked him down the hall. "Let's get out of here," she said.

Jackson looked small, his shoulders hunched, as he picked at the grass underneath his crossed legs. Spencer and Ripley sat next to him.

"They must be listening to the *Get Salty* podcast," he said. "How else would they know I'm helping you with Ethan's case?"

She didn't want to spiral down that rabbit hole. It felt like she was standing on the edge of a bottomless pit and Jackson was right there with her.

But the person who wrote that note knew where Jackson lived, and Spencer worried about his younger brothers, and his mom. What if they got caught up in the crossfire?

Spencer held Jackson's hand, finding his skin dry but smooth. His fingers wrapped around hers and a shine in his eyes broke her heart. His shoulders dropped and he hung his head low, but he didn't let go of her hand.

With a sigh, she said, "You need to take a break from this case."

His head snapped up. "What? Spencer, no."

"If you respect me at all, you'll take a step back. It's not worth it for you anymore. There's too much at stake."

"Spencer, I—" He saw the hardness in her eyes, and he clammed up. "Come on, we're a team."

"Ethan was right. I dragged you into this. It's my fault."

"You didn't drag me into anything."

"Okay, then I'm dragging you out."

"Spencer . . ."

"Please. Just for a little while."

Asking this of him looked like she was asking him to saw off his own arm. "I can't let you do this alone."

"I'll be okay." She hated the idea that whoever was writing these notes was getting exactly what they wanted. She was afraid, not only for herself, but now for Jackson, and the threats were working. "I'll be fine."

"Will you?" He looked at her, and she wished he hadn't. But he knew she was too stubborn to admit how she was feeling. She needed to be strong, for his sake.

He let go of her hand and stood. Ripley raised her head, watching him go. She let out a small whine, confused and sad that he was leaving without saying goodbye.

Spencer wanted to call out to him, tell him something that would make everything better, but she didn't. She should have known that it would get messy. Regret made her queasy.

Her phone buzzed in her blazer pocket and, for a hopeful split second, she thought it was a text from Jackson, but her heart lurched when she realized it wasn't a text, but a new email alert.

It was from the Admissions office at Caltech.

She opened her inbox with trembling hands and clicked on the email. She managed to read the first sentence, and then read it again, to make sure she had understood it correctly. Her body went cold the third time she read it. Ripley watched her patiently, sensing something was up.

"I didn't get in," Spencer said. "Look, Rip—it says—'we regret to inform you that we cannot offer you admission at this time.'" She dropped her phone into her lap and held her head in her hands. Ripley nudged her nose under Spencer's armpit, but Spencer refused to budge.

Spencer wanted to put on a brave face, but the well of tears shining in her eyes gave her away. Her voice cracked. "I didn't get into Caltech." She could barely say it, it felt like fiction. "I didn't get in . . ." She held her breath, trying to keep it all down deep, the sob burning hot behind her sternum.

This was her worst nightmare.

She'd been so optimistic and determined, all the essays and interviews, and all those extracurriculars, all that work to get on the lauded Headmaster's List.

And they said no.

She held in the tears so furiously, they burned like fire in her eyes. She didn't want to look any more pathetic than she already felt, didn't want to show how much it hurt.

Spencer heard the door to her bedroom creak open. From the sound of the floorboards, and on account of the fact that Hope usually barreled into her room like a bull charging a red cape, Spencer knew it was her mom. Hope must have told them when they got home what had happened, otherwise Mom wouldn't be walking in like she was there to defuse a bomb.

Spencer had been crying furiously into her pillow for hours, the kinds of sobs that racked her whole body, painfully seizing every muscle with each breath. Ripley had tried lying on top of her, but Spencer still wouldn't stop. Everything was terrible. Nothing was happening the way it was supposed to. Her life was in shambles, and it only now felt real. First field hockey, then Olivia, now college. Hadn't she worked hard enough? Hadn't she done everything everyone had told her to do to be successful? Wasn't this part of the deal: get good grades, get into a good school, start the future out on the right foot?

She felt so stupid for getting her hopes up about getting into Caltech. Of course, even though she had done everything she was supposed to do, it still wasn't enough.

The mattress depressed beside her and her mom lay down next to her, pulling up the comforter around them both. Ripley's hot breath remained on Spencer's back.

"It's okay to cry," her mom said softly. Giving her permission to cry only made it feel like she was a complete loser, which made Spencer cry harder. She went on like that for a long time, until finally there was nothing left, and exhaustion replaced the hollow hole in her chest. Mom let Spencer cry for a long time, until Spencer was sure she'd run out of tears, and it only came out in dry heaves. What had she done wrong? Was she not smart enough? Had she not joined enough clubs? Had she not participated in the right after-school activities? Did she not commit hard enough on the field? Wasn't being at the top of the Headmaster's List worth anything? Why wasn't she good enough?

Her pillow was damp with snot and tears, but she didn't care. All she wanted was to wallow in self-pity and defeat. Her entire future had felt so real and full, like she could hold it in her hands, but in an instant, it crumbled to dust between her fingers and no matter how hard she scrambled to keep hold of it, it blew away into the wind.

"It's not your fault," her mom said, rubbing soothing circles on her back with her palm. "It's not your fault."

Spencer rolled over; her face felt puffy and hot. Ripley

readjusted and hopped down to the floor. The spot where she'd once been felt cold. "You say that, but it is! I'm a failure!"

Her mom shushed her. "That's not true. One rejection doesn't make you a failure."

"Yes, it does!"

"Spencer Rose Sandoval, you stop it right now. You're being too hard on yourself."

"I don't know what else I'm supposed to do!"

"That school puts so much pressure on you kids, honestly . . . Always a competition. The Headmaster's List isn't everything, sweetheart. These parents in LA just think it is."

"I'm never going to be hired by NASA. Who would want me?"

Her mom didn't say anything, just let her cry it out some more. There was no use trying to reason with her. All her pain and regret bubbled up her throat like bile, and the best way to get rid of it was for Spencer to purge. She cried into her pillow a little more before it slipped into silent hiccups.

She must have dozed off, because the next thing she knew, her bed was empty except for Ripley snoring at her feet. Her mom had left some time ago. A plate of home-made fish tacos was waiting for her on her desk, already cold, and she scarfed them down, staring out the darkened window to the street below. Making the Headmaster's List had been a huge waste of time. What was the point any-more? All of it, for nothing.

All she had left was Ethan's case.

\* \* \*

If not for Jackson's text, she might have remained in bed forever. Her phone buzzed, reeling her brain out of a slog of Vicodin-induced haze. She'd stayed up most of the night, feeling sorry for herself and pouring over Ethan's case, reviewing the photos from the crash until she felt like she had gone cross-eyed, before the painkillers started to make her sleepy.

She fumbled on her nightstand for her phone. It was a text from Jackson. Her heart fluttered a little just seeing his name.

*Jackson: Thanks for doing all you could.*

Spencer sat up to reply, her whole body electrified. *What happened?*

**_Get Salty_: A True Crime Podcast with Peyton Salt**

*[Intro Music]*

**Peyton Salt:** Before we get into our main story, we've got an update on the Ethan Amoroso trial, Salters. You're going to want to find some place to park, because I know you listeners love to tune in on your commute, and if you're not driving, you're going to want to pop open a bottle of champagne!

Drumroll, please!

On the counts of aggravated reckless driving, child endangerment, and felony manslaughter, Ethan Amoroso has been found . . . Guilty!

*[marching band celebratory music playing]*

It's been a wild ride, for sure. I have to say, I'm surprised it unfolded the way it did. Usually, people of Ethan's pedigree get a slight slap on the wrist. Maybe from now on we'll be seeing more kids like him get their comeuppance. It only took the court two hours to come to a consensus, and boy, oh, boy, are we glad that they did. Just in time for the holidays!

Obviously our thoughts are with the Moore family, and me and everyone here in the studio hope they feel a sense of justice now that Ethan Amoroso will be facing his punishment. So far, the Moore family fund is over one hundred thousand dollars, thanks to our generous community. There's still some time to buy our merch. All proceeds go toward the Moore family fund, so get yours now before they sell out! And now, a word from our sponsors.

# THIRTY-NINE

**IT WAS OVER.**

All over.

With Jackson gone, Spencer felt like a part of her was missing. He had been a fixture at her side, looking into this case with her, getting deeper into the weeds together. Not having him there to talk things through hurt more than she had realized.

She didn't blame him for his decision. She blamed everyone else for pushing them to their limits.

Detective Potentas, Peyton Salt, even Dr. Diamond for putting so much pressure on them as the best students in school. They all ignored Spencer, made her feel crazy and alone, and maybe, with Jackson now taking a step away from the case, she really was.

Maybe she had truly lost it.

Like most nights, she spent it in her room, looking through every conceivable source of information because it might be the one thing she'd been missing this whole time, and if she could only find it, maybe then she could rest.

But Ethan's case was over. It was all for nothing.

She lost track of how many pills she'd taken during the last few days. It felt like she was taking more and more, just to get by without feeling like her skin was melting off from the pain. She popped one after another, because her whole body ached, probably because she was hunched in her desk chair, her posture turning into an old crone's hunch as she stooped over her laptop, scrolling, scrolling, scrolling. Definitely not taking too many. Definitely not.

She barely focused on her appearance anymore. Usually at school, she'd have her hair up in braids, but these days all she could manage was running her fingers through the tangles and letting her waves hang loose over her shoulders. She didn't even bother with makeup anymore. What was the point? Everyone saw what they wanted to see anyway. She was unraveling at the seams; once having been the chewed-up doll stitched back together, her stuffing was now coming out.

Perfect little Spencer, perfect little mess.

Ripley whined at the door, needing to go out, but Spencer didn't hear her. She'd rung the bell a few times already. Spencer's mind was elsewhere, blankly staring at the screen.

She also didn't hear it when her dad came in, saying her name a few times until he put his hand on her shoulder, making her jump.

"Hey, Ripley needs you," he said.

"Just one more minute," Spencer said, returning to stare at the screen.

"Spencer . . . she needs to go outside. She's your responsibility."

"I said one more minute! God!"

He stood up straighter, shocked at her outburst, but Spencer didn't notice. She was too honed in on the words on the page, even after they'd turned into a blur and she couldn't read them anymore; her focus slipped and she stared at nothing. The search for Ethan's appeal was getting farther away. It barely registered that she didn't sound like herself anymore. Without saying a word, her dad opened the back door for Ripley to go out into the backyard.

Jackson, Olivia, Ripley . . . Background noise. Spencer was on her own. One more pill. Just one more. She didn't want it, but she needed it. Just to get through the day. One more.

Weeks passed in a blur of monotony.

Homework piled up on her desk, forgotten. Messy mountains of trash overflowed on her desk, dirty plates and crumpled-up napkins. Bedsheets kicked to the foot of her bed. Spencer's room had become a sty.

All she could manage to do was sleep. Wake up in the night, crying. Ripley on her chest. Wake up. School. Start over. Numb.

Ethan's case was over.

She'd failed.

In class, Jackson and Olivia noticed how distant she seemed, retreated into herself, consumed whole by echoes of the past, and they shared worried glances. The nightmares didn't stop, the flashbacks during the day made her flinch and ask to be excused from class to walk with Ripley around campus, not caring about anything at all. She needed to move, she couldn't focus, she didn't feel like she was real anymore. Pain was constant.

Nobody understood what she was going through. Nobody could help her.

*Scream. Float. Crash.*

She was trapped in a time loop, repeating the same terror over and over again, and she just wanted out. She wanted to escape, one more pill, that was all. Then she'd be better. Then she'd be stronger, back in control.

On the periphery, she knew people were talking about her, hiding their words behind their hands, behind closed doors.

What do we do about Spencer?

Spencer hadn't heard Jackson come up behind her. She was at her locker, putting away her books when she felt a presence behind her, aside from Ripley. She whipped around, heart in her throat, and rammed her back up against the locker, making the door slam wider with a horrible clang. Jackson held his hands up, startled, eyes wide. He was in his soccer gear, his duffel over his shoulder, ready for practice.

"Spencer, I—"

"Don't do that!" Just as the words came out, she regretted saying them. She sounded feral, so unlike herself, and she noticed the hurt in his eyes. Her heart felt lodged in her throat and she swallowed it down. "Sorry," she said. Ripley put her nose on Spencer's hand and heat rose in her cheeks.

She hated that for a split second, she thought he'd been the person who had written the threatening notes, coming to fulfill their promise when her back was turned. Paranoia was getting the best of her.

"I called your name," Jackson said. "I thought you were ignoring me."

"I wouldn't ignore you on purpose."

Jackson let out a slow breath, watching her with a line drawn between his brows. "I wanted to check up on you. Since I'm not . . . you know, since you don't want my help anymore."

"It's all under control," she said. "This is for the best."

"Olivia and I have been worried about you."

"I'm fine. You two can rest easy."

Jackson didn't rise to the heat in her tone. She didn't want to snap at him, but she couldn't seem to stop herself. It was like there was a different Spencer controlling her tongue. Jackson, though, didn't take it to heart. He said, "I don't want you to feel alone, so I wondered if you wanted to go get some ice cream with me tonight. No pressure, just ice cream."

The way he looked at her disarmed the acid in her stomach. Something as simple as ice cream wouldn't fix her problems, but it wasn't about ice cream at all. She knew he cared about her, but she couldn't even care about herself. She was a mess, and it was difficult to wade through the wreckage. She had a hard time living with herself, and the ugly part of her had been winning for a long time, pushing everyone away when it was the exact opposite thing she wanted. It would have been easy for the people around her to walk away, leave her to her own destruction, but there Jackson stood.

"That would be nice . . . Yeah," she said. "I'd like that a lot."

"How about eight? Don't be late?"

Spencer managed a smile. "Wouldn't dream of it."

# FORTY

**THEIR PARENTS HAD A LATE** night in the clinic again. A Pomeranian puppy had gotten into an entire bag of Valentine's Day chocolate and needed an emergency stomach pump, so that left Spencer and Hope to fend for themselves on food. Spencer, too tired to make anything and definitely not in the mood to think about what she was hungry for, ordered a pizza from Little Italy's Pizzeria, and they ate their large mushroom and olive pizza on the couch. Spencer's headache had returned, so she sat on the couch with her icepack hat on and draped her arm over her eyes to cover the flickering light of the TV as Hope sat curled up in the reading chair watching another old rerun of *Murder, She Wrote*. Even Angela Lansbury's delightfully mid-Atlantic accent wasn't enough to soothe Spencer's throbbing head.

Ripley lay curled up at Spencer's feet, keeping her warm, and she wiggled her toes appreciatively. Midterms were coming up at school, some of the last tests Spencer would ever have to take as a senior, and the pressure was on to ace them all. Studying all afternoon, now that she didn't have Ethan's case to worry about or field hockey practice to attend anymore, was all she did these days. All the stress was what probably triggered her current headache. She knew she needed to rest, even for a little bit, because if she was remotely fatigued, it could be the determining factor between a 100 and a 99 percent, a fraction of a mistake she couldn't afford to make.

"Hey, Hope?" Spencer asked, without removing her arm from her eyes. She knew Hope was still there; she could hear her tapping away on her phone.

"What?"

"Can you do me a favor and grab my pills for me? They're by my bed . . ."

Hope sighed but got up anyway and padded to Spencer's room. A minute later, she came back, shaking the pill bottle in Spencer's face. Spencer took it, again without looking, and thanked her.

"Need anything else, m'lady?" Hope asked sarcastically. Spencer could practically hear her rolling her eyes.

"No, I'm fine." She didn't rise to Hope's level, too tired to say anything snarky back, which must have disarmed Hope because Spencer felt the couch compress near her knees as Hope took a seat.

"Jackson hasn't been around lately . . . ," she said, trailing off. "Have you two split up?"

"We weren't dating."

"Could have fooled me."

Spencer managed a smile. She finally twisted open the pill bottle and poured a dose into her palm and swallowed it without water, embracing the bitter taste. She hadn't needed to wash down her medicine for a while now.

"Is something the matter?" Hope continued.

"No, everything's fine. We're actually supposed to meet up for ice cream in . . ." She glanced at the clock on the wall, always keeping an eye on the time. "Forty-five minutes."

Hope crawled over Spencer's knees and squeezed herself onto the couch, sandwiched between Ripley and Spencer. Hope always liked to fit herself into tight spaces; it reminded Spencer of a bird in a nest. She felt safer when she was surrounded in warmth.

Hope said, "I think he's nice."

"He is nice. We're just taking it slow, that's all."

"You guys are confusing."

Spencer smiled.

They went quiet again as the episode continued playing. Spencer dozed off a little as the pills took their hold on her. She knew she needed to get up, but she was so tired. She just needed to rest her eyes for a minute.

"Hospitals in TV shows always look so much better than they do in real life," Hope said, referring to the television. She watched as the character Jessica Fletcher bantered with doctors.

"It's like that for most things," Spencer said. "Things are always better on TV. It's all fantasy."

"Yeah, that night in the hospital after the accident . . . Definitely not what they'd put on TV. I was there when you woke up. Mom and Dad didn't want me to see, because you were so out of it; they didn't want to scare me. You were freaking out on the nurses and they had to hold you down. You were screaming at everyone."

Spencer didn't say anything. It sounded like someone possessed, not her.

Hope laughed nervously. "You were shooing everyone out, like they were stray cats who had wandered in. I think you were hallucinating."

Spencer got very still.

*Shoo. Shoo . . .* , she'd told Detective Potentas when they first met.

"Hope," Spencer said slowly, and Hope looked at her. "What specifically did I say? The exact words?"

"Shoo! Just like Grandma used to shout when she was scaring off the squirrels hanging on to her bird feeder." Hope laughed at the absurdity of it all, but Spencer felt like the world had fallen out from underneath her.

She sat up so quickly, it startled both Ripley and Hope. "Watch it!" she cried, but Spencer was already tearing off her ice pack hat and hurrying to her bedroom.

She didn't bother closing the door behind her as she pulled Ethan's case binder from the drawer in her desk and flipped it open to the police photos of the accident, courtesy of Peyton Salt. Her heart raced as she scanned the pages, her stomach churning in knots, but she found what she was looking for.

She landed on the photo of the driver's side. Anyone looking at it would hardly believe anyone could have made it out of the seat as uninjured as Ethan had. But that wasn't important. She was looking for one thing, and she found it.

There, buried in the depths of the driver's-side footwell, hidden among the debris and chaos, was her missing flat. The sparkly ones she'd been trying to find for months, her favorite pair that she just assumed Hope had borrowed all this time. But the telltale bow lay there in the photo, and the truth buzzed loudly in her head, like a hornet's nest.

She remembered. She remembered everything.

Ethan wasn't guilty.

Because she was.

Spencer was driving the car that night.

# FORTY-ONE

**SPENCER DIDN'T SCREAM. DIDN'T GASP.** Didn't cry. She barely felt real in that moment as she stared at the photograph, everything coming into place in her mind, lining up the facts of that night like puzzle pieces finally nestling into place. It all made sense now. Clarity. Mystery solved.

The proof was right there, staring at her through the debris, looking like the rest of the car, all twisted and bent. But it was unmistakable, evidence that only she would know.

She collapsed onto her bed, eyes squeezed shut, as the memories rushed in.

The party, in full swing by the time she'd arrived. She could smell the smoke from the firepit, hear the band harmonizing, see the familiar faces of her classmates grinning and laughing as the last part of the summer felt it could never end.

A yellow Solo cup full of Diet Coke. She hadn't been drugged at all. *Where's Ethan? Have you seen Ethan?* Brent Lang saying he saw him behind the house. Skateboards in an empty swimming pool. Ethan and Hailey sitting on the edge, making out. Wipe away the evidence. Spencer feeling hollow.

Ethan chasing after Spencer, catching up to her in the

front yard, where kids were gathered around the firepit. He could explain. Yelling, rage making her vision all red, and Ethan saying it was a mistake. Trying to calm her down.

Spencer hated him then. She hated him so much. *Take me home!* She demanded. *I want to leave right now!*

Tabby underneath Chris, who was slobbering all over her, and Tabby asking Ethan, with dazed eyes, *Hey, can we get a ride?*

*Sure. He okay?*

*He'll be fine. Just drunk off his fucking ass.* Tabby and Chris piling into the car, asleep immediately. No seatbelt. No one remembered to put it on him.

*I'm driving!* Spencer had yelled. She was so angry, she wanted to be in control. Didn't want to give him anything. Didn't want to give him the satisfaction.

*How much have you had?* Ethan asked.

*Nothing!* She'd shrieked. *I'm fully sober!*

He had the keys in his palm and she snatched them out of his grasp. *Give them to me! I told you, I'm driving!*

Fast. Too fast. She was yelling at Ethan, about how he broke her heart, and how could he do this to her, and her shoe wedged between the floor and the gas pedal. The car roared forward. She got the shoe out, but she still can't stop. Can't brake. She tries. The pedal goes to the floor.

*I can't! There's no brakes!*

Ethan looking at her. The right side of his face lit up as the headlights reflected back as the tree loomed. That's why her memories were so wrong; the shadows on his face weren't right. Him looking at her now from the passenger's seat, the truth laid bare. But she can't stop. The tree.

*SPENCER!*

They are going too fast.

No—

Scream.

The car jumping the curb.

Float.

Breaking glass, breaking bones.

Crash.

Pain. Pain. Pain. Pain. Pain. Pain.

Her shoe was pinned underneath the gas pedal, the sparkling rhinestones easily mistaken for broken glass. But it was there. Clear as day. It couldn't have gotten there any other way.

She had been driving the car when it crashed at one hundred twenty miles per hour into a palm tree. It was her fault that Chris had died.

She hadn't been saying "shoo" in the hospital. She'd been saying "shoe."

She had tried to tell them what happened, but she was so drugged out, she wasn't able to articulate. Everyone thought she was in shock; no one listened. Why would they? Ethan had admitted to causing the accident. He'd said he'd been driving. But why?

It didn't matter now.

Her injuries had revealed the same truth. She'd broken her left clavicle—the driver's-side seat belt crossed her chest from left shoulder to right hip. The facts were plain as day on her body, and everyone wanted to ignore it because of Ethan. *Ethan.*

He was going to prison for her. He was protecting her and her perfect future.

She needed to confess.

It was the only thing she could do now.

She grabbed her phone, pulled on a hoodie, and hurried out of the house. Hope asked where she was going as Ripley bounded from the couch and rushed after Spencer. But Spencer didn't answer Hope's question as she hurried to the front yard and got on her bike. Her dad had been able to fix it after it got run over. She needed it now more than ever. She took off down the street, pedaling hard, Ripley galloping after her.

She needed to tell the truth about that night. All of it. And she needed to tell the Moores before it was too late.

# FORTY-TWO

**IT TOOK RECORD TIME TO** reach the Moore house, but Spencer was running on adrenaline and barely out of breath when she dumped her bike on the front lawn and pounded on the door, each knock as frantic and hurried as her racing heartbeat.

She desperately needed to tell the Moores what had happened. They deserved to know first. Once they knew the truth, all of them including Spencer could go to the police and sort everything out. She was the only one responsible for Chris's death, not Ethan, and they could all figure out what to do next. But they needed to know. She knew it would hurt to say it, but it had to happen.

And when the front door of the house opened, it wasn't Mr. or Mrs. Moore who answered, but Nick, Chris's older brother, still home from college.

"Spencer?" he asked, confusion written all over his face.

She barely had time to take a breath as it all came spilling out. "It was me! I did it. It was all my fault. It was me!"

"What? What are you talking about?"

Spencer swallowed, let out a ragged breath, and said,

"Are your parents home? I need to talk to them. It's important."

"No, they're out but . . . what's wrong? What happened? Tell me."

She did. She told him everything, holding nothing back. It flooded out of her, and once she started, she couldn't stop.

"I was the one who crashed. Tabby was trying to get rid of Chris and asked Ethan for a ride, but I was so angry at him that I insisted I drive, so I did it. I started driving, and I was so angry with Ethan, shouting at him, I didn't notice that my shoe got stuck under the gas pedal, the car was so fast. Too fast. I couldn't stop. I—I crashed. I did it. I killed Chris. It was an accident. Ethan is innocent. It was me." She gasped, her breath hitched, and her heart felt like it was going to explode as she watched Nick.

Nick listened patiently as she talked, his face set like stone and his pale skin growing whiter under his freckles. The reality of what happened that night was setting in. Now no one could blame Ethan. It had been Spencer all along. She had tried to do the right thing, tried to get everyone home safely even though she was so furious and had every reason not to. She could have just turned around and told Ethan to figure it out for himself. But she hadn't. She was trying to be a good person, and Chris died because of it.

Nick didn't say anything as he stared at her, frozen, an unreadable look on his face.

"We need to go to the police, tell them the truth," she said. "I need to clear Ethan's name. I need to turn myself in."

He nodded stiffly. "Give me a moment to grab my coat," he said and disappeared into the house.

Spencer paced on the front porch, barely managing to contain her shaking limbs. Ripley watched her from the lawn, head tilted, carefully following her with her eyes. Spencer was amazed she wasn't hysterical by now, but finally telling someone the truth of that night was validation that she wasn't crazy after all. She had been right the whole time. But she never would have thought she had been the one to do it.

It had really been an accident after all. But they pinned it on the wrong person. Spencer needed to see it through to the end this time, for sure.

Nick returned with his coat on and his keys in his hand. "Let's go," he said. "I'll drive you."

Spencer hadn't gotten into a car since her mother drove her home from the hospital. Her stomach nearly dropped to her shoes at the thought of getting inside one again. But Nick opened the back door of the car parked in the driveway and waited for her, allowing Ripley to jump in first.

Fear spiked hot through her bloodstream, making her feel somehow both freezing and boiling hot at the same time, and she took a faltering step back. It felt like an eternity, but it was probably only a couple of seconds to steady her nerves.

She needed to get over her fear. This wasn't about her anymore.

She took a breath, mustered up the courage, and got into the back seat.

Ripley put her head on Spencer's shoulder, doing her best to calm Spencer's nerves, as Nick drove them east toward the police station, but Spencer held tightly onto Ripley's collar and the ceiling handle as if her life depended on it. She didn't want to look too crazy. Nick wouldn't understand what she was going through, and she didn't want to show just how vulnerable she was, reliving the most painful experience of her life over and over again in her head. So she clamped her lips together and closed her eyes.

Ripley's happy panting against her shoulder helped a little bit.

"How are you doing over there?" Nick asked. His green eyes caught the lights from oncoming traffic as he checked the rearview mirror.

"I'm fine," she said. "Just trying not to have a panic attack."

"It'll be over soon. I promise."

She nodded. "I'm sorry it took me so long to remember. I wish I had been able to sooner."

"It's okay. I don't blame you for what happened. I really don't. And I'm not sure you're in your right mind right now," Nick said.

Spencer swallowed; words were difficult now as her throat closed up with the guilt of what she'd done. She put her hand on her forehead and forced herself to breathe. She focused on the interior of the car. It was a classic. Ethan would have liked it, and it smelled like exhaust and polished leather.

*Scream. Float. Crash.*

*Ethan's hands, carrying her out of the car. "Spencer, oh God, Spencer! Not like this. Please, Spencer, wake up." Blood on her face. Ethan blocking out the night, hovering over her, his eyes wide and afraid. Afraid for her. His nose bleeding, he was hurt too, but all he cared about was her.*

He'd taken the fall for her. To protect her. Because no matter what, he'd loved her.

Her stomach lurched when Nick took a turn, and she fell forward, almost hitting her nose on the back of the front passenger seat. She stared at the tape deck, a relic, and wondered what kind of car still had a tape deck these days. Her gaze slid over to Nick's grip on the steering wheel, his knuckles pale in the dark. Taking note of her surroundings helped ground her. She just wanted all of this to be over.

"Sorry," she said, gasping. "I still have a fear of driving. I know I'm being ridiculous."

Then she looked at where he was driving. They weren't going to the police station at all.

"Nick—where are we going?"

"I called your mom earlier, when I was getting my stuff. She's meeting me at the hospital. You're hysterical. I told her what you just told me, that you were confessing to a crime. I told her you were having an episode. It's normal for brain trauma victims to be confused."

"What? Nick! No! I'm not confused. I'm totally lucid."

Nick glared at her.

"Why—why are you doing this?" she demanded. "I'm telling the truth!"

"I told you to stop looking into the case, Spencer," he said grimly. "But you just wouldn't listen. I tried to warn you."

The letter in her locker. Somehow he'd gotten the number, probably asked someone who didn't even think twice about it. He might have even gotten it by using his father's login information as a teacher to get into the school's database and look up her profile.

"This doesn't sound like you, Nick," she said. She thought maybe trying to reason with him would get him to let her go. She kept her voice as level as possible. "Come on, let's go to the police and talk all this through—"

"NO!" he screamed. "STOP IT!"

Spencer cringed away from him when she noticed the car's logo on the steering wheel. It was a Dodge. Nick was driving a Dodge Charger. The car that ran her off the road.

"You were the one standing outside my house," she said. She licked her lips; they'd gone desert dry. "You tried running me over! You almost killed me."

"Because you WOULDN'T STOP." He turned around to her and the anguish in his eyes was hard to look at. "They found him guilty! You could have just walked away, let that rich smug asshole kid go to jail! He deserved what he got! Everyone says so! He's a worthless pile of trash! But Spencer Sandoval doesn't know when to quit."

"Why do you hate him so much?" she whispered.

"What do you think? Julianne was my girlfriend. Even if she wakes up, she'll never walk again. Ethan took that all away. Ethan was there when she fell. He didn't do anything. I was there that night, but I was too late. But I saw him. He just stood by and left her lying there, gasping for breath, back broken. It was Ethan's party; it was his fault people were up on the roof, he was always making people do stupid, dangerous things."

Spencer didn't argue with him. She just let him talk. The words spilled out of him like acid, making him sick until it all came out.

"After that, he strutted around the school like it didn't matter. Everyone forgot about Julie. But I didn't. And now Chris, too. He killed my brother. You say you were driving, but I don't believe you. It was Ethan, Ethan has to pay."

"It was me! Chris died because I couldn't stop!"

Nick snarled. "Chris died because of Ethan! Ethan killed him, whether or not he was driving!" It didn't make sense, but there was no reasoning with him. His warped, twisted view of what he'd done was justified in his mind and in the minds of everyone who already assumed Ethan was guilty.

Spencer's heart beat furiously, she couldn't help the anger that had risen in her chest. "Ethan looked after Chris! He saw that he needed help getting home that night. He felt terrible for what happened to Julie and treated Chris like a brother. He cared about him! You didn't see any of that!"

Nick didn't reply, just kept driving.

"You cut the brakes on his car," she said dully.

"Brakes? What are you talking about?"

That was when Spencer realized they were at her parents' animal hospital. Nick hadn't lied. He was taking her to her mom.

Nick's face was pale. "What are you saying?"

"You didn't—you didn't cut the brakes on Ethan's car?" she asked.

"No, why would I do a thing like that?"

"You just don't want me to tell the truth—so that Ethan rots in jail, is that it?" she asked.

"The case is closed, Spencer," Nick said. "Let it go."

Spencer saw her mom walk out to the parking lot. But she couldn't talk to her mom right now. She needed to find someone who would believe her.

# FORTY-THREE

**JACKSON CHEN'S HOUSE WAS LIKE** a French château landed in Bel-Air. When she arrived, it took a while for the butler to bring him down.

"Spencer, what's going on?"

She told him what she remembered about the crash, and that Nick had confessed to stalking her, sending those letters and trying to get her to stop looking into the case. But she remembered everything that happened that night now. It was all coming back to her. She was driving. It was her.

"Does anyone else know what you just told me?" Jackson asked.

"Just Nick, but he doesn't want to believe me. He wants Ethan to pay for what happened to Julie and Chris. I didn't even tell my family where I was going."

"Okay, good. We'll get this sorted out."

Jackson drove, and the two of them sat in silence. Then she realized, like Nick, he wasn't driving to the police station. He was driving somewhere else.

"Um . . . isn't the station that way?"

"No, this is a shortcut." He coughed.

Spencer was so confused. First she remembered the

crash, confessed to Nick, and then Nick confessed to his own actions. And now ... now ... Jackson was acting weird. But he hadn't said anything since they got into the car.

A million thoughts rushed through Spencer's head at once as she tried not to panic.

There had to be an explanation. Jackson couldn't mean to hurt her. She couldn't be getting kidnapped. That wasn't possible.

The rational part of her brain tried to tell her that she was being silly; of course, it had to be some misunderstanding. Maybe this was a shortcut ... Getting kidnapped just didn't happen. Especially by someone she trusted.

Still ... why were they driving so far out of the city?

And turning up to the hills?

A small part of her tried to believe it wasn't true. She wasn't even sure it was real. It didn't feel real.

She'd always thought being kidnapped was a lot more dramatic, a furious battle with screaming and kicking and clawing for freedom, and there she was sitting quietly in the passenger's seat, too frightened to move. To an outsider seeing her expression, she might look like she was carsick instead of being taken somewhere against her will.

She reached into the pocket of her hoodie, but just as her fingers wrapped around her phone, something shiny and black flashed in Jackson's other hand as he pulled something out of his pocket.

He leveled a gun at her. She didn't know what it looked like, or what kind it was. Her brain only registered *gun*, and she froze.

"Don't," he said. His voice was low and gravelly. He was not messing around. This was not a joke. This was real. And Spencer was terrified.

Spencer held up her empty hands, heart in her throat. She'd never even seen a gun in real life before, let alone had one pointed at her. She didn't know what else to do. Crying wasn't even an option.

Jackson kept his eyes on the road, driving her God-knew-where, but he didn't put the gun away. Ripley, oblivious to the situation, watched the world go by out the window, leaning with the momentum of the car as Jackson paused at a red light at an intersection.

Spencer had half a thought to jump out of the car and make a run for it. But then she would be leaving Ripley behind, and she couldn't do that.

He must have seen her eyes dart to the door handle because Jackson said, "I wouldn't do that if I were you."

Spencer was so afraid, she couldn't move. All she could focus on was the gun aimed at her. "Are you going to shoot me?"

Jackson didn't reply. The light had turned green, and the car started moving again. No one in any nearby cars, even if they glanced her way, would have seen the gun in Jackson's hand. No one knew where she was. No one knew she had gone to Jackson's house.

No one would know what happened to her. No one would know she'd gotten into his car. No one would know.

She was going to be the next great mystery.

# FORTY-FOUR

JACKSON HAD DRIVEN THEM IN silence all the way through the city, until Spencer saw the sign for the canyon up ahead. He'd taken her to Highwood Estates, the neighborhood under construction.

She tried not to panic as he pulled the car down a dirt trail through the woods, darker under tree cover. Her heartbeat was thumping so loudly, she was certain he could hear it, but he didn't say anything to her all the while until he parked in the flat space near the spot where the party had been, the party that started all of this. The houses, unfinished and unused, stood out like bleached skulls in the night.

Jackson turned off the engine but kept the headlights on. "Get out," he said.

It took Spencer a second to process that he was speaking and did as she was told. The air was crisp and cool, unusual for LA, but she hardly noticed. She fumbled with her phone in her pocket, but it was useless. There was no cell signal out here. She had missed her chance to call for help. She needed to think fast if she wanted to get out of this alive. So she pressed another button on her phone and shoved it into her pocket as Jackson rounded the car, aiming the barrel of the gun at her even when he let Ripley out of the car.

"Sit," he said, pointing to the dirt.

She didn't argue with him, and she sat hard on the ground. Ripley immediately went to her side. She sensed Spencer's panic, and she put her nose under Spencer's armpit, but Spencer didn't move to pet her.

"Why are you doing this?" she asked Jackson. "What's going on?"

"You said you remembered everything from that night," he said.

She blinked. She did remember . . . What was Jackson getting at? Then she remembered. Like a flash. "You were there. The night of the party. I saw you."

"You weren't supposed to see me. I had an alibi."

"You told everyone you were at an overnight soccer camp, but you were there. I saw you by the cars. In a soccer hoodie." The same soccer hoodie that Chris wore. All the soccer guys were so interchangeable in the dark. But she had seen him there. "Why?"

Jackson shrugged.

"He was your best friend."

"I never asked him to be," said Jackson. "But he was just—so insistent. I could have fought off those bullies in sixth grade on my own. But no—he had to. He had to be a hero! And it was always all about him."

*He was always faster than me.*

*He always got what he wanted.*

*I liked you first.*

"But why? Why cut the brakes?"

"I didn't think anyone would get hurt . . . He was always driving too fast, always endangering the lives of anyone else on the road. He never thought about anyone else but himself. He needed to be taught a lesson. I just wanted him to fuck up."

"So you could get his spot on the Headmaster's List. So you could prove you weren't like your family. That you were better." Spencer couldn't believe it. "Your dad . . ."

"Shamed us, no one would talk to us. Especially not the Moores, and Ethan, oh, it was just another of his hero moments to stand up to everyone and befriend a guy like me."

"But Ethan wasn't driving. It was me."

Jackson actually smiled, but it was distorted and strained, robotic. "I admit, I didn't expect you would be behind the wheel."

"Didn't you care about us crashing into anyone on the road?"

Jackson shrugged.

He didn't care. He had pretended to help her, so he could keep an eye on her. Because she was the only one who knew the truth.

Resentment was a disease. That's all it was. Everything that had happened these past few months was because of pure resentment. So many people got hurt to get it. It was so simple, and it left destruction in its wake. She felt sorry for him, even though he was aiming a gun at her. He was hurting, but he was dangerous. His eyes were cold. Spencer tried to talk to the Jackson she had known these past few months.

"You wouldn't do this. You're not a killer."

"Yes, I am," Jackson said with a laugh. It was high-pitched, unhinged. "I already killed Chris, didn't I? What's one more?" He tightened his grip on the gun.

He was going to kill her.

# FORTY-FIVE

**SPENCER'S BODY WENT COLD. SHE** held out her hands, the only thing she could do.

"Don't, Jackson."

She waited for the gunshot, but it never came. Jackson looked at her, his face screwed up like a demented mask, and Spencer wondered if he saw the girl he'd been spending all this time with, unarmed and defenseless in the dirt with her service dog pathetically trying to get her attention. She needed more time, she needed to get him talking.

"We can figure this out," she said. "We can get you some help. It'll be okay."

"SHUT UP," he screamed. Spencer's eyes never left the gun. She stared down the barrel. How a person could get this deep in their own grief, she understood too well. But to do something like this . . . Her heart pounded in her throat.

"I get it, Jackson. I do. But let's just take a breath—"

"It's too late, you always tell the truth, you'll tell them," he said, cutting her off. He adjusted his weight, shifting on his feet, antsy, and Spencer worried he'd squeeze too tightly and shoot. "But it doesn't have to hurt. We can make this painless." He licked his lips, his eyes dancing wildly. "I know you're taking medicine for your pain. Finish your whole bottle right now. It'll be just like falling asleep."

It would look like a suicide.

Someone would notice—her parents, Hope, Olivia—that Spencer was missing and call the police. Maybe it would take a few days, maybe more, but they'd find her body, sitting beneath the spindly tree, Ripley curled by her side, refusing to leave her alone. It would look like an accident, just like the crash. They'd have a funeral for her, with the same flowers they used at Chris's ceremony, pose her to look like she was sleeping in her casket, peaceful. Ripley'd refuse to leave her casket, choosing to stay curled up on the floor, perhaps hoping that she might wake up. People might say a few nice words about her, maybe shed a few tears, assume that she couldn't take the guilt of the crash any longer. Maybe it would come out that she was really the one behind the wheel, maybe someone would figure it out, maybe not. No one would look into her death. No one would have any reason to.

Tears burned the edges of her eyes. Instead of getting scared, she got mad. What Jackson wanted her to do made her insides turn to fire. When she got mad, it consumed her.

She stood up, hands clenched into fists at her side.

"Sit down," Jackson said, pointing the gun in the direction he wanted her to go.

"No." She lifted her chin defiantly.

Jackson worked his jaw back and forth, annoyed, as if

she was the one inconveniencing him. His finger twitched on the trigger. One small move, and it'd be over for her. But she was so angry, she didn't care. She almost wanted him to shoot her, because then there'd be an investigation and the truth would come out.

"You don't want to do this, Jackson," she said. She took a step closer. He took a step back.

"What are you doing? Stay where you are." He was the one who sounded scared now.

Anger had overridden her fear. She raised her voice. "You don't want to hurt me, Jackson. We're friends!" *I was falling in love with you . . .*

"No! You don't get it. My family's gone through enough."

"I get it. If something happened to my sister, God, I don't know what I would do. But if you kill me, you'll be ruining her life too, just like what happened to you. Do you want anyone else to feel that way?" Thinking of Hope made her voice quake, but she couldn't explode. Not yet.

Jackson's hand shook, but he braced himself with two hands on the gun. She took another step forward. She was not going to let him get away with another death.

"Shut up," he said. His lips pulled back into a snarl.

"You don't want to do this. There's another way. You can get help."

"No one can help me."

"Yes, they can. You just need to lower the gun . . ." He lifted it higher, pointed it at her face. She flinched. Would she even have time to realize he had pulled the trigger?

Jackson was beyond talking to, but she had to try.

Ripley put herself between Jackson and Spencer, shielding Spencer as best she could. She didn't know what was going on, but she knew something was wrong.

Ripley was trying so hard to help. That was all she ever tried to do. Spencer couldn't imagine her life without her. It was hard to believe she had been so hardheaded at first to think she could do anything without her help.

If anything happened to Ripley . . .

"Please," Spencer said, looking at Jackson as her voice cracked. "Don't hurt my dog."

She didn't realize what she was planning to do until she was already doing it.

When Jackson's eyes moved to Ripley, that's when Spencer tackled him. Head down, she dived straight for his chest, wrapping her arms around his body and knocking them both to the ground. No thoughts, pure adrenaline. The wind got knocked out of her lungs when she hit the dirt, but she fought through it. Jackson was taller, and stronger, but Spencer was not going down without a fight.

She grabbed for the gun, but he batted her away, writhing. They fought, kicking up a cloud of dust, but Spencer didn't give up.

Lights burst in her vision as something smashed over her head, the butt of the gun hitting her skull with a tremendous *CRACK*, and the world tipped sideways. Something warm trickled down the side of her head but Spencer was too stunned to do anything else.

Jackson let out an earsplitting scream as Ripley bit down hard on his arm holding the gun, her teeth breaking through the skin. The sound of fabric tearing, Jackson's cries, and Ripley's growls as she dragged Jackson away from Spencer.

Ripley shook her head furiously, not letting go, even though Jackson hit her repeatedly in the face, trying to get her to break free. Spencer tasted dirt and blood, and tried to get up, but her limbs weren't working.

Ripley was trying to save her.

She let out a yelp as Jackson hit her one more time, and the next moment Jackson was running away back to his car. The engine roared and dirt kicked up over Spencer. She tried to move, but it felt like her arms were made of lead. Something wet and warm dripped over her eyes, blinding her.

Ripley barked furiously at the car, each sound cutting through Spencer's head like a hammer on a gong.

As the car disappeared down the dirt road, Spencer puked, the world still spinning. Ripley came to Spencer's side, nuzzling up against her.

Jackson had gotten away.

But Spencer wasn't done.

She slipped her hand into her hoodie pocket and checked the screen of her phone. The audio recorder app was still going, and she ended it with a tap. Blood from her fingers streaked across the screen. She had captured Jackson's whole confession on audio, but the world was going dark.

She couldn't send the file to anyone. She still had no

signal. All she could do was lie on her back, feel the tickle of blood pooling under her head, and stare at the stars. They arced across the sky, like a long-exposure photo, getting bigger and bigger, swallowing her whole. She was floating, spinning in space, away, away. Spencer was going to throw up again.

Ripley whined, nudging Spencer's face with her wet nose, but Spencer was losing the fight against unconsciousness. Her head felt like it'd been cleaved in two.

The world became less and less real, the ground falling away from her as she ascended into the warm abyss of nothingness.

The last thing Spencer saw before the world slipped away was the blinking green light on Ripley's collar.

# FORTY-SIX

**A VOICE.**

*Spencer!*

*Spencer!*

*Oh God, Spencer, please!*

Olivia's face appeared above her, blocking out the stars. Spencer wanted to stay awake, to say goodbye, but it was getting harder. Lead weights were pulling her eyelids shut.

*She's over here!* she called to someone behind them. A girl's voice called back.

Hope? Spencer wasn't sure she said it out loud.

Red and blue lights illuminating her face. Sirens in the distance.

Tires crunching on the dirt. Barking incessantly. Ripley.

*Spencer, I'm here. It's okay.* Olivia's face took up her entire vision.

Then darkness took over.

# FORTY-SEVEN

**HEAVEN SOUNDED AN AWFUL LOT** like a hospital room.

Spencer heard the steady beep of a morphine drip machine, the distant murmur of doctors talking in the hallway, a TV soap opera with volume set to low.

Opening her eyes was a chore, but she managed to do it.

She was indeed in a hospital room, very much not in heaven. The dull reminder of a throbbing headache made sure of that. The bandage around her head was proof that she lived.

"Dang! She lives!" Olivia stood frozen in the doorway, her eyes shining with silver tears.

Spencer immediately started crying with joy. She couldn't help it. She had missed her best friend so much; it hurt deeper than discovering Jackson had been playing her for a fool all along.

Olivia ran at Spencer and threw herself on the hospital bed, holding her so tightly it snatched the breath from her lungs. But Spencer didn't care. She just wanted Olivia back.

"I'm so sorry," Spencer cried through her tears. "For everything. For not being there. For all of it."

"I know, I know!" Olivia sobbed.

They held each other for a long time, crying and saying how sorry they were to each other, like broken records. But Spencer felt like she could give herself back to Olivia, who hadn't deserved everything that had happened between them. Spencer had been a terrible friend, but Olivia would forgive her.

"How did I . . . ?" She wanted to gesture to the room, but her arms felt too heavy. "What happened? How did you guys find me?"

"Hope. It was all Hope. She had your mom call Nick, who told us you'd run off, and when you weren't answering your phone, they activated the GPS in Ripley's collar."

Ripley, the best girl, lay curled on a cracked leather armchair in the corner of the room, peacefully asleep. If it wasn't for her, Spencer wouldn't be here now.

"It was Jackson. Jackson Chen. He was there the night of the party. He cut the brakes in Ethan's car."

Olivia looked pale but nodded. "I know. The recording was on your phone. Your parents gave it to the cops. Hope you didn't mind. How did you solve it?"

Spencer didn't hold anything back as she explained everything leading up to her kidnapping, how it was really she who had been driving and how Ethan had covered for her, how she'd seen the proof in the police photos, how Nick had wanted her to stay silent, and how Jackson had let a toxic resentment build to murder.

"Ethan's innocent," she said. And so was she. She had been driving, but she hadn't caused this.

Jackson had cut the brakes.

Olivia let Spencer's parents into the room, and Hope followed but immediately went to Ripley's chair to give her a good smooch on the head.

Spencer allowed them to fuss over her, she was so relieved to see them. To think she might not have ever held them again was unbearable. They freaked out, rightfully so, about what had happened, but Spencer didn't care. She was just happy to see their faces again.

### *Get Salty*: A True Crime Podcast with Peyton Salt

*[Intro Music]*

**Peyton Salt:** I'm not sure what else I can say, Salters . . . But I'll try! In a twist of fate, we have an update on the absolute last case that I thought I'd be covering today. The one and only case of Ethan Amoroso, a fan favorite.

Turns out, there's been some new information that sheds some light on his case that may overturn his conviction in a new trial.

Thanks to the tireless efforts of Spencer Sandoval, it was uncovered that Jackson Chen was the one behind the tragedy. Early this morning, as I was recording this episode, police caught Jackson Chen trying to cross county lines. Ethan Amoroso may be innocent in all of this, after all. I am one to admit that sometimes I get it wrong, and this time, folks, I was very wrong. The details are hazy for me now as I'm waiting on my sources to confirm, but what I gather is that Spencer Sandoval uncovered the truth not long before being kidnapped and attacked by Jackson Chen to cover up his crimes. Needless to say, this case has worked its way into being one of the most compelling stories we've covered on this show. We've seen a lot of criminals get put away for less, so we can expect Jackson Chen's journey to be a long but certain one behind bars. Like father, like son!

# FORTY-EIGHT

**ONCE SPENCER MADE A FAST** recovery after a few days, suffering only a minor head wound that needed stitches, she was transferred to the rehabilitation wing. Doctors said she had been taking too much Vicodin, and they needed to monitor her as she cut back on her doses. They didn't say the word *rehab* lightly.

Everyone in school knew what had happened. Word spread fast. Both amateur and professional news outlets ran the story about Spencer's confrontation with Jackson Chen. Detective Potentas reinterviewed Ethan and he admitted that he lied about who was driving that night. He wanted to protect Spencer, so he took the fall after pulling her out of the car. A judge was going to review his sentence. He wasn't going to get away scot-free—he did lie to police, after all—but now that Spencer's testimony broke the case wide open, Ethan would likely be free in a few weeks. Chris's death could finally be solved.

One bright day, Ethan called her from home. He still wasn't allowed to leave his house until everything was sorted out, but it was nice hearing his voice after everything. She sat at the window on one of the two lounge chairs in her room, looking out across the hospital's quad, picturing him standing there just like old times out her bedroom window. Her heart galloped hearing his voice. The first words that came out of his mouth were "Thank you."

Heat rushed to her face. "You were willing to go to jail for me?"

"Yeah, well . . . It would have been worth it. People say I do stupid things all the time."

"Maybe you should stop being stupid, then."

He laughed easily, and she couldn't help but smile, too.

"All this time, I thought I was protecting you," he said. "But turns out you were protecting me. You never gave up. Think we can start over? Think we can try again—being us?"

She knew what he meant. Starting their relationship anew, with everything they'd done for each other, felt like a fantasy. And she wasn't sure if it was even possible. He'd still broken her heart. She wasn't sure she could ever recover from that. "Us? I think I need some time being me again." Without all the painkillers, she was starting to remember what that felt like. She read tons of books, and studied, and journaled under the careful eye of nurses and doctors, but she was feeling better already. Just like her old self: different, but better. "I'd like it if we can start over being friends," she added.

She could almost hear his smile. "Yeah. Friends."

"Congrats on CAL," he said. "I know it's not CalTech, but CAL's a great school."

"I think that's a double congrats, isn't it?" She smiled, because she knew Ethan had gotten in, too.

She'd gotten the acceptance letter at her second-choice school while she was in the hospital. It was close to home and had a great astrophysics department.

"I hear you and Hailey broke up," she said.

"Yeah," he said.

"I'm glad. You deserve better," Spencer told him, and meant it. "Take care of yourself, okay?"

"You first." Typical Ethan.

She hung up, still smiling as Olivia laid out a stack of papers on the table near the window.

"All good?" she asked.

"All good."

Ripley looked up at Olivia from her spot next to Spencer's chair. Spencer's trauma from the accident on top of what happened in the Highwood Estates wasn't going to fade anytime soon, and Ripley was fulfilling her duties most admirably. She was truly the best partner anyone could ask for.

"So . . ." Olivia said, staring at all their papers stretched out on the table, grinning despite the sheer amount of it all. They used to do this together all the time. She'd missed that.

"So," Spencer said, eyes shining bright with the prospect of homework. "Let's get started."

# ACKNOWLEDGMENTS

**HUGE THANKS ALWAYS TO MY** amazing team at Macmillan: my incredible editor, Kate Meltzer; my fabulous publisher, Jennifer Besser; and everyone who made this book shine. Thank you to my agents, Richard Abate and Ellen Goldsmith-Vein. Thank you to my awesome beta readers for such helpful feedback. Thank you to my friends and family. Thank you to my loyal readers. Thank you to Mike and Mattie always, top of my list in every book.